Pra...

"Elmer Kelton is a Texas treasure."
—*El Paso Herald-Post*

"Voted 'the greatest Western writer of all time' by
the Western Writers of America, Kelton creates
characters more complex than L'Amour's."
—*Kirkus Reviews*

"Kelton writes of early Texas with
unerring authority."
—*Fort Worth Star-Telegram*

"You can never go wrong if . . . you pick up
a title by Elmer Kelton."
—*American Cowboy*

"One of the best."
—*The New York Times*

"A splendid writer."
—*The Dallas Morning News*

"A genuine craftsman with an ear for dialogue
and, more important, an understanding
of the human heart."
—*Booklist*

Forge Books by Elmer Kelton

HANGING JUDGE

—— AND ——

BOWIE'S MINE

Elmer Kelton

FORGE®

A TOM DOHERTY ASSOCIATES BOOK | NEW YORK

This is a work of fiction. All of the characters, organizations, and events portrayed in these novels are either products of the author's imagination or are used fictitiously.

HANGING JUDGE AND BOWIE'S MINE

Hanging Judge copyright © 1969, 1997 by Elmer Stephen Kelton Estate

Bowie's Mine copyright © 1971, 1996 by Elmer Stephen Kelton Estate

A Forge Book
Published by Tom Doherty Associates
175 Fifth Avenue
New York, NY 10010

www.tor-forge.com

Forge® is a registered trademark of Macmillan Publishing Group, LLC.

ISBN 978-1-250-17792-6

Our books may be purchased in bulk for promotional, educational, or business use. Please contact your local bookseller or the Macmillan Corporate and Premium Sales Department at 1-800-221-7945, extension 5442, or by email at MacmillanSpecialMarkets@macmillan.com.

First Edition: June 2019

Printed in the United States of America

0 9 8 7 6 5 4 3 2 1

CONTENTS

HANGING JUDGE

AUTHOR'S NOTE

Judge Isaac C. Parker is sometimes portrayed as a ruthless and fanatical hangman, which is an injustice to a well-meaning, dedicated man. When he took over Fort Smith's federal court bench in 1875, Indian Territory was a haven for outlaws, from Texas gunfighters on the dodge to past, present, and future members of the James-Younger-Dalton-Doolin bands, not to mention miscellaneous whiskey runners, horse thieves, bank robbers, and assorted malefactors of every degree. The various Indian nations had their own tribal courts, but these exerted little power over non-Indian lawbreakers.

Like the rider who got the mule's attention by bringing it to its knees with a hickory club, Parker got the attention of the lawless his first year by dropping six murderers through the trapdoor of the big Fort Smith gallows, all at one time. A howl of protest went up in other parts of the country, but not in and around Indian Territory, where honest folk knew the true nature of the enemy.

Early in his career Parker appointed two hundred deputy marshals, whose duty it was to keep peace—or restore it—over 74,000 square miles of Indian Territory. The only other lawkeepers were the Indian tribes' own. Lighthorse police. Parker respected Indian law and left to the tribes those affairs which had to do only with Indians. But if a non-Indian was involved, either as culprit or victim, Parker took jurisdiction.

Tragically, Parker is remembered mostly for his hangings. Critics overlook the fact that his rough justice was a product of and perhaps a necessity for the times. He sent seventy-nine men to the gallows during his twenty-one years on the bench. During that time, sixty-five of his deputies were killed in the line of duty. The death toll among the lawbringers was almost as high as among the lawbreakers, at least those who died on the gallows.

The hangings seem less ominous when it is considered that during his hardworking career, he tried more than nine thousand defendants—more than four hundred a year—three hundred forty-four of them for capital offenses. He sentenced one hundred sixty to death, but half escaped the final penalty for one reason or another. None of those seventy-nine who actually walked up the thirteen steps to eternity was convicted for singing too loudly in church. They were a desperate lot, and the times called for desperate measures.

Parker believed in object lessons, which is one reason why he staged several of his gallows "spectaculars," multiple hangings of four to six men at one time. Whatever effect these events may have had on the outlaw element, they managed finally to cause a public outcry and a curbing of Parker's powers. Finally, in 1896, his court was eliminated. By then Parker was already a sick man, and the loss of his bench took the heart out of him. He died two months later.

To the end, the judge maintained that public sympathy was too often misplaced. "Sympathy should not be reserved for the criminal," he declared. "I believe in standing on the right side of the innocent, quiet, peaceful, law-abiding citizen. Is there no sympathy for him?"

George Maledon, Parker's official hangman, saw his own job in a stern perspective. Asked once if any of his victims ever returned to haunt him, he coolly replied that when he sent them away, they never came back.

1

Hanging day always drew a crowd to Fort Smith. Sam Dark had often pondered—without finding answers—the macabre side of human nature that made people travel long miles to watch a man die. If it weren't his job, *he* wouldn't be here. But he was a federal deputy marshal, assigned to keep watch on the people till the trap was sprung, to be on the lookout for any rescue effort or other disturbance. If he had been inclined to gauge crowds with a showman's eye, he would have said Barney Tankard was not a strong draw. Far larger crowds had gathered here on other occasions. Barney Tankard was just one man. The biggest crowds came to witness Judge Isaac Parker's spectacular multiple hangings, when they could see several men drop into Eternity together. Barney Tankard was not even a notable criminal. He was simply a farmer's son who had shot a friend in a drunken quarrel over a half bottle of contraband whiskey.

Folks said it was the Indian half of him that made him unable to hold his liquor and the white half that made him pull the trigger. He wasn't basically a bad man, just the wrong man to get drunk.

Sam Dark had been the officer dispatched across the Arkansas River into Indian Territory to fetch Barney for trial. Barney hadn't been wolf enough to get away, for he had never gone afoul of the law before. Catching him had been easy. This was the hard part, to stand here now watching the grim preparations on Judge Parker's big white-painted gallows.

Somebody was hawking lemonade at the edge of the milling crowd, catching his dollar wherever it might chance to fall. Dark angered, for it seemed to him a man ought to be allowed some dignity in which to die. Damn it, this wasn't a horse race or a summer picnic. He heard a child shout boisterously and another answer. He glanced around without patience, wanting to send them on their way. Buttons like that . . . they ought to be in school instead of out here waiting to see a man choke to death at the end of a rope . . . but this was hard country and these were harsh times . . . violence so common it was expected like the ague . . . temptation at every fork in the road. Lots of people figured that to see a hanging was part of a boy's proper education, an object lesson in what happens when one allows his feet to stray from the paths of righteousness and into the devious byways of iniquity. This was a thing to make a boy pause and tremble when tempted by an urge to steal a neighbor's ear-corn or to sneak a ride on somebody's mule, the first fateful steps on the well-marked road to the gallows.

Dark surveyed the crowd and found among

them a lot of good people—farmers, businessmen, riverfolk—and wondered what the hell they were doing here. A scattering of Indians watched placidly, people come over from beyond Arkansas to see a brother pay for breaking white man's law. If the crime had not been perpetrated against a white man Barney Tankard could have stood trial in tribal courts, for being half Cherokee qualified him as Indian. But it would have made no difference in the final outcome; even the tribal councils decreed death sentences for murder. An Indian convicted in tribal court might be given time to go home and straighten out his affairs, but the end was inevitable. It was a point of honor that upon the appointed day he would appear on his own volition before the council to meet his death like a man, in strength and in dignity. For Barney Tankard there was to be no dignity.

Dark saw a cluster of crib girls, gathered from down on the river, and a couple of them were weeping. He doubted they had ever seen Barney Tankard before. Perceiving little sympathy anywhere else, Dark was glad Barney received at least this much.

The lank, bearded hangman, George Maledon, guided the leg-ironed Barney Tankard onto the double-hinged trap door, and a hush fell over the crowd. Barney glanced up involuntarily at the rope that Maledon had earlier tested with sandbags to be sure it wouldn't kink. In his hands Maledon held the little black bag that would go over Tankard's head. He waited now for the end of the ritual, for the condemned man to speak his last words.

Dark had seen men pray in their final moments. He had heard others caution the onlookers to beware of mistakes that might lead them up these same fatal steps. He remembered a couple who had gone to Eternity cursing.

Given his chance, Barney Tankard stood in silence, a trembling young man still bewildered by a chain of events whose cause he could but dimly recall. He kept his feet only by great effort. His gaze searched the crowd until it found Sam Dark. Dark felt the despair in the dark Indian eyes and wanted to turn away but could not. Tankard summoned some inner strength to have his short say, and he looked straight at Dark as he said it. "What I done was wrong, that I know. But I've prayed, and I'm easy with the Lord. I didn't get here by myself. Them that sold me the whiskey, them that chained me and brought me to this place—they're as bad in their way as I am in mine. I wonder if they are easy with the Lord."

Seeing Barney was through the stern Maledon fitted the noose and the black cap. Methodically he reached for the lever.

Dark jerked his head away and shut his eyes. He had watched the first time; he had never made that mistake again. He flinched at the slam of the heavy doors and the sharp gasp from the crowd packed around him.

God, he thought, *what a wretched way for a man to die!*

When he looked again it was not toward the gallows. He knew nothing had gone wrong there. George Maledon was a precision craftsman who took satisfaction in a job well done. Dark turned to the ugly red brick courthouse, toward the high windows of Judge Parker's chambers. He could see the dim, portly figure of a man standing in the shadows, watching to see that the sentence was duly carried out as he had pronounced it in that austere courtroom. In a moment the figure disappeared.

Gone to pray now in solitude, Dark knew. *But whose soul does he pray for? Barney's? His own? Or maybe for mine and for the rest of us who've got a dirty job to do?*

Dark was particular not to look toward the gallows again. Though he turned away he could still see in his mind the accusing black eyes of Barney Tankard. There wouldn't be any sleep for Sam Dark tonight, not unless he drank himself to it.

The crib girls were walking away now, a couple of them weeping as if Barney were kin. *Every man ought to have somebody weep for him, even if it's just a girl from down on the river.*

The crowd was breaking up, though many people still stared at the grim white gallows as if hypnotized by the image of Death. There wouldn't be any trouble now; he could go. He pushed his way among the people, wanting away from here.

At the edge of the crowd he heard a youthful voice call: "Mister Dark! Could I talk to you a minute, Mister Dark?"

He didn't look around. "Talk to me tomorrow."

"I'd like to talk to you now."

"Boy, can't you see . . ." Dark turned half angrily, looking for whomever had spoken. He saw a man a little past twenty—fresh-eyed, smooth-faced but sunbrowned, wearing a floppy farmer hat and a loose-fitting homespun shirt probably made for somebody else. Sharply Dark said, "I got a right smart on my mind right now, button. I don't feel like talkin' to nobody. Hunt me up another time."

"I come a long ways."

"You shouldn't of. Right now I just want me a good stiff drink. By myself."

The young man went silent. But as Dark proceeded away from the courthouse toward the gin mills on Garrison Avenue, he sensed the lad was following him. Dark turned abruptly. "Are you kin of Barney Tankard?"

"No, sir."

"Kin of somebody else I've brought in for the judge?"

"No, sir."

"Then what's your grudge?"

"I got no grudge, sir."

"If it ain't a grudge, then I wish you'd leave me the hell alone!"

Dark resumed his walk, pushing on through the crowd. Acquaintances hailed him, but he passed them by. He fixed his gaze stonily on a certain saloon and tried to see nothing else. But his eye was caught by a heavy freight wagon standing in the street and a big man checking the trace chains. Dark stiffened at sight of him, and he rubbed a rough hand across his face.

The big man raised up. His mouth smiled but his eyes were hard. "Howdy, Sam Dark. Good hangin'."

Dark's fists knotted. "I don't expect Barney Tankard enjoyed it much."

"You don't need to look at me thataway. I didn't even know the boy."

"But you got his money in your pocket, Harvey Oates. And I expect now you're gettin' ready to go back across into the Territory and peddle some more of the same bad whiskey to other Indian boys who got no tolerance for it."

Harvey Oates kept his sham of a smile. "You want

to look in my wagon? You've done it before and you've never yet found a drop of whiskey."

"Someday I will. I'll drag you to the judge, Harvey."

"You'll never find what ain't there. I'm just an honest freighter, that's all. I take the necessities of life to the poor folks out yonder in the wilderness that can't come and fetch it for theirselves." He dropped the smile. "You're a sad case, Sam Dark. You've got to takin' your job too personal, and that's a dangerous thing. You're just supposed to bring them in; you're not supposed to worry about them."

"Most of them I *don't* worry about, Harvey. And when I bring *you* in I'll get a good night's sleep."

Dark turned away from Harvey Oates and elbowed through the swinging door of the saloon. The moustachioed bartender looked at him questioningly. Dark said, "I'm off duty, John."

"You wouldn't be drinkin' if you wasn't, Sam. You done your duty. I heard them doors drop. First drink's on me; I reckon you got it comin'."

Sam Dark had no dependence upon whiskey. He could go without it for weeks at a time and never miss it. Over in the Territory it was forbidden. But he respected whiskey's preventive and curative powers when used at the proper time and place. This was the time. He downed the glass, coughed, then slammed a coin on the bar. "So you don't lose money on me, John. Fill 'er again." He took the glass, careful not to spill anything, and carried it to a small table to nurse it with time and care.

He heard the bartender ask somebody, "What's for you, young fellow?" The reply was in the same voice he had heard at the edge of the crowd. "Nothin', thanks. Mind if I just set myself down here to wait?"

Dark scowled and flung a question halfway across the room. "What you waitin' for, button?"

"For you, Mister Dark. For you to get in the notion to talk to me."

That'll be a while, Dark thought to himself, looking away but not putting the thought into words. He sipped the whiskey, letting it burn his tongue, his throat, wishing it could also burn his brain and erase that image of those black eyes accusing him from the gallows. Times like this he wished he was still following a plow, his eyes looking past the brown rump of a stout Missouri mule. Times there was no price they could pay a man on a job like this that would be half enough. They paid little enough as it was.

He took a long time with the glass of whiskey, and when it was gone he filled it again. The tension had dulled a little. The black eyes that stared at him were blurred some and didn't cut quite so deep.

The farm boy still sat at a table across the room, patiently waiting. *Why don't he get tired and leave?* Dark asked himself irritably. But something sensed rather than seen told him the boy would wait there as long as Dark did.

Dark waved him over. "All right, button, you make as much noise sittin' there quiet as you'd make hollerin' in my ear. Come on and get it said."

The boy pulled out a chair but didn't sit down until Dark motioned for him to. "You don't know me, do you, Mister Dark?"

"Am I supposed to?"

"You was in kind of a fever at the time, but I thought you might remember."

"What time was that?"

"Time you rode up to our cabin bleedin' where

somebody had put a bullet through your arm. It had been a right long while, and you was sufferin'. Small wonder you don't remember."

Dark tried to. He reached through the haze of time and through the foggy memories of more than one wound received in the service of the United States District Court. "Would your name be Moffitt, boy?"

The young farmer nodded, pleased. "Yes, sir. Justin Moffitt."

Dark frowned, trying to bring the mental picture into focus. Young Moffitt was right; Dark had been fevered at the time and the whole thing was more like a dream than an actual experience. "Two years back . . ."

"Three."

"Your old daddy helped me into his house. You was a big gangly button but you helped too. Your ma, she cleaned up the wound and wrapped it and fed me some hot grits and pork."

The young man kept nodding. "Yes, sir, that's how it was. Pa tried to get you to stay a couple days and rest, but you rode out, still feverin', Pa followed after to be sure you made the settlement. We never did hear if you caught your man."

"Not that one. He got away into the Territory and disappeared. They was good to me, your folks. How is your daddy, and your ma?"

"Pa's dead, sir. Feller come by one day last winter and started to steal our mare. On the run for the Territory, I guess. Pa tried to stop him. It wasn't no match." Moffitt looked down.

"Sorry about your daddy. He was a Christian. How's your ma?"

"Still pinin' some after Pa, but she's otherwise all right."

Dark lifted his glass as if in a silent toast. He took another drink. "You said you come to talk to me. What about?"

"I'm needin' employment, Mister Dark. I want you to help me get on as a deputy marshal."

Dark's mouth dropped open. "What the hell for? You-all got a farm. Why would you want to take on a job like this?"

"Farm's small. Ma's got my brothers to help her. I need a job."

"Then get one choppin' cotton or sweepin' saloons or workin' the roads. This ain't no life for a boy off of the farm."

"I judge that *you* come off of the farm once."

Dark flinched. "Button, you're not old enough to know what you want."

"I got old enough the day we buried my pa. And I'm not a button. I'm twenty-two."

"When you're on the downhill side of forty like I am, twenty-two looks like a thumb-suckin' age. I bet you got some wild notion that this job'll help you find the man that killed your pa."

"Not likely. Chances are by now he's gone plumb to Texas, or even on to California. But there's plenty others left, just as bad as him. I want to help fix it so other boys won't have to bury their pa the way I done mine."

"A dream, son, that's what it is. And believe me, it'd turn into a nightmare if you stayed with it long enough. What makes you think I'd even consider helpin' you get a job like mine?"

"Maybe you forgot. Before you left our place you

said if ever there come a time any of us needed your help all we had to do was ask you. So here I am, Mister Dark, and I'm askin'."

"Best help I could give would be to send you packin' back to where you come from, and that's what I'm doin'."

"You promised you'd help."

"I *am* helpin', more than you know." Dark turned away from him, trying to dismiss him by showing his back. He sensed that the farmer stayed awhile, disappointed. Dark made up his mind to outwait Justin Moffitt. And presently the young man pushed back his chair. Dark heard the slow tread of Moffitt's feet as he retreated out the door.

"Damned buttons," Dark said finally to the bartender, "they never know when they're well off."

The bartender nodded and refilled Dark's glass. "Pity they ever have to learn. Pity they can't stay young and happy and dumb."

"Some do, till it's too late. Some like Barney Tankard . . ."

The afternoon wore away dismally. Some of the hanging crowd had come in for drinks, downed a few and long since departed. It was dusk when finally Sam decided he'd get up from here and go find something for supper. The crowd hadn't bothered him, though he had sensed that a few were talking about him, pointing him out as a Parker bloodhound who rode the dim trails of the Indian Territory, relentlessly seeking out candidates for Parker's judgment and Maledon's carefully oiled ropes. There was respect in their voices, even a touch of fear. But rarely did Dark find liking. That was a thing a man gave up when he took on the job.

He stepped out the door and paused, surprised to find it was so late. His belly was warm from the whiskey and the coiled tension had left him. He hadn't realized how time had slipped away. He turned to walk toward the shack that he used for sleeping and eating when he wasn't out on business for the court. It had been years since he had had a home.

Dark felt the hard pressure of blunt, cold steel against his neck. A voice fell on his ear, quiet and stern. "Just you take it slow and natural, Mister Dark. Don't act like there's nothin' wrong or I'll pull this trigger. We're takin' us a little walk down by the river."

Dark's pistol was in his waistband, beneath his coat. It had as well have been in the shack, for if he tried to draw it he would be too dead to pull the trigger. "Don't you get nervous with that weapon," he said. "Just tell me whichaway you want me to go."

The man moved the pistol down to Dark's ribs, and Dark glanced around enough to see him. In the bad light he thought sure he was Barney Tankard. His stomach went cold. *Damned whiskey,* he thought, *didn't know I'd drunk so much.* The man had Indian features, like Barney's, and a steady hand on that pistol. "Keep lookin' straight ahead, Mister Dark. You'll see me soon enough."

Dark walked with him, keeping an outward calm, which wasn't difficult. He realized he ought to be more excited than he was, and he knew the whiskey had dulled him. That was a thing he would have to take into account—that his reflexes were slowed. Anything he did he'd have to be damned fast about.

Presently they reached the river and walked beneath a canopy of tall trees into a patch of heavy shadow. There Dark made out a small spring wagon with a pine box in it. He saw a gaunt old man— farmer, by the look of him—and a heavyset Indian woman. A young girl stood by the wagon and she looked Indian, too—half Indian, anyway. The old farmer was white, but Dark knew those features. He had seen them in the face of Barney Tankard. He glanced again at the young man who had brought him here. No, it wasn't the whiskey; the man had Barney's look. These people would be Barney's family; his father and mother, his sister, his brother.

Dark was sober now. That cold feeling lay heavy in his stomach. "Mister Tankard?" he asked, knowing.

The farmer nodded. "Elijah Tankard. The boy with the gun, that's my son Matthew. The girl is Naomi. And this lady is Barney's mother, Dawn. Cherokee. Good people, the Cherokees."

Dark nodded. He'd known a lot of the Cherokees. "Yes, sir, good people. Mister Tankard, don't you think you ought to be takin' Barney home?"

"In God's due time we'll take him home." The old man's voice was deep and sad. "But we got a family debt that has got to be paid. Always taught my boys . . . a good man pays his debts."

"It'll be a mistake. You'll come to grief."

"Grief? Mister, we already come to grief. Just you look into the face of that boy's mother. She's been singin' a death song. Don't you think we know all there is to know about grief? He was a good boy, our Barney. He didn't go to do nobody any harm."

"He killed a man."

"Wasn't him that done it; it was that rotgut whiskey some of your Fort Smith peddlers sold him. It's them peddlers you ought to be hangin', sellin' that poison to good young Indian boys."

"He didn't have to buy it, Mister Tankard. He didn't have to drink it."

"A boy like that, he don't know. He don't understand the consequences. You forbid a thing and you make it look good to him. If Parker wants to clean up the Territory let him hang the whiskey peddlers that bring the ruin on these people."

"The judge does the best he can. He's sent many a peddler up the river."

"And let as many others get away. He can't hang a man for sellin' whiskey. Leastways he *don't*. And seems like if he can't hang a man he ain't very interested. That rope has gotten to be some kind of a religion with him. He gets drunk on it the way other men get drunk on whiskey."

Dark knew this was an unfair indictment; he also knew he wasn't in a position to argue about it. Far and wide, Isaac Parker was known now as "the hanging judge." He hanged them wholesale sometimes, by twos and threes and even by half dozens. Yet for every man he hanged, Judge Parker sentenced fifty to prison. It was human nature for people to forget about the fifty and remember only the one, and to call Parker a fanatic. "You had me brought out here at the point of a gun, Mister Tankard. That's a prison offense. But I'll forget it if you'll just take that poor boy home and not leave him layin' there on that wagon. He's due some respect."

The girl spoke. At another time and under other circumstances Dark might have looked at her as an individual, might have noticed whether she was pretty or not, whether her voice had a pleasant ring or an ugly one. But his only thought now was that she was an Indian woman, and that Indian men were known, among the wild tribes west, to turn their captives over to the women because the women could be the cruelest ones.

She said bitterly: "Don't you talk about respect for Barney. You brought him here tremblin' for that pious old hypocrite to hang. Barney done just one wrong thing in his life, and that wasn't really his fault. He killed one man. How many have *you* killed, fetchin' them in here like beeves to slaughter?"

Dark looked at the dangerous face of Barney Tankard's brother. He could tell this line of talk was bringing him close to whatever it was they had planned for him. To the father he said, "You better think, Mister Tankard. You already lost one boy. Kill me and there'll be a dozen deputy marshals out lookin' for you. You don't want to stand in front of Judge Parker. You sure don't want this other boy of yours to either. It'd be a pitiful waste."

The old farmer squared his gaunt shoulders. "We wasn't figurin' on killin' you, Sam Dark. But we do intend to fix it so you don't forget the Tankards. To the last day you live you'll remember us."

Dark saw the movement of Matthew Tankard's hand and thrust himself away, trying to escape the clubbing barrel of that six-gun. It struck him a glancing blow that sent his hat spinning and dropped Sam Dark to his knees. A fist—he didn't see whose—slammed into his face and sent wild colors spinning in his brain. The back of his head struck earth.

Fighting to find his balance and push to his feet, he

expected another blow. It didn't come. A young voice spoke taut and steely, "Step away from him. I'll shoot whoever makes the next move at him!"

Dark knew the voice. "Don't kill anybody, boy. Let them be."

"Looky what they done to you, Mister Dark."

"Let them be." Dark struggled to his feet, breathing hard. He tasted blood and ran his hand across his mouth, through his moustache. "They done it for cause. Leastways they thought they had cause. Don't shoot anybody, boy. One dead man today is enough."

Justin Moffitt stared hard at the Tankards, not comprehending until his gaze touched the pine box. Realization came into his eyes. "You-all would be Tankards, wouldn't you? From across the river."

The old farmer and his son stood off balance in mute frustration. The girl finally said, "We're Tankards."

For a moment Moffitt appeared to soften, but he looked again at Sam Dark and his mouth went hard. "Then you better be crossin' over. It's been a sad day. Let's don't make it no sadder."

"Boy," said the farmer, "you one of them marshals?"

Moffitt shook his head. The old man said, "Then you butted in where you didn't have no call. There's times when a man ought to just keep walkin' and not see nothin'."

"I got good eyes, Mister Tankard. Sorry about your boy. But Sam Dark here, he just done his job."

The men stared at each other a long time until the older woman said something in a low voice. When she got no response the girl said, "Come on, Papa. We better take Barney home."

Sam Dark still swayed. "Mister Tankard, I meant

what I told you—I'm sorry. And I pledge you one thing: I'll do all I can about them whiskey peddlers. They helped your boy fire that gun. I may be callin' on you for help."

Matthew Tankard took a step forward. "You ever show your face at our farm and I'm liable to kill you, Dark!"

The father firmly placed his hand on his son's shoulder. "Ease up, Matthew, you don't mean that. You growed up Christian." To Sam Dark he said, "Right now, tonight, I feel like Matthew does. Maybe in time I'll learn to feel different. If there comes a day when you need help agin them peddlers, and you feel like takin' a chance, you might come by. Maybe we'll shoot you and maybe we won't. Right now I wouldn't make you no promises."

The Indian woman sat on the wagon seat, her head down in silent grief. The girl climbed up beside her, and the old man followed the girl. His eyes hating, Matthew Tankard climbed into the wagonbed beside the coffin. Dark and Moffitt watched them until the night covered them up and only the creak of the wagon wheels indicated the way they had gone. Dark turned to the young man, who still held a pistol in his hand, his arm hanging straight. "You got that thing cocked? You'll shoot yourself in the foot."

His tone was one of mild reproach and Moffitt flared momentarily, having expected gratitude. "I know how to handle a gun."

"If they'd called your bluff what would you have done?"

"I wasn't bluffin'."

Dark decided he wasn't. This young man was serious enough to have shot somebody. "Well, then, I reckon you got me at a disadvantage. You got me owin' you. That's somethin' I don't like to do, is owe somebody."

"You owe me twice," Moffitt pointed out evenly. "Once for tonight, and once for the favor my pa and ma done you."

"And I reckon you'll dog my steps till I pay you?"

"That's exactly what I'll do."

"What'll it take for me to get rid of you?"

"Get me a job as a deputy like I asked you to."

"So people can hate you the way that family hates me? So they'll do to you what these folks almost done to me tonight?"

"Doin' the right thing ain't always popular. But it's always right."

Dark frowned. "First you got to always be sure what is right. Half the time nowadays I can't make up my mind." He shrugged finally. "I can't promise you a job, but I do promise you we'll talk about it. Where you stayin' at?"

"Noplace. Anyplace. I got a blanket on my saddle and a warbag with a little grub in it. I just sleep where night catches me."

"Well tonight it's caught you in Fort Smith. I got me a shack down here a ways. Only one bed and that's mine. But you can spread your blanket on the floor if you're a mind to."

"I'd be tickled, Mister Dark."

Dark turned and started to walk. In a minute he stopped. "I never did tell you thanks. I reckon I ought to." He sounded almost grudging.

"Get me a job, and that'll be thanks enough."

"Maybe. And then again maybe the day'll come that you'll wish you'd passed on by and let the Tankards do what they had in mind."

2

Justin Moffitt didn't sleep well. It wasn't the hard plank floor that bothered him; he could sleep on a floor or even the bare ground about as easily as on the best corn-shuck mattress in some nice hotel that changed the bedclothes every week. Most of the night he lay trying to frame the arguments he would use on Sam Dark in the morning. He sorted out all the facts and put them up in one-two-three order, like dry-goods on a shelf, and knew that when the time came to talk they would tumble out ingloriously, leaving him struggling for words. Justin Moffitt had always been handy with tools—an axe, a knife, a saw. He'd always been an easy learner with guns; whether a pistol or an old muzzle-loading squirrel rifle like the one his granddaddy had fetched down from the hills of Tennessee. With those things Justin Moffitt was in his element. But with words he was next to helpless. He couldn't argue or plead a case.

"You'll turn out to be a good farmer and not much

else," his father had told him. "There's nothin' to be ashamed of in that. You seldom see a rich farmer but you seldom see a hungry one, either. Long's he can grow a little somethin' to eat they can do their damndest against him and never quite starve him to death."

Maybe he *would* end up a farmer; Justin had no dread of the life. In fact he sort of liked it. But first he wanted at least to try for something that might be better.

Ever since they had moved into the big country near the Arkansas Justin Moffitt had been aware of the criminal element that constantly drifted through, much of it on the way to the vast obscurity that was the Indian Territory. He had been aware of his father's hatred for the type who dropped by isolated farmhouses and demanded food and horse feed as a divine right, a kind of forced tribute in return for leaving farmer and family unhurt. Like others of their kind, the Moffitts suffered these indignities because of the awesome price for fighting back individually. They observed the code of silence when lawmen came around, for lawmen never stayed long and the lawless were never far away. They sometimes exacted a terrible price from those who gave information.

Justin's father had stayed because he had faith that law would come here as it had come elsewhere and the land was rich with promise. "All we got to do," he said, "is hold tight and outlive the outlaw."

Justin had seen lawmen who seemed more inclined to avoid the criminals than to find them. Some, he thought, were little better than criminals themselves. One day Sam Dark had ridden up to the Moffitt farm, wounded and in need of help. He had accepted what treatment was necessary, then had ridden on doggedly in search of his assailant. This was a kind of man Justin Moffitt had never seen before. This was the kind of man he made up his mind he wanted to be. It was a tenet of the Moffitt family faith that a man owed a debt to his country and to the people who gave him life; he owed it to them to try to make the country better than it was. After meeting Sam Dark, Justin Moffitt thought he knew where his duty lay, how his debt was to be paid. When his father died, brutally murdered by a passing horse thief, Justin knew for sure.

He lay awake as daylight slowly penetrated the shack, bringing detail to the vague forms he had looked at through the night—a bare wooden table, two rawhide chairs, a small cast-iron stove with a stack of red bricks substituting for one lost leg. A lank, striped tomcat stretched idly under the edge of Sam Dark's cot, eyeing Justin distrustfully as an intruder, upsetting the accustomed order of his small kingdom. Sam Dark had slept fitfully, talking occasionally to Barney Tankard. Now he turned, causing the cat to rise up expectantly. Dark's eyes came open. He blinked a moment, then looked balefully at Justin lying on the floor, as if he had hoped Justin would lose heart and slip out during the night, leaving him alone.

His voice was gritty. "If you want any breakfast, button, you'll have to go out and chop some wood."

Justin flung his blanket aside. He had slept in his clothes—all but his shoes. He laced them hurriedly. When he returned with an armload of wood he found Dark had most of his clothes on and was fanning flame into some kindling. Dark took a little of the wood and motioned for Justin to drop the rest into

a box. "Ain't much to eat around here. Coffee . . .
sidemeat . . . biscuits." Dark ground some coffee beans
and poured them into a pot. He walked over to the
cabinet and picked up a wooden bucket, then turned
impatiently. "If the damned shack was to catch on
fire, first thing to burn would be the water bucket."
He thrust it at Justin. "Cistern's at the corner of the
house."

There wasn't room for two to work so Justin stood
back and watched Dark pinch pieces of sourdough
from a batch kept in a crock jar. The house was a
boar's nest and in need of sweeping, but Justin figured
he would raise dust and send Dark into a fit of irritation. He needed Dark on his side, not against him.

He silently studied the graying deputy, feeling that
here was an uncommon man and wondering if he
could somehow observe what it was that made him
that way. He saw nothing evident in Dark's face to
set him apart. Dark was well into middle age, creases
cutting around the edges of his eyes, down past his
moustache, under his stern jaw and down the stub-
ble of his neck. His hide was brown as any farmer's.
In fact he would pass anywhere for a farmer were it
not for something indefinable in his manner, something in the way he carried himself and in the watchful seriousness of his gray eyes.

Justin's father had once told him, "It's hard for a
good lawman to slip into a town and not be noticed.
He betrays himself by the way he walks, the way he
sits a horse, the way he looks at people like he was
judgin' them and sortin' the wheat from the chaff. He
develops habits he can't put aside. He don't have to
wear a badge. It shows on him."

The day Sam Dark had ridden up to the Moffitt

farm Justin had instinctively known him for what he was before he ever saw the badge. He never quite understood how.

He wanted to make conversation but he didn't wish to push himself, considering how badly he needed Sam Dark's favor. He waited for Dark to open the talk and Dark seemed in no mood for it. They ate in silence, Dark staring out the open door, eyes pinched, forehead furrowed in concentration.

At length Justin started to drop a strip of the side-meat to the tomcat on the floor. Dark frowned. "I wouldn't. Never feed him myself. I'm gone too much and he's got to stay used to makin' his own livin'. He'd suffer for it if I was to spoil him." Dark finished his third cup of black coffee before he stood up and walked to the door to pitch the grounds out into the bare yard. "You said you was pretty good with a pistol. Come show me."

Justin's pistol lay on the floor beside his rolled-up blanket. Dark stepped out into the yard, looking around a moment, then pointing. "Yonder's somebody's milk goat with a bell around its neck, stealin' my horsefeed. Let's see if you can hit the bell and not kill the goat."

Seemed like a safe gamble, using somebody else's livestock, and Justin raised the pistol and squeezed the trigger. The little bell exploded. The goat blatted in panic and sprinted away like a startled deer. Justin lowered the smoking pistol. "What else you want me to shoot?"

The shot had stirred a dozen or so dogs into wild barking, and in a house across the road Justin saw a woman and three children rush to the door to see what had happened. Dark shook his head. "Nothin'.

Just wanted to see what you could do." He watched impassively as the frightened goat disappeared around a turn in the weed-lined trail. "That goat wasn't fixed to shoot back at you, though. Think you could do as good against a man who was?"

Justin stared at the smoking pistol. "I might not. Never tried."

Dark nodded. "Honest answer. That's in your favor, anyway." He held out his hand for Justin's pistol and Justin handed it to him butt first. Dark turned it over in his big palms, inspecting it critically. "You've slept on everything I told you yesterday. Still got your mind made up?"

"Been that way a long time."

"Then I'll take you to Jacob Yoes. He's the chief U.S. marshal. He'll pass on you first and then most likely take you before Judge Parker. But if Yoes thinks you're all right the judge'll take him at his word."

"And if you think I'm all right will Marshal Yoes take you at your word?"

Dark's brow creased again. "You know you're usin' me, don't you?"

"I'm sorry. I wouldn't do it if I knew any other way."

"Well I gave you my feelin's, and you're of legal age. I won't stand in your way even though I think you're wrong."

"Thanks, Mister Dark."

"Thank me sometime when I've done you a favor."

Jacob Yoes was a preoccupied man with worry in his eyes and frustration in his manner. His desk was piled high with fugitive notices and unserved warrants; with expense claims from the dozens of deputy marshals riding the Territory in search of the lawless, who outnumbered the deputies by scores to one. That was reason enough to turn a man's milk into clabber. Dark introduced Justin, but Yoes showed more interest in the cuts on Dark's face left by the encounter with the Tankards. "What happened to you, Sam?"

"Oh, nothin', sir. Just fell off of a porch."

Yoes gave Justin the same careful, half-suspicious scrutiny Sam Dark had given him. The marshal asked Dark, "Do you vouch for this man?"

Dark said, "He comes from Christian folks. He's showed me he knows how to handle a gun." Justin waited for Dark to relate last night's incident, but he didn't. Dark thought a moment, then added, "That's all I can tell you about him." Justin felt disappointed. Dark probably didn't want to cause trouble for the Tankards, but that story would have impressed Yoes and strengthened Justin's case.

Yoes put his fingertips together and stared over them at Justin. "Young man, do you know how many of this court's deputies have died in the performance of their duties since Judge Parker has presided?" When Justin shook his head the marshal said, "Close to forty. And there'll be more. That's why there are vacancies in my force today. That's why there are almost always vacancies. One mistake, one stroke of bad luck and you could be just another name on this court's long, sad honor roll."

"I don't plan to make no mistakes, sir."

Justin realized instantly that he had sounded braggy. He hadn't meant to. "What I intended to say, sir, is that I'll be careful and I'll do my duty. I owe it to my father."

Whatever doubts he might have harbored, Yoes put them aside. "I see no reason to turn you down, then. But the final authority rests with the judge. We'll go and see him."

Yoes ushered Justin into an upstairs office, trailed by Sam Dark. In a desk by the window, his back half turned to the door, a tall, heavy-set man sat bent over several spread-out law books, the thick forefinger of his right hand laboriously tracing the lines of fine print. His black frock coat was a bit threadbare and there was about the man an air of austere dignity.

"Judge Parker, sir . . ." Yoes spoke with respect and with implied apology for the disturbance, for court was due to convene shortly and the judge seemed to be trying to establish some legal points in his mind. Parker turned slowly and without concern, for he evidently knew Yoes by his voice. It occurred to Justin that a man who had made as many enemies as Isaac Parker was taking a grave risk in leaving his door open and unguarded. Anyone could walk in here and murder him in cold blood. God knew there were plenty who might believe they had reason enough. But it was said the judge walked the streets of Fort Smith alone and unarmed, quietly demonstrating that his court would not be intimidated though it be surrounded by the most dangerous aggregation of unhung criminals west of the Mississippi.

For years Justin had heard awed talk of Judge Parker; he somehow expected to see a vindictive man sitting like an angry deity high upon a throne, hurling thunderbolts down upon the wicked. This man appeared to be anything but that. On the street Justin would have taken him for a minister. He was not old, probably not much more than fifty, for gray was just now beginning to streak his hair and beard. But to a man of twenty-two, fifty is old. Parker reached absently for the golden watch chain that dangled across his broad middle. He glanced at the time, his eyes blinking in uncertainty because his mind was still partly upon the lines he had been reading. He appeared relieved that it was not yet time for court.

This, Justin thought in surprise, could not be the legendary fanatic, the cruel-eyed hanging judge they whispered about all over Arkansas and across the Territory, the man who remorselessly played God with the lives of those unfortunates brought before him.

Parker saw the marks on Sam Dark's face. "What happened to you, Mister Dark?"

"Fell off of a horse, your honor."

Yoes blinked, for he had heard a different version. Parker's eyes shifted to Justin, plainly wondering if he were some felon hauled up for judgment. Yoes said, "Judge Parker, this young man is Justin Moffitt. He wants to join the service of this court as a deputy marshal."

Parker's blue eyes studied Justin as they might study a criminal in the dock, searching for some flaw. "Have you examined him, Marshal Yoes? Does he seem qualified?"

"As far as I can tell, your honor."

Judge Parker pushed slowly to his feet, and only then did Justin realize how tall and how large the man really was. He seemed to tower over Justin Moffitt. "You're young, Mister Moffitt, but we've had younger men in the service of this court. That won't weigh against you. What concerns me is your purpose, your reason. Is it money?"

"No, sir. I hear deputy marshals don't make much money."

"True, not from the government at least. But there is more than ample opportunity for a misguided man to use his badge and make money from illicit sources if he is of that type. We've tried to be careful in picking men, but we've made a few mistakes."

"Such a thing never entered my mind, your honor."

"Good. See that it never does, for let me warn you of one thing. This court is thoroughgoing against all the lawless, but it is absolutely merciless with a lawman gone wrong. I'll expend more effort to punish a man of that stripe than any other class of criminal except a murderer. A peace officer carries a degree of trust equal to that borne by a man of God. When he betrays it he forfeits all claim on the generosity of his fellow man."

"I'll be true to your trust, sir."

The judge studied him a moment more with a solemn, searching gaze that made Justin extremely self-conscious about his inexperience, his farmer look. He had an uneasy feeling that Parker could read in his face every little mistake, every petty sin Justin had ever committed. Finally the judge looked at Yoes. "I think he'll do, Marshal Yoes. How many young men today still remember to say 'sir'?"

Justin followed the marshal to the door. The judge called after him, "Mister Moffitt! I didn't ask you, but I take it you're a churchgoing man?"

"Yes, sir; when there's a church available."

"There are several here in Fort Smith. I hope I'll see you in mine."

"You will, sir." Justin would make a point of it.

The judge turned back to his desk. But now, instead

of the law books, he picked up a huge, black-bound Bible. He seemed to know just where to open it, and he immersed himself in the reading of the Word.

Walking down the hall with Yoes and Sam Dark, Justin was light-headed with relief. Outdoors he would have whistled, but here he sensed the dignity of the court. He restrained himself. "I want to thank you, Marshal Yoes."

"That's all right. We needed you."

Dark seemed disappointed. "Button, don't you know why they're so glad to see you; why they need you so much?"

"They're short-handed."

"But don't you know why they're short-handed?"

Justin shook his head. Dark said, "Marshal Yoes as good as told you. You hear a lot of talk about how many men Judge Parker has sent to the rope, but you don't hear much about how many deputies he's lost bringin' them men in. For every five men the judge has hanged he's lost four deputies killed in the line of duty. Almost one for one. You think about that a while, and then you figure out if I done you a favor."

3

Marshal Yoes took Justin into his office and explained the details of the job, the routine for claiming expenses, the manner of remuneration. "I'll assign you to one of the more experienced men. Since Sam Dark brought you here I'll let him take the responsibility of breaking you in."

Sam Dark's face creased in silent protest but he didn't give voice to it. He walked to the window and looked out, hiding his dislike for the idea. In a moment he said, "Then, button, we'll start breakin' you in right now. Yonder comes Rice Pegler and the tumbleweed wagon."

Justin wasn't sure he had heard. "The what?"

"The tumbleweed wagon." Dark gave him a quick look of impatience. "Come on, let's go downstairs."

Half suspecting he was being hoaxed, Justin followed. Outside and halfway down the broad stone steps he stopped. A small crowd was rapidly gathering around a long freight wagon. A Negro driver climbed down from the wagon seat. Two armed riders, each carrying a rifle in his lap, moved up on either side. One—a tall, angular deputy whose face was half hidden beneath a broad-brimmed gray hat—motioned sharply to half a dozen men seated in the bed of the wagon. "All right, you good citizens, climb out of there and be damn quick about it!"

The men moved stiffly, cramped from riding in an unaccustomed position. They wore leg irons and all were hitched to each other by a long chain.

Dark was on the ground and halfway to the wagon. Curtly he signaled Justin to come. "You wanted a job. Let's get after it."

The Negro driver walked to one of the horsemen who handed him a pistol. Justin surmised that he drove the wagon unarmed so no prisoner could grab a weapon from him. The Negro strode stiffly toward Sam Dark, smiling. "Howdy, Mister Sam. Glad we found you to home."

Sam Dark shook hands with him. "Howdy, George. Looks like you caught you a fair bunch of them at home this time."

"Fair haul, Mister Sam. But I reckon there ain't none of us as good a fisherman as you." He glanced at the horseman with the flat-brimmed old gray hat as if expecting rebuttal.

The horseman swung a long leg over the horse's rump and dropped easily to the ground. His bestubbled face broke into a hard, ironic grin. There was no humor in it but rather, if anything, a subtle malice. "I'd say we done pretty good, Sam. Even hooked one *you* been lookin' for a long time and never could catch." The tall deputy shifted his gaze back to the wagon. He shouted harshly, "Come on, I said climb out of that wagon! I don't intend to stand here all day!"

One of the prisoners, who appeared to be a half-breed Indian, muttered something under his breath. The words were muddled but the message was clear. The tall man took two steps forward and swung his fist, throwing the full power of his shoulders into it. The prisoner staggered backward and struck his head solidly against the wagon. "Anybody else wants to talk ugly to me I got another dose of the same bitters waitin' for him." His gaze fell distrustfully upon Justin Moffitt. "Who are you? How come you standin' here?"

Dark said, "Rice, he's a new deputy. Judge just hired him."

Rice Pegler eyed Justin half belligerently. "If you're drawin' federal money then get to earnin' it. We got prisoners to take to the cells."

Not sure what he was supposed to do but knowing he had better do something in a hurry, Justin drew his pistol. He moved around the back of the wagon where the last prisoner was awkwardly climbing down, carefully trying to avoid pain to a bandaged arm. Justin felt a little foolish pointing the pistol at the men. He had no real idea what he was doing.

The smiling Negro came to his rescue. "Howdy, boy. You want to help me take these men inside to school? I'll go and open the door. You stay behind them and make sure there don't none of them run off. Them leg irons costs money." He glanced at Justin's pistol. "And if you was to decide to shoot somebody, I sure do hope it ain't me."

His matter-of-fact manner took away much of Justin's uncertainty and his friendliness gave Justin ease.

It occurred to him that none of the prisoners could run unless they all did. They were chained together. He hadn't been afraid of them. Rather, he had been afraid of himself; afraid he would make a mistake at the start and look a fool.

The tall deputy made Justin feel like a fool simply by the way he looked at him.

But the deputy didn't watch Justin long. He concentrated on Sam Dark. "You owe me the drinks, Sam. I brung in the man that shot you a couple of years ago. He don't look like much now, does he?"

Sam Dark didn't reply. He stared at the prisoner with the bandaged arm. The deputy was badgering him and Sam Dark was plainly trying not to be graveled by it. Dark finally said, "Don't matter to me who got him long's he's got."

"I'm the one that got him," Pegler stressed.

Justin could tell it did matter to Sam Dark, despite what he said. Dark asked, "How come the bandage on him?"

"I shot him," the deputy replied.

"But why?"

"Why not? If *you'd* shot him when you had a chance to he wouldn't of put a bullet in you. You'd be surprised how a little chunk of lead weighs a man down and keeps his mind off of mischief."

Dark pondered soberly. "Then you must not be the shot you used to be, Rice."

"How's that?"

"You hit him in the arm. You always aim at the heart."

The Negro unlocked the door that led to the jail cells. Rice Pegler and another deputy followed him, then turned to watch the chained prisoners file in.

Sam Dark and Justin Moffitt brought up the rear. Justin was keenly aware that a considerable crowd had gathered outside, watching. He felt as if everyone had eyes on him. He decided that was foolish; they were curious about the prisoners.

Inside the jail he heard a cry go up among those men already in confinement. They were greeting the new crop. Some called individuals by name. One shouted, "Break and run! Better they shoot you than throw you in this hellhole!"

Justin had never been in a jail. He had thought he knew what to expect but the foul, choking air caught him by surprise. He took an involuntary step backward, toward the clean outdoors. Sam Dark caught his astonished look and grunted for him to stand his ground. Justin felt as if he would throw up, but he got control. The stench was overpowering. A low ceiling, a stone floor and the small barred windows conspired to trap the smells of human excrement. Slop pails stood partially filled, adding to the problem during the long, hot hours they waited for a guard or trusty to pick them up and empty them. Little fresh air found its way in here, much less circulated. Mopping the stone floors only intensified the problem by soaking down all the spillings and leaving the stone and mortar saturated with them.

The older prisoners were bearded and dirty for washing facilities were limited. Their clothes were filthy, every fiber penetrated by the grime and the stench of the place. Some expressed sympathy for the new prisoners being unshackled one by one and herded through the barred doors of the overcrowded cells. An Indian prisoner stepped up and embraced the half-breed. The new prisoners looked around anxiously among those already here, searching for old friends—or old enemies.

Sam Dark said, "We better get a doctor in here when we can, to look at that man's wound."

Rice Pegler scowled. "He didn't call no doctor to look after yours. If I was you I'd let him sweat. It'll either get well or it'll kill him."

"We'll get him a doctor," Dark repeated.

Pegler stared into the cell, his craggy face contemptuous. "Suit yourself, but I sure as hell ain't goin' to pay for it. Look at them animals there—Indians, niggers, white trash. Far as I'm concerned, they got nothin' comin' but jail or a rope." He watched the last cell door swing shut with a hard clang that must have had an awful finality about it to the men newly locked inside. Glancing once more at Dark he shook his head and walked out muttering about being hungry.

Justin didn't think *he* would ever be hungry again. He waited for Sam Dark to do something or say something. Dark just stood looking through the bars at the wounded prisoner who had shot him a long time ago. Justin finally said, "I expect Pegler's right. If they hadn't done one thing or another to deserve it they wouldn't be here."

Dark didn't look at him. "They're fugitives till I catch them. After that they're men." He turned and left the jail. Justin followed after him, sensing that in agreeing even a little with Rice Pegler he had somehow erred, had not raised himself in Sam Dark's eyes.

Justin found that much of the marshals' and deputies' work was routine. It involved a great deal of paperwork. Watching Rice Pegler laboriously scrawl

his way through a lengthy report of his mission with
the tumbleweed wagon, Justin wondered how many
people would ever eventually read all that writing.
The way it appeared to him the federal government
was more concerned with getting the papers filled out
properly than it was with capturing fugitives. Rice
Pegler expressed his view of it: "Way I see it it's all
politics, our government is. The party that gets in, it's
got to have a lot of jobs to give the people who
worked hard to get it elected. It don't matter how
good they work for the government; it's how they
worked for the party that counts. These people got
to have jobs so they make jobs for them a-readin' all
them reports. No reports, no jobs. No jobs the party
don't get back in come next election. So we write
reports when there's badmen out yonder that needs
hangin'."

    Of all the deputies Justin found himself on the eas-
iest terms with the Negro, George Grider. Grider had
an infinite patience in explaining things and there was
much that Justin needed to have explained.

    Rice Pegler had a certain crude attraction for Jus-
tin because of his tough, straightforward way of looking at things. Pegler never bothered himself pondering
the delicate balances between right and wrong. To
him each thing was either one or the other, instantly
recognizable, beyond question. Pegler asked him,
"You never did see the man that shot your daddy,
boy? Then how you goin' to ever know if you come
across him?"

    Justin confessed that he had no idea.

    "The thing to do," Pegler said sternly, "is to figure
them all the same. Figure every criminal might be the

one that killed your daddy. Look at him the way you'd look at a snake. Don't ever give one of them a halfway even chance because he's as liable to kill you as to look at you. When in doubt, shoot. And when you shoot, kill a man. It's a lot cheaper on the government to do a buryin' than to put on a trial."

Once he became accustomed to the smell Justin spent much of his spare time in the jail, quietly looking over the prisoners until he knew every face. He kept wondering if one of them just *might* be the man he had hoped someday to meet. The longer he looked at most of them the more inclined he was to share Pegler's view. They were a coarse, hard lot for the most part—rough-looking, rough-talking, showing no particular remorse for the crimes they had committed, though many were fearful of the consequences when once they were brought before the judge. A number already had had their day in court and were waiting here for the carrying out of judgment. It was a short walk out of the cell, down that corridor, out into the sunlight and up those fateful steps.

Times, Justin was detailed to help escort prisoners to court. Usually these men were bathed and shaved and an effort made to present them in a manner befitting the dignity and high purpose of the federal court. One prisoner he guarded was a murderer who had waylaid and coldly knifed an Indian cowboy for the meager wages in his pocket. Justin had only contempt for him. Yet a chill ran down Justin's back as the prisoner stood for sentencing and Judge Parker's usually benevolent mien gave way to a fearful vengeance. The judge reviewed the stark facts of the case, commented upon the cruel nature of the crime, then set the date of execution and said in a powerful voice: "I sentence you to hang by the neck until you are dead, *dead*, DEAD!"

During his confinement the prisoner had made a show of toughness, often bragging of the defiant statement he would make to the judge when he had the opportunity to stand before him in court. Now he stood cowed, face pale. As Justin helped escort him back down to the dungeon he noted that the man was wet, and not altogether from perspiration.

"They can't do that to a man," he whimpered to all who would listen. "They can't just take a man's life away from him thataway. It's murder."

It was on Justin's mind to tell him he should have thought of that before he took another man's life without any thought to rights. But the cold reality of the death sentence had never quite reached him before, and Justin stood in awe of the power concentrated in that huge man on the judge's bench.

Rice Pegler was in awe of nothing. He told the prisoner, "Quit your whimperin'. Bible says what ye sow, that shall ye reap. And you sure planted yourself a crop."

4

In the first weeks Justin Moffitt worked a lot of long days and nights, but all of them seemed to be in or near Fort Smith. He longed for an assignment that would send him out into that seemingly limitless, mysterious Indian Territory that lay tantalizingly within sight across the river. Other deputies were coming and going all the time, some bringing prisoners for the crowded jail, others telling stirring stories of exciting near-captures. But Marshal Yoes didn't choose to send Justin on these missions. Justin suspected Sam Dark was responsible for keeping him in town. Dark coached him, often curtly; more inclined to tell him of his mistakes than to acknowledge the far greater number of things he did right the first time. Justin continued to stay at Dark's shack, sharing the rent with him, helping buy the grub, but wondering sometimes if he ought to move out. After all he had the job now, and he had learned a lot about the way a deputy went about the performance of his duties.

He worried, when he had stretches of time on his hands, about Dark's attitude. To the sympathetic Negro, George Grider, Justin said, "I don't see no good reason for him to keep a-ridin' me the way he does. I do my job. I don't make too many mistakes."

Grider frowned, offering a nod but no advice. Justin expressed one recurring suspicion, that Dark was a strongly self-reliant man—he had shown that on many occasions—and didn't like to stand beholden to anyone. Perhaps it had offended him that Justin had reminded him of a moral debt owed the Moffitt family. Sam Dark had resisted help until resistance was futile. Perhaps he felt less of a man because in the end he had been dependent upon someone else.

"Sometimes I wish Marshal Yoes had assigned me to a man like Rice Pegler instead of to Sam Dark," Justin said.

Grider was surprised. "Rice Pegler?"

"Why not? He sure don't ever back away from nothin' or nobody, does he?"

Grider pondered a moment and avoided a direct answer. "He does his job, that Mister Rice."

"I'd like to be able to get along with Sam Dark. But if he don't want to get along I reckon I don't really need him anymore. I got the job now. What do you think, George?"

Not many people spent time with George Grider for to them his color was wrong. It pleased him that Justin Moffitt kept seeking him out for news and advice, for someone to share talk with. He said, "I'd give Mister Dark more time, if I was you. He don't mean you no harm."

"Then how come he acts like he does?"

"I think because when he looks at you he sees his-

self, young again, and sometimes he ain't too awful
proud of hisself nomore. Give him time, boy."

One night Justin was awakened by someone knock-
ing on the frame of the open door. Sam Dark was up
from his cot instantly, pistol in his hand. "Who's out
there?"

"I come peaceful," replied a voice far from young.
Justin could see the outline of a gaunt, slightly stooped
man against the moonlight. "I'm Elijah Tankard."

"Tankard?" Dark's voice was incredulous. "You
alone, Mister Tankard?"

"I'm by myself. I come for no harm; I come to help
you . . . and to help me, too."

Dark considered a moment. "All right, Mister
Tankard, I'm takin' your word. You come on in."

Justin felt a little foolish, standing there in his
underwear, but Sam Dark was the same way and it
didn't seem to be of the slightest concern to him. Dark
said, "I'll light the lamp."

The old farmer put up his hand. "Might be just as
well you didn't. I don't know that anybody in town
would recognize me, but there ain't no use takin' the
risk, is there?"

"Not if you got reason to think there is a risk." The
way Dark said it he was putting a question to the old
man without actually asking it.

Elijah Tankard found a rawhide chair in the reflected light of the moon but he didn't sit in it. He
braced his hands and leaned his weight against its
straight back. "You got cause to distrust me after
what me and my boy Matthew done to you. And I
reckon we got cause to hate you for you deliverin' my
youngest boy Barney to the hangman. I can't rightly
say I feel any kindness toward you, Dark; I doubt as

ever I will. But whatever I think of you I hate them whiskey peddlers ten times worse. It was them that put the devil in my boy's mouth. Now they're back in our parts again, lookin' for other boys to ruin with that poison. If you'd like to catch them, Dark, I'll take you ever step of the way."

Dark stood hunched, not over his surprise. "You know they won't hang for peddlin' whiskey. Worst they'll get is time in prison."

"They ought to hang like my boy did. But better a stretch in the pen than out runnin' free and leadin' good boys astray."

Dark peered a moment at Justin Moffitt, then turned his attention back to the farmer. "Mister Tankard, would you mind waitin' outside? I want to talk this over with Deputy Moffitt."

Disappointed, Tankard observed, "You don't believe me."

"I don't *disbelieve* you. But you can see how it'd be if you was in my place; I need to talk to Moffitt."

Tankard nodded and walked out. Justin could hear a horse stamping a foot. Just one horse. He looked.

Dark said, "He sounds honest."

Justin frowned. "He still hates you; he as good as said so. Could be he's baitin' a trap to snap your head clean off."

"Could be. But I want to believe him, Justin."

"Anyhow, is it worth the risk? Like you said, worst they could give anybody for runnin' whiskey would be a stretch in jail. They sell whiskey here in Fort Smith right across the bar, legal as anything. What makes it so bad when they do the same thing in the Territory?"

"You and me, Justin, we're white. White men been drinkin' that stuff since before God wrote the Bible. We got it in our blood, and we're immune to it, to some extent. But it's new to the Indian. He didn't inherit none of that immunity. He can drink just a little of it and go plumb roarin' crazy, do things he wouldn't ever consider doin' if he was of a sound mind, sell his land, rent his wife, kill a friend the way Barney Tankard did. You'd about as well kill an Indian as to sell him whiskey. Old man Tankard knows that."

"Just the same, I wouldn't trust him no further than I could spit. You ride off with him you just may not ever come back."

"I wasn't figurin' on goin' with him alone."

Moffitt's eyes widened. "You takin' me into the Territory?"

"You been faunchin' around here like a stud colt, wantin' to get out yonder. Maybe now we'll find out if you can really earn your keep."

"I can take care of myself."

"I'm more interested in whether you can help take care of *me!*" Still standing in his underwear, Dark put on his hat and then began reaching for the rest of his clothes. "We'll have to go report to Marshal Yoes. We'll get old black George to follow after us in the tumbleweed wagon, holdin' back a day or so to keep from flushin' the game before we're ready."

Justin began to tingle. "Rice Pegler's in town. Maybe we ought to get him to go with us."

Dark looked at him in sharp disapproval. "Not Rice Pegler. We can do it, you and me. And if you can't do it, then I'll do it myself—*by* myself."

"We can do it, Mister Dark."

"Then I want you to remember one thing: you'll do what I tell you. Don't hold back and don't ask no damn fool questions. Agreed?"

"Agreed."

It took them a couple of hours to get the legal necessities taken care of and proper directions given to the Negro. Elijah Tankard waited at Dark's shack, out of sight.

"It ain't like I was afraid of anybody," he explained later, after they had crossed the river and set their horses upon the trail west. "But there's folks in Fort Smith that know me. If they seen me with you they might figure out what I was up to and send word ahead of us. Especially a man like Harvey Oates."

The name meant nothing to Justin, but he saw Sam Dark come to attention. "What about Harvey Oates?"

"You know as well as I do; it's common knowledge in the Territory that he supplies most of them whiskey peddlers. Them freight wagons of his are just to hide his real trade."

"His wagons've been searched. I've done it myself many a time. Nobody's ever found anything that wasn't supposed to be there."

"And you ain't apt to. There ain't enough marshals in the whole United States to check everything that comes into the Territory."

"One of these days we'll catch him."

"I'd love to be there."

They rode all day across green hills and wooded lowlands, past clear-running creeks and through long, lush valleys that had never felt the bite of the plow. This was yet Territory land, officially reserved for the

Indian, though, through marriage to Indian women or with maneuvering of many types of available permits, it was home now to as many white men as red. Farm-raised Justin could tell by the look of it that this country was ripe for the picking, the flatlands fairly begging for the bull-tongue plow, the rolling grasslands waiting for the white man's herds. A good many cattle already were scattered upon it, some probably having no right to be there. But as a whole the land was not yet anywhere near stocked. No wonder men waited on the far side of the river, their hands sweaty with impatience as they bided their time for the day they could come here legally and lay claim.

And the time would come; Justin had little doubt of that. This was a white man's world, and what the white man wanted he always took. It had ever been so and would ever be so, he figured. He had never pondered the moral issues. He simply took those things for facts that were historically obvious. He felt no personal guilt in this obvious wrong because it was a thing not of his doing, a thing that would have happened the same way if he had never been born.

Once when old Elijah Tankard was a little way ahead, Justin said quietly, "If this is Indian Territory it sure ain't like I expected. It looks pretty much like the other side of the river except not as developed yet."

"You expected to see Indian villages and tepees and stuff like that?"

"Well, it is Indian Territory."

"Didn't you ever hear of the Five Civilized Tribes? They was brought here from back east. They're not like the wild Indians out on the plains; they live in houses like the rest of us. They got towns like everybody else. They've had their own schools since before

I was born, their own newspapers, their own law. They're a hell of a lot more civilized than the general run of white folks that've moved in amongst them, you can bet your last breath on that."

They skirted the few small settlements and they rode out of their way to avoid meeting people on the trail. Elijah Tankard was supposed to be along as guide, but it seemed to Justin that Dark knew this part of the country as well as the old farmer did. It was unlikely Tankard strayed far from his farm except on rare occasions when he had to make the long trip to Fort Smith.

Justin noticed that by afternoon the old farmer, who had seemed to doze in the saddle off and on through the morning, began to look around with interest and perhaps concern.

"Gettin' closer now to where he lives," Dark said quietly to Justin. "Further we go now the more chance somebody'll see us with him. Ain't always healthy here to be seen with lawmen."

Once they heard a wagon and rode quickly off to one side of the trail, dismounting and concealing themselves in a heavy motte. Directly the wagon came into view, driven by an Indian wearing a flat-brimmed black hat. The Indian saw the horsetracks leading out of the road and he glanced suspiciously toward the motte. Justin felt sure he couldn't see them behind the heavy foliage. The Indian would be nervous awhile. This country was as infested with outlaws as with snakes. He was probably thinking that men who would hide along a public road might well have mischief on their mind. Likely as soon as he could do so surreptitiously, he reached down and brought up a rifle or shotgun into his lap.

Pity to scare a man this way, Justin thought.

That was one of the things Judge Parker had said he was working toward: the day when people—white or Indian—could live here and travel this land and fear nothing more than a runaway horse or a bolt of lightning.

About dusk Elijah Tankard said, "My place is just ahead, around that bend in the road. I best ride in first and be sure there's nobody around but family."

Sam Dark dismounted to stretch his legs. Justin didn't feel secure enough to chance it. He sat on his horse, warily watching the farmer ride down a twisting wagon road past a cornfield and toward a long house which lay in a grove of trees that indicated a spring. He said, "There's a dozen places between here and that house where somebody could hide and put a bullet in you."

"In *me?*"

"It's you they got it in for."

"If they killed me, they couldn't leave you around to testify."

Justin frowned. "That thought has run through my mind."

"There's lots of places back up the road they could've got us if they'd wanted to. They've let us come this far. I reckon either the old man's tellin' the truth or else he's got somethin' awful interestin' waitin' for us down at the house."

"If that's the case, what do you plan to do?"

"Just go see what it is. When the other man holds all the cards only thing you can do is stand easy and stay awake."

Elijah Tankard returned up the road, shoulders slumped in weariness. He raised one hand as he neared the motte, a peace sign from his Indian in-laws. "Everything's fine down at the house. They're fixin' supper. You-all come on."

Sam Dark glanced at Justin and nodded. He swung into the saddle and pulled up even with the old man in the other rut of the wagon trail. Saddlegun across his lap, Justin hung back a length or two, following Dark so he could watch for any movement of the farmer's gun hand. He carefully watched on either side of the road, too, especially the cornfield where the rows came at oblique angles. A rabbit jumped up and skittered away into the green corn. By reflex Justin had the saddlegun halfway to his shoulder before he caught himself. If Dark or the old man sensed it neither gave any sign. Justin lowered the gun and rubbed a hand across his sweaty face. He wondered how Dark could be so icy calm.

The log house looked much like the one Justin had known at home. It had, from appearance, started with a single cabin, later augmented by a second section separated from the first by an open dog-run. Eventually, with passage of time and perhaps after the birth of the daughter, the dog-run was closed in for another room and the cabin stood now a solid unit. Its sections did not match, but that was probably of no real concern to anybody. Its purpose was utility, not decoration.

A floorless overhang served as substitute for a porch. Beneath its roof stood a young man, his shoulders stiff and square, his eyes openly hostile. It had been too dark that night in Fort Smith for Justin to have seen what color Matthew Tankard's eyes were, if it had mattered. It startled him to see that despite the strongly Indian features and darker hue of his face the grim eyes were a deep blue. The color seemed out of place, a legacy from his white father.

Sam Dark studied the young farmer. "I didn't come here for trouble with you. But if that's what you got in mind, let's get done with it."

Matthew Tankard's jaw clenched. He glanced at his father and he said nothing.

Sam Dark swung down, stretching his tired legs again. Justin waited till he was sure Dark was on balance, then he dismounted too. He kept his gaze on Matthew Tankard, for he felt that he was where the threat lay, if there was one.

"Fellers," said the old man, "the womenfolks'll have supper ready directly. You-all want to unsaddle your horses and feed them a dab?"

Justin glanced at Dark. "What about them whiskey peddlers?"

The farmer put in, "Matthew went and took a look at them this afternoon. They're still right where they was, sellin' to all who come. They'll keep."

Justin was hungry, sure enough, but he doubted he would enjoy supper much. He looked to Sam Dark to see what the older deputy would do.

"Much obliged," Dark said. "The horses need rest and a bit of feed. So do we all. Way I figure it them peddlers can wait till tomorrow."

Justin blinked. "Tomorrow?"

"If we was to take them now we'd have them on our hands all night. We're too wore out. First time we let up our guard they'd be gone. So we'll stay here and rest if Mister Tankard and his womenfolks don't object. Come mornin' we'll be up ahead of the rooster."

Whoever said an Indian didn't show expression hadn't seen many Indians, Justin thought. The expression in Matthew Tankard's face left no doubt what he thought about the deputies spending the night. He turned to protest but his father ignored him. "Dark, that's just what I was fixin' to suggest."

"We can sleep someplace away from the house," Dark said. "Any company that comes in the night, they won't stumble over us."

They led the horses toward the log barn and the brush pens. Justin had a hard time holding his tongue until they were out of earshot. "I can feel that Indian boy's knifeblade on my Adam's apple."

Dark didn't ruffle. "All life is a gamble. Day you was born your mother gambled her life for yours. Your folks gambled whether they'd be able to feed you till you was old enough to make your own way. You gamble every day you live till finally one day you make that last bet and it don't pay. Everybody loses sooner or later."

"What if it comes *your* time and I happen to be standin' there?"

"That's what gives life its flavor, boy."

A washstand stood by the door. The Tankard girl walked up from the spring, toting water in an oaken bucket. She set the bucket on the washstand, her eyes sharply telling the deputies they'd damn well better use it before they went into the house.

"Much obliged," Dark said. Her eyes held the same ungiving hostility Justin had seen in her brother's. She wore a washed-out cotton dress like any farm girl, but it didn't hide the fact that she was half Indian. Her skin had a brownish hue and her facial structure showed the Cherokee ancestry. Her hair was braided

Indian style, the braids reaching almost to her waist. And though she wore the dress as a concession to the father's blood, her feet were in beaded moccasins.

It was her eyes that startled Justin. Like her brother's they were blue.

Dress her up in a white woman's way from head to foot, comb out her hair, and you could almost pass her off as a sunburned white girl, Justin thought. In his mind he was doing her a compliment. It didn't occur to him that she probably would have no desire to do so, that she had not the slightest regret for the part of her that was Indian.

"Supper's waitin'," she said. "When you've cleaned up."

Justin had half expected to hear only a grunt from her, judging by her Indian look. But her speech was that of her father—without accent, without effort. He thought resentfully, *I expect we'll be clean enough for an Indian place,* but he didn't put it into words. He had a notion it wouldn't take much to provoke her into a fight. She might be figuring on it anyway, but he saw no use pushing her into it.

He kept watch until Dark had finished washing and had wiped his face and hands dry on a big raw-edged cloth hanging at the washstand. The cloth had been used before. The girl had fetched clean water but she was pleased to have them dry on an old towel. Dark caught Justin's angry look.

"Put yourself in their place and figure we're lucky, button. In their minds they got reason enough to kill us—me, anyway. But they ain't done it and I don't think they got any such notion."

"Right now they want to use us."

"Don't forget we're usin' them too. Think I'd of

come if I hadn't wanted so bad to get my hands on them peddlers? I wouldn't of set foot on this place for all the gold coin in the Territory after what I already done to these folks."

Elijah Tankard appeared in the doorway. "You-all come on in." His manner was more of tolerance than of welcome.

Justin followed Dark, still wary. He glanced distrustfully at Matthew Tankard, trying to determine whether the young man carried a weapon. If he did it wasn't apparent. Dark made a slight bow toward the aging Indian woman. His voice apologetic. "Miz Tankard, we appreciate you fixin' for us. You didn't have to."

She tried, but she couldn't bring herself to look at him without wavering. "You catch those peddlers. You do the same to them that you did to my boy Barney."

Dark looked down uncomfortably. "Ma'am, we'll do the best we can."

Justin was a little surprised, hearing Dark address an Indian woman as "ma'am." Most people looked down on Indians, sort of the way they did on George Grider. They didn't "sir" a man or "ma'am" a woman. But then Sam Dark wasn't like just everybody else.

Justin had been a little concerned over the kind of meal to expect in a largely Indian household. From stories he had heard he wouldn't have been surprised to be presented dog stew. He found he needn't have worried. The Tankard women had fixed cornbread, beans, pork, thick black coffee. Justin ate slowly at first, watching the family, still not convinced they didn't have treachery on their minds. He had a wild thought that they might have poisoned the food, but he shed that notion when he saw the Tankards eating, especially old Elijah. The ride had famished him. Justin gave in to his own hunger and eased his watchfulness enough to put away a big supper.

The girl Naomi sat across the table. Every so often Justin sneaked a glance at her. Once he found her looking at him and quickly jerked his gaze away. He had seen a few Indians in his life, for they crossed the Arkansas settlements now and again, but he had never seen an Indian girl he thought to be pretty. He couldn't make up his mind about this one, not entirely. He decided if she weren't Indian he would consider her to be at least attractive. She would look better if she would get rid of the resentment in her eyes.

Hate me, then, if it makes you feel better. We'll be out of here tomorrow and you can go back to your paint and feathers.

After supper the old man offered them tobacco. It appeared to be homegrown. Dark accepted, though Justin knew the deputy had tobacco with him that had been bought in town and probably would be a tastier blend. Dark and the farmer sat and puffed, glancing at each other now and again, each wanting to talk but denied by the barrier that stood between them. Justin had looked up several times during supper at a tintype on the mantel over the fireplace. Afterwards he tried to slip across inconspicuously for a closer look. The picture was of an Indian in white man's full dress suit. Justin pondered the incongruity of it.

The girl said, "My mother's father. My grandfather."

"How did they get him dressed up thataway?"

He could tell immediately that he had insulted her.

She said crisply, "He always went like that. He taught school."

Justin tolerated the close atmosphere as long as he could then went outside. Directly he heard the door open and he turned quickly. Matthew Tankard and his sister stood staring at him. In the dark, where the color of the eyes didn't show, Matthew looked pure Indian. The look was ominous to Justin.

"Stand easy, lawman," Matthew said in a voice like his father's, except younger. "We don't intend to fight you."

Justin looked from one to the other and weighed his words before he spoke. "Comin' to this place wasn't no idea of mine."

"Mine either, or Naomi's. If it was up to me we'd just slip out there and cut those peddlers' throats like my ancestors would've done. We'd bury them someplace nobody'd find them and then we'd be the dumbest bunch of Indians you ever saw. But Papa says that ain't the way; we got to call in the same law that killed our brother."

"Sam Dark is just doin' his job. And I'm tryin' to do mine."

"And so is Judge Parker. And so is his hangman. And so are them peddlers out yonder sellin' slow death to our people. Pretty world, ain't it?"

"It's all the world we got. Maybe we can make a better one out of it."

The girl said, "It *was* a better world, once, for the Indian. Till the white man came and spoiled it."

"You're half white."

The girl glanced at her brother. "We don't brag about it."

"Your daddy is all white. Where does that leave him?"

"He married into the Cherokees. He has more of their ways than of the white man."

"I'm white. Where does that leave me?" A little of exasperation was in his voice now.

The girl shook her head. "I don't know. Where do you want it to leave you?"

Dark came out eventually. He said nothing, just started for the barn. Justin followed. Dark scattered a little hay on the ground and unrolled his blanket. Justin did likewise, asking no questions until Dark wrapped a blanket around himself and rolled over, closing his eyes. Then Justin said, "Did you see the way them people was lookin' at us? They hate us."

Dark didn't answer. Justin went on, "That girl's eyes . . . she could carve us up like catfish on a riverbank."

"You expect me to stay awake all night and keep watch?"

"I thought we might take turn about."

"When these people decide to fight us again they'll do it in broad daylight and facin' us. Better get yourself some rest."

In a few minutes Dark was asleep. It took Justin a lot longer.

5

At something like four in the morning Dark shook Justin's shoulder. "Roll out." Justin got up slowly, rubbing his eyes. Sleep held on like a drug, for he had lain awake much of the night worrying about the Tankards. He stopped at the washstand in front of the house. Splashing cold water over his face helped bring him awake. The fact that he was still alive, that nobody had come to bother them in the night, made him feel a little foolish. He wished he had slept when he had the chance.

They ate a breakfast of pork and fried bread and dark gravy, then saddled their horses. The farmer and his son went along.

Dark cautioned the bent-shouldered Elijah Tankard, "Now, you-all stay out of it. You got to go on livin' here and there's no use puttin' you in danger of trouble after we're gone. Any fightin' to be done it's our job, not yours. That's what they pay us such a big wage for."

The farmer frowned. "Me and Matthew, we was talkin' last night. We agreed you'd have a right smart better case if you was to catch them fellers actually a-sellin' whiskey. We thought me and Matthew would go in and buy some."

"You ever bought any whiskey off of them before?"

"Marshal, you know I don't hold with that. Been my aim all along to keep them peddlers out of our country."

"So if they know you they'd be suspicious, you all of a sudden comin' to buy. But your boy here, they'd maybe expect it on account of him bein' Indian." He looked apologetically at Matthew. "No offense meant."

Matthew ground his teeth together. "None taken. We both know how the white man thinks."

"It'd look natural if you was to go in there smellin' of the stuff and actin' like you'd been on an all-night drunk and run out of drinkin'-whiskey. They'd be so anxious to find out how much money they could fleece you out of they wouldn't notice us till too late."

"How am I goin' to smell of whiskey? I ain't got none."

"I got some," Dark said. "Always carry a drop or two. Never know when a man might come upon a snake."

Justin frowned. "I thought it was against the law for anybody to carry whiskey into the Territory."

"It is."

"You're carryin' it."

"That law is for *people*."

They rode half an hour. Matthew Tankard raised his hand. "Down yonder in that thicket, that's where they're camped at."

It was still so dark that Justin could hardly make out the heavier gray of the dense foliage. He caught a faint smell of smoke from what was left of last night's campfire, the coals banked against the morning's need.

Sam Dark studied the layout, as much as he could see of it. "Mister Tankard, I'd rather you stayed up here, plumb out of it. They don't need to know about you. Me and Justin, we'll slip down into that thicket and get ourselves set while it's still dark. Matthew, you wait till good daylight, then start singin' and ride in. Act drunk. Minute you pay them and they hand you the goods we'll move. You step back and out of the way. Far as they need to know you had nothin' to do with us."

"Where's that whiskey I'm supposed to smell like?"

Dark brought a small bottle out of his saddlebag. "Before you go in pour a little on your clothes. Swish a little around in your mouth. I don't have to tell you not to swallow it."

Matthew's voice was testy. "You didn't have to, but you *did* tell me anyhow."

"No offense meant."

Matthew looked down, irritated. "None taken."

Dark tied his horse and leisurely circled to enter the thicket well above the camp. Justin followed close behind him, excitement beginning to play up and down his back. At length Dark paused, crouching behind heavy brush. Justin dropped down upon his belly and peered through the gradually lifting darkness. He could see a wagon and a staked team and two bed-rolls, the men sleeping with their feet toward the embers of last night's campfire. Dark leaned to whisper in Justin's ear. "You stay here. I'll slip on around to the far side of the wagon. When you see me get up and start in you come too. And be ready; you never know what a man'll do."

Dark left him and faded out of sight. Justin lay waiting, hand sweaty-cold on his pistol. Daylight came slower than he had ever seen it in his life, the darkness taking what seemed like hours to lift. Rosy streaks finally reached across the eastern sky. The sun came up, bathing the camp in eye-pinching light. One of the men stirred in his bedroll, turning a couple of times and then flinging his blankets aside. He sat up scratching his chest, then scratching his tangled hair and his scraggy growth of beard. He took a long drink from a nearby jug, rolled himself a cigarette and drew a long drag or two from it. He took his boots out from under the blanket where they had been placed to protect them from the dew. Justin heard him call to his partner to rouse his lazy something-or-other and go punch up the fire.

Justin looked up toward the hill, wondering when Matthew would ride down out of the sunrise. It was a while before he heard from far off a strange song that he took to be some kind of Indian chant. The men in camp looked at each other. One walked over to the wagon to fetch a rifle. Silhouetted in red against the early morning sun Matthew Tankard sat his horse a moment, then started down. He sang a discordant chant and slumped loosely in his saddle. The sun picked up a momentary glint from the bottle in his hand. Sam Dark's bottle. The two peddlers watched him curiously.

Riding into the edge of camp Matthew turned the bottle upside down to show that it was empty. He held it to his mouth and tilted it as if to lick away any last drop that might previously have escaped him. Then he flung the bottle aside and shouted, "You got whiskey?"

The men eyed him suspiciously. The one with the rifle held it pointed at Matthew. "What you want, Injun?"

"Friend give me bottle. Tell me he buy bottle from

you. Now I want to buy bottle from you. You got whiskey?"

"Kind of early in the mornin', ain't it?" one demanded.

The other walked close to Matthew for a good look. "Not for this one it ain't. It's still late at night. Smells like a still." To Matthew he said, "Maybe we got whiskey. You got money?"

Matthew slid down awkwardly from the saddle, going to one knee and grabbing at his stirrup to catch himself. "Sure, I got money. You think I'm some damn broke Indian?" He dug around in his pockets and came up with a couple of silver dollars. The peddler shook his head. "Not enough, Injun. Takes a heap sight more than that for our whiskey. This is good stuff, not some cheap farmyard squeezin'. You got three more of them dollars we might do business."

Five dollars. Little as Justin knew about whiskey he knew this was robbery. No wonder these peddlers liked to work the Territory.

Matthew dug some more. He dropped one coin to the ground. Both men stepped forward eagerly to pick it up.

He's sure got their whole attention now, Justin thought. *We could walk the whole United States Army in here and they wouldn't see it.*

Matthew came up with the five dollars. One of the peddlers reached for it but Matthew pulled his hands back. "First you give-um whiskey."

The taller of the two jerked his head toward the wagon. "Go fetch it, Willis."

The one named Willis brought a bottle. Matthew took it and held out his hand as if to pay. Then he drew it back. "One bottle not enough. How much more dollars for two bottles."

"Five dollars."

"No got five more. For two bottle, maybe you sellum cheaper."

The peddlers were engrossed now in haggling with Matthew. Justin glanced toward the place where he knew Sam Dark was waiting. Dark raised up cautiously, pausing to be sure he would not be observed too soon, then moved forward, saddlegun in his hands. Justin pushed to his feet, wiped his sweaty hands on his shirt and took a good grip on his pistol as he stepped out to meet Dark. The peddlers were still arguing with Matthew. Sam Dark was within two paces of them before he spoke.

"Raise your hands. You're under arrest."

The two whirled. One grabbed at his waist, but his pistol belt still lay on his bedroll. He hadn't gotten around to putting it on. The other stood stiff, hands half upraised, eyes startled. He had laid down his rifle. It was too far to reach. The surprise faded, and anger took its place. "Who the hell are you?"

"Federal marshals," Dark replied. "You're under arrest for sellin' whiskey to an Indian."

Matthew Tankard backed away, still holding the bottle and the silver dollars.

Sam Dark ordered the two men to lie on their bellies, their hands over their heads. One promptly complied. The other stood defiant until Dark moved menacingly toward him. The man sank to his knees, cursing, then finally to his stomach. Dark handed his saddlegun to Justin and leaned over the men, quickly searching them for weapons. He found nothing except a long knife, which he took. "Justin, you chase back up the hill and fetch our horses down. We'll need the handcuffs."

Justin did as he was told, the excitement running through him like floodwater down a draw. He found Elijah Tankard sitting on the hill, watching. "Everything go the way you-all figured?" the farmer asked.

"Seems like." He caught the horses. "You best stay put so nobody ties you into this."

Justin rode down, leading Dark's horse. He tied the animals to the wheels of the wagon and brought out the handcuffs. The men lay with arms outstretched. Dark motioned for Justin to put the handcuffs on them. It was easy but he remained wary, half expecting one of the men to jump up and challenge him.

"All right," Dark said when the men were cuffed, "you two can get up now. It's a long ways to Fort Smith."

"We ain't even had coffee," whimpered the peddler named Willis. He didn't seem overly bright. Justin guessed he was probably the swamper of the pair, brought along to do the heavy lifting and the dirty work.

The other glowered at Matthew. "Damn stupid Indian."

Matthew Tankard dropped all pretense of drunkenness. Gone, too, was any pretense that he had not been in league with the lawmen. His mouth took on a sardonic smile. "Not so stupid. Maybe you'd like a drink of your own whiskey." He made no effort now at the broken English people expected to hear from an Indian. He stepped over to Willis and extended the bottle he had bought. "You can have it back. I'll keep my five dollars."

"Matthew," Dark warned, "don't . . ."

The other peddler was quick. He reached for the bottle but grabbed Matthew's hand instead. The bottle smashed on the ground as the man twisted Matthew's arm and brought the Indian around backward. In one quick motion the man snaked the pistol out of Matthew's belt and brought it to bear on Dark, using Matthew as a shield.

"All right, lawman, drop that gun or I'll kill this Injun too dead to skin!" Dark lowered the saddlegun, cursing under his breath.

Matthew was stunned, but only for a moment. He brought up his booted foot and stomped down on the peddler's toes.

Justin hadn't lowered the pistol. As the peddler was momentarily distracted Justin rushed in, hoping to get past Matthew and jam the pistol into the man's ribs. Then he could fire if he had to, and he wouldn't hit Matthew by error. But the peddler saw him coming. He swung Matthew's pistol around and jerked the trigger. Justin saw the flash and felt something strike his head like a sledgehammer. He heard another shot and felt an impact to his shoulder. He spun around, seeing crazy flashing lights, and he tasted dirt as he fell on his face. He was vaguely aware of fast movement around him, and he thought he heard another shot. He was too far gone to know.

Sometime later he felt something cold on his face and became conscious of hands wiping his forehead with a wet cloth. He opened his eyes but saw only a painful, blinding light. He shut them quickly. His head felt as if someone had struck him with the sharp edge of an axe. And someone had built a blazing fire in his shoulder.

Sam Dark's voice was quiet and gentle. "Easy there, button. Just you lay there. Movin' is only goin' to hurt you."

It was a while before Justin could begin to orient himself. At first he had an odd notion he was back on the farm and a mule had kicked him. Gradually he began to realize he had left the family place weeks ago. Piece by piece he worked out the fact that he and Sam Dark had come here hunting for whiskey peddlers. He realized finally that one of them had shot him. Opening his eyes cautiously he found he could see a little. He could discern the worried face of Sam Dark, leaning over him. A couple more men stood nearby. He couldn't make out the faces, but he reasoned that they had to be the Tankards.

"Shot me, didn't he?" Justin asked weakly.

"Twice." Dark tried to smile, but it was thin. "Hit you once in the head. That wouldn't have caused much damage, but he put another bullet in your shoulder."

"Did he get away?"

"No."

Justin turned his head a little. Now he could see the peddler—the man named Willis—handcuffed to a wagonwheel. Another lay in the clearing, crumpled like a rag doll carelessly flung aside.

Dark said, "I couldn't shoot because of Matthew. But Mister Tankard, he shot him from the top of the hill."

Unnerved, the old farmer said, "I shot a man once in the big war. Never done it again in my whole life until today."

Matthew Tankard knelt beside Justin. "I pulled a fool stunt, showin' off to that peddler, tryin' to show him us Indians can do somethin' besides drink poison. I like to've got you killed."

Justin's left arm wouldn't move. He reached up with his right hand and touched his throbbing head.

The wound was warm and sticky to his touch. His hand came away bloody.

Dark said, "Lay back, button. We got to stop you from bleedin' before we can move you any."

Justin became aware he was lying on a blanket. The sky rocked back and forth, strangely red instead of blue. He shut his eyes, hoping things would stabilize, that the burning pain might diminish. "I don't understand," he murmured. "A little time in jail . . . I don't see why he'd of took the chance."

Dark said, "Peddlin' whiskey ain't the worst some of these people have done. Likely he was wanted for somethin' a lot more serious. Probably why he was out in the Territory in the first place. Knew if we got him to Fort Smith he'd be tried for somethin' else besides whiskey runnin' and that Judge Parker would stand him on that gallows with a rope around his neck."

"A bullet was too good for him," Matthew Tankard gritted.

Dark replied, "Too bad we got this other one here to witness. Otherwise I could report that *I* shot him."

Matthew frowned. "You want the credit, Dark?"

"It's no credit. But if I'd shot him instead of your daddy doin' it, it might've saved you-all some worry later on." He glanced at the old farmer. "You-all will be marked now amongst the peddlers."

The farmer said soberly, "It ain't a good feelin' to kill a man, even if he *did* deserve it. But I was in this country before his kind of trash ever come. I'll be here when they're gone."

Justin clenched his teeth as Sam Dark bathed the two wounds in whiskey out of the wagon. Justin wondered if the stuff might be poison. It didn't matter to the peddlers, once they got their money, if some of their customers went blind or died. The whiskey burned like the hinges of hell and Justin lapsed almost into unconsciousness. He was dimly aware that Sam was probing the shoulder wound, and later that he was wrapping it with cloth from the wagon. Justin knew the cloth was probably more dangerous than the whiskey but he was in no condition to protest. He could hear Dark and the Tankards agreeing that the thing to do now was to take Justin to the Tankard farm in the peddlers' wagon. To make room for him they pitched the whiskey bottles and jugs out. Elijah Tankard picked up an axe and solemnly smashed those that didn't break in the fall. Dark salvaged a few to keep for medicinal purposes.

The prisoner Willis had regained courage now, satisfied they wouldn't murder him out of hand. "Listen to me, farmer! They'll make you pay for every drop of that stuff!"

Tankard gripped the axe as if considering swinging it at the man. "We've already paid. More than you'll ever know."

Matthew Tankard pointed at the dead man. "What'll we do about him?"

"Throw a blanket over him," Dark said. "Damn if I'll put him in the wagon with that button. We can come back later and bury him here."

During this time Justin lay still, the sky swaying dizzily back and forth whenever he opened his eyes. He didn't open them much.

He heard Matthew Tankard call, "Somebody's comin' yonder, Dark. Couple of wagons on the trail."

Justin tried to raise up and look. He couldn't move anything but his head. He turned it, trying vainly to

see. Dark touched him gently. "Lay still. Just lay still."
Soon Justin could hear the creak of wagons and the
rattle of chains and the plodding of horses. He could
tell that Dark was staying behind the peddler wagon,
out of sight, letting the other wagons get close before
he showed himself.

"The devil's own luck," Dark said, half under his
breath. "Them is Harvey Oates' wagons. Harvey
Oates, the worst whiskey runner in Indian Territory."

Elijah Tankard and Matthew stood in the open but
within easy talking distance of Dark. Matthew said,
"All we done so far has been to cut off the tail of the
snake. Now we got a chance to chop off its head."

"No," Dark told him.

Matthew said, "I see one man on each wagon, three
men on horses. That's five. No, yonder's another man
bringin' up the rear. That's six. It's two to one, them
against us."

Dark replied firmly, "It's *nothin'* to one; you ain't
goin' to contest them. Matthew, I want you and your
daddy to stay out of the way. You're no match for the
kind of men Oates keeps around him."

"You can't fight them by yourself."

"I know. If it looks like a fight I'll back off. I never
play in a game where the other man has stacked the
cards. See that ugly one on the dun horse? That's
Quarternight. He's a gun fighter and a bad one. And
that Negro? That's Huff. They say he's got whip
marks all over his back from the slave days, when he
was still little. It made him mean. Harvey keeps him
and Quarternight for protection."

The prisoner Willis decided the men at the wagons
were near enough to hear him. He shouted, "Harvey,
look out! It's a marshal!"

The wagon drivers hauled up. The men on horse-back moved together, conferred, and then one rode forward, trailed by the others. The man in the lead held a rifle across his saddle and his eyes were watchful. Justin could see him now, through a crimson haze. Harvey Oates surely must be able to see that Willis was handcuffed to the wagon wheel, Justin thought.

"What goes on here?" Oates demanded.

Sam Dark stepped out into sight, saddlegun in his hands. "Howdy, Harvey. Didn't figure on runnin' into you so far out here in the Territory."

"I asked you what's goin' on here?"

"Friends of yours had a little trouble. I caught them sellin' firewater."

Harvey Oates was a big man with a red face, broad nose and hair in his ears. Heavy black eyebrows framed a pair of belligerent eyes. "Sam, I don't know that man."

"He called you Harvey. Sounded familiar."

"I been workin' this country a long time, haulin' freight. Lots of people know me, people I don't know atall. You talked like there was more of them. I don't see but one."

"Other one's lyin' yonder under a blanket. He's dead."

Anger leaped into Oates' eyes. But he kept a calm voice. "It don't mean nothin' to me. I got no friends in this camp."

"I don't believe that, Harvey. I figure they are customers of yours, or maybe even on your payroll. I figure you got more whiskey in them wagons. I figure you're out restockin' the peddlers."

The ugly one, Quarternight, glanced at Oates and pulled his horse up closer in silent challenge. Close beside him sat the third rider, the large Negro, whose right hand rested on his gun butt. Outlaws of every race found their way into the Territory. Oates glared at Sam Dark. "Figure all you want to. The point is, you don't know. Figurin' don't carry no weight in court."

"I thought maybe I'd take a look, Harvey."

Oates leaned back in the saddle and glanced toward the two horsemen flanking him. "I bet you ain't got no warrant to be lookin' in my wagons."

"I could get one."

"But you ain't *got* one. If you want to inspect my wagons you better head for Fort Smith and get you a warrant. Then you can look all you want to."

"Meanwhile you'd get shed of all your whiskey."

"You're figurin' again, Sam. Figurin' ain't provin', is it?" A harsh smile came to Oates' face, for he could tell he had all the advantage. "Sam, I've always went out of my way to be friendly with you. I never did know just what you held against me."

"You *do* know. It's out there in your wagons."

"You ain't seen nothin'. Get yourself a warrant and then we'll let you look. Now we're fixin' to move on down this road. You figurin' on standin' in our way?"

Sam Dark tried to stare the big man down. It came out a draw. "I'll stop you, Harvey. Not today, but one of these times."

Oates spat. "Well if it ain't goin' to be today I'd be much obliged if you'd move yourself out of our road."

Dark moved back reluctantly. Oates turned in his saddle and motioned for the wagons to come ahead. He and Quarternight sat on their horses and stared at Sam Dark as the wagons went by. When they were past Oates pulled on the reins and made his horse back up a step. "I'll see you in Fort Smith sometime, Sam, and I'll buy you a drink. A legal drink."

The prisoner at the wheel saw that Oates was not going to help him. "Harvey," he called anxiously, "you just goin' to leave me thisaway?"

Oates stopped. "Stranger, there ain't nothin' I can do for you. But I'll give you some advice. Sit tight and don't tell nobody nothin'. I bet you got friends in Fort Smith, and I bet by the time Sam gets you to town they'll have a good lawyer hired and waitin' for you."

Willis nodded, relieved. "Harvey, it was that old farmer yonder that shot Mitch. And that Indian boy with him, he helped these lawmen set the whole thing up."

Oates frowned at the Tankards. "Seems to me I know you, don't I? Name's Tankard, ain't it, farmer?" His eyes narrowed in malice. "None of my business, but I'm glad I ain't in your shoes. Some people around here don't take kindly to them that helps people like Sam Dark. Some have got a long memory."

Elijah said bitterly, "I had a boy named Barney. Is your memory that long, Oates?"

Oates shook his head. "Like I said, it's none of my business."

He rode after his wagons, the two gunmen flanking him. They talked as they rode, and Quarternight looked back once toward the Tankards.

Elijah said finally, "Too bad there was so many of them. I bet you was right about them wagons, Dark."

Dark nodded. He and Matthew Tankard carefully lifted Justin into the wagon and made him as comfortable as was possible on a pair of blankets. Dark started to put the prisoner Willis in with Justin but thought better of it. "The hell with him," he said. "A walk'll do him a world of good." He uncuffed the man from the wagon wheel and locked him to the rod that fastened the endgate of the wagon. "He'll be too busy keepin' up to study on any mischief."

Willis cursed. "You aimin' to make me walk plumb to Fort Smith? That's an awful long ways."

"Longer than you ever realized," Dark agreed. "But we won't go all the way today. That button needs to lay up and rest. As for you and me we'll wait at the Tankards' till George Grider shows up with the tumbleweed wagon." He glanced at the farmer. "That is, if it's all right with you."

Elijah nodded his gray head. "You and this boy here, you've earned anything you want to ask for."

They went to the Tankards' place, Dark driving the wagon, the prisoner walking along behind, complaining, threatening, begging. The Tankards followed, leading the extra horses. The jolting brought jarring pain to Justin Moffitt, but there was nothing he or Dark could do about it. Justin fought back tears. He had not felt such despair since the first night he had left the family farm and had camped alone by the bank of some unknown creek to eat a dismal supper and lie sleepless, listening to the wild cries of the night-roaming creatures. Justin was aware that his wound was bleeding some and he knew he could very well die. Fever was rising and in his misery the despair deepened. He opened his eyes and looked out the back of the wagon, past the protesting prisoner to Matthew Tankard, who appeared once again all Indian as he brought up the rear. He closed his eyes and saw visions of the farm and wished he were there. It had never looked so good to him in reality as it did now in the homesick glow of memory.

Sometime later he awoke, startled to find that he had either slept or lapsed into unconsciousness. The wagon was not moving. He heard Sam Dark unlocking the prisoner from the tailgate and moving him around to the side of the wagon, snapping the cuff shut over a spoke in the wheel. Willis cried anxiously, "What if that team takes a notion to run away with me shackled here?"

"Then," Dark said coldly, "you better be a hell of a runner."

Justin gritted his teeth against the pain as they lifted him over the tailgate and carried him into the house. Fevered, he could nevertheless see the two women hurrying out the door. Elijah said, "Dawn . . . Naomi . . . you women got a job to do."

They placed Justin on a wooden-frame bed and a cornshuck mattress. "My brother's bed," said Matthew. "Hope it's good enough for you."

Justin couldn't tell whether there was sarcasm in the young Indian's voice or not. At the moment he was too sick to care. He felt Naomi Tankard's deft fingers removing the cloth Sam Dark had wrapped around his shoulder, and she was cleansing the wound again. It didn't seem so painful now as when Dark had done it. The fever had dulled him.

Elijah Tankard matter-of-factly told the women what had happened. Justin could feel Naomi's hands go stiff. "Papa, you killed a man?" When he reiterated that he had she said, "And those other people, they know you did it?" He told her they did. She spoke gravely, "Papa . . ."

The older woman began talking, or perhaps it was some kind of chant. Justin couldn't tell because the words were strange. Cherokee, he reasoned.

Sam Dark had watched in silence while the women took away the bloody cloths he had put on Justin. "No bullet in there," he said. "I looked. It went clean through."

When the women had rebound Justin's wounds, Sam Dark stood up. "Mister Tankard . . . Matthew . . . I'm goin' to ask another favor. It'll be days before we can move that button without risk to his life."

"He's welcome here," said Elijah.

"I figured he would be. Now, I'd like to leave our prisoner here with you awhile, too."

"You goin' someplace, Dark?"

"Thought I'd trail after them wagons awhile."

Matthew asked, "What you got in mind?"

"Nothin' definite. Just thought I'd go and watch. I might get lucky."

"I'll go with you."

"No, that'd leave your daddy too much responsibility all by himself." He paused, looking at Justin. "Besides, whatever I do I've at least got a badge to justify me. You'd be on your own."

Justin tried to raise his hand, tried to protest against Dark going off and leaving him here among strangers. But he couldn't get the words said. He could hear Dark walking out, explaining that George Grider should be along by tomorrow sometime, bringing the tumbleweed wagon, and that Dark expected to be back by then.

Sometime after that Justin lapsed into sleep. When at last he awakened, he saw a candle flickering on a small table near the bed. He sensed a presence and turned his head slowly. Naomi Tankard sat rocking in a chair. Seeing he was awake she stopped rocking. Justin tried to raise himself up but couldn't. He lay blinking, trying again to orient himself. "Be still," she said. "Any movin' you try to do just makes it worse."

His head was hammering. He reached up cautiously with his right hand and felt a bandage wrapped around his forehead. "I can't help feelin' like that feller *did* shoot out some of my brains after all. I oughtn't be just layin' here."

"I don't see that you got any choice."

"Is Mister Dark back yet?"

"No."

"Sure wish he was. Wisht he'd stayed here to begin with."

"You don't think he'll come back for you?"

"He'll be here unless somethin' happens to him. I just wisht he was here. I think we've brought trouble for you folks."

"There's been trouble here before."

"Folks say these Territory outlaws, they stick together."

"So do us Indians."

Justin lay quiet, trying to think. "Funny, I'd sort of forgot you was Indian atall."

"Had you?" she sounded dubious.

"You talk . . . well, you talk just like everybody else."

"Not like everybody. I can talk two languages, English and Cherokee. Can you?"

"No," Justin admitted ruefully. "I reckon I talk English as good as nearly anybody, but I sure don't speak no Cherokee."

"So bein' white don't make you better than anybody else, does it?"

"I never said . . ."

"Yes, you did. With your eyes, the way you looked at us when you came here yesterday. You said it."

"I'm sorry. I didn't go to cause you grief."

"It didn't upset me any. I only worry about the opinions of people I like."

He burned under the scorn in her voice. "I didn't ask to come here, you know. I come on orders, and I wouldn't of got shot at all if your brother . . ." He stopped himself, for he saw the futility of argument. Her mind was made up and talking wouldn't change it. He hurt badly enough without compounding the misery by flaring up this way. He turned his head away a minute, then back again to look at her, somehow wanting to make her feel kindlier toward him. "Look, if it's any consolation to you I've never shot at an Indian in my life. The only ones I ever seen was just travelin' across the country, and when they'd ask us for somethin' to eat we always give it to them. My pa wasn't an Indian fighter, nor my grandpa nor any other of my kinfolks that I know anything about. We always let people alone and hoped they done the same for us."

She sat rocking, staring at him. He had heard the old fable that Indians never smiled, but she made a liar of it.

"You must be goin' to live," she said, "or you couldn't have gotten that mad."

Sometime after daylight Sam Dark rode in wearily, shoulders sagging. But even through the window Justin could see him grin. Elijah Tankard went out to meet him. Matthew Tankard walked down from the barn and reached for Dark's reins, wordlessly offering to take care of his horse. Justin heard Dark ask, "How's the button doin'?"

"A right smart better this mornin' but still feverin' some," the farmer replied. "How was your ride?"

"Tell you about it directly. Got any coffee?"

"Got coffee on and the women'll hustle up some breakfast. I'd judge by looks that you need it."

First thing Dark did was to come in and look at Justin. "Button, you think you're goin' to make it?"

"I expect so."

"I wasn't sure of it yesterday. Guess you got a harder head than we thought."

"You trailed them wagons. Find any whiskey in them?"

"Never did get to look. I'm satisfied the whiskey was hidden in the beds of the wagons and covered up with a lot of freight and trade goods."

"So you just had to let them go?"

"Didn't have no evidence I could take into court."

The old farmer took the news in dejection. "So Harvey Oates keeps on peddlin' ruination and linin' his pockets with silver."

"Not this trip." Dark sipped at a cup of hot coffee and a thin smile came. "Seems like Harvey had an accident. Somehow or other a fire started durin' the night. Burned both of them wagons clean to the hubs."

Matthew Tankard had come into the room in time to hear most of it. "Lightnin', maybe."

Dark grinned. "Maybe."

6

Later they heard horses and Dark went to the window expecting to see George Grider. Justin could hear him mutter. "It's Harvey Oates. Got his whole bunch with him." Through the open door Justin could see Oates and the gunman Quarternight. He took Dark's word that the others were there. He could see one teamster riding a workhorse bareback.

Dark told Justin, "You lay still, button. I doubt old Harvey'll make any trouble right now." He walked outside, motioning for the Tankards to stay in the house. The women did, but Elijah and Matthew moved out under the overhang. Justin raised up and dropped his legs off the side of the bed, then moved down far enough to watch out the open door. The voices came clear.

"Howdy, Harvey," Dark said when Oates came.

The prisoner was still handcuffed to the wheel of the whiskey wagon. He stood up, expecting release.

But Oates gave him hardly a glance. His hard gaze rested on Dark. "You look kind of sleepy-eyed, Sam."

"Age," Dark replied. "I don't sleep good of a night anymore."

"Guilty conscience, maybe."

"Possible. I done things in my life that I wasn't proud of."

"Do anything last night that you ought to've thought over?"

"Can't think what it might've been."

Oates stared, his eyes hating Dark. "Sam, you're a long ways from Fort Smith."

"Not so far that the judge's rope won't reach."

"Somebody done us a bad turn last night. Somebody touched off both of our freight wagons. Now the judge is keen on doin' things legal."

"So am I, Harvey. If you want me to I'll go investigate."

"You needn't bother. It's done. But nobody'll catch me unawares again. Next time somebody'll catch a bellyful of buckshot that he'll be slow to digest. I doubt as the judge'll object to a man protectin' his property." He paused, his gaze moving to the Tankard men. "I reckon you folks was here all last night?"

Dark said, "I'll vouch for them."

Oates gritted, "I figured you would." He frowned at the old farmer. "Good ways to your next neighbor, ain't it?"

"It's not so far."

"I hear there's people in this country that don't like a man gettin' thick with the Fort Smith courthouse crowd. I hear it's considered a hazard to a man's health." He jerked his thumb toward the prisoner. "I expect even a whiskey peddler has got friends. They might not take kindly to what you done."

Elijah said, "We got no reason to care what they think."

"Looks to me like you got lots of reason. Old Sam Dark, he can't stay here all the time. But you got to."

Matthew Tankard took an angry step forward. "You threatenin' us?"

"No, Indian, not threatenin'. It don't mean a thing to me one way or the other. Just pointin' out facts."

Matthew took another step and Quarternight brought up a rifle lying across the pommel of his saddle. The big Negro edged his horse closer. Sam Dark reached forward and touched Matthew's shoulder. "Stand easy. They ain't got an ace in their hand. Don't give them one." He looked at Oates. "Water your horses, Harvey, then get movin'. These folks don't welcome you here."

"They may come to wish they'd welcomed me instead of you."

In a minute they were gone, Quarternight looking grimly back over his shoulder. The prisoner at the wagon had a happier expression. "Farmer, you heard what he said. I got friends. If you was to turn me loose maybe they'd forget what you done to my partner."

Matthew seethed. "Let's *do* turn him loose, Indian style. Let's give him a three-minute start then see how far he can get before I catch up and kill him."

That sobered the prisoner who looked worriedly at Sam Dark. Dark said, "No, we got to keep it legal, the judge's way. Besides this is just a little fish. The big one has got away."

"He ain't gone far. We could catch him."

"And do what? When I take him before the judge I want to do it with evidence that'll hang him."

George Grider came eventually, all alone on the seat of that big freight wagon. It seemed almost a waste, all that mulepower going all that distance to haul back a single prisoner. The lanky Negro eased wearily down from the wagon and stretched himself, pressing hands against his sides. "Sure been a long ways." He shook with Sam Dark then balefully eyed the handcuffed man. "Where you got the rest of them hid?"

Dark said, "This is the only one we have."

Grider smiled. "Him? We could've took him to Fort Smith on a water cart. Old age must be gettin' you, Mister Sam."

"Maybe so."

"Where's the boy at?"

Dark led the way into the house. Grider took off his floppy hat and nodded politely at the Tankard men, giving a little extra surprised scrutiny to Matthew Tankard's Indian features. There was a sort of easy tolerance between Indian and Negro here in the Territory, though before the war some of the wealthier Indians had been slaveowners. Grider's eyes widened at sight of Justin lying on the bed. He eased a little when he found there were no potentially mortal wounds. He brought himself to make a crooked grin. "Boy, old judge is liable to fire you, layin' off on the job thataway."

Justin tried to think of something appropriate to say but there wasn't a funny streak in him. Grider said, "Might've been better if you'd got killed. You'd of gone on the hero list. This way you're just a laid-up deputy that the guv'ment's got to feed. They do git impatient."

Justin could sense deep concern behind the black man's banter. "I'll try to do better next time."

Grider said, "We got lots of room in the wagon. We can lay out a bed for you and you can keep the prisoner company on the way home."

Dark disagreed. "We better not try till he's better able to ride."

Justin frowned. "You fixin' to leave me here, Mister Dark?"

"You're not afraid of the Tankards, are you?"

"You know better than that."

"Well, then, it's settled. Me and George'll take the prisoner in. Longer he stays here the more apt he is to bring trouble down on the Tankards. You stay till you can ride then you come on in. You can find Fort Smith by yourself, can't you?"

Justin said impatiently, "How green do you think I am?"

"Don't you start till you know you're strong enough to make it. You're bein' paid to work, not to be layin' off on a roadside someplace."

The women fixed George Grider something to eat then he started east in the tumbleweed wagon, Dark following on horseback. The last thing Justin saw of them was the prisoner sitting shackled in the wagon-bed, bouncing as the iron-rimmed wheel dropped into a rut. Justin could hear the cry of protest but didn't see George turn his head. The Negro was probably grinning and looking for another rut.

For a couple or three days Justin didn't move much. The first day it was too painful. Naomi Tankard brought him just about everything he needed. The second day the pain was less severe, but by then he had become used to Naomi fetching things and found he liked it. There didn't seem to be much gain in upsetting a favorable arrangement. Not that he tried to make things look worse than they were. The wound had swollen, and for a couple of days it had a red and angry look before the swelling started down and the healing set in.

By then Justin was walking around, though he wasn't doing it very fast. He figured the bullet had trimmed him close for he was a while regaining his balance. He never made more than a couple or three steps before he had to grab something—a chair, a bedstead, a table. Once he reached out and there wasn't anything to grab except Naomi. He did, and his face went suddenly warm. Hers colored a little. Quickly as he got his balance Justin jerked his hand away.

"Sorry. I didn't go to do that."

"No harm done, I suppose." She sounded as if she weren't sure.

"Don't want you to think I meant anything by it."

"You're not the type to grab an Indian girl."

"Not *any* girl." The warmth in his face was slow to ebb. "You always make out like I got somethin' against you for bein' Indian. Maybe the trouble is that you hold it against me for bein' white."

"I guess you can't help it."

He figured a half Indian family like this was bound to live somehow differently from other people, but after several days he could see little to support that theory. Occasionally they lapsed into Cherokee language but mostly they talked English, and it sounded the same as his own. The women cooked white man's food, the same as any farm family raising and eating most of its own produce. He had kept expecting to eat dog stew or something of the kind, but it didn't turn out that way. They said grace over their meals, a habit Justin had lost since leaving home. An uncle, Naomi said, was a minister.

Everybody in the Tankard family worked hard for there seemed more to be done than time to do it. Even so, Justin noted that Matthew always managed to take off and hunt. Late every day a full-blooded Indian of Matthew's age would show up, rifle in hand. He was introduced to Justin as cousin Blue Wing who lived a couple of miles over the hill. Usually they got back about dark carrying fresh meat. Matthew's Indian strain was strong when it came to hunting.

Justin tried to join the women at hoeing the garden, but they kept the hoes out of his reach until he got dizzy and had to go sit down. They told him plants responded better to a woman's touch than to a man's, an Indian notion Justin suspected had been originated by some Cherokee male whose hand fitted better the bow than the hoe.

Feeling came back into Justin's left arm and he found he could get limited use of his fingers. When old Elijah brought some harness from the barn and spread it beneath the shaded overhang Justin was able to help him mend it. That much, at least, he could do to help repay for bed and board. And that night when Matthew came home without meat, the front sight missing off of his rifle, Justin took a silver coin and laboriously fashioned a new sight from it. Matthew stared at him in surprise and with a little new respect.

Elijah watched approvingly. "You'd of been a good

gunsmith. You ought to've taken up fixin' guns instead of shootin' them. You wouldn't be laid up the way you been."

Justin ran his fingers down the long barrel. It was an old rifle, a hand-me-down from before the big war. But it had been cared for, and in the hands of a careful shooter it could probably trim whiskers and not bring blood.

Matthew saw Justin's appreciation for the old weapon. "Like the gun do you, deputy? My old granddaddy—not the school-teachin' one—took that off a man in a fight. A white man." He paused, a harsh humor in his eyes. "My granddaddy scalped him."

Justin managed a half-hearted smile. "I expect it was a rifle worth fightin' for in its day."

"Still worth fightin' for. It could still fetch down a trophy for a scalphunter."

Justin held the rifle toward him. "You lookin' at my scalp?"

"I reckon not. They've taken all the fun out of life these days. But my old granddaddy, he'd of taken it."

Elijah rebuked his son. "Hush up, Matthew. It's not fitten to make light of death thataway."

"It comes to all of us, Papa, whether we take it light or take it hard."

As his strength continued to build Justin started going to the stock pens with Matthew and watching him break horses. Matthew had a skill and ease at this trade, so he broke horses for other people for a fee. It looked easy the way Matthew did it. Justin considered trying to help him but knew he would be refused. He had no business boarding one of those broncs anyway. His proficiencies were in work he could do with his hands, like smithing and carpentry. He could ride a horse as well as most any farm boy, but he was no bronc breaker and knew it. So he contented himself with helping saddle a wild one or with opening the gate so Matthew could ride a humped-up pony out into the open pasture and give it its head.

Matthew found he could go an increasingly long time without dizziness now and his conscience began to nag him a little. He ought to go back to Fort Smith and report for duty. He was still on the payroll; at least he assumed he was. Fact was he had grown to like it here and wasn't particularly eager to start toting that pistol again. In a way this place gave him a comfortable feeling of being home.

He knew Naomi had the most to do with it. It might be a long time before he would chance by here again. He had grown to like being around her.

But he decided finally there was no longer any valid excuse for staying off of the job. He thought he could make Fort Smith if he didn't push himself too fast.

"I reckon I'll be leavin' for town," he told the family at supper. He was looking at Naomi when he spoke, and he noticed that she lowered her head so he couldn't see her eyes. He tried to make light of it. "I been drawin' federal wages and not doin' any work. I reckon they could jail me for stealin'."

Elijah's heavy moustache seemed to droop. "We'll miss you, boy. Somehow you've sort of filled an empty spot that's been in this house since . . ." He let it trail off there.

Naomi finally brought herself to speak. "You shouldn't hurry yourself, Justin. You're not strong yet."

"I'm strong enough and I been a burden here too long."

Naomi said, "Papa, can't you talk to him?"

Elijah shrugged. "I'd like to, girl, but a man has got a duty. When it calls him he goes, like I went to serve in the big war. You can't hold a man back from that."

Matthew frowned, watching his sister as if he had just come to a sudden realization. "Look, deputy, one more day wouldn't make no big difference, would it?"

"I don't suppose it would if there was a good reason."

"Well, the reason is that I got to take a bunch of these fresh-broke ponies up the country. I could do it tomorrow. I'd feel better knowin' there was an extra man around while I was gone."

Justin tried to see a reason why he couldn't, though he didn't try very hard. "I don't suppose they'd fire me over just one more day." He saw Naomi lift her head a little and he decided he would stay whether they fired him or not.

Matthew was ready next morning at first light to head the string of horses out. "I'll pick up Blue Wing to help me," he said. "Ought to be home by dark." He left, going north.

Justin helped Elijah hitch his team of mules. He started to walk with him down to the cornfield where the plow had been left lying at the turnrow, but Elijah wouldn't hear of it. "You'd work yourself up to a heat and you ain't strong enough to face it. We'd have you on our hands another week. You just shade yourself, boy."

Justin shrugged and watched as Elijah walked the team down the hoof-worn trail to the field, trace chains jingling. Justin stood on first one foot, then the other. Finally he decided he could keep occupied by saddle-soaping the harness in the barn; he had noticed a lot of it getting dry and tending to brittleness. He dragged it into the shade by the barn door and went to work. There was more of it than he had realized. Presently the women finished their chores in the house and started down toward the field, hoes in their hands, to help chop out the green corn. Justin waved and he caught the quick flash of Naomi's smile.

The harness took him the better part of the morning. Finished, he looked around for something else useful to do and decided to grease the wagon wheels. They needed it. He used the wagon jack to raise the rear axle. The big rear wheel turned out to be almost too much for him. He wasn't as strong as he figured. But he managed to lift it off.

Naomi came up from the field, walking toward the house. Seeing Justin she cut across to the barn and stood watching him a moment. "You'll have to eat dinner outside," she smiled. "You'll never get that grease off of you in time to eat in the house."

"Never could grease a wagon and keep myself clean."

"You don't have to do this, you know. You don't owe us anything."

"You been feedin' me for a week and a half."

"You wouldn't've been shot if it hadn't been for Matthew. So we owe *you*, not the other way around."

"I'd as soon be doin' somethin' like this as sleepin' in the shade. I don't take it as work." He had finished one wheel and started to lift it back into place. Naomi moved to help him, and he shook his head. "I'll get it. This ain't for a girl to do." The job left him breathless. The strain set his head to aching, and he hoped his face didn't show it. He had bitten off too much but he wouldn't admit that now. He would just go ahead and chew it.

Naomi said, "I came to fetch a jug of water down to the field. I'll bring it by here for you."

"Thanks, but I'm able to walk to the well. You better see after your folks."

Jug in hand, Naomi moved barefoot down the trail. Still breathing hard from exertion of lifting the wheel, Justin leaned against the barn door and watched her, admiring the easy grace of her walk, the gentle flip-flop of her long braids. It was easy to forget she was half Indian, and even when he thought of it, it didn't make a difference to him anymore.

Well he couldn't stand here all day hypnotized by a girl. He turned to step back into the barn. A movement beyond the field caught his eye and he stopped. Squinting, he made out only a blur, obscured by the heavy green underbrush. His first thought was that Matthew was getting home a lot earlier than he had said. Half a dozen horsemen broke out into the clear at the edge of the plowed ground, and Justin knew it wasn't Matthew. He pushed away from the door, instinctively uneasy.

Elijah Tankard had the reins looped around his shoulders, his hands gripping the plowhandles. He leaned back against the reins, halting the team, and reached up to slip the reins over his head. His wife Dawn was working her hoe fifty feet from him, her back turned to the men. She saw Elijah halt and she turned to see what had caught his attention. She looked only a moment then began moving toward her husband.

Naomi had gone a hundred yards toward the field. She stopped, watching.

It could have been some of the neighbors; at the distance, Justin couldn't tell. But he sensed fear in the way Dawn moved to Elijah as if for protection. Justin reached instinctively for his pistol and remembered it was in the house. It wouldn't be any better than a slingshot at this distance anyway. He remembered that Matthew hadn't taken his rifle on the horseback trip. It was still in the house. Justin broke into a sprint.

Naomi stood watching. Justin shouted at her to come back. If she heard she ignored him. He wanted to run after her, but the first thing was to get that rifle.

Finding it was easy; Matthew had left it leaning in a corner of his room. But it was one of the old percussion cap kind, and finding caps and cartridges took a minute. Justin shoved a handful in his pocket and went out the door running.

Naomi was moving now toward her father and mother. The men had brought their horses to a halt in a semicircle and confronted Elijah and Dawn far down in the field.

"Naomi!" Justin shouted. "Come back here!"

She gave no sign that she heard him. She was running when Justin saw the puffs of dark smoke. The sounds of the shots came a second later. He saw Elijah Tankard fall. Dawn rushed at the men, swinging her hoe in fury. Two more smoke puffs rose, and she fell.

Naomi stopped. Justin heard her scream. The riders heard her too. They appeared startled for a moment.

Then one spurred into a run through the corn, the horse laboring over the plowed rows.

"Naomi!" Justin shouted at the top of his voice.

She turned and started in his direction like a frightened doe. All this time Justin had been hurrying toward her. He could tell he wouldn't reach her before the horseman did. Justin painfully raised the rifle to his shoulder and fired. He didn't have the range. He saw dust kick up in front of the horse. The rider kept pushing, confident Justin couldn't hit him.

"*Justin-n-n-n!*" Naomi screamed.

Damn an old slow rifle like this one, Justin cursed silently as he struggled to reload. He watched the horseman rapidly narrow the gap between himself and the girl. Other riders had lost interest in the farmer and his wife and also were moving across the field.

Dry-mouthed, Justin dropped to one knee to take steadier aim. He drew a bead across the silver sight that he had put on the rifle for Matthew. He tried to lick his lips but his tongue was dry. He took half a breath, held as steady as he could, then squeezed the trigger.

The horse stumbled and the rider pitched forward across its neck. Justin rushed again to reload. Naomi glanced back once and saw she was out of momentary danger, but she didn't slow. If anything she ran faster.

The rider was down only a moment. The horse struggled to its feet. The rider took a quick look, then swung back into the saddle.

I just must've creased him a little, Justin thought. *I'll do a damn sight better next time.*

He didn't have to. The wound must have been

worse than the rider thought for the horse faltered and went down threshing. The horseman jumped free in time to avoid being pinned. He kicked at the down horse, trying to force it to its feet.

Naomi was in the clear. None of the other riders could catch her now. A pair stopped running and began to fire pistols at her, but at the distance they had no luck.

Justin had the rifle reloaded but held his fire, for he had scant chance of hitting anything and might need that load later. Naomi ran into his arms, crying hysterically. "To the house," he shouted. "We can't afford to get cut off out here in the open."

The rider who had chased Naomi was still kicking futilely at his horse. He was a hundred yards away but Justin thought he knew him. He looked like Quarternight.

Justin and Naomi made the house in a hurry. Naomi cried, "They killed them! They killed Mama and Papa!"

Going through the door he took a quick look back. The horsemen spurred for the house. All of a sudden the house didn't look like a good idea to him. It was too big for two people to defend against someone who really wanted in.

"Out the back door," Justin said. "Maybe they'll think we've holed up inside." He took time to grab his pistol and gunbelt and a few more cartridges for Matthew's rifle. He took Naomi's hand and they sprinted across the back yard, crouching low. A tangle of brush came up within twenty feet of the outbuildings. Justin didn't let Naomi slow until they were in the protection of it. Then he dropped to one knee, breathing hard and looking back.

He saw the horsemen gallop up to the house. A pair circled around to the back and swung down, their attention on the building.

"They didn't see us," Justin whispered. "They think we're still in there. Maybe we got a little time before they find out." But not much, he knew. The men would be tracking them shortly.

Naomi wept quietly, but their own peril did not allow her to dwell upon grief. She tugged at Justin's sleeve. "This way." She led him through the brush to a gravel bed where their tracks didn't show. They followed the dry gravel bed awhile then went out from it onto a slab of rock. She pointed toward another heavy growth of brush a few lengths away. Justin broke a branch off inside a bush where it wouldn't show and he carefully brushed out their tracks as they moved toward the heavy cover.

Behind them the men were pouring gunfire into the house. *Sooner or later*, Justin thought, *they'll rush it and they'll find out we're gone. I hope it's later and not sooner.*

Justin and the girl were climbing. Justin figured they were a mile from the house. A little later he decided it was closer to two.

The shots had stopped. *By now they know. They'll be hunting us.* But he and the girl had left little trail.

Naomi dropped to her knees, exhausted. She no longer wept, but dust had settled on her face and the dried tears had left tracks easy to see. She looked at Justin a moment, then leaned into his arms. The tears began to flow again. Justin didn't try to speak comforting words for they would be idle and of little help to her. He just held her and let her cry herself out.

When she was done with it he said, "You've acted like you know where we're goin'. *I* sure don't."

Her voice was tight. "There's a place up yonder in the hills. Not many people know about it. It's got water; it's got protection."

Her eyes widened and Justin turned. He saw a column of brown smoke.

"They've fired the house," he said.

She nodded and lay her head against his chest a minute, silent. Then she said, "The smoke'll bring the neighbors if the shootin' didn't. Then I guess Oates' men will leave."

"How do you know they was Oates' men?"

"Who else's would they be? Anyway I saw the one who tried to catch me. He was with Oates the other day."

"Quarternight," Justin said.

"He's the one. Oates sent them, all right."

A chilling realization came to him. "Quarternight probably realizes you can identify him. He can't afford to let you live."

"The neighbors'll scare them off when they come to see about the smoke."

"But Quarternight and them, they'll be huntin' for you."

"They won't find us where we're goin', not if we cover our tracks. Just a few of the Indians know about this place. Barney and Matthew and me, we used to play up there. It's where Barney went to hide after he killed that man."

"Sam Dark found him," Justin pointed out.

"Barney was still half drunk and scared. He didn't hide his trail. We'll hide ours."

They moved slower and were careful to leave no

tracks. Weakness came over Justin now that the mortal urgency was past. He had to stop often and rest. Times his skull felt as if it would split open. He felt of his head, afraid the wound might be bleeding again; otherwise he didn't see how it could hurt so much. Whenever he stopped to rest he turned his left ear in the direction of the back trail, listening for any sound that would indicate pursuit. All he could hear was the wind rustling through the brush, or the humming of the warm-weather insects, or the chatter of birds disturbed by their presence.

Naomi bent over him once, where he had dropped. She put her hand to his cheek then carefully touched his forehead. "Justin, this has been too much for you."

"You see where I got any choice?"

She stared gravely. "Looks like us Tankards have brought you nothin' but trouble."

"Not you. It's been Harvey Oates. From the first, startin' with what his whiskey done to your brother, it's been Harvey Oates."

She cradled his head in her arms and her tears touched warm against his cheek. "I'm sorry for all that's happened to you, Justin. For your sake I wish you'd never come."

"I'm sorry for the way things turned out, Naomi. But I'll never be sorry that I came."

Daylight had faded when they reached the place she had told him about. It lay three quarters of the way up a mountain, a deep brush-filled header that could hide half an army. At the foot of it Naomi stepped barefoot into a tiny stream. All but exhausted Justin took off his boots and followed, carrying the boots and socks under his arm. The stream would leave no sign of their going. They moved up and up. Once they left the stream to go around a tiny waterfall and Justin brushed out the few tracks they made.

At last, most of the way to the top of the mountain, they came to the clear, gurgling spring that fed the stream and started it on its long journey down toward the Arkansas River.

"This is the place," Naomi told him. "We named it the Deerhorn Pocket. It'll take another Indian to find us here."

Justin flopped to the ground on his stomach and lay in silent misery, hiding his face from Naomi so she wouldn't know. But she did know. She lay down beside him, her head on his shoulder. Justin thought, *I ought to be the one to comfort her, not the other way around.* But all he could do was lie there.

"We got no food here," he pointed out finally. "We can rest a day or two, maybe three. But we can't stay forever."

"We won't be here long. But even if we are, there's game aplenty . . . deer, squirrels . . ."

"We can't shoot it. They'd hear the shots."

"This has been an Indian campground a long, long time. Matthew and Barney left snares up here. And over yonder, wrapped up in oilskin, is a bow and a quiver of arrows that the boys kept here."

"I couldn't hit nothin' with a bow and arrow."

"I can. But likely we won't have to worry about it long. Matthew will know where we've gone. He'll come."

"How'll he know?"

"This isn't the first trouble that ever came to the Tankards or their kin. We made it up a long time ago that if any of us was to ever get in trouble we'd come to this place. That way the others would know where to look. Matthew will come."

"If they don't get him first." The moment he said it he wished he hadn't.

"Oh, Justin," she cried, "they mustn't get him. They mustn't. He's all I got left."

Justin turned over on his side and took her hand. "You've got *me,* Naomi, if you want me."

She came into his arms.

7

Sometime in the night they heard brush crackle. Horses were moving up into the header. Justin raised himself onto one elbow, roused out of an uneasy sleep. He reached for the rifle but he touched Naomi instead. He found that she was listening too, holding her breath.

"It can't be *them*," she said, but the fear in her voice made a lie of it.

Justin got to his feet, rifle in his hand. He stood uncertainly, wanting to move away but not knowing which way to go. One place was about like another.

"Maybe it's Matthew," Naomi said. "I told you he'd know where we are."

"Maybe." Justin decided to move down the header a little, toward the horses and away from the sound of the spring. Down there he could hear better and keep better track. Silently he motioned for Naomi to follow him. They moved into the darkness of the brush and walked carefully, trying not to step on a dead limb or snag a branch that might give them away. Justin stayed in front, the rifle up and ready. The blood pounded in his temples, bringing the pain back with a vengeance. When they had moved thirty or forty yards he dropped to one knee and held his breath, listening.

He heard a man's voice call, "Naomi! Naomi, you up there?"

Naomi cried out, "It's Matthew. I told you he'd come."

Justin was cautious. "You real sure it's him?"

Naomi was. She called to her brother, and his voice came back strong with relief. "Stay where you're at, Naomi. We're comin'."

Justin and Naomi stepped down to the stream and waited. When Matthew sighted them in the pale moonlight, he swung from the saddle and came running, grabbing his sister. "Thank God. I was scared to death they'd killed you or carried you off."

Justin stood in silence, pondering the foolishness of an old notion that Indians never cried. When she could, Naomi told Matthew that Justin had saved her and that she had led him up here.

Justin said, "I was wishin' there was some way we could've got word to you. But we was afoot."

Matthew solemnly stared at him. "Wasn't nothin' you could do, except what you done. I'm glad you was here, Justin. As it is we got to go down and bury Mama and Papa. If it hadn't been for you I'd be buryin' my sister, too." Matthew shoved his hand forward. "From now on you're not a white man. You're a friend."

The young Indian Blue Wing had been riding beside Matthew and three more Indians had followed single file. These dismounted and came up, listening solemnly for what Naomi and Justin had to say. Naomi was too choked for talk so Justin told it as short as he could.

A middle-aged Indian whom Justin took for Blue Wing's father spoke gravely. "We heard shots. Pretty soon we saw smoke. When we came, the men rode away. Elijah, Dawn . . . they were both dead. We couldn't find Naomi. We thought maybe those men, they carried her away. Men like that, they like Indian girls."

Matthew pointed at his rifle in Justin's hand. "Kill any of them?"

Justin shook his head.

"A pity. Blue Wing's papa and the others, they didn't get close enough to recognize anybody. Did you?"

Justin glanced at Naomi and saw she couldn't answer. "I shot a horse out from under one of them. Naomi says he was Quarternight."

In the moonlight he could see cold fury in Matthew's face. "Quarternight. And behind him Harvey Oates. That's three Tankards he's put in the grave. He'll never kill another one."

Justin frowned. "Don't you take any wild notions, Matthew."

"Nothin' wild about the notion *I* got." He turned to Blue Wing's father. "Charley, if it's all right with you we'll take them down to your place." Charley Wing nodded and Matthew took his sister's hands. "You'll be safe enough there. When we've buried the folks Charley can take you and hide you out among some of our people. Nobody'll find you unless you want to be found."

Fear lay in Naomi's eyes. "And where are you goin', Matthew?"

"You know. Don't try and talk me out of it, little sister. I'm the only man in the family now. It's up to me."

Justin said, "Matthew, the law . . ."

"Don't talk to me about the law. It hung my brother, but Oates and Quarternight and his kind run free. My people, my mother's people—they've always had their own law. What they had to do they just went out and done it."

Blue Wing was dispatched to Fort Smith to bring Sam Dark, but it would be a long time before Sam would get here. Not much was left of the night when the rest of the party reached Charley Wing's log cabin, and Charley's sad-eyed wife took her niece into her wide-open arms. Justin lay on a blanket on a small porch, but he slept little. Exhausted, he was nevertheless kept awake by the terrible scenes which kept running through his mind over and over again. At daylight everybody was up. Justin doubted most of them had slept much better than he had, least of all Matthew. They ate breakfast in silence, saddled their horses and hitched a team to Charley Wing's wagon for Charley's wife and two daughters and Naomi. They rode over the green hills, gathering other neighbors on their way to the gray ruins of the Tankard house.

At the edge of the clearing, a hundred yards from where the charred logs lay in a heap, Justin saw two men standing by a single large, newly dug grave. The men stood in solemn silence and watched as the horsemen and the wagons approached. They took off their hats and helped the women down. One spoke words that Justin took to be Cherokee and Naomi grasped the man's hand a moment. Justin realized that this was the minister-uncle, brother to Dawn. The uncle read from the scriptures, and when he was done a few of the Indians broke into a chant that made the hair stand on Justin's neck. Directly the service was done. Matthew spaded the first earth into the grave, then turned toward his horse. He paused a moment and spoke so quietly to his sister that Justin didn't hear the words. He saw her nod and reply as quietly. Matthew turned to Justin for a final word. "See you someday, friend." He stepped into the saddle and was gone. He carried with him the rifle with the silver sight.

Justin knew what might lie in store for Matthew. He wanted to stop him but he knew there was no way. Sick at heart he turned back to Naomi, and all words failed him.

I wish Sam Dark was here. Sam would know what to do.

It was another full day before Sam Dark arrived. With him came the tall Negro George Grider and the lanky, hard-eyed Rice Pegler. Justin was glad to see Sam and George. He wondered why Dark had brought Pegler along, feeling about the man as he did. Probably he had had to; orders from Marshal Yoes, or perhaps even from the judge. Rice Pegler knew his business.

Dark had heard the story from Blue Wing but he listened to it again from Justin. His expression became more grave as the event was recounted. A deep bitterness came into his eyes and a sadness as profound as if it had been his own family. "Where's the girl at now?"

"They taken her away from here. Hid her out among some of Charley Wing's kin. Oates' bunch can't find her."

Pegler noted Dark's emotion. "I don't see why you need to take it so personal. It's just another job. Anyway these are nothin' but Indians."

Justin said tightly, "They're people."

Pegler chewed a cud of tobacco then spat a brown stream at one of Charley's chickens. "You get along real good with these folks, Moffitt. Never would've suspicioned there was any Indian blood in you."

"There ain't."

Justin couldn't tell if Pegler meant malice or not. Probably he didn't; his words probably simply reflected his lifelong attitude toward people different from himself. He said, "Careful, then, or there might be Indian blood in your kids."

Dark said impatiently, "You got any idea whichaway Matthew went?"

"North. That's what Charley's people tell me. They tracked Quarternight and his bunch a long ways. When Matthew left here they already had the trail started for him."

"They still with him?"

Justin shook his head. "He sent them back; told them it was his place to take care of it."

Dark worried aloud. "If he catches up to Quarternight and he's by himself it's apt to be the last mistake he ever makes. Reckon you could talk some of Charley's people into ridin' along and showin' us? The more trackin' we can save the farther ahead we'll be."

Blue Wing put in, "I'll go with you. And I'll get one

of my cousins who helped mark the way for Matthew."

Justin said, "Thanks, Blue. That'll sure help us."

Dark frowned. "Us, Justin, but not you. You ain't lookin' none too good. You'll stay here and rest."

"I've rested enough these last two days to do me for a lifetime. I could ride with you now plumb to hell."

"And that's about where you'd end up. You stay."

Angry, Justin squared his shoulders. "Them was good people and they was friends of mine. I'm goin'. Even if I have to take this badge off and ride as a civilian, I'm goin'."

Dark studied him a moment, surprised and weighing the possibilities of argument. "All right, but if you can't make it we'll just have to leave you where you fall."

"Any fallin' done it won't be by me."

They ate a quick meal prepared by the Wing women, then they started off in a long trot, led by Blue Wing and a cousin of Justin's age named Alvin James. It was a curiosity to Justin that most of the Indians bore English names like the ones he had heard all his life and that they spoke a brand of English not dissimilar to the kind he was used to. When he came down to analyzing it the biggest difference was in their faces. He had already found with the Tankards how quickly one could learn to disregard that.

The cousin pointed. "No use pickin' up the trail right away. We can cut across to where we put Matthew on it and save ourselves some travelin'."

"Let's be at it," said Dark. "The more time we save the more chance we got of keepin' Quarternight and his bunch from killin' that boy."

They didn't have a change of horses, so they had to protect the ones they rode. A couple of times Dark had to call the Indians down from trying to set up too hard a pace. "It's apt to be a long trail, and we can't afford to be makin' the last part of it afoot."

Blue Wing would nod agreement, but in a little while he would be pushing again, and the riders moved occasionally into a swinging lope. Sam Dark controlled the pace. He didn't let them stay at it long. Always when they slowed back to a trot impatience began bubbling in Justin. He had heard of runner Indians he was sure could have traveled faster than this afoot.

Normally tracking would have to end at dark, but because Blue Wing's cousin knew one of the forward points they were able to travel deep into the night. When at last Dark called a halt the two young Indians were still raring to keep moving. Dark firmly turned them down. "The horses need rest even if you don't. They're doin' all the travelin'."

It always surprised Justin how easily Sam Dark could make himself drop off to sleep. Knowing from long experience the importance of rest at critical times he had disciplined himself into the knack of catching sleep wherever and for however long he could. Justin lay awake much of the night, tossing restlessly, thinking of the Tankards, of Naomi, of Matthew. His shoulder hurt him, too, though he had studiously avoided letting it show when Dark was looking.

Sometime before daylight Dark awakened him by gently shaking him. He was careful not to touch the wounded shoulder; Justin decided Dark probably knew after all. "Rouse yourself from that blanket, button. We'll have us a little coffee and cold bread and we'll be on our way."

They had put an hour behind them before the sun came up to light their way. They had ridden deep into the day when they crossed a shallow stream and Alvin James reined up. "This is as far as we got before Matthew caught up to us. Trail's cold now, but I think if we're careful we can follow it."

Dark nodded at the Negro. "George."

George Grider, Justin had learned, was highly regarded for his sharp eyes and his ability to follow the dimmest of trails. He had patiently explained to Justin once that the trick was to know how things were supposed to look in nature and then find the telltale signs of disturbance that revealed a man or a horse or whatever it was had passed that way. He had tried to demonstrate a couple of times when they were in Fort Smith with a few hours to kill, but Justin had never been able to see half the things George patiently tried to point out to him. Justin had made up his mind that whatever other qualifications he might have as a deputy marshal, any difficult tracking job was out.

Justin soon decided Alvin James was a better tracker than his cousin Blue Wing and George was perhaps even better than Alvin. They faltered now and again on the trail. Occasionally it was Alvin who picked up sign; more often it was George. Between them they kept the riders moving along in a fairly decent way.

Once the trail played out altogether at one particular stretch. George and the Indians combed the area without luck. George, ranging far out, spotted an Indian cabin in a meadow and suggested they go ask if anyone had seen Quarternight's bunch, or perhaps the lone Matthew Tankard.

"Not you," Blue Wing said. "They won't talk to the law; they're afraid of the badmen. But they'll talk to me and Alvin."

The two young men rode to the cabin. Sitting back at a respectful distance Justin watched an animated conversation between an Indian at the front of the cabin and the two cousins on horseback. There was much movement of hands and much pointing. Presently the pair came back. Blue Wing reported. "He says we can probably pick up the trail yonderways. He saw them all—Quarternight first, then Matthew. Matthew was beginnin' to close up on them when he passed here." He looked northward worriedly. "If Quarternight stopped anywhere there's a good chance Matthew's caught up by now."

Dark observed, "If he did he's probably been killed."

Blue Wing nodded. "Maybe his horse came up lame or somethin'."

"Not likely."

"We can hope."

They cut across as the Indian had suggested and picked up the trail. Justin could see much of it now, despite his shortcomings as a tracker. He surmised that Quarternight's group hadn't been riding very fast. They probably hadn't expected pursuit of any serious nature, for a large band of outlaws was considered safe in this territory from everything except each other. The law seldom traveled in groups large enough to stop them and the natives were unlikely to challenge them. The possibility of revenge was a cardinal point of outlaw strength deep in the Territory.

Look the other way and live was the self-protective motto of people beyond easy reach of the judge's court.

The hard, steady riding was agony to Justin. In the first place he wasn't as strong as he had thought. The horse's jarring trot kept sharp pains darting through his healing shoulder. Times he couldn't keep his face from twisting. He dropped back a little to protect himself from Dark's sight, though he had an uncomfortable feeling that Dark knew and was simply waiting for him to give up and fall out.

The only way I'll quit is to faint, and I'm a long ways from that, he told himself stiffly. *Come night I'll still be with you, Sam Dark.*

And he was, though realistically he knew if things came to a sudden showdown he probably would be more a hazard than a help. A red haze lay before his eyes and he feared that when he tried to dismount he probably would go down on his face.

Dusk came. Justin expected Dark to call a halt but he didn't. George Grider said he couldn't see the tracks anymore. Dark replied, "It don't matter. There's a settlement up yonder a ways. I'm bettin' they was headed for it. It's been a restin' place for the outlaw breed a long time. Last year I was trailin' a man through here. When I hit town everybody in the country knew it. Come to find out a storekeeper had a system of warnin' people. Of a night he hung a lantern in a certain place at the front of the store. Of a day he ran up the flag. I was two days figurin' out that he wasn't just bein' patriotic."

It took a while in the dark to get lined out in the right direction. At length they came upon a well-marked wagon road and followed it. Justin rode along at the rear, head down, shoulder throbbing so that he wanted to cry out. He had no clear idea of time for it moved with a terrible slowness.

Lanternlight glowed downtrail and Justin straightened as he heard Dark say the settlement lay ahead. Justin managed to look a little more alive, whether he felt it or not. He sensed that Sam Dark turned in the saddle, watching him critically. Sam dropped back and waited for Justin to come up even with him. "You all right, button?"

"You hear me complainin'?" Justin's voice was raw and testy, a cover-up for the pain.

"If there's any trouble you let me and George and Rice Pegler take care of it. You'd just be in the way."

"Then how come I'm here?"

"That's what I been wonderin'."

Justin didn't see a sign showing the name of the settlement. It didn't matter; the name of a place had little to do with what happened there. He saw half a dozen buildings fronting on the road, most of them standing in darkness, for it was getting on into night. He made out a blacksmith shop and a mercantile. A lighted lantern hung in front of a building that had the word *hotel* painted across it. Except for lamps in windows of a few dwelling houses back away from the road the hotel was the only place in town that showed any real amount of light. Most folks either had gone to bed or were over at the hotel, it seemed.

It was plain that Dark knew the place. He rode straight to the hotel and dismounted, stretching himself and taking a quick look around. He walked up to the window and peered, hand on his pistol. He jerked his head in a motion for Grider and Pegler to follow him. "Button, you stay out here with Blue and Alvin."

Justin eased from the saddle and leaned a moment against his horse, the weakness coming over him and threatening to make him fall. When his head cleared, he made his way haltingly to the window. Inside the front room he could see half a dozen men gathered around a table, playing cards. He remembered a couple of the faces. They had been with Oates when Dark and Justin and the Tankards had taken those two whiskey peddlers. A middle-aged Indian woman drowsed in a chair against a far wall. Justin theorized she was the hotel owner's wife; marriage to an Indian was one way many white men found a legal means of establishing business in the Territory.

The men looked up in surprise as Sam Dark walked in the door. Justin drew his pistol, figuring to back Dark from out here if trouble started. But no one gave any indication of starting it.

At length Dark said, "I'm lookin' for Quarternight."

A man Justin took to be the hotel owner pushed away from the table and stood up. "You got a warrant, marshal?"

"I got a witness that says he done murder. Now, where's he at?"

"You're a little late, marshal."

"I'll be the judge of that. Where'd he go?"

Justin took that for an idle question, because he was sure these men wouldn't willingly tell anything. To his surprise, the hotel man said, "He didn't go far; I'll show you, marshal."

He walked to the door and stepped out onto the little porch where Justin stood. He glanced at Justin and the Indians then looked back for Sam Dark. He pointed. "You can't hardly see it in the night, but the graveyard lies yonderway a couple hundred yards. That's where Quarternight went. If you want to take him with you you'll have to dig him up."

Dark stared, incredulous. "He's dead?"

"I'll lend you a shovel. Go see for yourself." The hotel man paused, waiting for the impact to soak in. "Now if you really want to be doin' somethin' worthwhile, marshal, you can go get the man that killed him."

"What happened?"

"Last night, about this time or a little later, we was all settin' there playin' cards just like we're doin' now. No sign of trouble, everybody just enjoyin' himself, old friends together talkin' about old times and havin' a harmless little game. All of a sudden this young Indian steps through the door with a big old rifle in his hands. He don't say nothin' to nobody. He just puts that rifle up against Quarternight's head before anybody has time to make a move. He pulls the trigger and blows Quarternight all over the room. You want to go back in there and look?"

Sam Dark shook his head. "Anybody do anything to this boy?"

"Nobody had time. It happened so fast Quarternight never did even see him, I don't think. Had his back to the door. After the shot, the place was full of smoke. We was fallin' out of our chairs, tryin' to find our guns. The boy went back out that door and disappeared into the night."

Dark's fists clenched and loosened as his mind darted ahead to the many possibilities. "If it happened that fast I don't expect anybody got enough of a look to identify that boy if they ever seen him again." He sounded almost hopeful.

Whatever his hope had been one of the Oates teamsters dashed it. "I can tell you, marshal, and if you catch him I can stand up in court and put the rope around his neck. It was that friend of yours, that Tankard boy."

Dark looked sharply at him. "There ain't enough lamplight in that room to hardly see your cards by. You could be mistaken."

"No mistake, marshal, and you know it. I seen that Tankard boy right enough. He shot poor old Quarternight without givin' him a chance. I'll stand up in front of your hangin' judge and tell him so. I'll see the rope put around that boy's neck for what he done to Quarternight."

Dark said, "You could be lyin', all of you. You could've killed him yourselves in an argument over the card game." He was grabbing at straws and Justin knew it.

Rice Pegler put in, "What's got into you, Sam? It's open and shut. We been ridin' like hell to try and get here ahead of that boy so they wouldn't kill him. Didn't turn out like we figured, but there was murder done just the same. That boy's got a rope comin' to him now. It's up to us to see that he's brought in."

Misery was in Sam Dark's eyes. "Always anxious to hang somebody, ain't you, Rice?"

"One lawbreaker looks same as another to me. If Quarternight had killed that boy you'd've been hellbent to take *him* in. I don't see no difference."

Dark shook his head hopelessly. "No, I reckon you don't. You never could." He glanced a moment at Justin who leaned against the wall, his head down.

"We'll rest here the night then we'll start in the mornin' to see what we can find."

Justin cried, "Knowin' why he done it you'd still hunt him down?"

Dark snapped at him, "I told you there'd come times you'd wish you hadn't pinned that badge on. I told you there'd be jobs you'd hate yourself for. Now don't come cryin' to me about it." He turned away, not showing his face to Justin.

Rice Pegler said, "Sam, we could hunt around here for a month and not find him. You and I both know where we can go to catch him."

"He won't go home, not after this."

"Not home. You know who he blames for all that's happened. Even more than Quarternight he's blamin' Harvey Oates. All we got to do is go stay close to Oates. Sooner or later that boy'll show up and try to kill him. We'll be there and we'll have us one surprised Indian."

8

Sam Dark set a slow and easy pace going back to Fort Smith. Rice Pegler was impatient but Dark told him, "Justin Moffitt has been through a lot, his wound not bein' healed. I figure we ought to take it easy on him."

Pegler said, "I thought you was just givin' that Indian boy plenty of time to get in ahead of us and kill Harvey Oates."

"That," Dark said impassively, "sure would be a pity, wouldn't it?"

If such an event had been Dark's secret hope, however, he was disappointed. When after their leisurely trip they finally reached Fort Smith they found big Harvey Oates alive and considerably indignant. Beside him at his wagonyard was the large Negro who had been with him and Quarternight the morning the whiskey peddler was shot. "Huff here come and told me what happened to Quarternight. I reported it to the authorities. What I want to know is how come you all here instead of out yonder trackin' that killer down?"

"That's a big old country," Dark said bluntly, making no effort to hide his feelings against Oates. "We figure that boy knows it like he knows the back of his hand. Findin' him is goin' to be awful hard."

"You won't find him here in my wagonyard!"

"As a matter of fact that's exactly where we expect to find him. Way we got it figured you're his next target. He knows Quarternight was just workin' for you, that Quarternight killed the Tankards under your orders."

"That's a slanderous lie against Quarternight and against me!"

But Justin could tell the idea of his own danger was not new to Oates. He had probably sensed it as soon as he heard about Quarternight. Matthew Tankard was not an ordinary settler to be frightened into quiet submission. "What're you goin' to do about it, Sam? It's the duty of the law to protect an innocent taxpayer."

"I figure the thing for us to do is to hang to you like the bark on a log. When he comes to get you we'll catch him."

Oates' eyes narrowed, for he plainly disliked having so much law that close. "I don't need for you to do that. I got Huff here and I got some other men that know how to use a gun. They'll protect me. It's your job to head that boy off before he ever gets this far."

Dark made a show of regret but his eyes betrayed a grim enjoyment of the situation. "How, Harvey? You know there's been a notorious whiskey peddler operatin' out of Fort Smith for years, sellin' his wares across the river. We never been able to catch him at it. If we can't find whole wagonloads of whiskey how can we hope to find one Indian boy?"

Oates' eyes crackled. "When're you goin' to quit accusin' me, Dark?"

"When I've put you away."

Oates' face was splotched. "I can't afford to fight with you; I got too much at stake here. But someday you'll run into somebody who won't stand still for you."

Dark's voice dropped. "If ever you feel like takin' the chance, Harvey, I'll be tickled to accommodate you."

"I got a business to run. Somebody else'll do it; I'll just watch. Might even buy you a headstone, Sam, if I'm feelin' good."

"Don't do me no favors."

"No favor. It'd be my pleasure."

Justin went with Sam Dark to the courthouse. There, sad-faced, he made a full report to Marshal Yoes and Judge Parker. The judge slumped, frowning. "I've always been partial to the Indians," he said regretfully. "Under the circumstances I hate to sign this warrant."

Dark asked, "Do you have to, judge? You know how come Matthew Tankard to kill Quarternight. If anything he ought to have a medal comin' to him. If we'd got to Quarternight first you'd of hanged him anyway."

"In all probability." The judge pushed ponderously to his feet and strode over to peer out the window down upon the empty scaffold. He was silent a moment in thought. "But that would've been a legal death, done in full justification according to the law. What young Tankard did was, in effect, a lynching.

No matter how we try to justify him the facts still remain. Quarternight was as yet untried, unconvicted. That boy was his own jury, his own executioner. The killing was murder, and he must answer for it as such."

Justin had kept still, listening. Now he argued. "If you'd been there like I was and seen what they done to his father and mother, your honor, you couldn't bring yourself to convict him."

Parker kept staring out the window. "The law is clear. There may come a day when this court can afford to take liberties with it, but for now if law is ever to be brought to the Territory it must be applied as relentlessly to our friends as to our enemies. Certainly I feel pity for that boy. But I feel even more pity for the Territory. I cannot afford emotion in the courtroom no matter how much of it I have here in the privacy of these chambers. It's your job, Mister Dark, to find that lad and bring him in. It will be mine to give him a fair and impartial trial according to the statutes."

Dark looked at the warrant, as yet unsigned. "I hope, sir, that you'll let me do the job in my own way." He explained about the likelihood that Matthew Tankard would sooner or later come for Oates. "What I want to do is put a full guard on Harvey Oates for his own protection. If he sneezes I want me or somebody under me to be close enough to wipe his nose. We been wishin' a long time for a legal excuse to put this kind of guard on him and now Matthew has given it to us. As long as Matthew is out there we can stay so close to Harvey that he can't move a pint of whiskey across that river without us seein' it."

Judge Parker, for all his somber reputation, had a

streak of humor that let him appreciate a fine bit of irony. "If in the process of guarding Mister Oates you should happen to find evidence of illegal activity on his part, I trust you would not hesitate to fetch him before this court."

"I wouldn't hesitate a minute, your honor. I might even rouse you from your bed."

"Mrs. Parker might complain, but for me it would be a night's sleep well lost, Mister Dark. Whatever you need to set up your guard you have full authority from me through Marshal Yoes."

In the long days that followed Justin Moffitt was given much opportunity to lie in Dark's shack and catch up on his rest, to let his shoulder heal without complication from undue exertion. Officially he stood regular tours of duty, but unofficially Sam Dark relieved him from many of these or at least cut them short. Justin argued at first, considering this an imposition against Dark. But Dark, moodier than ever since the deaths of the Tankards, spent all but his eating and sleeping hours as near to Oates as he could get, on duty or off.

That this constant attention was a hindrance to the normal conduct of Oates' business was obvious. The first thing Justin saw in Oates' big warehouse was a very large store of whiskey, both bottled and in barrels. There was nothing illegal about it so long as it remained stored here or went into trade east of the river. But if ever a bottle of it crossed the Arkansas going west it was contraband. Sam Dark saw to it that a deputy marshal followed every wagon that carried a legal consignment to any of Oates' customers. He would watch until it was unloaded at final destination and the wagon sent away. Within very few days it became plain that Oates was chafing under this surveillance.

Sam Dark pointed his thumb at the large store of whiskey and told Justin, "We got him up a stump. You have any idea how much money he's got tied up in all that whiskey, button? It'd bust the back end out of a bank."

Justin nodded. "Looks like enough whiskey there to pickle every farmer west of the Mississippi."

"West of the Arkansas, anyway. His legal trade on this side of the river don't amount to a hill of beans. If we can keep him boxed in long enough and he can't get his money out of this whiskey we'll bust him flatter'n a wagonsheet."

The days were long and Oates' temper was short. He was given to raving at his men and more than once he lost a teamster who stamped away in anger. A couple of times he attempted a ruse to escape surveillance by throwing Dark's deputies off of the track. Always, when he paused to look back, he found Sam Dark quietly watching him.

More than once a wagonload of whiskey slipped out in the night and came close to the river before cutting east again when it was found that a deputy was trailing along, quietly watching.

One day Harvey Oates climbed to a wagonseat and cracked a whip over a newly harnessed team, causing them to break into a run as the wagon rumbled through the gate and out of the wagonyard. Sam Dark had been standing in the gate and he stepped aside just in time to avoid being run over. Harvey Oates brought the team back around, his face colored in anger. "Almost got you, Dark, and it wouldn't of been my fault. Got so a man ain't got room to turn around without he bumps into you or one of them deputies. When're you goin' to get the hell out of my way?"

Dark knew Oates had tried to kill him. Sardonically he replied, "When that Tankard boy comes you'll be glad you have us."

"If you was to see him you'd let him kill me; *then* you'd arrest him."

"Harvey, you got no faith in your fellow man."

Justin noticed that more and more Harvey Oates was having visitors. They would come, perturbed and demanding, and Oates would lead them off out of earshot to engage in animated conversations that included a lot of arm waving and hand motions. He figured these were people who normally bought Oates's whiskey, either in the Territory or for shipment to the Territory. They were running out of stocks and came in to find out why. Justin made it a point to study their faces so he would know them if he ever came across them again. Meanwhile that whiskey sat in the warehouse, unmoving, unsold. Harvey Oates was given to fruitless pacing in his wagonyard. At every opportunity he made it a point to crowd Dark and his deputies. One deputy, slammed against a wall by a span of mules, had to be treated for a broken arm.

Oates stamped across his wheel-packed loading area as Dark showed up to relieve Justin Moffitt. "Sam Dark, I've stood for this as long as I can. You got to do somethin' about it."

"Harvey, we've never stood in the way of your business. I've given the boys orders not to bother a soul. In no way at all have we kept you from the honest pursuit of an honest trade."

"In no way have you caught that damned Indian, either."

"We will. We'll outwait him if it takes till Christmas."

Oates couldn't wait till Christmas. In these several weeks he hadn't sold enough of his whiskey stocks to buy feed for his teams. Dark told Justin, "Sooner or later he's goin' to get desperate enough to try and go around us."

One night Justin was on guard at the wagonyard with George Grider. If he had been forced to it Justin would have had to admit he spent little time watching for Matthew Tankard. Dark's attitude toward Oates had become contagious, and Justin had accepted Dark's conviction that Oates would try to get out from under some of that big store of unsold whiskey. This particular night Oates seemed more nervous than usual, if that was possible. Usually after dark he would sit in his office and slowly drain about half a bottle of his own wares. This night, so far as Justin had seen, he hadn't drunk a drop. He would walk out into the wagonyard, look around expectantly, then return to his office. Presently he would come out again.

"Mister Oates," Justin told him, "if I was you I sure wouldn't be standin' close to the lantern thataway. You never saw Matthew Tankard shoot."

Irritably Oates said, "You was sent to watch out for that Indian, not to tell me what to do."

"Your neck," Justin shrugged, and he turned away.

He moved just in time. A bullet smacked into the office wall just behind him. The sound of the shot made him jump involuntarily. His next move was to grab the lantern and hurl it across the yard. That was a mistake. Instead of going out, it smashed open, and the spilled kerosene flared, throwing dancing light across the whole space.

Harvey Oates fired into the darkness and shouted, "Yonder he goes! Get after him! He tried to kill me!"

The bullet had struck closer to Justin than to Oates, but Justin had no time or inclination to argue. He had to take Oates' word that he had seen somebody in the darkness. The lanternlight had all but blinded Justin, and he saw nothing. Oates fired again. "Damn it, he's gettin' away. Go after him!"

A couple of Oates' teamsters hurried out of the barn, guns in their hands, and Oates waved them into pursuit. Justin moved out into the darkness in the direction Oates had pointed, though he still couldn't see anybody except Oates' own men and the lanky Negro Grider. "You see him, George? Was it Matthew?"

"I seen a man for a second or two. I lost him. Reckon he must've run for the river."

Justin looked back once, and he saw Harvey Oates still standing there in the open wagonyard. It struck him as odd that the man, having been shot at, would leave himself exposed that way. Light coming through the office window behind him and the still-flickering flame from the smashed lantern made him a fair target.

The teamsters raised a great hue and cry, and they fired into the darkness. Justin could hear them holler, "There he goes!"

"I still don't see him, George."

"Neither do I."

The teamsters were yelling for the deputies to come on. "We can catch him if you'll hurry," one shouted.

In moments Sam Dark and Rice Pegler and others had joined the pursuit. Trotting along beside Dark, Justin asked, "Leave anybody to watch out for Oates?"

Dark shook his head. "They're all out here tryin' to find Matthew."

"I think somebody ought to go back. I got a feelin' about this thing. It ain't right."

"You think it's counterfeit?"

"You said yourself that Oates would try somethin' to get out from under us."

Dark stopped running. He stared at Justin in the moonlight. "Go back, button, but don't let Oates see you. Stay out of sight and watch. I'll send George Grider back directly to join you. If Oates is fixin' to try somethin' I want him to think he's gettin' away with it."

Justin returned to the wagonyard in a slow trot, trying to regain the breath he had lost. He found the yard dark, the office lamp out. The big warehouse doors that opened into the yard were closed. He thought for a minute that Oates and everybody had gone. But he made out a dim light barely visible beneath the wide doors. Stealthily he climbed over the plank fence, keeping his body low, and hugged the fence until he had circled the broad yard and came up against the building. Ear close to the wall he could hear thumping noises inside. He knew the sound. Somebody was loading a wagon. The voices were subdued but he recognized Oates' among the others. He heard trace chains rattle and knew the wagon was being pulled up. Another wagon was rolled into place and it too was loaded. Quietly, beneath it all, Justin heard Oates' voice saying, "Hurry it up, damn it, hurry it up!"

He moved away from the door as he saw the dim light flicker out. He shrank back into the shadows and waited for the doors to open, but they did not. He could hear a long creaking noise from the other side of the barn, then the rattle of chains and the groans of heavily laden wagons. He realized that Oates must have hidden doors built in the back side of the barn, unnoticed unless one looked carefully for them. He was taking the wagons out the back way so they never appeared in the wagonyard. It was an exit he would have to reserve for emergencies, for the heavy wagons would soon leave permanent telltale tracks.

Justin started to climb over the fence but saw a quick movement and ducked low in the shadows. He saw nothing else for a moment. Then George Grider was standing almost close enough for Justin to touch. Justin whispered, "George!"

Grider hadn't seen him, and he jumped. "Justin, boy, what you tryin' to do to me?"

"Didn't know it was you at first. They've loaded some whiskey wagons and taken them out the back."

"Let's go see."

They moved cautiously around the building, staying in the shadows. The wagons already had passed out of sight in the darkness, though Justin could hear the faint rattle of the chains. The teamsters were being very quiet, not shouting at the teams or cracking any whips. Justin saw a man shoving the big hinged doors back into place and he dropped to his knees. When the move was finished the wall looked solid. A cross plank hid the tops of the doors. Inside the hinges probably were covered with something to keep them from being noticeable. The man who had shut the doors had a branch in his hand and was brushing the wagon tracks, trying to smooth them down to a point that they would not easily be seen.

When the man had disappeared around the dark barn, Justin whispered, "George, I'll follow after them afoot if you'll go fetch our horses. I'll hang back to where you can find me."

"Reckon I ought to tell Sam Dark?"

"Later, after we know pretty well whichaway they've headed. If you took time now we might not find each other."

George Grider faded out of sight. Justin set out in a gentle sprint after the wagons. At this point it was not difficult to follow the tracks, but he feared as soon as they turned into a public road he might lose them. He hurried along following the sounds. At length he was close enough to see the rear wagon. He had guessed there were two, but now he could tell there were three.

Mister Dark had Oates pegged right, Justin thought. *He was getting desperate to sell some whiskey.*

Justin couldn't tell whether Oates had come with the wagons. It was his best guess that Oates probably would not, for his disappearance would cause quick suspicion and possibly result in these wagons being found before they traveled a safe distance from Fort Smith. Likely Oates was hoping to get these wagons out with nobody the wiser. Chances were he had loaded them from the back side of the storage area to make the depletion of the stock less apparent to the eye.

Justin watched the wagons make a left hand turn onto a public road. The lead wagon clumsily cut a little short, leaving a heavy set of tracks that betrayed the direction of the turn. It seemed to Justin a stupid thing to do after they had gone to all this trouble to slip out of town without being seen or heard.

In a few minutes he was reminded how green he was, for he found the thing had been done with good reason. In a wide part of the street, where wagon tracks by the hundreds were cut afresh every day, the teamsters made a complete circle and headed the teams back in the direction they had started from. Come daylight, soon as vehicular traffic started moving at its normal rate, all signs of the turn would be obliterated.

Justin decided Sam Dark would have anticipated a move like this and been ready for it; it wouldn't have surprised him as it did Justin.

The road the teamsters took led southeastward out of Fort Smith, in a direction directly opposite the normal route into the Territory. That bothered him, but he knew that if this shipment were meant for legal trade east of the state line it wouldn't have been moved out in the dark of night. Sooner or later the wagons had to turn again.

Afraid George Grider wouldn't discern the clever switch in directions, Justin waited for him at the point where the original tracks had entered the public road. When George came leading Justin's horse he saw through the teamsters' ruse and pointed his chin eastward. "Thataway?" Justin nodded, again feeling green because he knew he would have been fooled if he hadn't personally seen the wagons turn.

"You reckon they'll run yonder a little ways and then cut across the river?" he asked George.

The tall Negro shook his head. "Not right off. They ain't sure yet that they got clean away. They'll go a ways east, I expect."

The Arkansas River made a bend just above Fort Smith and then was no longer the boundary for the territory. The wagons could cross, if they chose, without being on illegal ground. They could then bear westward and enter the Territory at a time and place of their own choosing.

Justin figured the wagons were a mile ahead of them when he swung into his saddle and trotted down the road. George Grider pulled up beside him and jerked his thumb toward the south. "We better stay off of the road. We can skirt along a ways out yonder and never get too far from it."

"Why?"

"I expect you'll see, directly."

Justin asked no more questions. He had seen enough to trust George's judgment whether he understood it or not. He also let George set the pace, which he did in a walk. It didn't make much speed, but neither did it make any sound to speak of. In a little while George reined up and cocked his head to one side, listening. He motioned Justin into a small clump of brush where they were hidden in black shadows.

A horseman came in a walk, warily scanning both sides of the road. George and Justin stepped to the ground and placed hands over their horses' nostrils to keep them from nickering. The rider went by and was soon swallowed up in the night. Justin was ready to move on, but George touched his arm and motioned for him to wait. Presently the man came back, in a trot this time and no longer looking very hard.

When he was well gone George Grider whispered, "Outrider checkin' up. Makin' sure there ain't no star-packers like us followin' along to mess things up for them. They'll go a little easier now, but I doubt they'll fall asleep. We still better give them room."

Justin and George moved into an easy trot to close the distance between them and the wagons but they didn't move back into the road. When they reached the point that they could hear the clop of hoofs and the rattle of chains they slowed to a walk again.

"They're still movin' east," Justin whispered finally. "They ain't done a thing that ain't legal."

"No use us doin' anything either, except just ride along and watch. If they don't do nothin' illegal we just had us a nice ride and plenty of fresh air."

After a while Justin thought he heard something and he raised his hand quickly. He and George both stopped. Justin stood up in the saddle to listen. George looked puzzled. "I didn't hear nothin'. Must of been the wagons."

"Wasn't in the direction of the wagons. It was out yonderway. I'd of swore I heard a horse."

He strained, but he didn't hear it anymore and George Grider's expression showed he never did hear it. Justin could tell George thought Justin had imagined it, but George was too polite to say so. "That outrider again," George suggested, "takin' him a little wider swing."

"Probably," Justin said. He didn't hear it anymore and now he was no longer positive he had heard it in the first place. He let the horse move into a walk again.

Later they both heard one sound, a rider loping away from the wagons, heading northeastward. Justin and George looked at each other, wondering and not finding any answers. A couple of hours passed and the wagons had made a few miles before the rider came back. The deputies were close enough now to see him in the moonlight. They couldn't hear the conversation but they could see him gesturing to the teamsters on the lead wagon.

Justin wondered if this might be Harvey Oates, but he returned to his earlier belief that Oates probably would stay in Fort Smith to avoid calling attention to these wagons.

Justin knew how to read time by the stars and by his judgment it was a couple of hours past midnight when the wagons left the public road, turning suddenly north on a faint trail evidently used only by farmers in the area. George Grider nodded knowingly. "They figure they're safe now. They're taking to the river."

Justin had been up this river a time or two. He knew of no ferry here and no bridge to span the Arkansas. He was curious how these freight wagons would be taken across the water. Before long he saw the full moon shimmering on the slow-moving river. "It'll be a dandy trick," he whispered, "and I'm lookin' forward to seein' them do it."

A couple of hundred yards from the point where the wagons reached the river Justin and George tied their horses. They proceeded afoot, taking their time and staying in the shadows, working their way down close enough to watch without being seen. Justin thought the men probably would lash logs against the wagon wheels on each side and float the vehicles. To his surprise he saw the teamsters were unloading their cargo. He glanced at George as if expecting an explanation, but George had none.

For the first time Justin saw a large boat tied at the river's edge. One of the freighters hoisted a whiskey keg onto his shoulder and carried it down, placing it in the boat. Then Justin knew. They weren't going to take the wagons across. Likely other wagons waited on the far side for a transfer of the whiskey. Those would make the run across into the Territory while these either went back to Fort Smith or proceeded eastward to pick up legitimate shipping elsewhere for Oates. The tracks leaving the public road would be little noticed by any but the sharpest eyes and there would be no reason to suspect there was anything wrong.

Surely, Justin thought, there must be easier ways for them than this. He doubted this was Oates' customary method of handling the trade but it was a device he could fall back upon in a tight squeeze. The beauty from Oates' viewpoint would be that if he were discovered in this transfer nothing could be proven against him. His wagons were still on legal ground.

Sure seems sometimes like they got the law stacked for the transgressor and against the poor old boy who's trying to catch him at it, Justin thought.

Moving the whiskey was a slow process for it took the boat three trips just to unload the first wagon. It started on the second wagon and Justin stretched out on the ground, taking his rest. He knew there was nothing he and George could do anyway but sit there and watch. He could make out the shape of wagons across the river. It appeared there were more of them—maybe five or six—small spring wagons of the farmer type. They would probably scatter from here like a covey of quail, hitting the Territory at several different points to make it difficult for the law to apprehend them all.

Two of us and five or six of them, Justin thought,

looking helplessly at George. *Even if we split up and trail them we can't get but one apiece. That means three or four go through.*

He made out a horseman circling the place and decided they had sent the outrider again to be sure they weren't surprised. Justin had a moment of worry about their horses, tied back in the brush. But the rider didn't go near them. As Justin watched, the man tied his horse in a clump of trees and walked to the riverbank, observing from the shadows a little while, then returning to his horse and riding downriver.

Justin glanced at George and George only nodded, puzzled too. The man had walked up as if he were part of the outfit, but he hadn't joined in and hadn't stayed. For all Justin could tell it might have been Harvey Oates himself, checking up on his men, then riding on. And there wasn't anything Justin and George could do about him. Justin could respect now the frustration he had seen several times in Sam Dark.

After a while the second wagon was empty and the boat started carrying whiskey from the last one.

Going to be a lot of celebration in the Territory before long, Justin thought.

The boat was almost across with the second load out of the third wagon when George Grider touched Justin's arm and pointed across the river. Justin became aware of sudden movement among the men who had been transferring the loads there from the boat to the wagons. He couldn't make out the cause of it. Then he saw a flash and instantly heard a shot. Oates' men resting on this side of the river jumped to their feet. The men in the boat stopped rowing and the boat began to drift gently with the current. Justin saw several men on the far side come splashing out into the water. At the distance he thought their hands were raised over their heads but he couldn't tell for sure. He heard shouts but couldn't make out the words.

The men in the boat began rowing back to Justin's side of the river. Again a shot was fired and Justin knew by the sound of it that it was a heavy rifle. He thought he knew which one. It spoke a second time. The two men jumped out of the boat and started to swim. Somebody on the far bank methodically kept firing at the boat.

"George," Justin said in wonder, "he's tryin' to sink it."

"If he puts enough holes in her she'll sure enough go down," George responded. "Wonder who . . ."

The two deputies glanced at each other, and Justin knew George was reading his mind.

Matthew Tankard!

9

The boat drifted aimlessly with the flow of the current and Matthew, across the river, was still plunking bullets into it. The boat began listing. It would sink bye and bye, carrying the load of whiskey down with it.

The shooting stopped. A flame flickered then flared into brilliance. Matthew was setting fire to the wagons.

Oates' men on this side of the river began firing random shots in Matthew's direction. Quickly shouts of protest rose up from the men Matthew had forced into the river. They were in the line of fire if any of the bullets dropped short. The firing stopped.

One after another the wagons blazed. Justin counted five. Of a sudden he began to laugh.

George Grider didn't smile. "Harvey Oates'll bust a gut when he hears about this. He ain't so rich that losin' all this won't hurt him. It'll be like bustin' both his legs. Ain't no tellin' what he might do."

"What *can* he do?"

"Put a price on that boy, for one thing. If he offers enough somebody'll fetch him Matthew Tankard's head in a sack."

"Matthew can hide out amongst the Indians."

"Even Indians—some of them—have learned that if silver jingles loud enough it'll drown out a bad conscience."

"Matthew'll take care of himself." Justin tried to sound confident, but George was raising some doubts.

George said sternly, "You know what we ought to be doin' right now, don't you? We ought to be goin' downstream out of sight—like he done—cross over and come back up to catch him before he leaves them wagons. He's wanted by the court."

"He's a friend of mine, George."

"Man who's got a badge on his shirt and a warrant in his pocket, he ain't got no friends. He's got to see every fugitive alike. That's what that oath said, remember?"

Justin frowned. "We could pretend we never seen a thing."

"We *did* see it. We got to report it. We don't want to report we was this close to a fugitive and didn't make no try at catchin' him." George paused. "Better we catch him than for Oates to do it. That boy'd never draw another breath."

Justin thought of Matthew's face as he had seen it when his friends were burying his mother and father. He thought of the sister Naomi and wondered how he could ever face her if he took Matthew to that bleak brick prison. But he knew the Negro was right. "We'll make the effort, George."

They did, but to Justin's relief it was only an effort.

By the time they swam the river and got back to the smoldering wagons, they found only the wagon men on the riverbank, cursing bitterly and swearing vengeance. They were soaking wet, all of them.

Justin and George introduced themselves as deputy marshals and asked what had happened.

One of the men swore vigorously. "Some damned Indian. He come up on us while we was busy and there wasn't a one of us could reach a gun. Halsey yonder tried, and he's got a hole in his leg. Damned Indian tried to drown us."

Justin said, "May be lucky for you it turned out thisaway. If we'd of caught you after you got to the Territory you'd of all had a long stay in Fort Smith, with expenses paid."

"Ain't no way you can prove we was goin' to the Territory."

"No reason now for us to have to. That Indian took care of it for us." He said to George, "We'd as well be gettin' on back to Fort Smith. We got a report to make."

George's eyes accused him a little. "Ain't we goin' to trail after your friend?"

"We'd have to wait till daylight."

"That ain't long. Look in the east."

Trailing the wagons, then watching the excitement, Justin hadn't realized the night was almost gone. He had thought of the darkness as an excuse. It wasn't good enough. "All right, George, we'll wait for daylight."

It was gratifying to look at the charred wagons, their loads destroyed. Only about one boatload was left across the river and the whiskey runners couldn't risk trying to get that into the Territory now. The freighters came over from the other side to survey the wreckage in profane anger. The first light of morning showed no sign of the boat. Somewhere out there it had gone down.

A freighter eyed the deputies suspiciously. "What was you-all doin' while all this was goin' on? It's your job to help protect a man's property."

"Even if it was about to become illegal?"

"If you catch the man that done this to us I hope you let us get the first crack at him."

"Likely," said Justin, "you'll be in jail before he is."

When it was light enough George Grider began looking around for tracks. He wasn't long in finding them. Matthew had evidently made no effort to hide them. He had crossed a little way downriver. The deputies did the same and picked up his tracks without much trouble on the far side.

Justin was disappointed. "I hoped he'd head for the Territory as hard as he could run. Instead, looks to me like he went right back toward Fort Smith."

George nodded. "Didn't finish his job yet. He come after them wagons hopin' to find Oates with them. Now he's gone back to where he knows Oates is at." He was silent a minute. "I know he's your friend, but I think you better make up your mind to one thing."

"What's that?"

"You'll likely have to help bury him."

After a while it became obvious they were wasting their time fiddling along following the tracks. There could be no doubt that Matthew was heading for town. Justin and George struck up a stiff trot in a straight line.

A long time before they got there they saw the

smoke. It could have been from any number of things but Justin had a feeling about it. "Matthew's a great hand with fire," he remarked. "Looks like he didn't take time to rest none."

Matthew hadn't. Justin and George found Harvey Oates' warehouse lying in piles of gray ash and heaps of black charred timbers, still smoldering, the heavy smoke rising into a cloudless summer sky. Harvey Oates paced the open wagonyard, his shirt soaked with sweat, his face begrimed from a vain battle to save his property. Sam Dark stood calmly watching him, a cold, humorless smile matching the grim satisfaction in his eyes. He looked up surprised as Justin and George rode in. "Thought you-all would be over in the Territory by now, catchin' us some fish."

George Grider let Justin tell it. Justin said, "The fish didn't make it, Mister Dark. Seems like they was crossin' the river over east a ways and they met with an accident."

Oates was suddenly interested and suspicious. "What're they talkin' about, Sam?"

Dark said, "Some wagons left your warehouse last night."

Defensively, for he plainly thought his men must have been apprehended on illegal ground, Oates declared, "Any wagons of mine that left here last night, they was stolen."

"All right," Dark conceded, "they was stolen." To Justin he said, "What happened?"

"Same thing that seems to've happened to the warehouse here. What didn't get burned got sunk with the boat, all but about enough to drown a squirrel in."

Oates' face went scarlet. "Who done it?"

Justin shrugged. "It was dark. We never seen his face."

Oates slammed a rough fist into the palm of his left hand. He turned on Sam Dark. "That same damned Indian, I tell you, Sam Dark, you better get me that Indian!"

Crisply Dark declared, "The only thing I ever want to get for you, Harvey Oates, is about six foot of good stout rope."

"You're the law . . ."

"And we'll get that boy, but it'll be for the law, Harvey, not for you. I wisht he'd caught you in your warehouse and burned you with it. A little fire like that ain't much to what you got comin' later anyway."

Oates stared into the ashes, and the misery in his face would have brought sympathy from Justin if he hadn't known the man. This loss had staggered him financially; the wound might even be mortal. Oates rubbed a hand over his face, leaving the black streaks smeared even worse. To Dark he said, "You're purposely standin' around here lettin' that Indian get away. He's over the river by now and to hell and gone."

"I ain't movin' till I hear from Rice Pegler. He was on duty here when the fire started. Ain't nobody seen him. I figure he took out after that boy. We won't know whichaway they went till we hear from Rice Pegler." He turned back to the two newly arrived deputies. "Justin, you and George better go get you some fresh horses. No tellin' when we might have to ride out of here in a hurry. And get you somethin' to eat, too. I expect you're hungry."

Justin was. He had been too excited to notice it up to now. They got the horses fed first then went to Sam

Dark's shack to fix breakfast. Most restaurants in town wouldn't accept George Grider. They might let him stand guard for them against a robber but they wouldn't feed him.

Finished, they got fresh horses and rode to the federal courthouse to wait for word and to rest. They didn't rest long for Sam Dark came along directly, Harvey Oates dragging his heels. Oates was raising Hail Columbia about getting all the marshals in the Territory on the trail of that Tankard boy. Dark would have struck him if Marshal Yoes hadn't been there and if Judge Parker hadn't at one point come striding heavily down the hall. The judge glanced at Oates' agitated face and Justin thought he saw a hint of a smile tug at the ends of the jurist's graying moustache.

Presently Sam Dark had to go out to check on a rumored sighting of the Tankard boy. While Sam was gone Rice Pegler rode up to the courthouse on a winded horse that Justin knew at a glance wasn't his. It looked as if it belonged pulling a plow. Harvey Oates went trotting down the courthouse steps demanding excitedly if Pegler had caught that Indian.

Obviously tired Pegler shook his head. "Almost did," Justin heard him say as he walked out to listen. "Way yonder, the other side of the river, I caught up to him. We swapped a few shots. One of the bullets took the horse out from under me. I had to commandeer this plug off a farmer and come back for help."

Oates was anguished. "He got clean away?"

"Not clean. I put a bullet in him; I could tell that." Pegler seemed pleased with himself.

Anxiously Justin demanded, "How bad was he hurt?"

Pegler turned his attention momentarily to Justin,

his eyes disapproving. "You look like you'd rather it was *him* that put a bullet in *me*."

"I asked you how hard is he hit?"

Pegler shrugged. "Couldn't tell. If it had hit him where I aimed it I'd of drug him in by his heels. One less outlaw to cost the taxpayers."

Harvey Oates said, "You're a good officer, Pegler. Wisht we had a hundred like you. Let's get you a fresh horse out of my corral, and we'll help you run that boy to the ground."

"You ain't no marshal, Oates."

"But I got horses and I got men. I'm the aggrieved party; I got a right." He paused, eyeing Pegler speculatively. "And I got somethin' else—a thousand dollars that goes to you if you nail that Indian for me. I want to hang his hide on my fence."

Pegler's jaw dropped a little. He was plainly considering it. But in a minute he shook his head. "I'm a deputy marshal in the service of the court. Ain't no thousand dollars goin' to corrupt me."

Oates stared at him. "Two thousand dollars."

That staggered Justin for he had never seen two thousand dollars. It seemed to shake Pegler, too. His tongue flicked across dry lips. He glanced at Justin, evidently wishing Justin weren't present to overhear. "Two thousand dollars." He rubbed a hand over his face and looked back at Oates. "Is that a promise?"

"Ironclad."

Pegler's hands trembled at the prospect of getting so much money at one time. But only a moment. He turned to Justin. "That boy's a friend of yours. Where do you figure he'd head now that he's got a bullet in him?"

Justin knew Oates' offer had gotten to Pegler. A

cold chill ran through him at the thought of Matthew Tankard crippling along out there somewhere like some young wounded elk, this wolf pack howling on his trail. Justin had a notion where Matthew might go but he wouldn't tell Pegler. "How should I know? He's got friends all over."

Pegler frowned. "He's got a sister. Where's she at?" That had been part of Justin's notion and it shook him that Pegler so quickly thought of it too. But Justin could honestly say, "I don't know. They hid her out for protection from Oates and his men."

Oates colored, his eyes hostile. "You and Sam Dark with your loose accusations." He jabbed a finger at Justin. "You got a duty, boy, to tell this officer everything you know."

"So he can make himself two thousand dollars?" Justin's voice was bitter.

"So I can do my duty," Pegler said stiffly. "There's a warrant out against Matthew Tankard for murder. The way you feel about him don't make no difference in your duty to help see that the law is served. You know anything, you better tell it."

Justin tensed. "All I know I told you. Anything else you got to go and find out for yourself."

"When we get back," Pegler threatened, "I'm goin' to report all this to Marshal Yoes and Judge Parker."

"You goin' to report the two thousand dollars too?"

Pegler's eyes were flinty. "With two thousand dollars in my pocket it won't matter to me whether they like it or not. I couldn't save that much in five years workin' the way I'm doin'." He turned back to Oates. "You promised me a horse. Let's be about it."

Pegler swung up onto the tired farm horse and

turned in toward Oates' stables. Justin said, "I'm goin' with you, Mister Pegler."

Pegler stopped. "I don't want you, boy."

"You'll have me anyway."

"I'll tell Marshal Yoes and he'll keep you here."

"I'll tell him about the two thousand dollars and he'll peel that badge off of you."

Pegler flamed, suddenly hating Justin, but he realized he was boxed. "I'm tellin' you we got no need for you."

"Matthew Tankard is liable to have need of me. If you catch up with him I'm goin' to be there to protect him."

Pegler's voice dropped, almost inaudible. "Come, then, and be damned. But I'm warnin' you—if you get in my way I'll set you afoot." He jerked his horse angrily and turned again toward the stables.

Justin hung back. George Grider moved up gravely. "Don't you think you'd ought to wait for Mister Dark to get back?"

"I can't afford to. If they get the chance they'll kill Matthew. They'd even kill Naomi if they could get away with it. It's up to me to see they don't. You tell him to come on as quick as he can."

10

Of the eight riders the big Negro Huff took the lead, and it was evident from the way he started that he knew these trails well. During the days and nights the deputies guarded Harvey Oates it had been plain to Justin that this black man was Oates' chief bodyguard now that Quarternight lay six feet under. Though it was not common for white men to accept orders from a black, Justin had noticed that when Huff spoke the Oates men around him paused to listen. They feared him and this was enough to offset his color. He made it a point not to lord it over them, but he made it a point also that they not forget who and what he was.

Justin tried to ride close enough to Pegler and Oates that he could hear anything they said to each other.

Oates asked Pegler if they couldn't find Matthew's tracks where he had shot the horse out from under the deputy. Pegler nodded. "We could but there's no need. We'd be a week trailin' him. I figure we can shortcut him. If I was in his shape I'd want to try and get back to home country where family or friends could take care of me. He's got a sister out there, and other relatives. I figure he'll go to them. All we got to do is scour the country and we'll get him."

Justin remembered the region they rode over. The Negro took a slightly different route from the one over which old Elijah Tankard had led Justin and Dark. This was understandable for Huff was probably used to the whiskey runners' trails. He had no doubt guarded many a wagonload of contraband making its way across these long miles of rolling hills and deep green valleys.

They rode all afternoon, pushing much harder than Justin and Dark and Elijah had pushed the time they came this direction. Whenever they reached a house or found a traveler Oates and Pegler and their five would gather close around, bristling with guns, and attempt to cow whoever they had cornered. They would demand to know if anyone had seen a wounded Indian boy, and Pegler would forcibly give the threat of taking them to the stinking cells in Fort Smith if they lied. This badgering of people brought no result, for either no one had seen Matthew or they were made of sterner stuff than Pegler thought. Pegler always left them with a final threat. "If we find out you been lyin' we'll be back thisaway."

Justin had wondered once why Sam Dark had so little respect for Rice Pegler as an officer or as a man. Justin had begun to sense the reasons weeks ago. Now he no longer harbored any doubt. Pegler gloried in power. By some accident of circumstances, no doubt, fate had decreed that he become a law officer rather than an outlaw. He could as well have been the other,

Justin thought, and his manner need have been little different. There was a streak of cruelty in him that constantly sought release.

Pegler was eager for that two thousand dollars and he kept pushing Huff to set a faster pace. The Negro was inclined to give more consideration to the horses but Pegler crowded him. At times they swung into an easy lope that would carry them a quick mile, then drop back to a trot. Pegler complained when darkness came and they had to camp.

Next morning they came upon ground that had become very familiar to Justin. This was the Tankard farm. As they reached the edge of the field Justin saw Huff turn his head and glance involuntarily toward the spot where Elijah and his wife had been killed. Justin's jaw set hard. *I couldn't prove it in court, Huff, but you just settled it for me. You was here that day.* He wondered how many of the others with Oates now had also been here. Any who were had good reason to want to see the last of the Tankards dead and buried—including Naomi.

Pegler called now for a slowdown and for watchfulness. "Look out for fresh tracks," he warned. "He could be laid up here someplace drawin' a bead over his sights."

The riders spread apart, trying to watch the ground and at the same time keep a wary eye open for Matthew possibly hiding with a rifle, trapped now and determined to sell out at the highest price. They combed the field and the pastureland around it but found nothing other than a scattering of horsetracks, some of them days old. "Neighbors," Pegler grumbled. "They probably been comin' over here takin' care of things. With all them tracks how do they expect us to find the ones we're lookin' for?"

Justin had ridden in worried silence all the way from Fort Smith. He couldn't resist putting in now, "They don't. You wouldn't expect the neighbors to pitch in and help you, would you?"

Pegler gave him a hard glance but made no reply. The riders regrouped finally around the charred wreckage of the big log house. A hard smile crossed Oates' face as his gaze drifted over the cold ashes. "Whoever done this," he said, "it was a thorough job."

Justin put in again, "Like Matthew done to your wagons and your warehouse. You taught him real good, Oates."

Oates turned a shade darker. "I wasn't nowhere around when this took place, boy."

"But Huff was. And some of the others you got sittin' here."

Huff looked startled. Oates gave him a quick glance that told him to stand easy, then turned to Justin. "Loose talk can get a man killed. You have no proof. From what I've heard you was too far away to identify anybody. It was your loose talk about Quarternight that led the Indian boy to kill him. You got Quarternight's innocent blood smeared all over your hands."

Justin could have said that Naomi could make identification, too, but he knew they were well aware of that fact. For Naomi's sake it didn't need any pushing. Justin said, "You can save the lies for people in Fort Smith ignorant enough to believe you, Oates. I know you're a whiskey runner. I know you sent Quarternight and Huff and the others to kill the Tankards.

You took revenge for what happened to your peddlers and your wagons and figured to scare other people into keepin' their mouths shut."

Oates glanced at Rice Pegler. "Pegler, you better hush him up or I can't be responsible for what happens to him. There are men here with strong feelin's when it comes to bein' lied about."

Pegler fastened a hostile gaze on Justin. "You heard him, boy. You got no proof so you just keep your mouth shut."

"You know I'm tellin' the truth, Pegler. You've let the flash of that money in your eyes turn you blind. You've let them make you a party to it. They're guilty and you're lettin' it rub off on you. You won't be able to wash it away, not with two thousand dollars' worth of soap."

Pegler grunted. "That's enough. I done listened to all I intend to. You've went as far with us as you're goin'."

"I'm a deputy marshal. I can go where I damn well please."

"But not with us." Pegler drew his pistol and ominously spun the cylinder. "You could have an accident. I could be checkin' my gun and let it go off and hit that horse of yours between the eyes. Then you'd be afoot and couldn't come along. Sure would be a pity to have a thing like that happen to a good horse."

Justin swallowed, for he knew Rice Pegler would do it. He might even do more if he had no witnesses or was sure of those he did have. Pegler said, "You better listen to me, boy. I'm readin' you the gospel."

"I'm listenin'."

"Then hear the rest of it. We're goin' on. We're goin' to comb every farm in this part of the country.

I figure that sooner or later, we'll find that Tankard girl. And when we find the girl we'll find the boy too."

Justin felt the blood rise to his face. "I'm bettin' you don't find either one of them. But if you do, and you hurt them any worse than they already been hurt, I'll be huntin' for you, Rice Pegler."

Pegler said stiffly, "I'll remember you threatened me, boy."

"You'd damn well better."

Justin swung to the ground to stretch his legs, and he watched in anger as Pegler and Oates and the others rode away from him, heading in the direction of the Wing house. He realized now what he should have known when they left Fort Smith—that they wouldn't tolerate him when they got into the country they were heading for, that they would do whatever was necessary to get rid of him.

Well, he thought, they wouldn't ride up on the Wing place and catch everybody asleep. Justin drew the saddlegun from its scabbard, took a firm grip on the reins and fired three shots into the air. The startled horse nearly tore his hand off and the hard jerk made pain jab through Justin's nearly healed shoulder. Justin watched the riders stop and look back at him. Oates shook his fist.

Now, Justin thought, *just try to slip up on anybody*.

He had it in mind to ride along a safe distance behind them and continue to harass them this way. But he figured this series of shots—and perhaps one more—would serve to alert the Wings. They would send somebody out, spot the riders and spread the alarm. Wherever Pegler's posse went the word would travel ahead of them.

Justin decided he could make better use of his time

in another way. He let his gaze drift toward the range of hills where Deerhorn Pocket lay. He remembered what Naomi had told him about it as he and she had ridden together up there in that timbered header: "We made it up a long time ago that if any of us was to ever get in trouble we'd come to this place. That way the others would know where to look."

Up there was sanctuary. Up there was food and water, a place to hide, a place to heal. Pegler's posse, even if it should try to comb those hills, wasn't big enough to flush out a man who knew its secrets.

If Matthew had gotten this far he would have gone to the Deerhorn Pocket, Justin was convinced. No lawman knew about it except for Sam Dark, who had trailed a drunken Barney Tankard when Barney was in no condition to hide his tracks; and Justin Moffitt, who had fled here with Naomi. But even Dark and Justin probably couldn't find Matthew in the denseness of that Indian stronghold if he chose not to be found.

Justin fired three more shots in quick succession, just to insure that the Wings were well warned. Then he turned his horse toward the hills and Deerhorn Pocket.

11

Justin wished he knew the Indian tricks about hiding his trail. George Grider had tried with little success to teach him how to find other people's trails; no one had thought to teach him about covering his own. He went about it in the most commonsense manner he could, tying the horse periodically and walking back to brush out his tracks. When he reached the creek he turned into it and rode in the water, slowly moving up the hill. He paused from time to time to look behind him. He had a nagging feeling that the posse might become suspicious and come back to watch him, but he saw no sign of that and he gradually became confident.

As he moved he watched for any sign that someone else had preceded him. If so, the tracks had been smoothed over. Increasingly he began to feel that perhaps he had guessed wrong this time; maybe Matthew hadn't headed for the pocket after all.

He found fresh horse droppings, and this renewed

his earlier conviction. If Matthew Tankard hadn't gone up this hill somebody else had. Quietly, so his voice wouldn't carry back to the bottom, he began to call Matthew's name.

"Matthew, it's me, Justin. I come to help you. Matthew?"

He worked back and forth across the lower reaches of the header, stopping often to look, to listen. He kept calling. No one answered, but instinct told him he wasn't alone. He could feel another presence here in this timber, could feel eyes watching him. If he hadn't been up here before and if he hadn't established a relationship with these people, it would have been enough to spook him back down the hill. He thought he knew a little of how some early trappers and hunters must have felt, ranging out into deep and hostile Indian country. It was enough to raise the hair on the back of his neck.

He kept calling, "Matthew. You up here, Matthew?"

At length he heard a loud metallic click and involuntarily he shivered to a sudden chill. He knew the sound of a rifle hammer being cocked back. "It's me," he said shakily. "Justin. I come to help."

He saw a movement of leaves and a young man pushed his way out of the brush, rifle leveled at Justin. He recognized Matthew's cousin, Alvin James, the tracker. Alvin's eyes were not friendly. "Justin, you made a mistake comin' up here."

"I come to help."

"You still a deputy?"

Justin nodded.

"Then I don't see how you can help Matthew none. You're his enemy."

"I'm not his enemy, I'm his friend. But he's got aplenty of enemies down below that hill. I come to do what I can to see he stays out of their hands. Where's he at, Alvin?"

"If you come to take him back you just forget it."

"I won't do nothin' he don't want me to do. Take me to him."

Alvin James studied Justin a while longer before persuasion overcame suspicion. Finally, he said, "I'll take you to him, but first you shuck that gun. Any guns go up there I'll take them."

Justin pitched Alvin his gunbelt and holster, the pistol in it. Alvin looped it over his shoulder and lowered the muzzle of the rifle, using it to point. "Tie your horse then come on thisaway."

He led Justin up the side of the little stream then on across to a ledge of rocks. There beneath an overhang he saw Matthew Tankard lying on a blanket. Matthew's face was twisted and he looked weak. He was wearing an oversized shirt somebody evidently had given him to replace a bloodied one.

Justin asked, "How bad is it, Matthew?"

Matthew eyed him with the same suspicion Alvin James had shown. "You askin' me as a friend or as an officer?"

"As a friend."

"He got me in the side. Bullet went clean through, but I bled like a stuck hog at first till I finally got it stopped. Sure did take the vinegar out of me."

"You did good just gettin' here."

"Couldn't of done it without help."

"They're lookin' for you, you know. Harvey Oates is headin' a posse himself, him and Rice Pegler."

Matthew's hate was plain in his blue eyes. "Oates! Seems like every bad thing that's happened to us Oates was behind it one way or another."

"He's offered Rice Pegler two thousand dollars to get you and Rice has got his badge to back him up."

Matthew grimaced. "Glad to know I'm worth so much to him. I must've damaged him worse than I thought."

"You gouged him awful deep. They figure to scour every farm in this country lookin' for you. They're startin' with the Wings. That's how come I fired the shots a while ago, to stir the Wings up and have them ready."

"You fired them shots? We heard them, me and Alvin. We figured it was the Wings or some of the others signalin' us to lay low."

"They're not just huntin' for you, Matthew. They're huntin' for Naomi, too. She's a witness against them. I hope you got her hid out good."

Matthew glanced quickly at Alvin. "She *has* been. They couldn't of found her in six months where we had her. But now I don't know . . ."

Justin caught the sudden uneasiness and it set him back on edge. "What do you mean?"

"We sent Blue Wing to fetch her here to help take care of me. They're apt to be travelin' now."

Justin fretted, "She could ride right into that posse."

Matthew picked up a small stone and hurled it away in frustration. "I told them I didn't need her but they kept after me. Said she'd want to come; you know how kinfolks are." He looked up at Alvin James. "Alvin, you better slip down off of this hill and see if you can find Naomi and Blue. Head them off before they get here."

Alvin glanced suspiciously at Justin. "I don't know about leavin' you, Matthew, him bein' one of them and all . . ."

"Go on, Alvin. I can take care of myself. You find them and get them the hell out of this part of the country, away from that posse. And don't get yourself caught."

Reluctantly Alvin agreed. "But only because Matthew says so," he told Justin, his eyes narrowed. "You do anything to hurt Matthew and I'll hunt you till hell freezes solid."

It amazed Justin how quickly Alvin disappeared. That was what made this place so good for a hideout. One moment he was there and the next he was gone, unseen and unheard. Justin knelt by Matthew. "Anything I can do to help you?"

"You've already done it, lettin' us know about that bunch of manhunters. But what about you? You're still an officer. You can't just forget you seen me up here, or can you?"

That touched on Justin's conscience. "I promised Alvin I wouldn't do nothin' you didn't want me to do. If you don't want to go in I won't force you."

"Don't that violate an oath or somethin'?"

"It does."

"How can you go on bein' an officer knowin' you've broken your oath, knowin' you had your hands on a wanted man and then let him go?"

"I don't know. I been doin' some worryin' over that."

"I sure don't figure on givin' myself up. I figure I'll lay up here till I get some strength back then I'll head west. They tell me out west I could pass for a Mexican if I learn how to talk the way they do."

"That wouldn't be your country. You wouldn't ever feel at home."

"I wouldn't feel at home on Judge Parker's gallows, that I'll guarantee."

"The judge is sympathetic to you, Matthew."

"But the law is the law. If he lives up to it and a jury finds me guilty he's got to hang me, ain't he?"

"A jury might not find you guilty."

"They'd have to. And then he'd have to hang me."

"He could give you a jail sentence if he found cause. He's let a lot of people off who've done killin', if he thought they had just cause."

"Can he guarantee me that?"

"No, I asked him. He can't make no guarantees and neither can I."

"Then I ain't goin', not of my free will."

"And I won't force you."

Matthew lay in silence a while, staring at the blue sky and at a bird soaring high. Justin wasn't sure but he thought it was an eagle. Now and again Matthew bit his lips and Justin knew he was feeling pain. In spite of it Matthew smiled. "I had to leave soon's I got the fire started in Oates' warehouse. I must've burned it good, didn't I?"

"You burned it good."

"You didn't know it, but I burned a bunch of his wagons, too."

"I knew it," Justin said. "I was there." To Matthew's look of surprise Justin explained how he and George Grider trailed the wagons, hoping to arrest the teamsters as they crossed over into forbidden ground. "You shootin' at Oates in his wagonyard gave him a chance to load them wagons and try to move them while the officers was out lookin' for you."

Matthew said, "I didn't shoot at Oates. I was there all right, waitin' for the chance to do it close enough to where I wouldn't miss. You-all was always around him, though, and I didn't get to. I figured Oates sent one of his own men out to shoot at him and lead all of you off. I stuck tight, right where I was. When the wagons went out the back of the warehouse I figured Oates was with them, so I trailed along."

Justin was nodding. "I thought so; I *did* hear you go around us."

"When they stopped at the river I took a chance and walked in amongst them while they was busy, close enough to find out Oates wasn't with them. Then I got the idea about burnin' the wagons and sinkin' the boat. So I done it. Then I went back to town and broke into the warehouse. Oates wasn't there, just a watchman. I set the warehouse afire, drug the watchman out and took off a-runnin'. But there was a marshal out there and he chased me."

"Rice Pegler."

"He was like a grassburr. I done all I could but I couldn't shake loose from him. I finally shot his horse, and that's when he put the bullet through my side."

"You was wrong to shoot Quarternight the way you done. You made another mistake when you didn't leave the country right then and there."

"I got no regrets about Quarternight. He didn't give my folks no chance; why should I give him one? The only mistake I made was in not gettin' Oates first. He was the big one, the one I really wanted. Now I may not ever get him."

"Somebody will; he won't last forever."

"Sometimes it looks like his kind *does* last forever."

Much later Alvin James came back. Justin could tell

by the look on his face that something had gone badly wrong. Matthew knew too. He demanded, "What is it, Alvin?"

"I was too late, Matthew. That bunch, they already caught Naomi and Blue. They was close up and they rode onto that marshal before they knowed there was anything wrong. That marshal, he sent word to you."

"They catch you, too?"

Alvin shook his head. "No, but when I seen they had Naomi and Blue I rode in to see if they'd hurt them any. I didn't let on we was kinfolks or anything; thought I'd just play dumb. But that marshal, turned out he was one who went with us when we trailed you and Quarternight; he knowed me. He said he knowed that *I* knowed where you are. Said he'd be waitin' for you down where your house used to be. He'd have Naomi and Blue there and he'd turn them aloose if you gave yourself up. Otherwise he'd haul them to Fort Smith and throw them in prison for harborin' a fugitive. Said they could stay in there for years."

Matthew cursed. "They'd never live to Fort Smith. Oates don't want Naomi able to identify any of his men." He pushed himself to a sitting position, his hand going quickly to his side in a moment of hard pain. "Had they been mistreated any?"

Alvin glanced worriedly at Justin, then back to Matthew. He was hesitant in his answer. "Matthew, don't you do nothin' foolish."

Matthew read the answer in Alvin's oblique reply. His voice was angrily insistent. "Tell me, Alvin."

"They'd beaten Blue unconscious. I don't expect he told them nothin'."

"And Naomi?"

Alvin looked down. "She was bruised some."

Justin cursed and started in long strides down the hill. "That damned Pegler . . ."

Matthew called after him. "Justin, you come back here. You can't stop him."

"I'm a deputy marshal, same as he is."

"But you got no authority over him. And if he's got two thousand dollars at stake he'd as soon shoot you as not. Maybe rather. He could always tell them *I* done it."

Justin stopped. He hadn't seen it that way and the realization jarred him. "I'll figure out a way."

Matthew held up his hands in a sign that he wanted to be helped to his feet. "No, I'll stop him. I'll go down and give myself up. You said the judge'd be sympathetic."

"You'll never live to see the judge. They'll kill you if you go to them."

"They'll kill Naomi if I *don't* go. And maybe Blue Wing too. It looks like they've left me with no choice."

"There's bound to be somethin' else."

"If so, what? Tell me what it is."

Justin had no answer. Matthew looked gravely at him a moment. "Justin, if you was to take me down as your prisoner, maybe *you'd* get the two thousand dollars from Harvey Oates."

"I wouldn't touch it."

"You could hire me a lawyer with it. Anyway, maybe it'd keep your friend Pegler from gettin' it."

Justin frowned, wishing there were some other way. "You sure this is what you want to do?"

"Hell no, it ain't what I want to do. But I don't see that they've given me any choice."

"Then I'll take you down and declare that you're

my prisoner, under my protection. Anybody that lays a hand on you, I'll file charges."

"Don't get yourself on thin ice, Justin. They might not let you live to Fort Smith, either." Matthew tried walking but he was weak. He had to lean on Justin for support as they moved down the hill toward where his horse was hidden. When they reached the horses Matthew turned to his cousin. "Comin', Alvin?"

Alvin nodded. "I'll stay with you, Matthew."

Justin had been doing some quick thinking. "No, Alvin, you can be more help doin' somethin' else. I want you to go round up all the kinfolks you can find in a hurry. Bring them to the Tankard place. You-all can ride along with us as an escort to Fort Smith to be damn sure we all get there."

Alvin nodded, accepting the idea as a good one. "Take your time gettin' down. I'll have Tankard kin there in an hour."

But Matthew was not inclined to take his time. "They could kill Blue and Naomi while we're on our way. Let's move, Justin."

The hill was steep, and more than once Justin had to catch Matthew and hold him in the saddle. Matthew sagged, holding one hand tight against his side much of the time. His eyes glazed in fever, and his mouth hung open. "Matthew," Justin said, "you ain't goin' to make it. How about me goin' down and bringin' them here?"

"And give away this hideout? Some other Indian'll need it someday. I don't want all the law findin' out about it."

At the bottom of the hill they rode in the creek a way, making no tracks that might lead one of the idle curious into a discovery of the Deerhorn Pocket. Their horses left a trail of water on the bank as they rode out and slanted down toward the Tankard homestead.

Matthew reeled in the saddle, and Justin rode in close to grab him. Matthew got hold of the horn, steadied himself and said, "I'll make it now. Let's go."

Justin could see the horses down by the burned-out house and barn. He could see the men gathered beneath the shady trees, waiting. He looked in vain for Naomi.

"They've seen us now," he said. "Keep your hands on the horn in plain sight so they won't have no excuse to shoot you." Justin reached down and drew the saddlegun up from its scabbard and laid it across his lap. He made it a point to keep his horse as close as possible beside that of Matthew, preventing Matthew from being a clear and easy target. He saw a couple of the men start to move out and meet them. Rice Pegler called them back. Pegler and Oates and the others made a ragged line as they stood forward of the trees, waiting in the sunlight. Every man had a pistol or a rifle in his hand.

Justin's blood was like ice as he looked them over one by one, trying to decide where the greatest danger lay. He took an extra long look at the Negro Huff, then at Pegler. "Rice," Justin said, "he's my prisoner."

"Our prisoner," Pegler said.

"No, mine. He's got my protection. I'll kill the first man that makes a move at him." He looked up and down the line again, making sure everybody heard him. To be certain, he repeated the threat.

Pegler gritted, "If you think you're goin' to do me out of that money . . ."

"The hell with your money!"

Justin got down cautiously, the rifle ready, his gaze taking in all the men. He stepped to Matthew's horse. "Ease down on me, Matthew." He had to shift the rifle over to his left hand and give Matthew his right arm. Even so, Matthew went to his knees. Justin helped him to his feet, watching Pegler and Oates and the men. "He's in bad shape," Justin said.

"Good enough shape to hang him," Oates said. "Let's do it right here."

Justin pointed the rifle. "Say that one more time and I'll kill you where you stand. I got a right to protect my prisoner."

Oates swallowed, for he knew Justin meant it.

Justin heard Naomi cry, "Matthew!"

He saw her where she had been seated on the ground beneath the trees. Beside her, lying still and silent, was Blue Wing. Justin saw the blood on his clothes and he knew at a glance that Blue was unconscious. Justin glanced bitterly at Pegler. "Some of your work?"

Pegler said, "I got a right to question a prisoner."

Justin saw the marks on Naomi's face as she hurried toward her brother. "You questioned her too, I guess."

"An Indian. You always got to be a little tough on an Indian; show them you're not runnin' no bluff."

Naomi threw her arms around her brother and buried her face against his chest. When she looked up it was at Justin, and her eyes accused him. "I don't see how you could do it . . ."

Justin tried for words and didn't find them.

Matthew told her, "I asked him to bring me in. Else I was afraid they'd kill you and Blue."

Pegler heard. His eyes narrowed. "Then you

knowed all along where this boy was. You wouldn't've brought him in if he hadn't wanted you to. You sold out, boy."

"If I did it was for a friend. You sold out for money."

Harvey Oates moved up and Matthew pushed his sister gently aside. Matthew said, "I'd of got you, Oates, if I'd had half a chance."

"But now," Oates taunted him. "I've got *you*."

Justin said, "Wrong. *I've* got him and you better not forget it."

"It's a long ways to Fort Smith."

Matthew's hatred overcame his caution. He lashed out at Oates. Missing, he overreached himself and went to his knees. Justin saw that Oates was drawing back his foot to kick at the boy and he stepped quickly forward, pushing the rifle at Oates. "You make one move . . ."

He was aware of sudden movement behind him. He tried to turn, but he heard a *swish-h-h,* and his head seemed to explode. He felt himself falling forward and his face struck the earth. He was aware of loud and angry voices, of Naomi's quick scream, and of a gunshot. He tried to push himself up but he couldn't find his hands. Nausea came and he knew only the blackness of a deep, deep pit, angry lights swirling in his brain. He lost all sense of time, all sense of anything except an agonizing struggle to find his hands, his feet.

When finally the nausea subsided and his eyes once more opened to a sustained level of light he found himself on hands and knees. It took a minute for him to begin to see through the clouds that seemed to have gathered around his face. He made out a shapeless mass that slowly became a man lying on the ground and a lump that became Naomi, huddled over her fallen brother.

Justin didn't have to ask. He knew. Matthew Tankard was dead. Justin tried to push to his feet but fell. He crawled on hands and knees and reached forward to touch Matthew and found no life in him. He kept reaching and found Naomi's hand and heard her begin to cry. "He's dead, Justin, he's dead."

Voices spoke to him, but it took a while for them to come clearly. He thought he knew what had happened but he asked anyway. A voice he knew was Oates' said, "You turned your back on that Indian and he tried to brain you. I shot him."

Justin kept blinking until he could see. His eyes found Pegler. "What happened, Mister Pegler?"

"Oates told you."

"I'm askin' *you*."

"And I'm sayin' Oates told you."

Naomi cried brokenly, "They're lyin'. It wasn't Matthew that hit you; it was that black man. Oates shot Matthew in cold blood."

Justin said, "You're under arrest, Oates, for murder."

Oates laughed harshly. "By whose testimony?"

"By mine."

"You didn't see nothin'. You had to ask what happened and we told you. The girl lies because he was her brother. Every man here will testify that I shot that boy to save you."

"Every man?" Trembling in anger, Justin looked again at Rice Pegler. "How about you, Mister Pegler?"

Rice Pegler looked Justin straight in the eye. "What do you think?"

A little of the nausea came again. "I think you've earned your two thousand dollars."

Justin put his arm around Naomi's shoulders and let her weep until the first anguish was drained from her. He heard horses and thought it was Alvin James coming with the Tankard kin—a little too late. Instead it was Sam Dark and George Grider. They dismounted and Sam Dark walked up silently. He stared at the lifeless Matthew Tankard, and Dark looked as if a mule had kicked him in the stomach. His voice was barely audible. "So you got him, did you, Rice?"

Pegler nodded. "Oates fired the shot, but you could say it was me that got him. Without me it wouldn't of been done."

Sam Dark bent forward and gently placed his fingers under Naomi's chin. He turned her face upward and saw the darkening bruises, the flesh beginning to swell. His voice went icy cold. "What happened to the girl?"

Stiffly Pegler said, "She gave us a little trouble, that squaw."

Sam Dark looked at Justin. "Seems like somebody gave you a little trouble, too, button."

Bitterly Justin spilled the whole story. He saw the hatred rise in Dark's face as the older deputy stared at Harvey Oates. Dark's fingers spread and stiffened as if he were choking the whiskey runner. "You and me, Harvey," he spoke finally, "seems like we don't bring these poor people anything but trouble and death."

"He was a killer."

"But you and me, we made him one. You with your rotgut whiskey, me with this badge. Well, you're through, Harvey. You're one evil that this country's had enough of. Justin says he placed you under arrest; all right, I'm takin' you in for the murder of Matthew Tankard."

Oates backed off a step, suddenly alarmed. "You got no case, Sam. Ask Pegler."

Dark turned to the tall deputy. "We been tryin' a long time to stop Harvey Oates. You ain't goin' to lie for him, Rice."

Rice Pegler tried to face Sam Dark's hard gaze. He had to look away. "Oates told you how it was, Sam."

"I also heard about that money he offered you."

Pressured, Pegler was angering. "Don't badger me, Sam."

Sam Dark stepped close enough to put his face a few inches from Pegler's. "You're a four-flusher, Rice, but I'm not lettin' you stand here and lie. I want the truth."

Pegler's face went to flame. His fist came up and struck Sam Dark beneath the chin. Dark staggered back, caught his balance and surged forward, his own fist swinging. It caught Pegler in the belly and buckled him forward.

The Negro Huff had been holding a pistol in his hand; the same pistol, Justin was sure, that had knocked him off of his feet. Huff stepped in, trying to position himself to swing it at Dark. George Grider, quick as a cat, shoved the cold muzzle of his own pistol against Huff's left ear. "Back away there," he said.

Huff turned on his heel, swinging the gun around. He stopped in his tracks at sight of George Grider's long-barreled .45. George jammed the muzzle of it against the man's front teeth, hard enough that Justin heard it connect and almost felt the pain. George held it there.

For a long moment the two black men stared at each other, each in a position to blow the other to kingdom come. But George Grider was cold as winter frost and in his eyes was something dreadful that Justin had never seen there before, something he had never suspected lay hidden behind the man's kindly face. It froze the big man Huff. The muzzle of Huff's pistol slowly sagged, and finally he let the weapon drop to the ground.

A savage smile crossed George Grider's face. He lifted his pistol, then brought it slashing down across Huff's head. The big man fell like a sack of oats.

George said, "That'll teach you about clubbin' folks."

Sam Dark and Rice Pegler were oblivious to the deadly confrontation between the two Negroes. They were pounding each other back and forth across the yard. The mutual dislike that had lain submerged for a long, long time came to the surface now. They struggled and puffed and swung their hard fists. They made little defense against each other. Each took what the other gave and tried to give better. The spectacle reminded Justin of a pair of bulls butting heads, backing away and butting again, equally strong, equally angry. Dark's face was streaked with blood, and so were his fists. Rice Pegler's shirt hung off of his shoulders in ribbons. Pegler went down first, staggered to his feet and put Dark down. They backed off at arms' length and slugged each other, and when their arms were too tired for that they closed in and jabbed fists into each other's ribs with what tiny remnant of strength was left to them. It was brutal and senseless but Justin made no move to stop it, nor did George Grider or anyone else. Justin sensed that this had been inevitable and a long time coming. When he couldn't watch anymore he shut his eyes. He could still hear the scuffling and the hard breathing. When that stopped he looked up again. The two men faced one another on hands and knees, swaying drunkenly. They fought each other to the ground.

"Rice," Sam Dark wheezed, "you're a . . . dirty . . . lyin' . . . four-flushin' . . . blood-thirsty . . ."

Rice Pegler's mouth hung open, the lips torn. "I'll get you . . . Sam Dark . . . I swear to God . . . I'll get you!"

12

Alvin James brought the Tankard kin, half an hour too late. Appalled, outnumbering the Oates men by three to one, they seemed inclined at first to annihilate the whole bunch. Sam Dark, touching a wet cloth to his swollen face, talked them out of it. "Been killin' enough for one day. The law's slow but the law finally gets it done. That boy yonder, he wouldn't be dead today if he'd waited and let the law take its course. Sooner or later men like Harvey Oates always get caught up with. Now we got him under arrest. He'll never run loose again; for that I give you my personal guarantee."

Charley Wing looked like an angry eagle. His son was conscious now but groggy and badly beaten. "I want Oates dead," Charley said.

"The court'll do that."

"Those men . . ." Charley Wing pointed at Oates' crew, "they tell it one way. Naomi tells it another. Who will the court believe?"

"Everyone knows what these men are. The court won't believe them."

Wing's gaze shifted to the battered Rice Pegler, who sat hunched, one eye swollen shut, the other showing his hatred. Wing said, "That man, he is a deputy. He also says it as the other men say it. Will the court believe him?"

"He'll tell the truth when the time comes because he knows what *we* can tell if he don't."

Justin comforted Naomi as she laid her head on his shoulder. "You got to go in with us now, Naomi," he told her. "We'll need your testimony to convict Harvey Oates." When she didn't reply he told her, "You'll have protection. There won't nobody hurt you ever again."

"I'll go, Justin. I'd take any risk now to see that he gets all he's got comin'. But do you think they'll really convict him?"

"Your word and mine against all them whiskey runners? Why wouldn't they?"

"I don't know, Justin. It's just a feelin' I got. He's been around here so long I just can't picture this country ever really bein' rid of him."

"Matthew got rid of him. He stopped him as sure as if he had shot him."

"I don't know, Justin. I'll believe it when I see it."

"You heard Mister Dark; he gave his guarantee. Now we best be goin'."

Charley Wing and many of the Tankard kin rode along as an escort to see that nothing went wrong on the way to Fort Smith. George Grider handled the team hitched to a light spring wagon borrowed from the Wings so Naomi wouldn't have to ride horseback. Keeping his horse in a walk, Sam Dark watched the girl, his face deeply sad. "She's went through an awful lot, button," he said to Justin. "She sure needs somebody now."

"She's got a lot of kin."

"That ain't what I mean."

"I know what you mean. But what kind of a life could I give her? I'd be gone the biggest part of the time workin' for the court."

"The hell with the court. You don't need it and it could get by without you."

Justin made no effort to argue with him further. Presently they began to talk about today. "What I don't understand," Dark said, "is how you found Matthew so easy. How did you know where to look for him?"

Justin told him about the Deerhorn Pocket. Dark nodded, remembering. "I never could've found Barney Tankard up there if he had been sober."

"The Indians have used it a long time," Justin said.

Dark nodded. "Beautiful. Sometimes a man needs solitude, a quiet lost place where he has time to be alone and think things through. If ever I had to run I think that's the place I'd run to."

Next day the procession came across the tumbleweed wagon lumbering along with a couple of prisoners other marshals had picked up. Sam Dark took a cold pleasure in chaining Harvey Oates ignominiously to the bed of the wagon. Harvey Oates' face flushed in outrage as the padlocks were snapped. Beside him—against Oates' protests—went Huff, for on the strength of Naomi's word he would be charged with striking Justin. George Grider would add his own charge: attempting to strike a second peace officer and threatening a third with a pistol.

Oates wheezed, "I refuse to have you drag me through

the streets of Fort Smith this way, chained to the bed of a prison wagon and alongside a nigger at that."

Huff looked at him in angry surprise for Huff had been his bodyguard. The first surprise at betrayal turned slowly into a simmering hatred. Justin watched hopefully, thinking Huff might become bitter enough to turn evidence against Oates. But he reconsidered, for any testimony Huff gave against Oates would go indirectly against himself. They could expect no help from Huff.

Sam Dark rode just in front of the tumbleweed wagon, or beside it when the ground was smooth. Rice Pegler rode in the rear, well apart from Dark. George Grider was a-horseback now, and Justin drove the spring wagon and sat beside Naomi. She rode in silence most of the time, head down, her eyes closed against the sun and the dust and the ugly reminders brought by sight of the tumbleweed wagon ahead. She no longer wept for that was behind her. Justin suspected she was not thinking back so much as looking ahead.

"What'll I do when this is over, Justin? I've got no one left back there, no one to go to."

"You've got the place. The house can be rebuilt. Your friends and kin will help you with the crops. You got a fine place to live."

"But no family, Justin. I can't live there without family."

He didn't know what to tell her. The obvious answer was on his mind but he didn't want to state it.

She said it for him. "You're a farmer, Justin."

"I used to be a farmer. I'm an officer now."

"You don't have to be an officer."

"It's what I've wanted for a long time."

"Are you enjoyin' it, Justin? How did you feel about it when you went up into the Deerhorn Pocket where Matthew was? Or when you had to take him down there where those men were waitin' to kill him?"

Justin didn't answer.

She said, "There'll always be a Deerhorn Pocket of one kind or another. And there'll always be men like Matthew that you'll hate to bring down." He still didn't answer, so she went on. "It takes a certain kind of hardness to be a marshal in the Territory, Justin. I don't think you have it. You were goin' to let Matthew go free. You wouldn't've brought him down if it hadn't been for Blue Wing and me. That isn't the mark of an officer."

"Matthew was different."

"Everybody is different, in his own way. There'll be other Matthews."

The tumbleweed wagon always attracted a crowd as it rumbled through the streets of Fort Smith on its way up to the federal courthouse. Harvey Oates sat sullen and redfaced, his head down as far as it would go. He was the center of attention, for he had left here a widely known if not widely respected businessman. He had come back a prisoner chained to the wagon. Oates tried to cover his face with his arm but it didn't help. He was trembling in silent rage when the wagon pulled up in front of the courthouse to discharge the prisoners. Several deputies came hurrying out to help. Spectators' eyes were mostly on Oates as he climbed down wobbly-legged, dragging his chains. He made it a point to go ahead of the Negro Huff, whose eyes touched Oates, then turned away in resentment.

Oates wasn't in the stinking jail half an hour before a lawyer came running.

Judge Parker was conducting court, and he was not in the habit of being disturbed for the everyday comings and goings of the tumbleweed wagon. He dispensed justice on a tightly operated schedule, starting at his regularly appointed hour each morning and staying faithfully on the bench as long as necessary to dispense with a creditable number of cases. Sometimes this took until dusk and occasionally far into the night. He was not swayed by his own fatigue or by the complaints of the hard-working attorneys who practiced before the bar. Not until late afternoon did he pause long enough to hear the report of Sam Dark and Justin Moffitt. He summoned them to his chambers and was smiling as he welcomed them. The smile dimmed at sight of Dark's battered face, and at the bandage on Justin's head.

"I was told you brought in Harvey Oates and lodged him in a cell," Parker said in his heavy voice. "They also told me the Tankard boy is dead. But nobody told me you had sustained injuries yourselves."

Dark shrugged uneasily. "Nothin' serious, your honor."

"What charge is to be brought against Oates? Selling whiskey illegally? I've waited for years to get him in front of me."

Sam Dark said, "Your honor, we're chargin' him with the murder of Matthew Tankard."

"Tankard was a fugitive," Parker reminded him.

"But not at the time he was killed. Moffitt had him under arrest and under his protection. Harvey Oates wilfully shot him in cold blood."

Parker looked quickly at Justin. "You were a witness, then?"

Justin stammered. "Well, sir . . . I didn't exactly see

it myself." He touched his bandaged head. "It happened just after I got this."

Dark said, "Oates' men are goin' to swear that Matthew Tankard slugged Moffitt and that Oates shot him to protect Moffitt. But that's a lie."

"You'll need a witness."

"We have one—Matthew Tankard's sister. She's waitin' in the next room."

They brought Naomi in. Parker was dismayed at the sight of her bruises. "Did Oates and his men do this to you, young woman?"

She nodded, uneasy in the presence of this dreaded man. "Yes, sir." To his questioning she told the story as she had told it before. Judge Parker frowned. "You realize, of course, that it will be your word against all those men?"

"I'm only tellin' what's true, sir."

Parker looked at the two deputies. "It's plain these men believe you. And so do I. Now, if only the jury does . . ."

Dark's eyes narrowed. "Why wouldn't they, your honor?"

"You can never be certain about a jury."

"They *got* to hang him," Dark exclaimed. "One way and another, he's got the blood of fifty men on his hands. I gave those people out yonder my guarantee . . ."

"Never guarantee a jury." Parker placed his hands together and spread the fingers, studying them blankly. "It occurs to me that Deputy Pegler was out on the hunt for Matthew Tankard. Wasn't he there at the time this all took place?"

Justin Moffitt nodded soberly. "He was there, your honor."

"Was he a witness?"

Justin nodded again. "Yes, sir."

"Then I see no cause for concern. The word of an officer is all we'll need to see that Mister Oates never draws another free breath. Where is Deputy Pegler?"

Justin and Sam Dark looked at each other and Dark shrugged. It occurred to Justin that he hadn't seen Pegler since they had arrived in town. Parker strode to the door and called for Marshal Yoes.

"Yes, your honor," Yoes said. "I saw Rice Pegler. He said Sam Dark and Deputy Moffitt would take care of the written report. He asked to be assigned on another job far out in the Territory. He left an hour ago." Yoes looked narrowly at Sam Dark. "I gathered that he and Deputy Dark have had a violent disagreement. Pegler thought it would be better if he and Dark stayed out of each other's way awhile."

Judge Parker frowned at Dark. "What's the trouble between you two?"

Ill at ease Dark said, "A private matter, sir."

"Any trouble between deputies of this court can hardly be considered private, Mister Dark, if it affects the performance of their duties and the conduct of this court. I trust that in the future you and Mister Pegler will restrain yourselves."

"We'll sure try."

Parker turned to Marshal Yoes. "I don't know how soon the trial will come up for Harvey Oates but I'll want Rice Pegler here for his testimony. We can't leave anything to chance."

Yoes said, "He'll be here, sir."

Harvey Oates' attorney was in and out of the federal courthouse several times a day demanding that

his client be released on bond so he could continue
with the normal conduct of his business. At length
Judge Parker set bond and Oates strode out of the cell
and up the basement steps to sunlight and freedom.
Sam Dark and Justin Moffitt stood at the top of the
steps watching. Justin sensed the depth of Dark's hatred; the killing of Matthew Tankard had affected
Sam more than Justin had realized at first. Perhaps it
was an extension of the guilt he had felt over bringing in Barney Tankard for hanging. In a sense Dark
seemed to blame himself for Matthew's death. And
behind the whole melancholy chain of events had
been Harvey Oates.

Dark blocked Oates' way. Oates stopped short of
the top of the steps. "Move aside, Dark. I'm a free
man."

"You're on bond. There's a difference. One day soon
I'll get to yank you back in here. And then . . . ." he
pointed at the white gallows . . . "You'll climb another
set of steps. A short trip up and a shorter one down."

"Don't count on it," Oates told him.

Rice Pegler's manhunt turned into a long one. The
weeks went by and little was heard from him. It suited
Justin, for with Oates' neck almost in the noose and
Pegler out of sight Sam Dark was fairly decent to live
with. He sent Justin off on a few assignments but
never any extended ones that kept him out of Fort
Smith and away from Naomi for long. They had
found a family for Naomi to stay with in town until
time for the trial. As an important prosecution witness she was given the constant protection of the
court. Sam Dark gratuitously saw to it that most of
the time the duty was delegated to Justin.

The day came for the trial and it was a relief to

Justin. After all this waiting it would be pleasant to get the thing under way, he had thought.

He hadn't realized how wrong he could be.

The opening part was easy. The prosecution was allowed to present its case first, and Justin was called to give his part of the testimony building up to the death of Matthew Tankard.

"I could tell Harvey Oates was fixin' to kick the prisoner," Justin said as he came to the end of his statement. "I moved to stop him. That's when Oates' bodyguard Huff hit me over the head and Oates shot Matthew Tankard."

At that point the complexion of the case began to change. Oates' attorney objected strenuously to Justin's interjecting an account of events that had occurred when he was obviously not conscious enough to see them for himself. Judge Parker sustained the objection. The defense attorney came around to cross examine. He explored Justin's relationship with the Tankard family.

"Am I to understand," he asked, "that you considered yourself a friend of this fugitive, this Matthew Tankard?"

"I liked him," Justin admitted. "I knew him before he was a fugitive."

"I gather from your testimony that you knew right where to go to find him. Where was that?"

"Up in them hills."

"So all the time another duly appointed officer, Rice Pegler, and a group of aroused citizens searched high and low for him, you knew exactly where to find him and you did not share that information with your fellow officer?"

Justin's fingers began nervously drumming against

the arm of the witness chair. Up to now neither he nor
George Grider nor Sam Dark had said anything to
anyone about Oates' promise of money to Rice Pegler.
This had been their ace in the hole to keep Pegler in
line. Justin had been trying to avoid indicating that
Pegler had any stake in the situation beyond his duty
as an officer. Justin pondered his answer a while before he gave it. "I was afraid the men with Deputy
Pegler wouldn't allow the prisoner to live. And they
damn sure didn't."

The attorney turned quickly to Judge Parker. "Your
honor, will you please caution this witness against interjecting extraneous testimony?"

Solemnly Parker admonished Justin to answer the
questions only.

The attorney said, "It has become my impression
that you are well acquainted with the young lady
seated yonder. Who is she, Mister Moffitt?"

"Naomi Tankard."

"She is the sister of the deceased, is she not?"

"She is."

"What is the nature of your relationship with this
young lady?"

"We're friends."

"Nothing more?"

Justin colored. "Nothin' more."

The attorney stared a moment at Naomi, making a
show of his approval. "Quite a comely young woman,
wouldn't you say? Hardly shows her Indian blood."

Judge Parker leaned forward, mouth turning down-
ward. "Counselor, if you're trying to make a point it
escapes me at this moment."

"I am on the verge of an important point, your
honor."

"Well, I don't see that the young lady's Indian blood has anything to do with the matter at hand."

"I meant no disrespect, sir. I was merely trying to show that this is indeed a most handsome young woman, one who might easily catch the fancy of a youthful deputy marshal used to the long, lonely trails one must ride in the performance of that type of duty. Now we've all been his age and we're all human. I submit, gentlemen of the jury, that a smile in the eyes of such a girl might blind an impressionable young man like a glance into the sun, so that he might tend to see only that which would be favorable in her sight. I submit that this family had a mistaken vendetta against my client and that this girl's pleasant face and winsome smile were used to prejudice this young officer against him."

Justin said, "Your honor, *I* object to that."

Parker shook his head and Justin knew he had erred.

Sam Dark was called, as next prosecution witness, to describe the scene as he had come upon it after the death. He referred to "Harvey Oates and his whiskey runners" and brought the defense attorney angrily to his feet. The attorney headed off any of Dark's attempted references to Oates' whiskey trade on the basis that it was hearsay, unproven, unfounded and purposely aimed at prejudicing the jury.

Listening, Justin began looking nervously back toward the door. Marshal Yoes was supposed to have had Rice Pegler here today to testify. So far Rice hadn't been seen.

When Sam related that upon his arrival Justin had told him about Huff clubbing him and Oates shooting Matthew, the attorney objected that this was an unsupported statement from an unqualified witness who by his own testimony had been suffering from a severe blow on the head and whose knowledge of the event was limited to what the girl had told him. On cross examination he asked Dark if the story told by Oates and by all the other witnesses had not varied sharply from the one told by the girl, and if all these had not agreed upon the details.

"Them whiskey runners will all lie," Dark declared, drawing another objection.

It had been the prosecution attorney's plan to take testimony first from Justin, Dark and Pegler, then to cinch the case with the emotional impact of Naomi's stark description. But Pegler still hadn't arrived. Judge Parker whispered instructions for deputies to go out and seek him. Meanwhile there was nothing to do but go ahead with Naomi's testimony. The prosecutor elicited from her the story she had told about the sequence of events culminating in the death of her brother while Justin sprawled unconscious. At length the defense attorney was given the right of cross examination.

He paced the floor in silence a few moments, stern gaze fixed on the nervous girl. "Young lady, would you please point out Harvey Oates to me?"

She did. The attorney asked her, "Had you ever seen him before the event you had just described?"

"Once. He came to our house with a group of men the day my father shot one of his whiskey runners." The attorney admonished her about earlier rulings on testimony of this type. "Did you—I'll broaden the question—did any of your family ever see Mister Oates sell whiskey to anyone?"

"We all knew he did it."

"You all knew, even though nobody ever saw it happen?"

"Some things people just know."

"So that your family hated him on the strength of these reports?"

"We hated him for what he done to our brother Barney."

"And exactly what was that?"

Haltingly Naomi went into the account. When the prosecutor tried to object the defense attorney pointed out that the girl herself had opened this line of testimony. Naomi told about Barney's hanging because of a crime committed when he was drunk. "It was Harvey Oates' whiskey that done it to him," she said positively.

The attorney turned to the jury. "Gentlemen, you can see the attitude of recrimination and hatred that had built up in this family, simply on the basis of an unfounded rumor, so that they were willing to go to any lengths to correct what they considered to be a woeful injustice."

"It *was* an injustice," she cried out. "He killed my brother Barney with his whiskey. Then he sent and had my mother and father killed. And finally he killed Matthew with his own hand. I saw him do it!"

She was standing in the witness box, her dark hands clenched, tears shining on her cheeks.

The attorney gave the jury time to look at her then said, "I ask you, gentlemen, if you have ever seen a woman who carried more hatred in her heart? I ask you, if she hated him so much and had a chance with one small lie to send him to the gallows would she hesitate? I submit, gentlemen, that her hatred was such that she might even have forced herself into believing she actually saw something she did not, because what she imagined suited her need for revenge. Look at her, gentlemen, and pity her. But I implore you, do not allow your pity for her to lead you into an injustice against an innocent man, my client. The testimony of our own witnesses will soon establish the real truth."

Watching first the jury then Naomi, Justin sensed that the defense had at least established some doubt in their minds.

That damned Pegler, he thought angrily, *where's he at?*

The prosecutor, all his present witnesses used up, had to plead to Judge Parker for patience. "We have one more witness whose testimony is vital to this case, your honor. He is Deputy Rice Pegler. He was supposed to be here before now, but apparently some outside duty has detained him."

"I've sent men out to hunt for him," Parker said. "When and if he arrives you can still put him on the stand. In the interests of time I suggest we proceed with the defense witnesses."

One by one the defense paraded its witnesses, who gave virtually identical testimony and who all saw clearly every move that everyone had made in those fateful moments. Not one of them had been standing in the way of the other. The defense attorney saved Harvey Oates for last and let him tell his story. It was like the others except that he could explain his motivation.

"Tankard had grabbed the deputy's pistol, you see, and had struck him from behind. He had raised it to strike again. Now I knew the next blow was sure apt to be fatal. There was nothin' else I could do, your honor, except what I done. I shot him. The way I see it I saved that deputy's life. I'm sorry he feels the way he does about me; it's the girl who done it to him. If you could've seen him the way he clung to her afterwards . . ."

The prosecutor tried to shake Oates' testimony as he had tried to shake that of the men before him. He made a dent or two but he didn't punch any holes.

The judge had called for the attorneys' summations when a slight commotion started at the back of the courtroom. Rice Pegler stood there.

Judge Parker said sternly, "Mister Pegler, you are woefully late."

"I been held up, sir."

"Are you ready to testify?"

"I suppose I'm as ready as I'll ever be, your honor."

"Then, Mister Prosecutor, I suggest you proceed with your witness."

It seemed to Justin, watching, that Pegler avoided looking at him or at Dark. In fact he avoided looking at almost everybody except, perhaps, Harvey Oates. The opening part of the questioning was similar to that given the other witnesses, establishing his presence at the scene, his reasons for being there.

"Now, Mister Pegler," the prosecutor said, "we come to the point at which Deputy Moffitt and his prisoner dismounted and moved toward you. We know from a reading of the officers' report what has been attributed to you, but we want you to describe for us in your own words the sequence of events that followed."

Pegler rubbed his hands nervously, looking at the floor. "Sir, I don't know what's in the report. I didn't write it myself; I got sent out on another assignment

right away. I expect Mister Dark wrote the report."
He glanced at Sam Dark then back to the floor.

"Just tell us what happened."

Rice Pegler raised his head, bringing his gaze from
the floor to the ceiling then back to Harvey Oates.
"What happened was that the prisoner grabbed the
deputy's pistol out of his belt and hit him with it. Then
Mister Oates, he shot the prisoner. That's all."

The courtroom buzzed. Justin Moffitt was on his
feet. "Damn you, Rice Pegler, that's a lie!"

The judge rapped his gavel and called for order.

The prosecutor stared wide-eyed and stunned, as
if Rice Pegler had struck him in the face with a shovel.

Justin shouted, "Damn you, Pegler, Oates has paid
you off!"

The judge rapped again. "Mister Moffitt, if you
don't sit down and be quiet I'll have to cite you for
contempt. I *will* have order in this court." The judge
himself was shaken and plainly disappointed. He
turned to Rice Pegler. "Mister Pegler, what were you
doing during this time? If you were doing your job
properly it should not have been up to Mister Oates
to shoot the prisoner."

"I was there, your honor. I was on the point of
shootin' him myself. But Oates was closer and had a
clearer shot."

The judge's face was florid. "Mister Pegler, this
court has proceeded for weeks on the assumption that
the material in the marshal's report was substantially
the same as your own observations. If what you have
just told us is true Harvey Oates should never have
been arrested in the first place. Why was he?"

Pegler looked at the floor. "Me and Deputy Dark,
we had us a fight over that, sir. I didn't think we ought

to bring Harvey Oates in and I told Sam so. But he
hated Mister Oates. He gave me a bad beatin' and he
said if I crossed him he'd shoot me. So I took another
assignment to get out of his way. But I made up my
mind when the time come I'd be here to set things
right."

Enraged, Justin glanced at Sam Dark. He found
Dark hunched in his chair, his whole body trembling,
his face flushed with silent fury. He made Justin think
of a barrel of powder, the fuse smoking. "Mister
Dark," Justin said. He didn't like what he saw in
Dark's face. He feared Dark would bound across the
short space to the witness chair and grab Rice Pegler
by the throat. "Mister Dark," Justin whispered, "don't
do nothin' sudden."

Sam Dark just sat there.

It was hard to tell from the judge's face whether he
believed Pegler or not. Justin decided the judge knew
the man was lying.

But the jury didn't know it. The outcome of the
case was evident even before the attorneys went into
their final arguments. When the jury was led away to
the jury room it was gone only long enough to vote.
It brought in the inevitable verdict: not guilty.

Harvey Oates' friends in the back of the room
shouted and whooped and stomped their feet. Naomi
Tankard covered her face with a handkerchief. Sam
Dark sat in a stunned silence, trembling.

Judge Parker rapped vainly for order. He saw he
wouldn't get it. He said heavily, "Deputy Dark . . .
Deputy Pegler . . . I want to see both of you in my
chambers in five minutes!" He dismissed the court
and retreated angrily from the room.

Oates' attorney triumphantly slapped the whiskey

runner on the back, then Oates' friends began crowding around, offering congratulations. Oates was all
laughter and smiles. Rice Pegler strode slowly across
to join the Oates group. Oates called, "Boys, you all
know where to meet me in about twenty minutes. I'll
buy drinks for the crowd." He had a special greeting
for Pegler. "You timed it just right," Justin heard him
say. "I owe you somethin'."

Pegler glanced over his shoulder. "You owe me two
thousand somethin's."

"You'll get it."

Sam Dark had heard, too; Justin could tell by the
way he finally moved, turning his face toward Pegler
and Oates. The look in his eyes was terrible. Dark
pushed carefully to his feet and turned his back on
the crowd. He strode out of the room and down the
hall.

Justin put his arm around Naomi's shoulder and
led her away. "We'd best get out of here, Naomi. This
is no place for you now."

He passed by the marshals' office and saw Sam
Dark strapping on his pistol belt. "Mister Dark," Justin asked worriedly, "you goin' someplace? The judge
said he wanted to see you."

"I heard him."

Oates' crowd swept down the hallway and out the
wide front door shouting, laughing, pulling Oates
along. Dark started for the hall then turned to look
at the bewildered girl. "Honey," he said, "don't you
waste any more tears. Harvey Oates has run out his
string."

Sam Dark strode down the hall and out the front
door. Justin called after him, "Mister Dark! Sam!"
Then he followed.

He stopped at the top of the steps. Below, he saw that Harvey Oates had turned and that the crowd had spread apart a little. Oates was looking at Sam Dark, taunting him with his eyes. "What was it you was sayin' about me walkin' up them thirteen steps, Sam? Had me all but hung, didn't you, but I pulled out of it. Now it's you that's on the way out, Sam. After today there won't nobody pay any attention to you. You'll be lucky to get a job catchin' stray dogs."

"You're through, Harvey."

"Me through? I ain't even started yet."

"You've started and you've finished. You've killed your last Indian boy, Harvey."

Justin knew what was going to happen but he was powerless to move. He stood on the top step and watched as if hypnotized. Sam Dark's hand went down then came up with the pistol in it. He shoved the hand forward, thrusting the pistol almost into Harvey Oates' shirt. He fired once and he fired again.

Men shouted. Women screamed and went running in panic. But Harvey Oates never heard them. All he ever heard was that first shot.

Then, in the excitement and the frightened scurrying of the crowd, Sam Dark was gone.

13

Reluctantly Justin walked into the judge's office, following half a dozen other deputies. He glimpsed Rice Pegler standing halfway across the room, and for a moment Pegler stared at him, eyes bitter and challenging. Justin thought about it a little then edged toward Pegler. The tall deputy turned his face away.

Justin said, "You're not goin' after him, Pegler." He had dropped the *mister*.

Pegler stood in gray silence, trying not to hear him.

Justin said, "You lost two thousand dollars. If you want to take it out on somebody, try *me*. I'll fight you from here to the river."

Pegler still didn't answer, didn't look at him. Justin pressed. "Sam Dark called the turn on you. He called you a liar, a four-flusher. Now I'm callin' you the same. I'm sayin' Harvey Oates bought you off and hid you out till the last so nobody would have a chance to work on you, to get the truth out of you. I'm sayin' you sold us out for two thousand dollars."

Judge Parker was hunched over his desk, which was half covered by a set of warrants. He looked up in irritation. "Mister Moffitt, this has been a bad day. You're making it even worse." The shock and the strain were showing in Parker's stocky face. He looked incredibly weary, infinitely sad.

Justin moved closer. "Your honor, you're not really goin' to swear out a warrant against Sam Dark, are you? You know the kind of a man he is. You know the service he's given to this court. And you know the kind of man Harvey Oates was. You know, if the jury didn't, where the truth was in that courtroom today."

Parker gave the young deputy a long look of pity. "Mister Moffitt, you know my feelings toward Sam Dark. You also know where my duty is. This court has always stood for one thing: justice. For friend and foe alike."

"After all he's done for this court you can't send me out to hunt him down like a dog."

Parker shook his head and he made a point of extending his patience. "Not like a dog. Like a man. These marshals are his friends, most of them. They'll treat him with respect."

"But bring him in just the same, and throw him in that hellhole downstairs like any common criminal, and try him, and walk him up those thirteen steps."

"This court will do all it can for him. It will treat him fairly."

"And in the end it'll hang him."

Judge Parker shrugged, his face grave. "It might."

Justin stood in angry frustration, staring at the portly judge. Of a sudden he realized that the judge was as helpless as he, a prisoner, in a way, of his own harsh code. Justin reached up to his shirt and un-pinned his badge. "I won't be a party to it, sir."

He started to place the badge on the desk but Judge Parker caught his hand and squeezed the fingers shut. "Don't act in haste, Mister Moffitt." He sat a moment that way, his hand gripping Moffitt's. He called to Marshal Yoes to clear the other men out of the room. When they were gone Parker said, "You call yourself a friend of Sam Dark's. You know that when this warrant is issued he'll be considered an outlaw. No matter how far he runs, how well he hides, sooner or later someone will find him. That someone could be a friend, like you, who will treat him with kindness and respect and pity. It could be a stranger, cold and indifferent. It might even be an enemy like Rice Pegler, who would go after him in malice."

"You'd let Pegler go?"

"There'll be a hearing for Rice Pegler, but right now there isn't time. He's still on duty. And like every other officer of this court it will be his duty to find Sam Dark if he can. I have a feeling that is one duty Rice Pegler will relish." The judge got up and slowly walked to the window, peering out upon what once had been a military parade ground. "Many a time I've stood at this window and wept for the soul of a man I had condemned to that gallows. But I've never let my feelings sway me from my duty, however harsh it might be. Sam Dark has been a man like me. He has never flinched from his duty, even when he personally hated it. His soul has known the torments of hell more than once. It's not unthinkable that in the end a man like him would have to break. But when he does he has to face the same judgment as anyone else. Better he face it at the hands of his friends."

Parker turned back around. "What I'm saying is that as a friend of Sam Dark you may have some idea where he would have gone. I'm saying that it would be far better if you went and fetched him rather than have it done by someone like Rice Pegler." He paused, his somber gaze dropping to Justin's closed hand. "You still have that badge, Mister Moffitt. What're you going to do with it?"

Justin closed his eyes a moment, then raised his hand and pinned the badge back to his shirt.

He stopped by the cabin to pack some food in a warbag and tie a blanket behind the cantle. Then he rode by the house where Naomi stayed. Her eyes were bleak as she looked at the horse. "I didn't think you'd go after him, Justin."

"I didn't intend to. But the judge made me see that I have to try. If I don't find him Rice Pegler might. Pegler would track him to China now if he had to. Better me than Pegler."

Naomi leaned to him and he held her tightly. She said, "I'll be here when you come back."

"I'll *be* back."

The Territory was big and wide and open country lay west of it all the way to the mountains and finally the Pacific, room enough for a man to run. If Sam chose to run far Justin would have no idea where to seek him.

But in his mind was a conviction that Sam Dark would not run far. Dark was not a man to move blindly and in panic. He had always been one to study a problem through and to move with deliberation. He would hole up somewhere and survey his situation. He would think out a solid plan then act upon it.

Sam Dark knew the Territory as well as any Indian and Justin had no doubt he knew dozens of places to find security and to give him time. Justin knew only one, the Deerhorn Pocket. He realized it was a long shot but it was the only one he had. He recalled his conversations with Dark and how Dark had been taken with this hidden sanctuary deep in the Cherokee country.

"If I ever had to run," Dark said, "I think that's the place I'd run to."

This was the first mission Justin Moffitt had ridden alone in the Territory. He had wanted to bring George Grider but George had been too overcome. He could not bring himself to search for Sam Dark so he had remained in Fort Smith, on duty at the jail. "I ain't takin' the tumbleweed wagon out again," he had told Justin, "not till this is all over with. I couldn't live with myself if somebody was to bring in Sam Dark and I was to have to chain him in that wagon."

It was strange, riding alone this way. It gave Justin time and solitude in which to think and he wished it didn't, for the thoughts that kept forcing themselves upon him were no comfort. He camped on a clear-running stream and caught some fish for his supper but they had no flavor. He lay wide-eyed most of the night, staring sleeplessly at the stars. At daybreak he was up and moving.

He came at last to the Tankard place and he rode by the family cemetery above the field. A fourth mound was there now. His throat tightened as he remembered the days he had spent with these people, those last days before a smothering black blanket of tragedy fell upon them. Justin's gaze lifted then to the hills, toward the hidden place where he might find

Sam Dark. He passed by the black ruins of the house and barn and started the long climb.

He made no effort at covering his tracks now for he saw no need. Either Dark was here or he wasn't. Justin found the little stream and rode beside it letting the horse pick its way along in a slow walk. Justin was startled by a sound in the bushes and a buck deer suddenly burst into sight, sprinting across in front of him and disappearing into another thicket.

The suddenness of it unnerved him a little and he found his hands shaking. *What am I scared of?* he asked himself. *Sam Dark won't shoot me.*

But a nagging thought came for the first time and a little doubt began to arise. Sam Dark had never been a hunted man before. That could change things. Justin felt an impulse to reach down for the saddlegun but he quickly pushed that notion aside. *What would I do with it if I had it? Sam Dark is a friend of mine. I couldn't shoot him.* But that tiny worry persisted. *Maybe he could shoot me.*

High up in the pocket he began to call for Sam Dark as he had called for Matthew Tankard not so long ago. "Mister Dark! It's Justin. I come to talk to you."

He rode slowly now, stopping often to rise up in the saddle and listen. He would call then ride again.

Near the upper end of the pocket he found him. In a tiny clearing Sam Dark suddenly appeared, rifle in his hands. His face was lined with weariness. He seemed somehow older, grimmer than Justin had ever seen him. "You shouldn't of come, button."

Justin said, "Can I get down?"

Dark seemed only then to realize how he was holding the rifle. He dropped it to arm's length at his side.

"I don't know why you'd want to, but help yourself."
He motioned with his left hand. "I got a little fire over
thisaway and a can of coffee on."

Justin tied his horse. He made a point of removing
his gunbelt and looping it over the saddlehorn so Sam
Dark would feel no threat. Then he followed Dark
through the trees to a rock overhang much like the
one under which he had found Matthew Tankard.
Dark had only one cup. He filled it with steaming
black coffee, careful not to pour in too many grounds,
and he handed it to Justin.

Dark said, "I expect things was in an uproar when
you left."

Justin nodded. "They was."

"They got warrants out on me by now, I suppose."

Justin nodded again.

"You got one of them, Justin?" Dark asked.

Justin said, "I do. Everybody has."

They went silent a long time, occasionally looking
at each other, most of the time looking off into space.
From up here one could see for miles out across the
Territory. Off in the distance Justin could see a couple of cabins and wondered idly whose they were.

At last Dark asked, "You figurin' on takin' me
back?"

Justin stared into the cold and empty cup. "If you'll
let me. I didn't want to come at all; the judge talked
me into it. Way he said it, somebody'll get you sooner
or later. He'd rather it was a friend. I don't have to
tell you that you got enemies, Mister Dark."

"Rice Pegler?"

"Among others."

Sam Dark's face twisted bitterly and his knuckles
went white from clenching his fists. "I figure a man

could stay up here a long time and not be found. There's plenty of game to keep him from bein' hungry. I found a snare this mornin' and a cache with a bow and arrows."

"The Tankard boys!"

"The Indians around here know this place and they might figure out I was up here. But they wouldn't tell nobody. And you wouldn't tell nobody, Justin. I could stay a year if I needed to."

Justin knew better. He knew Sam Dark wasn't the kind who could live long hiding like an animal. Sooner or later he would have to come down and rejoin the human race. Even if it killed him.

"The judge said he'd give you every possible chance, Mister Dark. He said he'd see to it that you got justice."

"But in the end you know how it'd have to come out. There's been men hung on his gallows for less than what I done."

"He likes you, Mister Dark. He'll do all he can."

"If he didn't hang me he'd have to send me off to prison. That's just another kind of death. Slower, but death just the same. I've put too many men into that kind of a place. No, Justin, I won't do it."

"You're already in prison, Mister Dark, can't you see that? This place up here: it's a prison of its own if you can't leave it. Someday you *will* leave it and somebody'll kill you."

"Better a bullet than a rope or the rot of a stone cell."

Justin frowned, trying to frame his words. He had never been good at that. "The judge sent me to bring you in, Mister Dark. For your own good I got to do it."

Dark stared at him curiously. "You goin' to shoot me, Justin?"

"I couldn't do that."

"Then you're not takin' me. That's the only way you'll get me down from here. It's the only way *anybody*'ll get me down."

Justin realized then the hopelessness of it. He knew he would never persuade Sam Dark and he knew he couldn't shoot him. He pushed to his feet. "Then I reckon I'd as well be goin', Mister Dark. I'm doin' no good sittin' here—not for me and not for you."

"You just goin' to let me stay?"

"You said it yourself. I can't shoot you."

"You goin' to tell the others where I'm at?"

Justin shook his head. "You know me better than that. I won't betray you, Mister Dark."

Dark grimaced then pointed to the badge on Justin's shirt. "In that case you better shuck the badge. The minute you ride down from here without me you've violated your oath."

"The badge don't mean as much as friendship."

"That's what I'm talkin' about. When you wear that badge you got to make a choice. You're not cut out for it, Justin; I been tryin' to tell you that from the first. A man like me could do it. A man like Pegler, even. But not you, Justin; you got too much heart for it. You think I haven't got scars for the years I put into it? I got a lot more on the inside than ever show on the skin. The judge . . . he come to this country with all kinds of dreams of makin' it a fit and proper place, and he will, but he'll go to his grave grievin' over the things he had to do to change it. Stay with the job long enough and it'll kill you, button . . . your spirit, if not your body. You was born to be a farmer. Go back to it while you still can."

"This Territory is a long ways from bein' tame yet, Mister Dark. That's what I put the badge on for."

"There's other ways to tame it. The plow can do it better than the gun ever will. There'll be farmers in these hills when the outlaws and the marshals are all gone, when the judge is forgotten and the courthouse fallen down. That girl, Justin . . . do you feel about her the way I think you do?"

Justin nodded.

Dark said, "She's got land down yonder and she needs help. She can't keep it by herself. Put the badge away and go marry that girl. Love her like she was meant to be loved, and love this land, too. It'll be good to you. All that badge will bring you is grief and maybe an early grave."

Sam Dark followed Justin down to his horse. They stopped a moment and looked at each other and Dark shoved his hand forward. "Goodbye, button. Do what I said: marry that girl."

Justin nodded and turned away, reaching for the reins.

From the brush came a harsh voice that Justin knew only too well. "Raise them hands, Sam Dark! Raise them high!"

Justin whirled. Rice Pegler stepped out from behind the green foliage, letting a branch swing back with a slapping sound. He held a rifle pointed at Dark. Justin glanced at Sam Dark and saw the moment of doubt reflected in his eyes, the suspicion of betrayal. Justin cried out, "Sam, I didn't . . ."

Pegler grinned cruelly. "I followed you, Moffitt. I had a hunch you'd know where Sam was holed up

and that you'd go to him, same as you did to Tankard. And I knowed when it come to the tawline that
you couldn't bring him in. But *I* can bring him in. Step
away from that horse, boy."

Justin measured the distance he would have to go
to reach the gunbelt. Dark knew his thoughts. Dark
said, "Don't try it, button. He'll kill you."

Pegler grunted. "Damn right I'd kill him. I come to
fetch you in, Sam, and I'll do it dead or alive. The
choice is up to you. It don't matter to me one way or
the other."

Sam Dark was somber. "I told Justin and I'll tell
you. I ain't goin' in to a rope."

"I don't see as you got a choice."

Sam Dark looked a long moment at Justin Moffitt,
then back to Pegler. "I've got *one*," he said, and he
reached for the pistol at his hip.

Pegler's rifle thundered and after it, like an echo,
came the crack of the pistol. Justin's horse reared and
broke loose and tried to run. Justin grabbed the reins
and was dragged a few feet before he brought the
horse to a stop. Dry-mouthed, heart hammering, he
turned to look.

Rice Pegler sat on the ground, holding his stomach and groaning, one leg buckled under him. His
hat was off. Justin tied the horse and warily moved to
Pegler's side. Pegler looked up at him, his eyes begging
for help. The rifle lay on the ground. Justin reached
down for it, cursed bitterly and flung it away into the
trees.

He walked then to Sam Dark. He knew at a glance
that it was over for Dark; the rifle bullet had torn a
hole in him that nobody could fix. Dark moaned as
Justin tried to lift him and Justin eased him gently to

the ground again. "Why did you do it, Mister Dark? Why did you do it?"

But Justin knew, though Sam Dark would never tell him. The pulse was gone; Sam Dark was dead. Justin slumped over him and broke into sobbing. When he was done and had control again he pushed awkwardly to his feet. He fetched his horse and laboriously lifted Sam Dark into the saddle. He would carry him off the hill and see that he was buried somewhere down below, among friends.

Rice Pegler was still hunched, arms tight around his belly, his face deadly pale. He sat in a spreading pool of blood. He raised one hand, the fingers outspread, groping. His eyes pleaded. "Help me," he rasped. "Help me."

Justin Moffitt stared at him, making no move toward him.

Pegler cried out, "Help me, boy. Help me or I'll die here."

Bitterly Justin said, "Then, Goddamn you, die!" And he led the horse down the hill.

BOWIE'S
MINE

1

His name was Daniel Provost, and it was the time of the Texas Republic. Once, years ago, he had heard Sam Houston's Twin Sister cannons at San Jacinto, and from sanctuary beyond the rain-flooded bayous he had watched smoke rise over the battlefield. He had been a boy then, too young to fight. Now the 1840's were well along and he was a man, but no adventure was left. Modern times and civilization seemed to have stilled it forever. His world was restricted to the narrow confines of Hopeful Valley along the Colorado River in what was considered western Texas, and it was seen mostly over the narrow-pinched rump of a lazy brown mule.

The man riding the bay horse and leading three packmules was the first stranger Daniel had seen in three months. Daniel leaned to pull against the leather reins looped around the back of his neck and let the heavy wooden plow ease over as he watched the horseman slowly work his way down the gentle hill toward the field. The man wore buckskin and an old Mexican sombrero that had seen too many rains, and too much sun. Daniel watched in silent curiosity as the man reined up at the end of the plowed rows and raised his hand in peace.

The man's longrifle lay across his lap, but Daniel saw no threat in it. The face looked friendly enough, what he could see of it through a considerable growth of brown whiskers.

"Stand there, Hezekiah," Daniel needlessly admonished the mule; any time Hez was given a chance to halt, he wouldn't lift a foot until he had to. Daniel slipped out of the reins and trudged across the rows, studying the man. "How do. Anything I can do for you?"

The man looked around, and Daniel sensed he was searching for sign of a rifle. Daniel had none. The man said, "I come in peace, brother, as any good and honorable man." A benign smile shone through the whiskers, and Daniel could see this was a young man, thirty possibly, maybe even less. "Name's Milo Seldom. Is that water you got in yonder jug, or somethin' stronger?"

"Water," said Daniel, and fetched the canvas-wrapped jug from where it hung in the benevolent shade of a huge and ancient live oak.

"Sure am obliged," said Seldom, and tipped the jug off his shoulder in the style of a man drinking whisky. He took several long draws, then wiped his sleeve across his mouth and handed back the jug. "Mighty good water. Many a place I been, folks'll offer you hard liquor first off; glad to see that you-all here have got a bent toward religion."

Daniel shrugged. "Ain't religion, exactly. Whisky

and hot sun and hard work don't mix too good. My name's Daniel Provost. You come a long ways?"

"A long ways. Still got a fair piece to go." He pointed his chin. "Seen a cabin as I topped the hill. You got a wife there, and family?"

"Ain't married. I live with my folks."

"Seen a deer back yonder a mile or so. If I was to go fetch it in, reckon the woman of the house might see fit to share vittles with a lonesome, hungry stranger?"

"You don't need to bring nothin' to be welcome at the Provost house." But Daniel reckoned it wouldn't hurt any; the menfolks had been too busy with the planting to fetch fresh meat.

"I always like to bring more than I take away," the stranger said. "Leaves folks thinkin' good of ol' Milo Seldom. If you'd kindly see after my packmules a bit, I'd go see after that there deer."

Daniel took the lead rope and led the mules to the tree where he had kept the water jug. Knowing mules, he didn't put the jug back where it had been. Hezekiah moved his head interestedly, looking at the packmules and watching Seldom ride away on his bay horse. But he showed no inclination to move his feet; he never did until he was forced to.

Daniel studied the bulging packs and tried to make out the vague aroma that came from them. It was somehow familiar, but mixed with the strong mule-sweat it was too evasive to identify. Curiosity nagged at him, and when the stranger was out of sight, Daniel went so far as to put a hand on the rope that held one canvas bundle. But he changed his mind; a man didn't poke where he had no business. He walked back to Hez and put him and the plow into service again, his mind on the stranger rather than on the job.

He sensed that Seldom had come from far-off places, and maybe was headed for far-off places Daniel hadn't even heard of, let alone seen.

Daniel had no fear of work, and the plow-handle fit his hands, but he had often thought it would be good, just once before he settled finally into harness and took up wife and land of his own, to go out and see what lay beyond the hills that rimmed this valley; to see the lands from which the few travelers came; perhaps even to see the mysterious western country from which the Comanches used to materialize wraith-like to strike suddenly and kill and burn and fade away again.

He sensed that Milo Seldom had been to these places—some of them, anyway—and that his hands were not made for the plow. Briefly he envied the man as he had envied a couple of men in Hopeful Valley who had been in the thick of the battle with Sam Houston. They never talked about it much; they talked much easier about crops and horses and cattle and the like. Maybe that was the way of it for most men—one big adventure and they were ready to settle down for a quiet, steady life of hard work. Trouble was, Daniel hadn't had his adventure yet. He sensed that Milo Seldom was a man given entirely to the kind of experience Daniel hungered after.

Before long he heard the crack of the long rifle. There was no second shot, which did not surprise Daniel; he suspected those keen gray eyes needed but one chance to look down the barrel and over the sights. By the time the stranger came back, the deer properly gutted and draped behind his saddle, Daniel had finished to the end of a row. The sun was still an hour high, but on such an occasion as having a stranger call, he doubted that anybody could fault him for calling it a day. He unhitched Hezekiah from the plow, climbed up onto his bare back and rode to the tree where the packmules were tied.

The stranger sat idly pitching up a flattened chunk of lead and catching it in his hand. It was the ball which he had used to kill the deer. Lead was not to be wasted, and a hunter usually made every effort to retrieve it and melt it to be poured for another day, another deer.

Daniel said, "You just shot once."

"Poverty makes a man a good shot. Takes coin for powder and lead, and precious little coin ever crosses my palm. But it's a-fixin' to, my friend."

"What do you mean?" Daniel knew it wasn't any of his business, but the stranger had opened the subject.

"Them packs there, they're goin' to open the door. I'm goin' to find out if gettin' rich spoils a man's shootin' eye."

"You need any help?" Daniel joked.

The stranger took him seriously. "Matter of fact, I just might, was the right man to come along."

Daniel stopped smiling. "You didn't say whichaway you was headed."

Seldom eyed him a moment in silence. "Was headed for your house to find out if your kind mother would like some fresh venison."

Daniel took that as a sign that the subject was closed, and he didn't press it. But as he rode he glanced back at those big packs, jouncing along on the quick-footed Mexican mules. He noted the easy, almost slouchy way Seldom rode, as if he had been hatched in a horse barn. But if his riding was slouchy, his gray eyes were searching.

"Ain't nothin' here you got to watch out for," Daniel told him. "Last Indian trouble we had was several years ago. Just a little bunch huntin' for horses, mostly."

"Them Indians ain't dissolved off of the face of the earth, friend Provost. Just because there's more settlement now than there used to be don't mean they won't show up again; more settlement means more horses. Indian, he always has a powerful want for more horses."

"I'll bet you've fought Indians."

"Ain't we all? Fought Mexicans, fought outlaws, fought bears and cougars. Fought sin, too. Life's an eternal struggle for the right thinkin' and the true believer."

"You sound like a preacher."

"I ain't, but now and again when I find somebody in need of the Word, I carry it to them the way it's been carried to me. Figure I owe it to folks to pass on the blessin's I've received. You strike me as bein' a good true Christian, Mister Provost."

"Name's Daniel," Daniel reminded him. "I've read the Book. Never done no hard studyin' on it, though."

"Man don't have to study it; it's all around him—in the blue sky, in the green hills full of game, in the runnin' streams and the rivers full of fish. The Lord's work is all around us plainer than words in a book. Ain't everybody can read a book, but anybody can see the Lord's good work."

That led Daniel to wonder if Seldom could even read; lots of people couldn't. There wasn't a great call for reading in this country anyway; long as a man could do a few ciphers and plow a straight furrow and sight down a barrel, they would have to get up

awful early to starve him to death. It was often said
that Texas was overrun with lawyers and bookish
people; what it needed was men who knew how to
build something and bring in food and fiber. The ed-
ucated folk were considered like scavengers who took
secondhand what someone else's labor had wrought.

Daniel observed, "The Indian is part of God's work
too, I guess."

Seldom grunted. "Put here to test us. The good
Lord gave us the gun to shoot him with."

Daniel nodded. "I reckon."

Seldom studied Daniel's brown mule and the tangle
of harness. "You don't carry a gun to the field with you?"

"Last three-four years ain't been no need. The only
feathers we ever see any more are on wild turkeys."

Seldom gave him a look that plainly said he doubted
a farmer was apt to be much of a shot anyway. Daniel took this as a challenge. He said, "You mind if I
try a shot with that old longrifle of yours?"

Seldom stared at him in doubt. "Ol' Betsy's a shade
contrary." It was fashion for Texans to name their rifles after the one David Crockett had carried into the
Alamo. "Keep in mind that she bears a hair to the
left." He poured powder into the pan and handed the
rifle to Daniel as Daniel slid off the mule. Daniel
picked a dead limb on a lightning-struck live oak fifty
yards away and dropped to one knee. The pan flashed,
the rifle shoved hard against his shoulder, and the
limb splintered and fell.

Seldom's eyes flickered in surprise. "You ain't always been a farmer."

Daniel had, but he let the statement stand.

The Provost home was a big double log cabin.
Aaron and Rebecca Provost had taken literally the

Biblical injunction to be fruitful and multiply. Daniel was the eldest of a considerable brood, old enough now to take up his own land if ever he could raise the money it took to put in a claim.

Aaron Provost watched with interest by the open door of the long log barn. He stood six feet tall and more, shoulders broad, tough hands the size of a cured ham. He could lift a wagon while someone fitted a wheel, or he could throw a bull yearling to its side and hold it down by sheer muscle and weight. He could have broken a man's neck with one blow of a huge fist if he were so inclined, but Daniel had never seen his father strike a man in anger. Provost was a friendly bear.

Aaron's eyes were boldly curious as he watched Milo Seldom, but he addressed himself to his son. "In early, ain't you, Daniel?"

"Brought a visitor for supper, Papa."

"So I see." Milo Seldom winced a little at the crush of Aaron Provost's hand; the big farmer didn't realize his own strength. "Name's Aaron Provost. You make yourself at home here, friend."

Seldom rubbed his throbbing hand. "Much obliged, Mister Provost. Brung meat for the table. Don't like to be a cost to nobody."

"A visitor's always a gain around here, not a cost. Daniel'll see after your stock, and I'll take you up to the house to meet Rebecca. She'll be tickled that there's somebody come."

Daniel asked Seldom, "Any special way I ought to handle them packs?" He hoped this would prompt Seldom to tell what was in them.

"Just throw them over the fence is all right. Nothin' there that can bust or leak out."

Aaron swung the deer carcass over his shoulder as if it had been a rabbit. He started walking toward the house with Seldom, but turned. "Daniel, you'll want to wash up and slick your hair before you come in. Lizbeth's here."

Daniel looked at the dusty patched clothes he wore and wished there were some way for him to change. But he owned only two pairs of britches and three homespun shirts. Lizbeth Wills was used to seeing men come in from the fields; her father and brothers were farmers like the Provosts. And if she and Daniel married, this was the way she would see him the rest of her life. She had just as well get accustomed to it.

Normally the thought of Lizbeth being here would crowd everything else from his mind. It did something to him he never quite understood to put his arm around her when nobody was looking, and to feel the quick, shy response as she leaned to him. Sometimes she put something sweet-smelling on her neck—he never did know what it was—and it got him to breathing hard and thinking things he would be ashamed to tell her about. He was not naive; he knew exactly what this sort of thing eventually led to, though he had never so far let himself go beyond a furtive pinch or two where he had no business. Lizbeth always slapped his hand gently to let him know he shouldn't, but never stingingly enough to make him retreat altogether. She let him know without saying so that once the proper ceremonies had been attended to, he would be welcome.

The stranger was heavier on his mind now, however, than Lizbeth. Tomorrow Milo Seldom would ride out with hardly a backward glance, while Lizbeth would be here forever.

As he struggled to lift the heavy packs from the mules and hang them on the fence, he heard the girl's voice. "How do, Daniel."

Lizbeth Wills was tiny; he could almost reach around her waist with his two hands. This had caused Rebecca Provost to worry aloud that she might not be strong enough to attend to all of a woman's work, though Daniel had noticed that the Mexican women of the Hernandez place upriver were small and seemed to have an unbounded capacity for labor. Daniel had never fancied the chunky or the big rawboned type of girls anyway; there were a few of them in the valley if his preference had run in that direction. Tiny or not, Lizbeth could cause him about all the excitement he was able to restrain.

Daniel glanced toward the house, saw nobody looking and gave her a quick promissory kiss. She touched him with both hands, then pulled back, remembering herself. "Supper'll be ready directly," she said. "Your mama is fryin' up venison from the deer the stranger brought in. I already helped with the bread." She was forever reminding him she could cook.

"What did you think of him, Lizbeth?"

"Not very fat, but he'll make passable venison."

"I don't mean the deer. I mean Milo Seldom."

She shrugged. "Never paid much attention to him. He's another rollin' stone without no moss on him. I like to see a little moss."

"Don't he make you itch to know the places he's been to, the things he's seen?"

"Why? I'm not interested in goin' anyplace. I like it here."

"Sure, this place is all right, but—" He broke off, knowing he couldn't explain it to her. It was a woman's nature to be a nest-builder, to cling to what she knew. She couldn't know the way a man's eyes lifted to the horizons sometimes, the way a man's nature strained to shake the bonds and cross over the unknown hills. He said, "I'll go with you in a minute, soon's I get through here. Will you wait?"

"You know I'll always wait."

The children were noisy but the venison was good, and Rebecca Provost had fixed fresh bread from wheat Aaron Provost had carried way over east to the flour mill. Milo Seldom wolfed food as if he hadn't eaten in a week, and perhaps he hadn't. A drifting man usually carried coffee and salt and little else, depending upon game for whatever sustenance he got. But even venison cooked on a spit over an open fire could become tiresome after a while. A woman's touch was probably a treat indeed. Daniel noticed that Seldom gave Lizbeth much of his attention. Not that he tried to talk with her much; but simply that his eyes seemed always to stray back to her. Daniel supposed this ought to bother him, but somehow it didn't. It seemed confirmation of his own good judgment in latching onto Lizbeth himself.

Later, when supper was done and Aaron and Daniel and Seldom repaired outside to the brush arbor to cool themselves in the spring breeze, Seldom pointed his chin toward the door. "Mighty comely little girl, that one in yonder. She spoke for?"

Daniel shrugged. "Sort of."

"Smart of you, friend Daniel. A man needs a good woman if he's got him a place and go' to stay put."

"Ain't got me a place of my own. Maybe someday, if I can raise the money."

Daniel's twelve-year-old brother Lod came out and

flopped down on the ground to stare at the bewhiskered Milo Seldom in flagrant and unapologetic curiosity. Seldom commented that he looked nearly a grown man and won Lod's friendship for life. Then Seldom looked toward the cabin again. "Always wished for a little woman like that myself, only I'm always on the move, and a man can't ask a woman to follow along after him like a pet dog. Indian woman, maybe, or even a Mexican, but white women ain't made thataway. Sort of brings me up close and reminds me of my shortcomin's when I see a woman like yours. You're lucky."

Am I? Daniel asked himself. "Must be somethin' to get to come and go when and where you please, to stay where you want to, move on when the notion strikes you, to see new country all the time."

"The restless foot. I've always had it; been both a blessin' and a curse to me. A blessin' when I see somebody who's worked himself into the ground on one little place for years and got no more to show for it than I have. A curse when I see a pretty little woman and know I can't ever have one like her, just an occasional night or so of sinful pleasure in one of the settlements, bought the way a man buys a bar of lead or a little parcel of powder. But I can't change my ways; they're settled too deep in me even if I wanted to get shed of them. Be content that you ain't got my rovin' nature, friend."

How do I know I haven't? Daniel asked himself. I've never tried.

Aaron Provost got out his old pipe and the leather pouch in which he carried his tobacco. Seldom blinked as if he had just thought of something. "Where'd you get the tobacco, Mister Provost?"

"San Felipe. Was down there on some land business with the guv'ment. Like to smoke?"

Seldom pushed to his feet. "Put it back in the pouch. I bet I got somethin' you'll like better." He strode to the barn. In a few minutes he was back, carrying a huge handful of leaf tobacco. "Try that. Bet you ain't had the like of this in years. Fine burley, prime stuff if prime was ever growed."

Aaron Provost smelled of it, and his mustache lifted in a broad smile. "I swum, lad, you are most certainly right." Eagerly he shredded tobacco for his pipe, lighted it and drew on it, eyes closed in pleasure. "Land o' Goshen, how this takes me back."

Daniel knew now the aroma he had smelled. "You mean that's what you got in them packs, is tobacco?"

"Not just tobacco, friend. Pure gold. I'm on my way down to Mexico to sell it. Them Mexicans will near give you gold ounce for ounce in trade for that kind of prime tobacco."

"I hear they got a mighty stiff tariff on it."

"Tariffs is for them that don't know the Mexican ways."

Daniel frowned. "You fixin' to smuggle it in?" He remembered an old rascal named Noonan who used to neighbor them here and who had told of smuggling tobacco into Mexico long before the big war with Santa Anna.

"Ain't nothin' sinful about a little smugglin'. Border lines is a thing of man, and contrary to all the laws of God and nature."

Aaron Provost's eyes were open again, and he was close to a frown. "There's talk we may be movin' toward another war with Mexico. You reckon a man

ought to be goin' down there under them circumstances, sellin' stuff to people who may be fightin' us
again one day?"

"I fought in the last war, Mister Provost, and if it
comes to that, I'll fight in the next one. But maybe
there don't need to be no war if people understand
one another, and what's a better way to learn that
than by trade? I say set up trade with a man and you
don't have to war with him."

"Depends on how you trade," the farmer said.

Seldom shrugged. "Better tradin' than fightin'."

Daniel remembered what Seldom had said about
standing on the threshold of wealth. Even granting
that tobacco was worth a lot in Mexico, he couldn't
see much wealth in three packs of burley. He said as
much.

"The tobacco," Seldom responded, "is just the
startin' place. It's to give me money enough that I can
go where the real riches are."

Little Lod asked, "And where is that?"

Aaron Provost admonished his son, "Another man's
business is best left alone."

Milo Seldom studied the boy a while. "No harm
done, Mister Provost. I see no reason I shouldn't tell
you; there's no harm you good folks would do me.
You remember Jim Bowie?"

"Him that died in the Alamo?" Aaron Provost
looked over at Seldom. "He'll always be remembered
in this part of the country."

"You ever heard about his lost silver mine?"

Daniel's backside began to prickle. "There was always talk that he found an old Spanish mine. Nobody
ever knew where, or even if there was truth in it."

"He found it," Seldom said with confidence. "Way

to the west, out in the middle of that Comanche and Lipan Apache country. Wasn't far from where the Spaniards built their fort on the San Saba and left it a long time ago. He found it, then he lost it. With what I get out of this tobacco, I'm goin' to go find it again."

Aaron Provost said soberly, "You'll find your grave, is all. There's Indians out yonder in that western country, thicker'n hair on a buffalo hide."

"But there's silver, too, and I'll have my share of that. Then the world will stop and tip its hat to Milo Seldom."

Daniel suspected nobody ever paid much attention to Seldom, and that probably rankled him. Come to think of it, he told himself, outside of family and a few friends there ain't nobody heard of Daniel Provost.

The women had come out into the cool and heard the last part. Rebecca Provost, a gaunt and patient woman, nodded knowingly, for she had heard many a dream spoken in words but had seen few lived out in deed. Lizbeth Wills listened with mouth open. She hadn't been around half as long as Rebecca.

Aaron Provost puffed contentedly on his pipe, enjoying the richness of the tobacco. "Every man to his own brand of religion I always say, and seekin' after riches is a religion to some. But the silver I want is right here on my own ground, in reach of my plow. It comes up fresh with every plantin' when the Lord sees fit to send the rain and withhold the pestilence."

Seldom replied, "And a good life it is too, brother, for them as has the gift to live it. But the Lord turned me another way, and who am I to deny Him?" He pushed to his feet. "I'll see after my stock before I roll out my beddin'. I'll want to rise early and be off in the cool of the mornin'."

Rebecca said, "Not without a good breakfast to give you strength."

"I wouldn't think of it, good lady. Cookin' such as yours is a blessin' that comes rare to a man of my nature." He bowed and walked to the barn.

"Strange man," Lizbeth said, watching with eyes showing awe. "Scares me a little."

"Nothin' strange about him," said Aaron, drawing on his pipe. "We seen a many like him back in Tennessee, and there's aplenty of them in Texas— backwoodsmen, men of restless foot, akin to the wild creatures that migrate with the seasons. There ain't no mystery to them; they're just men that ain't ever found their way."

"Idlers," said Rebecca. "Likeable, some of them, but idlers and misfits. They raise no crops, build no cabins. They move across the country like Indians. They contribute nothin' and leave no sign."

Aaron disagreed. "They contribute. They're the first ones into every new land. They're the ones that test the mettle of it and learn its ways. They open it up for the farmers and the others that set down roots. God made all kinds of men, and for every kind there's a reason."

Daniel's brow furrowed. "You reckon he does know how to find Jim Bowie's mine?"

Aaron shook his head. "A dream, that's all. But he knows how to hunt for it, and to some men the hunt is more important than the findin'."

2

Invited to spend the night with the Provost boys in the loft over the cabin's open dog run, Milo Seldom listened to the noise and politely declined, indicating he had rather sleep out by the barn than be a disturbance to anybody.

Lizbeth Wills stayed over and would sleep among the Provost girls, and as usual on such occasions, she and Daniel took a short walk hand in hand past the garden and down to the stock well and back toward the house. Also as usual, Lizbeth did all the talking. Most times Daniel would listen contentedly, enjoying the music of her voice and the exuberance of her dreams, but tonight he heard only a little of it here and there. His mind was on the stranger who rested out by the corrals; the stranger and the three packs of tobacco and the exciting times that must surely lie ahead of Milo Seldom.

Crisply, Lizbeth reproached Daniel for not listening

to her. "Some other girl got you thinkin'?" she demanded.

"Been studyin' on that Milo Seldom, and the things he said. Been thinkin' what a farm I could buy if I had me a share of that Jim Bowie silver."

"He's crazy even talkin' about it and you're crazy listenin' to him."

"It's enough to set a man's mind a-runnin', all that silver out yonder waitin' for somebody."

"You'll find yours, Daniel, where your daddy found his—in the crops that come up out of your own ground."

"But that's painful slow. A man gets in a hurry sometimes."

Her tone softened. "I'm not impatient, Daniel; I ain't pushin' you."

"It's me that's impatient."

Her hand squeezed his fingers, and she leaned against him. "There's time."

When she stirred him like that, he didn't know if there was time or not.

It was customary for everybody to be up and about by first light, for the day was never long enough to do all the work that needed doing, but Daniel quietly climbed down from the loft even earlier than usual. He moved uncertainly toward the barn, half afraid Milo Seldom might have taken a wandering notion and be already gone. To his relief he saw the tobacco packs still slung across the fence, and the packmules and horse hobbled on grass, waiting time to be on the move.

Lod came trotting along barefoot, tugging at his

britches. Daniel motioned for him to go back to the house, but Lod gave no sign he understood either word or gesture. Daniel decided to try to ignore him.

Milo Seldom was awake and dressed, if indeed he had ever taken his buckskins off. Daniel figured he probably had slept in everything except perhaps the heavy boots and the Mexican hat. "Mornin', brothers," Seldom greeted Daniel and Lod, sitting on his single blanket and scratching first his head, then his backside. "Womenfolks ain't already got breakfast, have they?"

It was still dark, and no candlelight yet showed through the open windows. "Not yet. They'll be up directly."

"Then I reckon I'll be packin' my mules and be ready. The early miles are the easiest. Late in the day a mile is hard won."

"I'll help you." Daniel took down a rawhide *reata* the Mexicans had taught him to use, for he suspected from the wild look that they carried about them Seldom's horse and mules might be mean to catch. But Seldom waved the rope aside. "I'd as leave not spoil them none. Feller uses the rope a few times, he can't catch them without it no more."

Seldom approached them with the bridle and halters, talking softly, reminding the animals of the biblical injunctions about hard work and faithfulness, and the penalties of sloth. In a minute he had all four properly caught and the hobbles removed. "When God gave man dominion over the beasts of the field, He meant him to use it with kindness," he told Daniel. One of the mules balked, so Seldom kicked it in the belly. "And firmness," he added.

Lod scurried around getting in the way, but Daniel

knew something about packing mules and was able to help Seldom. He pointed this out in an oblique way. "I reckon it takes you awhile when you got no help."

"Time means mighty little to a mule."

"It can mean a right smart to a man."

"I trust the good Lord to give me time for what needs to be done."

The Lord gave Seldom time to put away breakfast the likes of which even big Aaron Provost seldom ate. When he was done and had wiped his sleeve across his mouth the last time, Seldom thanked the women for their kind attention and good cooking. Rebecca had made up some extra corn dodgers and put them in a sack. Daniel hoped Seldom would tie them where they wouldn't get taken up with the flavor of horse-sweat. Seldom said, "I'll remember you good folks when the weather turns cold and rainy, and it'll bring a little sunshine to warm my soul."

Daniel followed him out to the horse and the pack-mules, itching with the things he should already have said. "Mister Seldom, you'll be needin' help on this thing you're doin'."

Seldom frowned, sensing the rest of it. "I got some people down the way that I expect'll be willin' to go with me."

"You got one right here that's more than willin'."

Seldom looked him full in the eye, regret in his expression. "Been thinkin' you'd say that, and been wonderin' how I could answer you without causin' bad feelin's to either of us. You ain't the kind, Daniel. Maybe you think you are, but you ain't. You was born for farmin' and tendin' stock and for raisin' babies with some pretty little cornfed girl like the one I seen here."

"Farmin' is not soft life; I know aplenty about hardship."

"But of another kind. A man can stand hardship when he's on land that he knows, when he's got his own people around him, when he knows where he's goin' to lay his head down come dark. It takes another breed of man to stand hardship where he don't know no landmark, don't have no friend, don't know if he'll live to see the sun come up. I'd be doin' you a wrong in the eyes of the Lord was I to let you go with me and you not meant for the kind of trouble we'd ride into." He tried a weak smile that didn't work, and reached out to grip Daniel's hand. "You'd best stay home, friend Daniel. This is a growin' country. Texas needs farmers a heap sight more than it needs tobacco merchants and treasure hunters. A man like me don't leave nothin' but tracks; a man like you leaves the land better than he found it."

Seldom gave Daniel no chance to argue. He swung easily up into the saddle, waved his hand in a broad motion meant for everybody, and rode away in a brisk trot, leading the Mexican mules.

Daniel's throat was tight with frustration as he watched Seldom move out across the rolling green prairie. At length he was aware of Lod standing beside him, eyes shining in admiration of Milo Seldom.

"You know somethin', Daniel?" Lod said. "When I'm old enough I'm goin' to get me a horse and some packmules and I'm just goin' to travel the country the way he does."

"The only mules you and me will ever handle is

plow mules," Daniel said, a touch of bitterness in his voice. He turned away, knowing it was time to harness Hezekiah.

Daniel tried not to dwell upon his disappointment. He went to the field and attacked the plowing with an angry drive he hadn't had in a long time. The mule seemed to sense that he was not to be trifled with, for it stepped briskly and gee-hawed to every command. Daniel finished more plowing in less time than he had done all year.

He saw the mule's ears point forward and head go up in sudden interest, and he looked. Over the hill came two men on horseback, strangers.

Traffic has sure got heavy here of late, he thought, wiping sweat with his sleeve and licking dry lips as he thought of the water jug waiting in the shade. He finished the row and left Hez standing while he went for the water and waited for the men to reach him.

He decided right off that he didn't like their looks. Neither was inclined to show friendliness; if anything, they were suspicious.

"You!" one of the men said sharply. "Come here!"

He was a tall man in a badly worn beaver hat and a swallowtail coat which hung down on either side of the saddle. The command roused a stubborn streak in Daniel.

If he wants to talk, he'll have to come to me! He stayed where he was and took another drink from the jug. The men moved their horses into motion and came up to him. That gave Daniel a sense of satisfaction, a skirmish won.

The other man spoke next; a smaller, chunky fellow whose belly pushed against the front of the saddle. "We're lookin' for a man."

Daniel said, "Will I do? Name's Daniel Provost."

The tall man took it up impatiently. "Man we're lookin' for was leadin' three mules. Tracks show he come right by this field; I'd say from the sign that it was yesterday. Whichaway did he go from here?"

"You're friends of his, I reckon?" Daniel said innocently, knowing by the look of them that they were not.

The two men glanced at one another, the tall man scowling, the fat man snickering a little. The fat one said, "You could call us acquaintances. We're awful anxious to meet up with him again. Now tell us whichaway he went."

"What did he look like?"

The tall one said angrily, "There ain't been so many people by this direction but what you'd know the one we're talkin' about. He had three mules with him, and a pack on every mule. Now, we don't aim to be unfriendly about this thing, but we're askin' you one last time."

Daniel sensed threat about the two, not to himself but to Milo Seldom. He knew that lying about his having been here would do Seldom no good; if they had tracked him this far, they could track him more. "Yes, there was such a man here. Come by late yesterday and asked if we'd feed him. Did he break the law?"

The fat one smiled without humor. "He done an unfriendly thing."

They know he's after the Bowie silver, Daniel decided, becoming increasingly concerned. They're after it too. "Us Provosts don't hold with lawbreakers or shelter the criminal," he said. "If it was a thing like that, I'll tell you all I know about him."

The fat one said, "All you got to do is tell us which-away he went when he left here. That'll gain us time we'd otherwise lose followin' tracks."

"West," Daniel lied, "toward Austin town, where they're buildin' the capitol. Said it would be a good place to sell some tobacco."

The two men looked at each other, then stared at Daniel. He stared back, trying to keep his face from betraying him. He felt no guilt, so he knew there was no reason for his face to give him away. The tall man gritted, "If you was to lie to us, we'd take that as an unfriendly thing."

"I don't know you or him either. Why should I lie?"

"He's got an easy way with people; they'll always lie for him."

The fat one nodded. "Come along, Bodine. We're keepin' a farmer from the tillin' of his fields."

The tall Bodine grumbled under his breath as they rode away. He kept looking back, but to Daniel's satisfaction they rode west. They had taken his word—maybe. But they probably wouldn't take it for long. When they had ridden awhile and hadn't cut any sign of a trail, they would probably come back. What they might do then he didn't know.

What he *did* know was that he had to warn Milo Seldom. He itched to be about it immediately, but he held himself in check, knowing they might be suspicious, knowing they might be watching. He had to go back to his work and give them time to decide he had told them the truth. It was hard going, plowing the length of that field, then back again, itching to be on his way but fearing to move from the job at hand.

By the time he had made it back to the starting

point, he could not hold himself any longer. He un-hitched Hezekiah from the plow, jumped up on the mule's back and bareheeled him into a reluctant trot, then finally into a rough lope toward the house.

He picked up his roan horse Sam Houston grazing the green grass and hazed him into a pen. Not paus-ing to unharness Hezekiah, Daniel bridled Houston and threw his saddle up onto the horse's back.

Lod trotted barefoot from a garden where his fa-ther had left him hoeing. "What's the matter, Daniel? You see Indians?" His voice was hopeful.

"Not Indians. There's a couple of hard-lookin' fell-ers after Milo Seldom. I sent them the wrong way, but they'll be onto me soon enough."

"I'll go with you."

"Like hell you will! You'll slip the harness off of Hezekiah and see that he gets somethin to eat." Lod opened his mouth in protest, but Daniel cut him short with an angry glance. "You argue with me and I'll wear a hole in your britches with a harness strap! Do what I tell you now, and keep out of my way!"

Daniel led the roan out and, swinging into the sad-dle, loped him toward the house. His mother looked up in surprise from the fireplace as he burst through the door. "Land sakes, where you goin' in such a hurry?"

"Maybe to Mexico; I don't know." He grabbed his old longrifle from its pegs on the wall, and the powderhorn and shot pouch that went with it. Face stunned, his mother demanded to know what the matter was.

"Got to go help Milo Seldom," he blurted. "Lod can tell you."

"Son—" She tried to grab him. He gave her a kiss

and was gone before her hands could clasp him and hold him back.

"Mama, if I don't come back awhile, you'll know I went with Milo. Tell Lizbeth so she won't worry."

"So *she* won't worry?"

She followed him, throwing out questions so rapidly that he couldn't have answered them even if he had been so inclined. "*Adiós,* Mama," he shouted back at her as he quickly mounted, the powderhorn swinging wide from his shoulder. He pulled the roan around and set him quickly into a run, wishing he had spurs. That was something that as a farmer he had had no reason to buy or have made for him. He swung around the garden and the near cornpatch, and then he was on his way south as hard as he could push the roan.

He knew the trail Milo Seldom had taken, for it led by the Hernandez place and ultimately joined with other trails that eventually would take a traveler into San Antonio de Bexar. Nearly every trail into Mexico went one way or another by San Antonio, for this ancient town had been the heart of Mexican Texas, pumping the lifeblood that had kept it alive for almost a century and a half under the flags first of Spain, then of Mexico. When a traveler skirted around San Antonio there was usually a reason, and not an honorable one. Daniel saw no reason why Milo Seldom should want to avoid town.

He found a horse and three mules no problem to track, especially since they stayed on the trail; the sign was plentiful. Daniel pushed the roan as much as he dared, loping him awhile, then slowing him to a trot to keep from breaking him down. The trot kept him impatient, and in a short while he jumped the roan into a run again.

Finally, ahead of him, he saw the man and the mules. Shouting and waving his hat, Daniel tried to get Seldom's attention. If Seldom saw him, he gave no sign.

If I was an Indian, Daniel thought, I could kill him and he'd never know what hit him.

Milo Seldom dropped out of sight over a hill. Frustrated, Daniel kept heeling the roan.

Two men burst out of a thicket and stopped their horses in the trail directly in front of him. Too late, Daniel tried to rein around them. His roan bumped one of the horses, and Daniel almost went down. When he grabbed Houston's mane and pulled himself back into the saddle, he was staring into the awesome bore of a rifle that looked like a San Jacinto cannon.

"Now, farmer," the fat man said, that mirthless smile cutting across his face again, "I'm purely disappointed in you. If ol' Bodine here wasn't of a suspicious nature, we'd probably be halfways to Austin now. Always been my misfortune that I trusted people too much, and often as not they've cashed me in. Now, you wasn't figurin' on goin' on down yonder and tellin' Milo Seldom we was comin', was you?"

It was a useless question not meant to be answered. Daniel's throat was dry all the way down. The longer he looked at that rifle, the bigger it got.

"Farmer," the tall man growled in evil temper, "if there was any profit to be got out of it, I'd shoot you. I might decide to do it anyway just to see whichaway you fall."

"Now, Bodine," said the bewhiskered fat one, "he wouldn't be of no earthly use to us thataway. Besides, folks around here might get fussy over a man shootin' a farmer, though Lord knows the country's purely overrun with them these days. No, seems to me like ol' Milo might be tickled to see this friend of his. Might be glad to treat with us, knowin' we wouldn't shy from takin' desperate measures." He glanced at Daniel and added, "If we was forced to it."

Daniel tried to swallow, but his throat was shut.

Lanky Bodine said, "You know that shootin' eye of Milo's. If he was to take the notion, he could pot you quick as we come in sight. Time I could get to him, he could be reloaded and get me too."

"How do you know I'd be the one he'd shoot first?"

"You're the broadest target. A man like Milo who's been hungry all his life just mortally hates a fat man anyhow. Smart thing for us to do is to take this farmer and follow along and keep out of sight. First time he stops, we'll work around him and get ahead. Then we'll step out and surprise him as he comes up on us."

It seemed to Daniel that if Milo Seldom had even one eye open or his ears weren't plugged with dirt, he ought to be able to see or hear them going around him and be on the *cuidado*. He made it a point to hit the hard ground where he could, for the hoofbeats drummed louder there, and he popped brush when it came handy. If Milo Seldom was half the frontiersman he appeared to be, he would end up doing the trapping rather than being trapped.

It was all for nothing. Bodine and his fat partner set up position in a motte beside the trail. Bodine kept the long barrel of his rifle pointed at Daniel's head. "Now, farmer, don't you even breathe loud."

Daniel hardly breathed at all.

Milo Seldom came along directly, head down and whistling a tuneless ditty. If thirty war-painted Comanches had been astraddle the trail, he would not have seen them.

The fat man eased out of the motte, and Bodine followed, silently motioning for Daniel to do likewise. "Well now, Milo, ain't this a pleasant surprise?"

Milo Seldom stared in astonishment. He never made an effort to lift the rifle from his lap. He swallowed and finally said, "Naw, Fanch, it ain't overly pleasant."

Fanch grinned. "Depends mostly on which side you look at it from. Me and Bodine, we're mighty pleased about the whole thing. See you taken good care of our mules."

"They *was* your mules. They been mine the last several days."

"We're mighty glad you got the use of them, Milo, but now we're takin' possession again. We hope you got no strong objections."

"I sure do."

"They as strong as ol' Bodine's rifle that he's got pointed at your farmer friend? Or as strong as this Jim Bowie frogsticker I got here in my hand?" Fanch waved his big Bowie knife and passed it so near to Seldom's throat that Seldom could almost taste the forged steel. Seldom shook his head in resignation. "Naw, they ain't that strong."

Fanch said, "Many a thing I don't like about you, Milo, but one thing a man's got to give you credit for: you're reasonable."

Daniel decided they weren't going to hurt him or Seldom; if that had been their intention, they would have done it by now and not wasted all the talk. He could see that Seldom was losing the mules and their burden, and with them the dreams of the silver mine. Daniel's fear subsided, and anger rose in its place. He was angrier at Seldom than at Bodine and Fanch. He said critically, "If you'd been payin' attention, you wouldn't of let yourself get caught thisaway. I done everything but set off a cannon."

Seldom made no effort to reply; he looked like a dog that had been given a couple of licks with the double of a rope.

Fanch said, "You'll find that's somethin' else about Milo; he ain't dependable. He's a dandy at hatchin' up schemes but mighty slack at seein' them through. Careless is what he is." He reached for Seldom's rifle.

Bodine still had his own rifle pointed at Daniel. "You'll have to get off of that horse, farmer. We got to take your horse to keep you from any notion of followin' after us. A little walk back to the farm will give you plenty of time to consider your follies."

"You got no right to take my horse."

"We'll turn him loose down the trail someplace. If he decides to come home, fine. If he don't, maybe you can get Milo to work it out." He poked at Daniel with the rifle. "Now git on down."

A clatter of hoofs came from atop the hill, and a rattle of chain. And down rode Lod Provost heeling the plow mule Hezekiah, the plow harness still on him. Bodine turned in surprise and let the rifle sag. Daniel grabbed it and pushed it away from him, trying to twist it from the tall man's hands. Instinctively Bodine pulled the trigger. The big blast went off close to Daniel's ear, though the ball passed harmlessly by.

The suddenness of it spooked Daniel's horse, and

he plunged forward into Bodine's. Off balance, Daniel sailed out over the horse's neck and straight into the tall man. Together they went over the rump of Bodine's startled mount, which kicked and wheeled away. Bodine hit the ground, Daniel on top of him. Something snapped. Bodine howled in pain.

"My arm! Damn you, farmer, you done busted my arm!"

Daniel desperately grabbed Bodine's rifle by its hot barrel, not realizing for a moment that it was useless until he took time to reload it. No, not useless; it would make an awesome club. A rifle barrel heavy as that could brain a man.

He thought then of Fanch and the Bowie knife and spun around, the rifle over his shoulder and ready to swing in self-defense. He held it that way, for in the moment of confusion Seldom had come into possession of the knife, and the situation had reversed itself. "Now, Fanch," Seldom said quietly, the point of the blade at Fanch's belly, "you just hold yourself real still. I always had an evil temptation to slice a fat man open and see if anything besides grease would spill out. Don't do nothin' foolish that might help Satan overcome my Christian nature."

Bodine squirmed on the ground. "My arm! My God, ain't nobody goin' to pay attention to my broken arm?"

Seldom showed no concern. "Which arm is it, Bodine?" He looked for himself, and seemed disappointed. "His left one. Friend Daniel, you ought to've broke his right arm instead; that's the one he shoots with."

Daniel momentarily turned his attention to his younger brother, sitting on the lathered mule. "Lod,

what the devil you mean followin' after me thataway?
I told you to stay home."

Lod ignored the question. "How come you to bust
that feller's arm?"

"Lod, it's a wonder you didn't kill that poor ol'
mule, runnin' him thataway. Now you get yourself
home and tell the folks I'm goin' on with Mister
Seldom."

Milo Seldom blinked. "I don't remember sayin'
nothin' of that kind."

"It's plain to me that you need help, even if you
don't see it. I can at least keep you from ridin' off into
a ditch or somethin'.."

Bodine kept crying about his arm. Seldom paid no
attention to him. "Well, you did show a right smart
of gumption toward these two evildoers."

Lod Provost asked, "Daniel, how come you broke
that feller's arm?"

Seldom finally gave some attention to Bodine, who
sat in the trail holding the arm and hollering. "Fanch,
you git down there and see if you can't do somethin'
that'll shut him up. I swear, there ain't nothin' gets my
hide to crawlin' like listenin' to a growed man cry."

Daniel sent Lod to catch his and Bodine's horses.
Daniel's rifle was still tied to Bodine's saddle.

Not trusting Fanch with the knife, Seldom cut the
sleeve from Bodine's dirty homespun shirt. The arm
was crooked, all right. Seldom put his foot against
Bodine's shoulder and pulled the arm. Bodine bawled
and fainted. Seldom said, "I believe I got the bone set,
Fanch. You find a stick and use that sleeve to wrap it
around his arm."

Bodine came back to consciousness, groaning and
acting grievously sinned against. Fanch said, "You got

any whisky, Milo? It'd sure help him with his miseries."

"A clear head will let him contemplate his sins and help him decide to set his feet aright upon the path to glory. And now it's time for me to be settin' *my* feet upon the path to San Antonio. I swear, interruptions like this sure do slow a man up."

Daniel said, "You didn't say yet, Milo, if I'm goin' with you."

"I thought *you* had already said it. Come along; you've earned a share."

"I ain't got no money with me, not a dollar, not a peso."

"Who *has*, this day and time?" Milo swung into the saddle and took up the lead line for the pack-laden Mexican mules. "Catch Bodine's and Fanch's horses, will you, Daniel? Them two boys won't cause us no worry if they ain't mounted."

The fat Fanch was sweating. "You ain't stealin' our horses and settin' us afoot out here, are you, Milo?"

"Not stealin'. Like Bodine told my friend awhile ago, we'll turn the horses loose someplace down the way. If they decide to come back to you, that's just fine. If they don't, you'll find walkin' is good for your wind."

"But Bodine's got a broken arm."

"He ain't goin' to walk on his arm."

"You goin' to leave us our guns though, ain't you? Else how'll we eat?"

"Use a snare, Fanch. You and Bodine, you always been good with snares of one kind and another."

Daniel told Lod again to go home. He wanted to see his brother well on the road before he left these men here. He didn't want them catching up to Lod and taking the mule away from him. Lod said, "What'm I goin' to tell Pa? He's apt to be a little pouty; the plowin' ain't finished yet."

"Tell him when I come home I'll finish it with a *silver* plow."

"Lizbeth, she ain't goin' to be overly happy either."

"She'll have silver rings for her fingers."

Lod nodded. As he turned to leave, he said, "You never did tell me how come you to bust that feller's arm."

"Go home, Lod." Daniel watched his brother ride over the hill and wondered what tangled tale he would tell when he got there.

Fanch stood glumly watching, hands clasped under his sagging belly as Seldom and Daniel rode off, leading the packmules and the two men's horses. Bodine sat in the trail, long legs stretched out in front of him, splinted arm hanging in a sling made from the other sleeve. He was hoarsely crying something about having pity on a poor, crippled old man.

Daniel rode a long time in silence, quietly studying the calm countenance of Milo Seldom. Seldom seemed unshaken. Looking at him, a stranger would not know he had been through anything more eventful than stopping to fix dinner.

At length Daniel asked suspiciously, "What's that they said about these bein' their mules? And it was their tobacco, too, I reckon."

"All in how you look at it. They'd stole it all off of somebody."

"How'd you happen to come by it?"

"We had us a little game of cards."

"Way you talk, I wouldn't think you'd hold with gamblin'."

"I don't. But when I play cards it ain't gamblin'. I was taught by masters."

"You mean you cheat?"

"Now, *cheat's* a strong word. I just take all the opportunities the good Lord sees fit to offer me. I don't ever play against a righteous man. I play only agin the evildoer."

"I don't see where that makes it any better."

"Anything I get takes it out of the hands of the unrighteous and robs the devil of his due. Them two, Bodine and Fanch, they'd of just sold that tobacco and spent the money on spiritous liquors and lewd women and such. I intend to use that money in ways pleasin' in the sight of the Lord."

"Such as?"

"I don't rightly know yet. I'll study on it."

3

Much of his life Daniel Provost had heard men speak in hushed tones of San Antonio de Bexar as if it were some sacred city. Perhaps in a way it was, for many men had shed their blood here in the name of their country, whether Texas or Mexico or Spain. He would not have been surprised to see roofs of shining silver and streets of gold. Instead he saw a motley scattering of rock and adobe structures small in size and indifferent in flat-roofed architecture. Dust curled in the streets as the wind sought its way past battle-gutted houses that had never been rebuilt. Standing much taller than the one-story buildings was a single church tower somewhere toward the center of town.

Daniel stared in awe at a collection of two-story ruins surrounded by a half-ruined rock wall. Before Seldom told him, he already knew what it was.

"The Alamo," Seldom said. "A hundred and eighty men, *mas o menos*, lie buried over yonder—what was

left of them after Santa Anna had the bodies burnt."
The crumbled walls were half overgrown with weeds,
and the facade of what had once been a stone chapel
was pockmarked by cannon balls and smoke-darkened
from fire and shell. Chills played down Daniel's
back.

"I'd like to go over and take a closer look," he said.

"Did you have somebody die in the Alamo?"

Daniel considered himself a Texan, the name given
to those settlers already here when the war was fought.
"A hundred and eighty men."

"There was a time before the war when this town
must of had seven-eight thousand people. You'd have
to scratch now to turn up a thousand. I doubt as San
Antonio will ever amount to anything any more. Or
Houston, either. You watch—these wide-awake towns
like San Felipe and Harrisburg will take it all away
from them."

They crossed the clear-running San Antonio River,
which Seldom said was fed by springs above the city.
Daniel had noticed many Mexican dams and ditch
systems or *acequias* carrying water to fields and gar-
dens. Cattle and sheep wandered unattended, grazing
at will on the property of all who had not bothered
to put up fences. A wonderful place for lawyers, Daniel judged.

He was disappointed at the extent of abandonment
he saw here, rock and adobe houses crumbling away,
roofs caved in either from cannon fire or from neglect.
Even many of the standing buildings bore deep scars.
At least three times in a decade this city had seen
bloody turmoil. Farther back, when Mexico had won
its independence from Spain, the city had violently
changed ownership more than once. And when settlers

and soldiers were not fighting one another, there had been the Comanches. At times they had seemed to consider this city their own private hunting preserve. They had stalked stragglers at its fringes and more than once had boldly raided along its streets.

"An unhappy place when you come down to it," Seldom commented. "Twenty years from now there won't nobody even remember this town, and a good thing that'll be."

They rode along the river in the waning daylight. Daniel saw some young Mexican girls bathing openly in the clear water, splashing and giggling, innocent of any clothing whatsoever. He turned away in shock but was compelled to look again.

"We can join them if you'd like to," said Seldom. "We could use a little washin'."

Daniel shook his head, his voice lost. He felt guilty staring at the girls because the thought came unbidden that this was how Lizbeth must look undressed. He felt as if in so thinking he had somehow violated her virtue. Just the same, he kept looking.

Seldom volunteered, "Place we're goin' to is a little farther up the river. This is where we'll join up with ol' Cephus Carmody. He's the man who can lead us to the silver."

They came at length to a small adobe house surrounded by a crude picket-type fence built of mesquite limbs, rawhided tightly together and stood on end, reinforced by a row of heavy cedar posts standing ten or twelve feet apart. "Cephus' place," Seldom said and waved for Daniel to follow him through the open gate.

A slender girl knelt at the edge of the river, rinsing clothing and beating it against a rock. A big pile of wet clothes lay beside her. Daniel thought she glanced back once, though he wasn't sure.

Milo Seldom stepped down and dropped the reins. He walked up behind the kneeling girl, swung his hand and gave her a smart slap on the rump. "Howdy, Flor."

She came up from her knees and whirled to face him. In one single unbroken motion she brought up the flat of her hand and fetched him a slap that sent him staggering back, a flash of red fingermarks on his cheek. He raised his hand in surprise and rubbed his stinging face.

"Wait a minute, Flor; it's me, ol' Milo."

"I know damn well it's you, Milo Seldom," she stormed, "and you're makin' mighty free with your hand. One of these days I'll take me a knife and cut it off for you one finger at a time!"

Daniel stared openmouthed. From her appearance he had taken this to be a Mexican girl, though her voice carried only a hint of accent, not nearly so much as the Hernandez girls had back home.

Seldom remonstrated, "Now, Flor, I got me a friend here. What's he goin' to think, hearin' that kind of language comin' from such a pretty girl?"

The girl's dark eyes fastened briefly on Daniel Provost, giving him a quick appraisal and coming up with a negative reaction. "If he's runnin' with you, Milo Seldom, I'll wager he's seen and heard a damn sight worse. Now, I've heard you say howdy. Let's hear you say *adiós*."

"I've hardly just come."

"You could've not come at all and I'd be happier."

"My friend Daniel is goin' to get the notion you ain't in love with me."

"If he's smart at all, he's done figured that out.

Though if he was very smart, he wouldn't be with you in the first place."

Seldom watched the girl warily, trying to pass over her hostility as if it were nothing. "Flor Carmody, this here is Daniel Provost. He's a farmer from up the country aways. He done me a good turn, and I've made him a partner in a venture. We're here to see your daddy."

Flor Carmody shrugged. "What do you want with that old sonofabitch?"

Daniel spoke Spanish, and he knew that *flor* meant flower. Whoever had named this girl had been overly optimistic.

Milo said reproachfully, "The Good Book tells us we should honor our father and our mother."

"I honor the memory of my mother. My father never had any honor."

"He's bound to've had some, Flor. He married your mother."

"Barely in time. My grandfather and my uncles had a lot to do with that."

Milo dropped the argument. "I sure do need to see ol' Cephus. Where's he at?"

"In Mexico. Some damned *Americano* of about his own stripe came by a few months ago and they went off to smuggle goods across the river."

Crestfallen, Seldom seemed to try to find a reason not to believe her. "I can't picture ol' Cephus runnin' off and leavin' you here by yourself."

"Why not? He's done it aplenty of times. I take care of myself."

It dawned on Daniel then why she was washing so many clothes. Seldom nodded his chin at the pile and said, "You makin' your livin' like that?"

Flor Carmody picked up a wet black dress and held it in front of her. It was twice her size. She snapped, "You can tell it's not mine."

"Looks to me like there ought to be an easier way."

"There's one," she gritted.

Seldom stared, suddenly alarmed. "Don't even joke about a thing like that."

"I ain't jokin'. I just ain't got that hungry yet."

"Maybe we could find you somethin' better than washin' out other people's dirty clothes, else you'll be an old woman before your time. Maybe we could find somebody willin' to marry you."

She doubled her fist as if to swing at him. "Milo . . ."

He backed off, putting up his hands. "I swear, girl, I don't see why you always got to be so hostile this-away. I never done you a bad turn in my life."

"Like hell you haven't!" Slowly she loosened her fist. "It's no use. You're what you are and don't even realize there's anything wrong with you. It's your nature and I reckon you couldn't do anything about it if you wanted to. It's just that you're so much like the old man—restless as a cat and about as responsible. He wore my mother out tryin' to follow him; she's buried God knows where along some damn horsetrail between here and San Felipe. He's wore two more women since, to where one quit him and the other one died. I swore when I got old enough to make my own livin' that I wouldn't follow him no more, and I don't."

"You don't have to take it out on *me*. I ain't in no way responsible for what Cephus has done, and I sure ain't ever asked you to marry me."

"No, Milo, you haven't. A better man might've."

"You'd of turned me down."

"If I'd had any sense."

"One thing I got to say about you, Flor, is that you've always had good sense. No manners at all, but plenty of sense."

"I'm fixin' to show my bad manners and ask you-all to leave. I got work to do."

Milo seemed not to hear. "Flor, I got to find ol' Cephus. It's important."

"Nothin' you or him ever did was important."

"This is. This time we're goin' after ol' Jim Bowie's silver."

She brought her hands to her hips and stared at him in contempt. "You and the old man have been talkin' about that silver for years, sayin' you'd go after it soon's you had the money to hire the men and buy horses and mules. You'll never live that long; neither one of you could ever hold onto a coin."

"I got the money."

She snorted. "I'll believe it when I can count it in my hands."

"Well, I ain't exactly got the cash, but what I got here'll bring me the cash."

She looked at the three pack-laden mules and shook her head, more in pity than derision. "Most people do their dreamin' when they're asleep."

"I got three packs stuffed full of prime tobacco. You know how them Mexicans like good tobacco, and how they'll pay for it."

"And you know what they'll do when they catch you smugglin'."

"They've never caught me yet; well, not but once or twice. When this is over I'll be richer than the king of Sheba."

"That's *queen* of Sheba. And if I remember my readin', she finally got snakebit."

Daniel had read a little history and knew they were both wrong, but he had read enough human nature to know this bout was deeper than any question of historical kings and queens; something strongly personal went back a long way with these two.

Milo shook his head. "No snake's goin' to bite me this time; I got the good Lord on my side."

"He's been on your side all along or you'd been killed in some folly years ago. How'd you come by them mules and that tobacco anyway? I'll take a vow that you never done no work for them."

"The Lord provides for them that watches out for theirselves."

"Good thing he watches out for you, too."

"You got to help me locate Cephus."

Her sarcasm was strong. "Split that silver with me?"

"I'll bring you ten times the clothes you got layin' there. They'll all be yours, too."

She told him Cephus Carmody had teamed with an old bandit named Notchy O'Dowd out of his own native Redlands, that stretch of unpoliced outlaw country that lay between the western settlements of Louisiana and the easternmost of Texas. Mexico imposed a high tariff on imports of foreign merchandise, and there was such a strong demand for such goods that a man with a little daring could make himself a small fortune if he remained uncaught. Cephus Carmody had been smuggling goods since the filibustering days long before Stephen F. Austin had set up his first American colonies in Mexican Texas. He had guided a couple of ill-fated Texan expeditions to invade Mexico, these excursions failing because of Texan exuberance and underestimation of the enemy rather than any shortcomings on the part of the guide.

Cephus Carmody had made a lot of money in his time, and spent it faster than he made it. One day silk, next day patches.

"That's where you'll find him, is in Mexico. Last I heard, the town of Colmena Vieja."

"Then that's where we'll go, is Colmena." Milo walked back to one of the mules and began to untie the pack. Daniel, who had sat on his horse and listened all this time, did likewise.

Flor Carmody demanded, "What do you think you're doin' now?"

"We'll stay in San Antonio a while, at least till tomorrow. Got to rest up the stock. You got some grain around here, ain't you?" He didn't wait for her answer. "I thought I'd try to find a couple more good men to go with us. You know if Lalo Talavera and Paley Northcutt are around anywheres?"

"Birds of a feather!" she said sharply. "You'll find Lalo wherever the most women are at. Paley Northcutt'll either be in jail or just gettin' out or puttin' himself in a fix to get back in. Try the *calabozo* first and then the *cantinas* and the alleys. You know all the places."

"I swear, Flor, you are the most cuttin' woman." Milo slipped the pack off one mule and hoisted it with heavy effort onto his shoulder. He carried it toward the rock house.

Flor took a few steps away from the riverbank and demanded, "Where you goin' with them packs?"

"Puttin' them in the house. You don't think I want to get all this money rained on, do you? Come on, friend Daniel, we got some huntin' to do."

She ran ahead to the door and blocked it, eyes blazing. "That's *my* house."

"Sure it is," Seldom said soothingly. "You think we'd leave this stuff with somebody we didn't trust?" He pushed past her, dumped that pack and went back for another. Flor Carmody watched in silent anger.

Daniel felt sorry about the way Milo Seldom was putting upon her. "Ma'am, I sure hope we ain't bein' no bother."

Her eyes cut right through him. "Now that," she jabbed, "is even dumber than anything *he* said."

Daniel retreated to the horses. Flower, he thought, mulling over her name. They ought to've named her Cactus; they'd of been closer to the truth of it.

Seldom turned the mules into a mesquite-limb pen and fed them grain he found in a rawhide-and-willow barrel. He walked to his bay horse and swung into the saddle.

Flor Carmody shook her fist at him. "Milo Seldom, you come back here and take your mules and your packs with you. I don't want them."

Milo smiled and started riding away. "We'll be back tonight, Flor. Don't you be waitin' up for us."

She cursed him in bristling Spanish till they rode out of earshot. Seldom said, "She speaks both languages, one as good as the other. Her mother was Mexican." He smiled, satisfied with himself. "You wouldn't think so, but that girl's been in love with me for years."

"It'd be easy to fool somebody."

"I might even let her marry me someday, if my foot quits itchin'. Man needs a gentle little woman to take the rough edges off of him and help him find the Lord's true pathway to peace."

4

Though it had dwindled to a thousand people, San Antonio was the biggest town Daniel had seen. He stared in awe at the mass of rock and adobe houses which in many cases stood wall to wall, more like prison compounds in appearance than like individual homes. Whatever yard they had was in the back. A person who stepped out of his front door was immediately in the street and in some hazard of being run over by a passing wagon or wooden-wheeled *carreta* if he was not on the *cuidado*. The danger was not great, however, for the traffic moved at a leisurely pace; tomorrow was time enough for a task not finished today, and if not tomorrow, then the day after.

Many of the houses were deserted and caving in, but as Daniel and Seldom rode toward the heart of the city, he saw that the larger percentage there were lived in. The streets in the cool of the late afternoon were increasingly coming alive with horses and burros, dogs and children. A sow and her pigs rooted in a muddy hole left by a recent rain, and scrawny chickens scratched for bits of grain in the dried droppings of animals.

Seldom pointed. "Ol' Paley Northcutt used to live over thisaway."

"That girl made out that he's somethin' of a drinker."

"Paley has pulled a few stoppers in his day. The Lord gives most every man a weakness to test him. But you get Paley away from the big city, away from the demon spirits, and he's as good a man as it ever pleasured you to ride with. Got nerve like a Mexican cougar."

He stopped in front of an adobe house where a sagging wooden door stood open, and a tiny brown-skinned girl stared big-eyed at the two *extranjeros* on horseback. She was clad in nothing but a curious expression. "*Chiquita,*" Seldom asked, "*donde está tu mamá?*"

A Mexican woman stepped into the open doorway, a baby clasped against her ample breasts, her long black hair hanging in wild disarray. Seldom bowed in his saddle and swept his hat from his head. Daniel hurried to copy him. Seldom said in as florid a Spanish as Daniel had ever heard, "Ah, *señora,* you look as beautiful as ever. The years touch on your features as lightly as the passing shadow of the dove in flight."

She was unimpressed. She answered crisply, "If you seek the *Americano* Northcutt, who is totally without value and should be cast naked among the wolves, he is not here."

"Where then might he be?"

"In prison, if justice were truly done, though there is no justice in this city under *Americano* rule, or

Tejano. When last I saw him he owed me four month's rent. I chastised him with a broom and sent him fleeing like a whipped dog into the street."

That, Daniel thought, ill fitted the image of the cougar.

Seldom gave her mild reproach. "To sleep in the mud, with the cold rain beating down upon him and the bite of the night air chilling his poor tired bones? Woman, is there no charity in your heart to match the beauty I see in your face?"

"It would be a charity to this good city if the Northcutt were to die in a drunken stupor, or drown in a goatskin of *pulque. Adiós, señor.*"

"*Adiós,* fair lady of the flowers." Milo Seldom pulled the bay horse around and shrugged at Daniel. "Don't fret, good friend, we'll find him."

If Daniel fretted, it was over the possibility that they might. "I never heard Spanish as pretty as that. Where'd you learn it?"

"From Lalo Talavera. A better hand with the ladies you'll seldom see."

They rode through the heart of the city, which lay a little to the west of the Alamo ruins. Daniel marveled at the size of the big stone church which stood on the main plaza, and at the long rambling structure which had been the palace of the Spanish governors and later the Mexican officials who had overseen this part of Mexico until brutal Santa Anna discarded Mexico's constitution and threw Texas away in an ill-managed campaign to drive the *Americano* settlers back across the Sabine.

Seldom said, "It was right here in these streets that the idea first come to Jim Bowie about the silver mine."

"How?"

"Them Lipan Apaches, they used to come into San Antonio to trade for goods. They'd always bring silver with them. Now, silver didn't mean much to an Indian except for the ornaments he could make out of it, but he learned quick that it meant somethin' to the white man, and that he could trade it for things that meant somethin' to him, like powder and lead, and cloth and such like. Well, the Mexicans in San Antonio tried at first to trail them Indians and find out where the silver come from. Some of them never come back; most of them just lost the Indians somewhere out yonder to the wet and come draggin' in afoot and hungry. Time come when the Mexicans quit worryin' about it and took it for granted.

"But you've heard stories about Bowie; he wasn't no man to pass up a chance at treasure. The kind of life he'd lived, he'd charge the fires of hell with a bucketful of water. A man who'll let them nail his britches to a log and set there and fight a knife duel with somebody else nailed down the same way—he ain't goin' to let a few feathers scare him. He wanted that silver, and he set out to get it. But he was smoother'n a card player about it and took his time.

"He made friends with them Indians; they could tell he wasn't no ordinary man—he was somebody come. He got to goin' west and tradin' with them and huntin' buffalo with them and all. Lived amongst them awhile, even, all the time keepin' his eyes open. And finally one of them Indians showed Bowie where the silver was at. Now, the way it was told to me, it was out yonder close to the old San Saba mission. Them Spaniards had them a silver mine, workin' it with Indian slaves. Come a time finally when the other Indians killed a lot of the Spaniards and run the rest of them off. They left silver bullion that they had smelted but didn't have no chance to carry away. Ain't no tellin' how much—thousands of dollars' worth, maybe, or hundreds of thousands, or millions. *Quién sabe?*

"Now, Bowie knowed that Indian shouldn't of showed him the place; soon's the other Indians found out, they'd kill them both. So Bowie took note of where it was at, then he got his horse and he rode for San Antonio as hard as he could go, movin' like the devil beatin' tanbark. He got him up a party of men, a dozen or more, with plenty of horses and guns, and they went back to find that mine.

"When they got near the place they found Indians, dozens of them, and hostile to the bone. Them treasure hunters, they had to fort up in a big live-oak motte. When the battle was over, there was dead Indians scattered up and down the creek but a lot more live ones still rarin' to fight. In the end there wasn't nothin' for the bunch to do but retreat. They come back to San Antonio badly whupped. Jim Bowie always said he was goin' back, but what with one thing and another he never did get another party together. Then come the war, and the Alamo. I wonder sometimes if he died thinkin' of all that silver that he never did get ahold of."

Daniel said, "Bowie's long dead. What makes you think that after all these years we can find the mine?"

"Bowie's dead, but not all the men that went with him out to the San Saba. There's a few that outlived the war. I got one who says he seen the mine with his own eyes, and he's been waitin' for years till we could get men and guns and stock enough to go."

Daniel felt his heart quicken. "Cephus Carmody?"

"The same."

"He's sure he can go back and find it after all this time?"

"A thing like a mine full of silver a man ain't goin' to forget. Sure, he'll find it for us. We'll all be rich, friend Daniel. The Lord will open up his bounty and bless us like kings of old. But first we got to have the men." He pointed. "There's a couple dozen *cantinas* where we might find Paley, but the easier thing might be to find Lalo Talavera first. Maybe Lalo'll know where Paley is at. They run together now and again. Over thisaway used to be a lively Spanish girl that Lalo had eyes for."

In a few minutes they sat their horses before a stone house, somewhat more substantial and better kept than the adobe where they had sought Northcutt. Seldom said, "I could get interested in this girl myself if ol' Lalo didn't have a prior claim." He dismounted and drummed his knuckles against the wooden door framing. As before, he bowed and swept his hat gallantly at the appearance of a strikingly handsome young woman. "*Señorita,* my eyes are dazzled by the brilliance of your smile. Each day that passes makes you more beautiful. I am seeking our mutual good friend Lalo Talavera. I know he has never been able to remove himself far from your beauty, and I thought by chance he might be here now."

A man's voice replied from inside the room, and an angry-faced young Mexican pushed himself in front of the woman. "He is not here. If ever he comes here again, he will be dead in a moment, as you will be, *señor,* if you do not leave this place immediately."

The woman said shakily, "My husband, sir."

"And my error," said Seldom, bowing again but pulling back toward the horse as he did so. "Surely I have mistakenly come to the wrong house. My apologies." He moved quickly away, glancing once over his shoulder as the man and woman disappeared back into the room's darkness. Shaken, he said, "Like to've turned over the whole pot of beans there. Reckon the best bet now is to look in on the *fandangos* tonight. Lalo has an eye for women and an ear for music."

A feeling of mutual suspicion still persisted between the Mexican majority in San Antonio and the American minority, though the war had been several years ago and though most of the Mexican people still here had taken no strong side in it one way or the other; the ones who had given heavy support to Santa Anna had mostly fled after his defeat. And there were some in San Antonio such as the powerful Seguin family who had fought beside the Texans against the man they considered a tyrant.

Despite the suspicion, friendships had grown between individual Mexicans and individual Americans. Daniel noticed that Milo Seldom had friends here, drawn to him perhaps because they were somewhat kindred in spirit, taking today for the pleasure that was in it and letting tomorrow's troubles await the sunrise of another day.

Seldom made the rounds of friends' houses, greeting the men with the *abrazo* and the women with a high-blown line of exaggeration. He and Daniel visited in the city awhile, then at the suggestion of one of Seldom's friends rode out to the edge of town to one of the many *ranchos* clustered there within reach of mutual protection should Indians strike. Around these *ranchos* grazed uncounted Mexican ponies and mules. Seldom tried to talk first one friend then another into selling him horses on credit. But there was a point at which friendship ended. When finally they accepted an invitation to a supper of goat meat and beans and flat *tortillas* of pounded corn at an adobe ranchhouse a couple of miles from the city, Seldom still had not talked anyone out of a single animal.

"A tribute to their business judgment but a poor reflection of Christian generosity," Seldom complained.

At full dark he and Daniel rode once more down the narrow, dusty streets. Fiddle music rose on the night air. It came from several places. "Now maybe we'll find ol' Lalo and Paley," said Seldom. "This is when they shine the brightest, after the moon is up."

Daniel had never been to a true Mexican *baile* or dance, so the first one held considerable interest for him. He and Seldom followed the fiddle sound to a stone building perhaps thirty feet long. He had to duck just a little to pass through the door, for the Mexican people were generally of smaller stature. The women and girls were mostly seated on benches lined along the sides of the room, and the men were either standing or walking around, talking to each other or to the girls. The arrival of two *Americanos* attracted momentary interest and suspicion, for some of the rowdier of the blue-eyed breed had been known to descend *en masse* upon such a gathering, throw out the men and take charge of the womenfolk. But some of the people here recognized Milo Seldom and pronounced him harmless.

Daniel noticed a couple of the handsome girls staring at him and whispering to each other, hiding all but their eyes behind their fans. The attention made him self-conscious and ill at ease, but not so much that he was ready to leave when Seldom told him Lalo Talavera was not here.

"Let's stay and watch a few minutes," Daniel said. The fiddle struck up a Mexican waltz, and the floor quickly had all the couples who could conveniently dance in the limited space. Daniel tapped his toes and watched the swirling feet, trying without much luck to pick up the secret of the step. It went too fast for him. He wanted to ask one of the girls to dance and see if he could master the waltz; he also wanted to see if these girls would feel as good in his arms as Lizbeth. But he didn't muster the nerve. It might be easier, he thought, fighting Indians.

At length Seldom took him out, assuring him there would be other *bailes* down the street, even better ones. They visited a couple more *fandango* places and still didn't see Talavera. "Maybe a little early for him," Seldom mused. "He might be otherwise occupied."

He had heard there was to be a *maromeros* show of rope dancers and actors in a nearby courtyard, and suggested that perhaps Lalo might turn up there. They went to a place where a couple of fires had been built in a large private yard to provide light for the show. Daniel watched with interest the rope dancing and the acrobats' tumbling. A couple of the older Mexicans complained that it was being clumsily and amateurishly done by this younger generation, but to Daniel who had never seen anything like it, it was a grand show. Then a handful of actors and actresses put on a couple of farcical skits so earthy in the visual aspects and so explicit in the Spanish language that Daniel found himself blushing in the darkness. He looked about, puzzling at the complacent attitude of the women in the audience. He had not thought women ever heard such words or even knew their meaning.

Lalo Talavera did not appear. Daniel could tell Seldom was becoming impatient. They left the firelight and started walking up a dark narrow street. Seldom was saying, "We better find them before the sun comes up, or they'll both take to the shade where they can't be seen."

Daniel heard what he took to be a groan and, catching Seldom's arm, silently pointed. The sound came again, only this time it was more a belch, then a short siege of coughing.

Seldom slapped Daniel on the back. "Luck's with us, Daniel; I'd know that belch in the devil's own barroom."

Paley Northcutt lay on his back, sprawled half in and half out of an open doorway, a jug of *tequila* strangle-gripped in his right hand. Daniel could smell him easier than he could see him in the dark shadows of the moonlight. Paley hadn't shaved in a long time, and his whiskers were long and matted; he hadn't bathed for even longer, Daniel judged.

Seldom crouched over his old friend, who lay in a stupor, totally oblivious to everything around him. Seldom said, "My, Paley, but you're a sight for sore eyes."

They'd have to be awful sore, Daniel thought.

"Well," Seldom said, "at least we know where he's at. We can come back and get him later; he won't be goin' noplace."

It was Daniel's judgment that Northcutt wouldn't be going anywhere for a long time, unless somebody carried him.

"Still a couple of dances we ain't been to," Seldom said. "If we don't find Lalo there, we'll start over. If he's in town and ain't got a broken leg, he'll probably show up."

They visited another dance place, and Daniel saw as pretty a set of dark-brown eyes there as he had ever seen. The girl all but asked him aloud to dance with her, and Daniel brought himself to take the bait. He bowed from the waist and asked her in the best Spanish he knew. She curtsied and came into his arms and the fiddles struck up a fast one. For a moment Daniel gave himself to the intoxication of the girl in his arms, the sweet smell of whatever she had put on herself. He fancied this could have been one of the girls he had observed earlier in the afternoon, bathing in the river.

The step became too fast and intricate for him, and he found himself stepping on her feet as she gamely tried to set him aright without taking the lead herself. He spun and spun with her, and almost lost his footing. Daniel decided it would be wise to admit the music had beaten him and make as graceful a retreat as possible under the circumstances. The girl tried to keep her composure and held a forced smile, but he could tell she was relieved when he led her off the floor and back to her place on the bench. It would probably be a while before her eyes flashed invitation to another clumsy *Americano*. Chagrined, Daniel jerked his head at Seldom to let him know he wanted to leave.

"They'll respect you for tryin'," Seldom said.

"But laugh at me just the same."

"Probably you was meant for the fields and the

prairies, not for the dance floor. Dancin' is an instrument of the devil anyway, arousin' fires between man and woman and leadin' to all manner of sin." He walked along in the darkness, keeping his head cocked to one side, listening. "Bothers me that we ain't seen Lalo. He's one of the most popular men in town."

At this moment they heard another fiddle and Seldom said, "That'll be a place we ain't looked yet." The fiddle stopped before they could locate it, and for a moment they were at a loss as to where the music had come from. Then they heard a woman's scream and several excited shouts. Seldom began to trot. Rounding a corner, they saw people spilling out of a candlelit stone house.

Seldom stopped at the door and looked in. From his expression revealed by the candlelight, Daniel could tell he was suddenly disturbed. "Lalo," Seldom said beneath his breath and stepped through the door.

A handsome young Mexican stood with back to the far wall, his face twisted in desperation. Facing him were three other men, two carrying knives which they held outthrust, one toward the man's throat and the other toward his belly. At a glance Daniel knew they were about to use them.

Seldom did not hesitate. He strode across the room and shouted, pointing his finger at Lalo Talavera. "There he is, Daniel. That's him, the *cabrón* who has been after my wife!"

The Mexicans turned to stare at him in astonishment. None seemed more astonished than Lalo Talavera, whose eyes stayed open wide right up to the instant Seldom's hard-swung fist landed squarely between them. Seldom's other fist drove into Talavera's flat belly. As Talavera sagged forward, Seldom caught him, hoisted him neatly up over his shoulder and turned belligerently on the men who stood there.

"I've found him, and don't none of you try to help him! He's got a good stompin' comin' to him, and by the Eternal, I'm the one that's a-fixin' to give it! I'm sorry if I've went and disturbed the *baile*. You-all go right on with your dance; I'll take care of this outside."

Before the men were over their surprise, Seldom had toted Lalo into the darkness. Looking back over his shoulder, he carried him around the corner, then began to trot, bent under the heavy burden. Daniel followed, keeping a watchful eye behind them. If there was pursuit—which he doubted—it was quickly lost in the dark.

In a few moments they reached the bank of the narrow San Antonio River. Seldom walked into it, unceremoniously dumped Talavera and came back to dry ground. He squatted and watched Talavera sputter and thresh. The Mexican crawled part way out on hands and knees, threatening all manner of reprisal.

Seldom said calmly, "Better speak soft, Lalo, else you'll draw them boys with the knives down here. What was they, jealous husbands?"

Talavera, still on all fours, wiped a wet sleeve over his face and stared at Seldom. "Milo, it is you?"

"Anybody else ever hit you thataway?"

Talavera watched him a moment, as if trying to decide whether to laugh or fight. He chose to laugh. "One was a husband. A mistaken one, of course."

"Of course." Seldom looked at him quietly. "But them boys was fixin' to dice you up or make jerky of you. If you had any brains, you'd stay out of other men's yards and not provoke them thataway. There's aplenty of girls that ain't married."

"One tries to work where one is most appreciated." Lalo rubbed a hand cautiously over the bridge of his nose and flinched. "One eye will surely be black tomorrow. And I think my nose may be broken."

"Didn't help my hand none either. You got a hard head." He rubbed his knuckles ruefully. "When you get through wadin' out there, Lalo, come along with us. We got places to go."

Lalo Talavera came out of the river, the water streaming from his clothes. "Go? Go where?"

Milo Seldom explained briefly that they were leaving in the morning for Mexico, there to sell his tobacco and finance their trip west to search for the lost mine on the San Saba. "It's the big chance we've talked about for so long, Lalo. I'm offerin' you the opportunity to go and earn a share of all that silver."

Lalo whistled under his breath. "The many times we have talked, I have never thought it would ever happen. It is a thing to dream of, like marrying the beautiful daughter of the governor of Coahuila. A share, you say? A full share?"

"A full share. Everybody that goes gets an even share. Since I'm furnishin' the stock and the supplies, my even share is bigger than the others."

"How can they be even shares when some are more even than others?"

Seldom looked at him a moment, then at Daniel. "I hadn't thought on it thataway. We'll work it out." He told Talavera that they had located Paley Northcutt and would go pick him up. "We got the goods at Flor Carmody's place. That's where we'll leave from."

"Ah, *sí*, the pretty Flor. A lovely flower to behold."

Seldom's eyes narrowed. "That's one flower you'll leave alone, Lalo. Any pickin' to be done there, I'll do it."

Talavera smiled. "That proud beauty will have none of us, you *or* me. She has a wish for better things."

"And what's the matter with *me*?" Seldom demanded.

"Nothing, old *compadre*, nothing. I am but remarking upon the foolishness of women."

"Well, it's time we went and got some rest; that's why the Lord gave us the night. Comin', Lalo?"

"In the morning. I will be there by the first light. But for now, I must go and have my wounds bound up."

"What wounds? Any little scratch you got, I can fix it."

"But not with the gentle hands and soft manner of one I know."

"If she's got a husband, you better leave her alone. You won't be much use with a knife in you."

Daniel and Seldom went back to the dark street where they had found Paley Northcutt. So far as Daniel could tell, the man hadn't wiggled a finger; he lay there just as he had before. Seldom picked him up and hoisted him onto his shoulder.

Daniel suggested, "Couldn't we dump him in the river like you done Talavera? He could sure stand the bath."

"It wouldn't keep. Give him a week or two and he'd be the same again."

Daniel hoped Seldom would make it all the way back to the Carmody house with his burden, but he didn't, and Daniel had to carry the man awhile. He kept his head turned to one side and breathed through his mouth.

At the Carmody house they found the tobacco packs all lying out in the open yard. Flor Carmody came to the door when she heard them. She was dressed in some flimsy shift for sleeping. Even if scandalized, Daniel still could not help but stare. Seldom said, "Flor, we put that tobacco in the house to keep it safe."

"You think I want this house smellin' like tobacco for six months? I drug it back outside and there it's goin' to stay. You try to move it in here again and I'll shoot you in the foot. That's where all your brains are."

"I swear, Flor, you can be the most unreasonin' woman."

"You've seen only my good side." The wooden door closed, and Daniel heard a bar fall into place.

Seldom muttered the Lord's name in vain. "Sometimes I don't see why He didn't let Adam alone and leave that rib where it was."

Daniel eased Northcutt to the ground and laid his head on a tobacco pack, trying to make him comfortable. On second thought he doubted it would make much difference; in his condition Northcutt could sleep on a rock pile.

Seldom said, "A thing like this needs guardin', Daniel. Me and you'll take turns. You stand the first watch and I'll stand the next. Wake me up in about two hours."

Daniel sat on one of the packs, rifle close at hand, and watched Seldom fall quickly into a sound sleep. In the distance he could still hear the sound of a fiddle, and he thought of that dark-eyed girl whose feet he had so clumsily abused. He guessed that was something he would tell Lizbeth about sometime, though it might be wise to keep it to himself. She might take it as disloyalty, his wanting to dance with some other girl so soon after leaving her. She wouldn't understand how he could be attracted by some other woman's flashing eyes; he didn't entirely understand it himself. But he found himself thinking more about that Mexican girl than about Lizbeth; perhaps there was something to the saying that a man's eyes began to wander when *he* did.

He stared awhile at Milo Seldom, and at the unconscious Paley Northcutt. Maybe Milo knew what he was doing, but Northcutt and Talavera seemed an unlikely choice for a trip like this. For that matter, he had some doubts about Milo Seldom.

At length he judged that the time had passed, though he had no watch to go by. He shook Seldom's shoulder and roused him. Seldom yawned and scratched and raised himself up, looking around as if unsure for a moment where he was.

"Your time to guard the packs," Daniel reminded him.

"Oh, yes, almost forgot. You get yourself some sleep, friend Daniel. We'll travel aways tomorrow."

Daniel stretched out on his blanket. The last thing he saw before he drifted off to sleep was Milo Seldom, sitting on a pack and yawning.

Sometime later—he couldn't judge how long—a mutter of voices awakened him. He started to turn over and felt something cold press against the back of his ear.

"Just you move nice and easy, farmer boy," a rough

voice said. "Don't do nothin' that'd give us cause to burn powder on you."

Daniel turned over carefully, suddenly wide-awake and knowing that what he had felt was the muzzle of a rifle. The first thing he saw was Milo Seldom, lying against a pack and not fully awake. Raising his eyes, Daniel then saw four or five men standing in the moonlight, all carrying rifles or Mexican *escopetas*. The one nearest Daniel had his arm bound up. This was the gaunt Bodine.

Bodine said, "You-all raise yourselves up slow and careful. We've done took over."

5

Daniel got to his feet, no sleep left in him. He counted four men, Fanch, Bodine and a pair whom he took in the moonlight to be Mexicans. Milo Seldom was still blinking; he hadn't quite comprehended it all yet.

Daniel felt like hitting him. "You-all got no right. This tobacco belongs to Seldom."

"Well now," grinned Fanch, slouching back on his heels so that his belly seemed to stand out even farther, "first it was ours, then it was his, now it's ours again. Only thing a man can be sure of in this world is change."

Daniel wondered if they knew about Seldom's idea for going after Bowie's silver. Surely Seldom wouldn't have been dullard enough to have let them hear of it; no, on second thought, maybe he would.

One of the Mexicans who had only a knife nudged Paley Northcutt with his toe. Northcutt hadn't made any response to the command, and the Mexican wanted to know what was the matter with him. Seldom said, "He'll do you no harm. He's had a little to drink."

"That," said Fanch, "is the one thing you've ever said that I would believe." He surveyed the packs, kicking at one of them with a booted foot. "Looks like our merchandise is still all here, Bodine."

"You got no right," Daniel said again.

Bodine thrust the muzzle of the rifle forward. "Farmer, you better put a hobble on your lip. I ain't forgot who it was broke my arm."

The one-handed way Bodine held that rifle made it probable that the recoil would break his other arm if he fired it. But from the direction in which it was pointed, Daniel wouldn't have lived to enjoy the satisfaction.

Seldom said, "I wouldn't provoke them none, Daniel."

Daniel turned his anger on Seldom. "Damn you, Milo, you went to sleep. If you'd been on guard, they wouldn't of slipped up on us thisaway."

He might have predicted Seldom's reply. "Like the Book says, the spirit was willin' but the flesh was weak."

Daniel had heard about all the biblical quotations he was interested in for a while. He cut loose with a vehemence that comes by nature to a man accustomed to dealing with mules.

Head down, Seldom said quietly, "It grieves me to hear such language spill from the lips of one I took for a Christian."

"And I took *you* for a frontiersman. All you are is talk!"

The exchange pleased Fanch. He moved in closer

like a better at a cockpit. "Go after him, farmer boy. Eat him up!"

Fanch wasn't as careful as he should have been, either. He stepped between Daniel and the other three men and let his rifle barrel dip in his enthusiasm for the verbal hiding Daniel was giving Milo Seldom. Daniel saw a chance to grab the fat man, wrest the rifle from him and use him as a shield to force the others back. He swung both hands down and got a grip on the rifle, then twisted suddenly and started to bring the muzzle up in an arc that turned it away from him.

That was the moment Paley Northcutt chose to turn over; he bumped against Daniel's leg. Daniel staggered, losing his footing. He saw Bodine's rifle barrel come swinging at him and was powerless to get out of its way. His head exploded and he felt himself fall back across Northcutt. Someone stepped on his belly and took most of the breath out of him. He saw nothing but bright flashes whirling behind his eyes.

He heard Fanch say, "No, Bodine, ain't no call for killin' him."

"I ought to," Bodine growled, "for what he done to me."

Milo Seldom wasn't saying a thing. He just stood there, hands about half up. He made no move toward Daniel because any suspicious move on his part might draw a rifle ball. At length he said, "Kind of a surprise, Fanch, you-all showin' up. Didn't figger to see you again."

"Bet you didn't," replied Fanch. "But the Almighty must be smilin' on us because you hadn't been gone hardly no time till a couple of Mexican travelers come along. We took the borry of their horses and rode off down the trail to where we found our own that you had turned loose. When we got here we found a few friends and done some askin' around. Wasn't no trick to find you, Milo. Ain't hard to outguess a man who's set in his ways."

Bodine pointed his chin suspiciously at the rock house. "We better take us a look in yonder."

One of the Mexicans said in Spanish, "It is where the girl lives, the prideful halfbreed."

"We better get her out here where we can watch her. If she's half Mexican, she's probably got a knife." He motioned for the man to follow him and went to the door. He found it barred. "Open up in there. Open up, I say!" When nothing happened, he had the Mexican try it with his shoulder. The door still held. Bodine said, "Bust in one of them windows."

There was no glass in Flor Carmody's house, or in most others around. The windows were nothing more than small wooden doors hinged to swing in and fixed so they could be barred. The Mexican threw his weight against the wooden window until finally the bar snapped and the window flew open. He leaned inside for a glance around. "Too late, *hombre*. There is a window in the back also, and the little bird has flown away."

Bodine shrugged. "If she's gone, she can't be stickin' no knife in my back. Let's get them packs loaded."

Daniel had lost a great deal of interest in the whole affair; his head throbbed so much that it was hard to keep up with anything else. He found warm blood beginning to stiffen his hair. He wished he was home.

But he *wasn't* home, and he could see the rogues forcing Milo Seldom to saddle his horse and Daniel's as well. Daniel wondered vaguely where Fanch and Bodine planned to take them, though he hurt too much to care.

The mules were quickly packed. Fanch said with obvious relish, "All right, Milo, you and the farmer git into your saddles. No use lettin' this fine night air go to waste."

Milo gave no argument and Daniel couldn't. It was all he could do to grope his way to the horse and find the stirrup with his foot. His head felt as if an axe were splitting it when he put his weight onto the stirrup foot and swung up. He almost fell over the other side.

Milo said, "Daniel is in no condition to ride."

Bodine gritted, "I wasn't in no condition to walk, neither, but you left me afoot."

"I'll be havin' to hold him in the saddle," Milo grumbled.

"No you won't," said Fanch. "You'll be too busy holdin' this other one here." He motioned to the Mexicans and they lifted the drunken Paley Northcutt up behind Milo's saddle, leaving him lying with head down on one side, feet on the other.

"You," Milo said, "are the cruelest of Philistines."

Fanch smiled. "We try not to do a job halfways and leave it."

They rode out of the yard, Fanch's and Bodine's rifles pointing the way. Daniel couldn't see much of the path they followed, but he could see the rifles well enough.

Fanch and Bodine soon reined up. Seldom had one hand entirely occupied keeping the occasionally struggling Northcutt from slipping off onto the ground. Sooner or later the jouncing on his stomach would have to bring up the *pulque* or *tequila* or whatever it was he had been drinking.

Fanch said, "Well, Milo, this here is where us and you part company. Miguel and Paco here are goin' to take you-all for a pleasant ride in the country. A nice long ride, so lean back and enjoy it. Any scenery you miss on the way out, you can get a good look at on the way back. You'll be walkin'."

Milo said, "I done insult to the Philistines. You-all are worse."

"You try to remember that," Bodine replied, and he pulled away. Fanch followed him, leading the mules.

One of the Mexicans motioned with his rifle. "There will be time enough for talk as you walk back. Right now you will ride and be quiet."

They rode silently for a long time. Finally Seldom said, "At least they don't figure on killin' us."

"Don't they?" Daniel said painfully. "It's killin' *me*."

It wasn't doing Paley Northcutt much good, either. They had to stop eventually to let him rid himself of a night's indiscretions; when he was done he was more or less awake but deathly sick. The Mexicans showed him little patience. They prodded him to his feet and made him get astride the horse behind Milo. A couple of times he slid off, so Milo had to put Northcutt in the saddle; Milo rode behind the saddle and held the man to keep him from hitting the ground again.

Daniel moved in something of a daze; the wound had long since stopped bleeding, but he could feel dried blood matted in his hair. They hadn't picked up his hat for him; it still lay in the yard at Flor's. He would miss it when morning came and the sun came up. Things would get worse before they got better—a lot worse. He wondered if that gun barrel had cracked his skull. He guessed it hadn't, or he wouldn't be here.

He had no idea where they were going, not even the direction, for when he tried to look up and find familiar stars the pain would grab him and he had to let his chin sag. He knew only that they were in rough hills, where big live oaks stood tall and awesomely dark in the light of the moon. One Mexican rode in the lead, the other in the rear. They had the thing figured out pretty well. Daniel was too numb to make a move against them, and Milo Seldom had his hands full keeping Paley Northcutt on the horse. In his own way Northcutt was in as much or more pain than Daniel; another time, Daniel might have felt sorry for him, if he hadn't felt so sorry for himself. Northcutt was a totally innocent victim; he had joined Milo Seldom without even being aware of it. Daniel, at least, could not make that claim.

Sunrise was beginning when the Mexican in front drew rein. "This," he said in Spanish, "would be a good place to die."

Daniel swallowed, not really believing. In Paley Northcutt's face he saw an expression almost of hope; Northcutt was so sick that death would come like a friend bearing money from home.

Milo Seldom argued with the lead Mexican. "Now, I know ol' Fanch well enough that I'm fair certain he didn't tell you to kill us. Stomp on us a little, maybe, but not kill us."

A mocking smile touched the Mexican's face; to him it was a joke. "Bodine said we should kill you. But the Fanch he said that would be a poor way to end a long friendship. He said you left him to walk;

now we are to leave you to walk. It is a long way back to San Antonio de Bexar. If you move with diligence, you should be there by tonight. By then the last of the tobacco money will have been spent on *pulque* and *tequila* and the bright-eyed women with fire in their blood." He took the reins from Seldom's and Daniel's hands and nodded his chin in a way that said he did not care if all the *Americanos* killed each other. "If ever you get back to the city, seek me out. I have an uncle who is a good maker of shoes." He paused, the smile fading. "But come in peace, for I have another uncle who is an undertaker. *Adiós, mis amigos.*"

The two men rode away leading the horses. Daniel Provost found a fallen live-oak trunk and sat down. Paley Northcutt sprawled out belly down on the green grass. Milo Seldom just stood and watched until the horses and riders were out of sight. When he turned he was not so much angry as sad. "Good Lord only knows when I'll ever get a chance again at Jim Bowie's lost silver."

As far as Daniel was concerned, that silver was no more lost than *he* was, and he said so. Seldom shrugged. "No trouble gettin' to town, except it'll take us awhile. Yonderway's San Antonio." He pointed. But watching the sun come up, he was taken by doubt. "I could be mistaken, maybe it's a little more in that direction."

Daniel looked at the ground, disgusted, but seeing no gain in showing it. Maybe it was a good thing it had turned out this way; Seldom probably would have taken them off into Indian country and gotten them lost. It would probably have been their luck to ride into a Comanche campground and be guests of honor at a scalp dance.

To his credit, Milo Seldom showed concern for Paley Northcutt. He knelt by the suffering man. "You all right, Paley?"

Northcutt tried to heave but had nothing left to lose. He said, "I feel like I been hit in the face with the afterbirth of a buzzard."

Daniel thought he smelled like it, too.

Northcutt got up finally into a sitting position. Through the flushed red of his eyes there peered an incongruous touch of curiosity. "Milo, I been scratchin' my head and doin' my damndest to remember, and still it don't come to me what the hell I'm out here for. Last thing I remember I was sittin' in an alley with a jug in my hand. Did I do somethin' foolish?"

"It's a long story, Paley." Milo looked back to where he thought San Antonio was. "I'll tell you sometime when I feel better myself. Right now we'd as well be a-walkin'."

Milo Seldom, bearing neither wound nor sour stomach, struck out in the lead, setting a pace that quickly proved too much for the other two men. Paley Northcutt staggered, fell and pushed to his knees. Milo Seldom said, "Maybe this will be a lesson to you, friend Paley; the worst miseries that flesh is heir to is the ones that go down the throat."

Northcutt managed to get to his feet again. He staggered along, stubbornness and anger keeping him going. Not very peart himself, Daniel began to admire the man's determination. His admiration was not that strong, however, that he let himself get downwind of him.

At length they came to a stream, and Daniel asked which one it was. He could see worry in Seldom's face; though Seldom quickly gave a name, Daniel suspected he had arbitrarily picked one.

Paley Northcutt waded out into the water and began bringing it up to his dry lips in cupped hands, trying to put out a fire in his belly. He lost his footing and fell threshing, going under once, coming up shouting for help and going under a second time. Daniel waded toward him, but Seldom said, "Water ain't over his hips if he ever finds his feet. The bath'll do him good."

Daniel considered that a moment; the idea had some obvious merit. But he had heard of a drunk drowning in a foot of water, so he grabbed the man under the arms and brought him to his feet. Northcutt pawed and choked and sputtered. He blinked, trying to get the water out of his eyes, but it kept running in from his hair that lay plastered across his forehead.

"Be easy, Mister Northcutt," Daniel said, holding the man's arm. "You'll be all right directly." He led the man across the shallow stream and up the opposite bank. Northcutt sat gagging. "I swear, if the good Lord meant a man to drink that much water, he'd of made him a duck."

Whatever else it had done, the stream had washed some of the stench from him. And once he was over the near-strangling, he seemed stronger than before; he stood steadier, walked easier. Daniel had taken a good soaking himself and felt better for it, though his head still ached as if someone had kept striking him with the flat edge of a Mexican sword.

They walked on through the morning, pausing now and again to rest. Northcutt began to complain of being hungry. No telling how long since he had last put a good meal under his belt. Now that the liquor was wearing off, he had nothing left to keep him going.

Seldom said, "It's a good sign, you feelin' the pangs like that. I been seein' some bees. I expect there's a bee tree around here close." While Northcutt and Daniel sat down, he went out to look around. Daniel had noted long ago that some backwoodsmen had a second sense when it came to finding honey caches. He supposed that living on little but wild meat most of the time gave them a craving.

It wasn't long before Seldom hallooed from a couple of hundred yards away and indicated he had found the tree. When Daniel walked over to help, Seldom sent him back. "I don't want you to angry up the bees. I got a way with them; they don't ever give me no trouble."

Daniel walked back to Northcutt and sat down. Presently he saw Seldom begin to dance and swing his arms excitedly, then break into a hard run toward the creek. Even at that distance his shouts of pain came strong and clear, and the names he used in vain had not all come out of the Bible. He dived into the water and stayed there.

Daniel and Northcutt waited awhile, giving the bees plenty of time to get over their mad and be on about their business. Seldom waded out of the water, face swelling angrily in several places. "Paley, I don't want to hear no more about your stomach. I'll be lucky if my eyes don't swell to where I can't even see."

Daniel couldn't resist asking him what had happened to his easy way with bees. "Bound to've been somebody messin' with them; got them all spoiled and suspicious," Milo replied.

Sometime after the sun had started its afternoon

slant, Milo commented that he was having trouble seeing through his swollen eyes. "Boys, I can't say I'm right sure where we're at."

Daniel thought that had been the case even before the incident with the bees, but he had had no inclination toward mutiny. He studied Milo. "No disrespect, Mister Seldom, but I'm powerful disappointed in you."

"It was them bees that throwed me off. I think now that San Antonio is yonderway."

Paley Northcutt squinted. His eyes were dull and tired, but the sickness was gone. "I say you're wrong, Milo. I say Bexar lies in that direction." He pointed differently.

Daniel listened to them argue until he tired of it, then decided to try his own instincts. "I got a notion it's thataway," he said, pointing in a third direction, "and that's the way I'm goin'. You-all try your own ideas, and whichever one of us makes it into San Antonio will try to borrow some horses and come back lookin' for the others."

He struck out walking. Presently he looked back and found both men following him.

Well, he thought, it ain't the first time the blind led the blind.

In normal circumstances it would have gratified him to have other men follow him, but this time he had no particular faith in his own ability to find the way; the fact that they fell in behind him simply revealed they had no faith in their own. The more he thought about it, the more dismal the prospect became. On top of the pain and the weariness, he began to be aware that his stomach was empty. They had not even the makings of a snare, and it was obvious they wouldn't try to rob any more bee trees. Well, they would do the best they could; precious little edge they had for doing otherwise.

It seemed to him they had walked three times as far as they had ridden through the night, though he guessed that was an exaggeration. The sun bore down heavily upon his bare head, and the heat and the wound together brought nausea. It was as bad when he stopped as when he walked, so he kept walking each time until his legs caved, pausing then to rest and let the other two catch up with him. It surprised him that despite his condition he seemed always to be out ahead of them. It didn't occur to him at the time that they might simply be letting him take the responsibility for the direction so that if it turned out wrong, they wouldn't share the blame for it.

Afternoon wore into evening, and evening into night. He had a thirst that water wouldn't slake; he suspected he was running a fever. He dragged one foot dully past the other and somehow kept himself moving. He no longer looked back to see if Seldom and Northcutt were following him. If they were, fine; if they weren't, the hell with it.

He came finally upon a narrow trace that appeared to have been used by the high-wheeled Mexican *carretas,* though not enough to have worn it deeply. In this part of the country all trails led to San Antonio. Or *away* from it. In this case he couldn't tell which. He looked back for counsel and saw the two men too far behind him for consultation; they wouldn't know anyhow, he decided. He picked a direction and moved on. Seldom and Northcutt followed him.

He was about to quit and lie down on the bare ground for a night's fitful sleep when he saw flickering lights ahead. Blinking, he made out the glow of lanterns and candles, tiny and elusive spots of yellow in the night. He said in relief, "San Antonio. I'd about give up."

Seldom wheezed, "I knowed you was goin' right. If you hadn't been, I'd of corrected you."

It was still a long way into the city, but he found strength he didn't know he still had, and he plodded along doggedly ahead of the other men. By now he knew the dark streets well enough to have no trouble finding Flor Carmody's place. He walked past barking dogs and idly curious loungers and came up finally into the open yard of the little rock house on the river. He saw the girl standing there, and three or four men with her, shadowy figures in the moonlight. It came to him that they might be Fanch and Bodine for all he could see. He was too bone-tired to know or to care.

Flor walked out and stared at him a moment; he sagged, but he kept his feet. "Where's the rest of them?" she asked. Too weary to speak, he jerked his thumb. Flor said with a hint of respect, "Outwalked them, did you? Better man than I took you for. Don't reckon you've had a lick to eat?" He could only shake his head. "Come on in and I'll get you some *frijolis* and *tortillas*. It's the best I can do."

Beans sounded good to him. She paused long enough to tell one of the men—all were Mexican—to watch for Milo Seldom and Paley Northcutt. One of the Mexicans trailed in after him, and he recognized Lalo Talavera. Daniel was in too much distress to worry whether Lalo had been here paying court to Flor despite what Seldom had told him.

Flor gave Daniel a jug of *pulque* and told him to

take a long drink. "It'll help you more right now than anything else you could take," she said. When he tilted his head up with the jug, she saw for the first time the ragged wound across his scalp. She held the candle closer and swore in unabashed Spanish. "You walked all day with that, and bareheaded? You *are* a better man than I gave you credit for."

By the time Seldom and Northcutt got there, Daniel had wolfed down one plate of beans and was working on a second. Flor gave the two men a good drink out of the *pulque* jug. When Northcutt looked around for another drink, the jug was gone. "I can't afford to keep *you* in whisky," Flor said. "I ain't fixin' to try."

Methodically she cleaned Daniel's wound. "If they'd hit you any harder, the brains'd be oozin out," she told him. "But I'm not sure you got any; if you did you wouldn't of took up with the likes of Milo Seldom. Anybody can tell you he's got two left feet."

Seldom shrugged off the insult. It was of small moment to him in the face of a good meal. "Flor, I reckon you know they got that tobacco."

She nodded.

"There goes our trip after that silver. All the hopes I had was ridin' in them packs. Times it seems like the good Lord has got a grudge against me, and be damned if I can figure where I ever done Him a wrong turn."

"I saw it through my window, before I took out the back and left here. It ain't your tobacco no more, Milo."

Milo said dejectedly, "I'm glad I at least had the use of it awhile and could favor a few good folks like Daniel's daddy with a handful of it. I tried to be generous while I had it. Now I'm hopin' you'll be generous, Flor."

She looked at him quizzically, not answering. He went on, "We been left afoot. No horses, no guns, not a morsel of food to keep us from starvation. I was hopin' you'd find it in your heart, Flor, to help us get a little stake. If not for me, for this good farmer who left home and family to come help us. If we'd of found the silver, we'd of done well by you, Flor. We'd of bought you finery like you've never seen, and a house bigger than the San Fernando church."

"I'll bet," she said dryly.

"It's the Lord's truth. Have I ever lied to you, Flor?"

She just stared at him.

"We've come upon evil days, Flor. I know that in spite of tryin' to act like Jezebel, you got the heart of a sweet angel. We're on your mercy."

No mercy showed in her eyes. "If I'll stake you, will you turn over to me all claim you got on that tobacco or the money that comes out of it?"

"You're just a woman, Flor. You got no chance . . ."

"I didn't ask you that; I asked if it's a deal."

Seldom shrugged, having nothing to lose. "Sure, it's a deal."

She glanced at the other men, each in turn. "You all heard that. You're my witnesses." Daniel nodded dully, figuring it was a waste of time. Soon as he was able, he would leave here anyway, striking out for home. He didn't know how he would explain his coming back afoot, no horse, no saddle, no rifle. It would be a humbling thing.

Flor said, "Was I to get the tobacco, I'd need help to go down to the border with me to sell it and to find my no-account father. Would you-all go with me?

Would you take orders from me and not argue like a bunch of burro traders?"

Seldom said, "Flor, you're talkin' idle."

"Fine one you are to call somebody else idle. I want an answer—yes or no."

"Sure," Seldom said. "Only, it ain't goin' to happen."

Flor turned to Daniel Provost. "You showed fight against them *ladrones* last night, even if you didn't show sense. And you come in ahead of Milo and Paley awhile ago. I think you might be a good gamble; I'd like you to go."

Daniel looked at her with growing interest; he sensed this wasn't all idle talk. "I don't know that I'd want a woman for a boss."

"Would you rather it was Milo?"

Daniel shook his head. He didn't figure Flor could do any worse.

Flor turned to Paley Northcutt. "No use you sayin' anything, Paley. I don't intend to take anybody that can't leave a jug alone."

Northcutt shook his head in puzzlement. "I don't even know what the hell everybody's talkin' about." Daniel remembered that nobody had ever told him. Daniel said, "He took a right smart of punishment today that was none of his affair. Somebody owes him somethin'."

Flor studied the man in silence. "You know why I can't take you, Paley. How long since you been cold sober?"

"Countin' today?"

"Before that."

Paley rubbed his chin, eyes narrowing in deep thought.

"There was a couple of days back in January. Or maybe it was February. Mexican family run plumb out of wood, and I went to help them gather it against the cold. Dropped my jug and busted it before we got out of sight of town. But I done all right."

"Think you could stay sober for a long time, maybe several weeks?"

Northcutt shrugged. "So far I ain't heard no good reason."

Milo grunted sarcastically. "There *ain't* no good reason. We lost it all."

Flor's face glowed in triumph. "Lalo, you want to show them?"

Lalo smiled. "My pleasure. If you will follow me, Milo; you too, my farmer friend." He walked out the door into the moonlight. Milo grumbled about the foolishness of listening to any woman idle away the time, but he followed.

Lalo Talavera pointed toward the brush arbor. "Are those the horses you lost? And the mules?"

Daniel blinked in surprise. There stood his roan horse Sam Houston that the Mexicans had taken from him this morning. There was Seldom's horse, and there were the packmules. He smelled the tobacco even before he saw the packs slung across the rough fence.

Milo Seldom shouted in joy. "The angels will bless you in heaven, Flor. You got it all back for me."

Flor Carmody had come out behind him. Her voice bristled in sarcasm. "For *you?* I'll take my blessin's here on earth. You lost it; it's all mine."

Milo stared in disbelief. "Flor! You wouldn't do that to me!"

She stood like a rock. "The hell I wouldn't."

Milo's voice began to soften, to implore. "Flor, all them things you said in yonder—I took them for idle talk."

"I never idle, Milo; you ought to know that. You heard what I said and you agreed to it. I got enough witnesses to take you to any court in the republic of Texas. But I won't take you to court. Give me any trouble and I'll turn you over to the same friends of mine who took care of Fanch and Bodine."

Milo looked at the tobacco packs. "You didn't have them killed, did you? Ain't no tobacco worth gettin' men killed, even men like them two."

She shook her head. "They're all right, but they're goin' to enjoy the hospitality of some awful stubborn people a few days while I go south with this tobacco."

Milo grumbled. "One thing I don't understand. If you knew where them Mexicans was takin' us, why didn't somebody come fetch us instead of lettin' us walk all the way back?"

Flor said, "I knew you'd get lost soon as they turned you loose. We wouldn't know where to look for you."

"We could've wandered around out there and starved to death."

She shrugged. "Then I'd of had to get somebody else to help me take the tobacco to Mexico."

6

South of San Antonio, Daniel found the country gradually changing. First it was green rolling hills, then the land took on a drier, harsher aspect hinting at the desert which lay ahead. Vegetation was still plentiful but different in character, much of it cactus-type growth, more of the thorny brush, the catclaw, *guajillo*, mesquite. Prickly pear grew in abundance. Along the dim trail Daniel could see evidence of last winter's hard times when Mexican freighters had impaled pear pads on pitchforks and burned the thorns away so they could be fed to the oxen which pulled the lumbering *carretas*.

At one point he saw the charred remnants of several oxcarts. From the looks of them he judged it had been two or three years since they had burned. He could picture shouting Comanche warriors suddenly charging from a nearby motte of heavy brush and overrunning the cart men before they could get into position to stage a defense. Wooden crosses leaned at angles over five graves.

A chill ran up Daniel's spine, and he gave the motte a long study, his hand tight upon the rifle Flor's Mexican friends had recovered for him. He knew it had probably been a while since that brush had hidden a warrior, for raids along these trails were becoming much less common than in an earlier day. But it would be foolhardy to think the Indians were gone forever. Sooner or later they would be back; if it were sooner, Daniel had no intention of being caught asleep.

The thought of Indians made him take another good look at his companions; he had already made several such appraisals and at the end of each was still in doubt. There was, of course, Flor. Her being along gave him cause for worry at the outset; it wasn't seemly for a woman to come on a trip like this. Milo Seldom—well, Daniel had to admit he was still drawn to this lanky, likeable back woodsman, but he no longer had faith in Milo's ability to find the back side of a box canyon. Lalo Talavera—he had not yet formed any definite opinion except that for some reason he had not analyzed, the attention the man paid to Flor bothered him; he couldn't say that she encouraged him, but neither did she run him off. Finally, bringing up the rear and leading the packmules, were four Mexicans, friends of Flor's. In two days' riding he had learned little about them except that two were brothers, Armando and Bernardo Borrego. The word *borrego* in Spanish meant sheep, and he hoped they didn't act that way if trouble came. The way they followed Flor and jumped at every word she said made him wonder. But then, Flor had a way of making people jump.

Flor had stood by her decision not to take Paley Northcutt. On the face of it, Daniel thought it was a prudent decision, though he regretted the ordeal Northcutt had undergone without even knowing why. Milo Seldom had finally explained to him, after it was too late and Flor had taken over.

"Silver? Solid silver, you say?"

Milo had nodded. "Pure silver cast into shiny bars. Maybe more bars than there are horses in San Antonio de Bexar, just layin' there waitin' for somebody to come and carry them away."

"How come there ain't nobody already done it?"

"Very few men still alive have any real idea where to look." Milo frowned. "Sure wisht you was goin' with us, Paley. Maybe I could talk Flor into another frame of mind."

"I ain't sure I'd even want to go. I try to never make an important decision when I'm sober, and I'm sober now."

Daniel Provost was sober, too—he had never been any other way—and he found himself looking back over his shoulder occasionally, resisting an impulse to turn around and go home.

Twice today he had looked back and thought he glimpsed a man on a horse, far behind them. Both times he had blinked and then stared into the heat waves, but neither time could he find again what he had taken for a man; all he could see was brush. Nerves, he thought. Thinking about Indians always got his hair up a little, and he had thought about Indians a right smart.

He was surprised when Flor Carmody pulled her horse over next to his and rode beside him awhile. She asked, "How's your head?"

"Don't hardly feel it any more, except that it itches a little."

"Healin'. Looks like you'll live." She studied him, and her unabashed curiosity made him uneasy. In a way he wanted to pull away from her, but he didn't. He had the feeling he sometimes got when Lizbeth Wills was near him but not quite touching. She said, "You been worryin' over somethin'. Want to talk about it?"

"Just been thinkin' about Indians some."

"We don't none of us live forever. Anyway, you know there ain't been much Indian trouble on this trail in a long time. You're bothered by more than Indians."

"I'm bothered by you bein' here. This is a man's job, not a woman's."

"Mexican women have always gone with their men; they're not like white women. There were Mexican women with Santa Anna at the Alamo who came all the way up from Toluca to cook for their men and see after their other needs. There've been Mexican women at all the missions and all the outposts. Besides, I've got a lot at stake here; I figure I'm smarter than any man on this trip."

He had no argument with her on that. "Why bring this bunch, then? Why not find you some better men?"

"If they were any smarter, they wouldn't take orders from me. I settle for what I can get."

He glanced back in suspicion at the packmules. "The more I've thought about it, the more I doubt that there's enough money in three packs of tobacco to buy the supplies and mules and such that's goin' to be needed for an expedition out west."

"That was Milo's notion, and he never did have

much head for figures. He's a dreamer, not a book-keeper. You're right; three packs won't buy near enough. But I won't be sellin' three packs; I'll sell a dozen or fifteen."

Daniel decided she wasn't much of a bookkeeper either. "I can't see where you'll get them."

"You ever hear them talk much about my father?"

Daniel shook his head. "Not much."

"He's a real blackleg, that old man—a scoundrel if ever one was born. But he taught me aplenty. There'll be a dozen more packs of tobacco when the time comes. Just trust me."

Late in the afternoon Daniel let himself drop back near the packmules, where Lalo Talavera was standing rear guard. He looked over his shoulder and caught a glimpse of what he had taken before to be a horseman. He squinted, but the man—if it had been a man—seemed to melt into the dotting of dark brush.

Talavera said in Spanish, "He is there, then he is not."

"You been seein' him too?"

"Since yesterday."

"Indian, maybe, scoutin' us?"

Lalo shook his head. "Possibly, but Indians would not wait so long to try us out. It is a robber, perhaps, hoping to come at night and find us sleeping. It is probable he tried us last night and saw men on guard."

"Makes me nervous, him trailin' along like that. Keep thinkin' it could be Bodine and Fanch. Next time around, that Bodine's likely to kill somebody."

"When it does not itch, I do not scratch. But since it itches *you*, then perhaps it is best we scratch a little, if you are game for it."

Daniel's mouth went dry. Lalo Talavera was testing him. On reflection, Daniel decided it was high time he tested himself; he might find he did not care to finish this trip. "What'll we do?"

"You ride up and tell Flor that the next time we pass a motte of brush you and I are going to drop out and wait."

"Think I ought to tell her what for? I'd hate to scare her."

"Scare Flor?" Lalo shook his head. "You could not scare that woman if you tied her to the mouth of a cannon and touched fire to the fuse. Believe me, I have tried. She has not given me so much as a chance to touch."

Daniel told Flor what they intended to do. She seemed more angry than alarmed. "Somebody talked too much," she said grimly. "I'll bet I can guess who it was." She cast a hard glance at Milo Seldom, who rode along head down and unaware, his mind a hundred miles away, probably in the midst of that huge cache of silver bars.

Daniel waited until the strung-out group passed by him and Lalo came, bringing up the rear. As they topped a small hill, Lalo pointed to two stands of brush, the faint trace running between them. "When he comes even with us, we shall ride out and take him."

"Alive?"

"If possible, but dead if he shows resistance. We are a long way from sheriffs here, and judges. Where there is no law, one makes it."

Daniel's nervous hands gripped his rifle, and realization came that in a few minutes he would be looking down the sights at a man, possibly to kill him. It was an awesome thought, and he tried to think instead of the farm. It seemed a long way off.

Lalo motioned for Daniel to take the motte on the right, and Lalo rode for the one on the left. Daniel noticed that Lalo was careful to ride where the grass was heaviest, to mask his tracks. Daniel was chagrined that he hadn't thought of it himself.

He hadn't realized how still and close a brushy motte could be, for the heavy foliage cut off any breeze; it cut off any visibility as well, which heightened the feeling of imprisonment. Daniel sensed that the man probably had topped the hill by now and should be on his way down, yet he could not risk stepping out to see. He wondered how he could sweat so much, yet his mouth be so damnably dry. He continually had to wipe his hand on his britches to keep it from being slick against his rifle.

Presently he heard slow hoofbeats against the soft ground, far away at first, then closer. Peering through the foliage, he caught a glimpse of color, but that was all. In a minute now the man would be even with him. Foliage was its lightest at the lower levels of the mesquites, and he caught sight of a horse's feet picking up and setting down. Daniel spurred out into the open, rifle at the ready. Lalo spurred from the other side.

"*Manos arriba!*" Lalo shouted.

The man thrust both arms straight up over his head. "Fellers, don't you-all shoot! Lalo, it's just me, Paley Northcutt. Farmer boy, don't you let your finger get nervous on that trigger."

Daniel lowered the rifle, but Lalo held his steady. "All right, *borracho,* perhaps you will tell why you have followed us so far."

Paley Northcutt trembled in surprise at being caught this way. "Didn't mean no harm, Lalo; you know there ain't a particle of harm in me."

"Maybe there is and maybe there is not. Answer what I asked you."

"I give a lot of thought to what Milo said about that silver. More I studied on it, the more I wanted to go."

"Why?"

"A few bars of that silver would sure buy a lot of whisky."

Lalo glanced at Daniel. "An honest answer."

Daniel demanded, "How come you followed us instead of comin' in like a man?"

"Flor'd of run me off. I figured if I was to wait a couple or three days till we was a long ways from San Antonio, she wouldn't have the heart to turn me down and send me back through Indian country all by myself."

Lalo said, "You don't know our Flor."

The more Daniel thought about it, the angrier he became, remembering the anxiety that had risen in him like fever while he waited in that hot, still motte. "You know, don't you, that you give us quite a turn?"

"Wouldn't of done it for the world. You-all ought to've ignored me."

"Ignore you?" Daniel demanded incredulously.

Paley Northcutt looked down ashamed. "Seems like folks have always found me easy to ignore."

Daniel's anger ebbed, and he found himself touched by remorse. "I didn't go to holler at you, Paley."

"Everybody does."

Lalo said, "Come on, Paley. We shall see if Flor's

heart is as soft as ours. I think she will probably kick you."

She would have, had the long riding skirts not made it impractical. Hands on her hips, she gave Paley Northcutt a bilingual threshing that would have moved a reluctant team of Mexican mules through east Texas mud in a run. She turned finally to Lalo and Daniel. "You ought to have shot him. We got no use for a drunk on this trip, and we can't just send him back. Minute he gets to babblin' over a jug, he'll have half of San Antonio trailin' us to get the silver."

Paley's slumped shoulders straightened. "You mean I can stay?"

"I mean I've half a notion to shoot you myself."

"I ain't drunk now, Flor, and I didn't bring nothin' to drink. Search me; search my saddlebags and blanket. Only thing I got liquid is a goatskin of water."

Flor studied him narrow-eyed and angry. "I don't know . . ."

Milo Seldom put in, "He's a good ol' boy, Flor. He's a right smart of help when he's sober."

"You can't remember that far back," she declared.

Lalo Talavera nodded Flor over a little closer. "True, he does not look like much, and when he finds whisky he is little of a man. But if you had ever seen his body, *hija,* you would have seen many battle scars, and none of them on his back."

Flor paced the ground, stopping to stare at Paley, then pacing and stopping to glance at the other men. "Looks to me like you-all want to keep him. Damn if I can see it your way, but there ain't nobody ever accused Flor Carmody of bein' difficult. All right, he can stay, but I want one thing understood: he ain't to have a chance of findin' anything to drink. If there's a man here got a drop of anything stronger than water hid out, I want it turned in to me right now."

Lalo Talavera dug into his blankets and fetched a jug. The Borrego brothers looked at each other a moment, then gave in and brought out one apiece. Flor looked sharply at the men. "Is that all? You sure?" One of the Borregos then brought out a second jug. Without ceremony Flor took Daniel's rifle from his hand. She pounded the butt of it against all the jugs and broke them. The liquor disappeared quickly into the sand.

Paley Northcutt stared at it as though someone cut the throat of his pet horse.

"We've wasted enough time," Flor said. "Let's get this outfit movin'."

7

It was a big, empty land where no one lived. The terrain became drier and hotter, the vegetation increasingly scrubby and thorny. Daniel sensed they were approaching the Mexico border even though he had never been there. He knew it by description from men who had fought and bled along that broad, muddy river. He noticed that the nearer they came to the Rio Grande, the more apprehension crept into Milo Seldom's nervous face. Eventually Milo pulled his horse in beside Flor's.

"Flor, I thought you said you knowed this country."

"I do."

"Well, don't you know where this trail is takin' us? There's a thousand miles of river to choose from, and you're stayin' on a trail that takes us right to a Mexican customs house. They'll catch us before our clothes dry out."

"Remember the rule, Milo: *I'm* in charge of this outfit."

"They got a prison across yonder with stone walls twelve feet high that they built just to put smugglers in. You act like you're tryin' to get the whole bunch of us throwed in there for twenty years."

"Did I ever say I intended to smuggle this stuff into Mexico?"

"Is there any other way? They got a customs duty over there that'd stagger a Tennessee plow mule. Time we pay it, we won't have enough left to buy a sack of cornmeal."

"We won't pay it."

"The only way to keep from payin' it is to smuggle past customs. The way we're goin', we'd just as well be carryin' a red flag and a Mexican brass band."

"You've got lots of imagination, Milo, but it doesn't always run in the right direction. You've known my ol' daddy Cephus a long time. Did you ever know him to do anything straightforward and honest?"

"Can't say as ever I did."

"Well, I'm his daughter. Just be quiet and let me handle this thing."

Milo Seldom pulled away but was far from quiet. He rode up first beside Paley Northcutt, then Daniel, then Lalo and finally the Borregos, telling each in turn that this wild-eyed woman was fixing to get all of them killed or flung into a dungeon to rot. None of them gave him any satisfaction. He came back finally to Daniel. "Farmer, if you're smart, you won't be no party to this. You'll tell her we're taking that tobacco and crossin' the river someplace else."

Daniel had no idea what scheme Flor Carmody carried inside that pretty head, but he had a feeling she was more to be trusted than Milo. "If you'd of been smart," Daniel retorted, "you'd still have the tobacco yourself."

They came to the river at midday. Daniel rode ahead to take his first look at this fabled Rio Bravo whose waters through the years had washed many armies, advancing and retreating, from both the south side and the north—Spanish, Mexican, filibusterers, Texan, not to mention Indian raiding parties which periodically swam south in the full moon and came back with horses and stolen women and children and their lances festooned with fresh scalps from Mexican people who could not conceivably have done them any harm in their own accustomed roaming grounds. This had been a violent river far beyond the memories of living men, back through the times of their fathers and grandfathers. Daniel suspected it might be a violent river for a long time to come.

On the far side, a fair distance up the bank and probably well beyond the flood limits, stood a rambling stone structure with corrals beyond it, flanked on either side by simple *jacales,* small houses of brush and mud. Past that, half a mile or so, stood a town, its mud walls gray, its rock walls catching the sun. This, Daniel thought, would be the place they had been talking about, Colmena Vieja. The word *colmena* meant beehive, *vieja,* old. Probably somebody had kept bees here at some time in the distant past, though on first sight Daniel could not see a thing a bee could make honey of.

He saw activity at the stone building across the river and noted that several men were looking their way. Milo Seldom rode up and said bitterly, "Well, she's went and done it now. That's the customs house, and they've seen us. Ain't no way we can cross that river now without they'll pounce on us like a bobcat on a rabbit."

Flor Carmody heard him but seemed to make a point of ignoring his comment. She said, "Daniel, I'd like you to go across with me to talk to the customs officer." She glanced at Milo. "You can come too if you'll promise to keep your mouth shut no matter what you see or hear."

Milo nodded sarcastically. "Sure, I'd like to go. I'd like to see how you get us out of this mess."

"We're in no mess. Long as the goods stay on this side of the river, we ain't broken no law."

"And we get no money for them."

"Have faith, o brethren, and all things will be revealed unto you."

Grimly Milo said, "Don't be makin' light of the Word."

She turned to Bernardo Borrego and said in Spanish, "You keep a watch on Paley Northcutt and see that he does not cross that river. I do not want him within a mile of any whisky."

Paley said in a hurt voice, "I heard that. You can trust me."

"So long as Bernardo watches you, I can." She dropped everything off her saddle, touched a spur to her horse, trotted him down the bank and plunged off into the river. Her skirts flared out as the water lifted them, and she slid out of the saddle to give the horse an easier go of it. She held onto the reins but left them loose, and she gripped the saddlehorn.

Daniel let his blanket and his warbag to the ground and knotted the powderhorn string up tight so that the horn was close to his neck. He followed Flor into the river, despairing of being able to keep his rifle dry. But he decided it wouldn't make any difference; he wasn't going to shoot anybody over there.

The river was deeper and swifter in the middle than he had expected. He almost lost his hold on the saddlehorn and let himself slip back to wrap his hand in the horse's tail. Daniel did not dare lose his hold; he was not a swimmer. He caught a mouthful of water and nearly strangled.

By the time they reached the other side he was thoroughly tired of the Rio Grande. He waded out, still holding the horse's tail and letting it pull him along. Coughing heavily, he tried to clear the muddy water from his lungs, his legs shaking from the ordeal. The wind went through the wet clothes and made him cold. He turned his gun barrel down and let the water pour out of it. He would have to give it a good cleaning tonight to keep rust from setting in. Abusing a rifle this way went contrary to all his frontier instincts.

He saw Flor trying to brush her soaked clothing, a lost cause. He supposed it was a woman's nature to try to salvage something of her appearance in even the most adverse of circumstances. And these were very adverse.

Three horsemen trotted down from the customs house. The one in front was an officer, Daniel figured, because his uniform had once been brighter and more colorful than the plain dingy white of the others. All were threadbare now and showed the results of hopeless battle against sweat and grime and heavy wear. The officer looked first at Daniel, then at Milo, trying to decide which man was in command here. Flor left him in doubt for only a moment.

"Captain," she asked in Spanish, "are you the customs officer here?"

He smiled then, eyes warming to the slender girl, her wet clothing clinging tightly to her body. "*Sí, señorita,* I am in charge here. But you give me a promotion my superiors have not chosen to do. I am but a lieutenant."

"Surely," said Flor, "you should be a captain, or perhaps even higher. One can tell from here that you keep a tight discipline and an efficient post."

"Again my thanks, *señorita.* If there is any way I may serve you, I am Lieutenant Zamaniega, *a sus ordenes.*"

"And I," said Flor without a sign of guile, "am Flor de Zavala y Campos. My father was Rafael Zavala the merchant. Surely you knew him."

The lieutenant shook his head. "The name unfortunately does not bring the man to mind, but I am sure it was my loss not to have known him. Again, how may I serve you?"

"I have across the river the remnants of a packtrain of goods my father was bringing to Mexico for sale. Alas, he was killed along the way." She crossed herself, and for good reason, Daniel thought. "We were lucky to escape Comanches with our lives, and to bring even this much of the goods."

The lieutenant was squinting, trying to see what lay across the river. "It is a great pity, *señorita.* I shall notify the priest, that he may light a candle."

"I shall see the priest myself, thank you. Meantime, there is the matter of three packs of prime tobacco."

The officer's brown eyes lighted. "Three packs. I fear that will carry a heavy duty, *señorita,* a most heavy duty. I wish there were something I could do for you."

Daniel figured he was giving Flor a chance now to offer him a *mordido*, a bribe to undervalue the goods. He could see larceny in the calculating eyes.

Innocently Flor said, "I feared that would be the case. I hope there will be money enough left to buy mules so that we may go back and get the rest."

"The rest?"

"The other twelve packs of tobacco. We lost most of our mules in the attack. We had to secrete the packs until our return."

The officer looked toward the river, his eyes calculating even faster. "Three packs—twelve packs. That is fifteen packs altogether, a great deal of money."

"Far too much money for a woman like myself, whose business experience is so sadly limited. My father was skilled at the bargaining, but I fear that I know little. I will be gobbled alive like a lamb by the wolf pack. I probably will never be able to retrieve the rest of the goods. I wish I could find an honest and reliable man here to become my partner, to see that I get full value and am not cheated. And that the import levies are fair. He would be rewarded." She looked at him with eyes helpless as a cornered fawn's. "*Well* rewarded, *capitán*."

Lieutenant Zamaniega bowed from the waist. "*Señorita*, you are most fortunate that you have come to this place rather than some of the thieves' dens that one finds at many points on this river. Our merchants are honest, and generous to a fault. Besides, I shall be vigilant that no man cheats you; on the contrary, I think they will be happy to pay you a premium. I shall personally see to it."

"I had thought that I would test the market here. If it is good, when I retrieve the rest of the packs I shall bring them here also."

"Rest assured, beautiful lady, there is not a better market on the entire Mexican border than you will find right here. We shall see that you are bountifully paid for the goods you have now, and for the rest when you bring them. It is the least we can do for so lovely a woman, so newly bereaved."

Daniel could not trust himself to look at the officer any longer, or at Flor. He looked instead at Milo and found the backwoodsman slumped, mouth slacked open in total disbelief. Daniel beckoned Milo to one side where the officer would not hear. "She always been able to lie like that?"

"She's her daddy's daughter. Ol' Cephus never drew an honest breath."

"I thought he was your friend."

"Cephus Carmody is nobody's friend. I always liked him, but I never turned my back on him when I had anything I thought he'd steal."

The officer told Flor he would be glad to cross the river and give her a customs valuation on the tobacco so she would know exactly what the duty would be before she left the Texas side. "We have a boat tied just upriver," he said. "It will not be necessary for you to swim and cause yourself further discomfort. Would you care to accompany me?"

"I would be delighted, *capitan*. What of my two employees, these *Americanos* here?"

"Do you always give employment to *Americanos?*" The lieutenant plainly disapproved.

"My father's doing. But I must say they fought well against the Comanches—for *Americanos*, at least."

The lieutenant frowned at them. "Alas, the boat is small. If you wish them to be there, I fear they must swim."

A little of the devil was in Flor's eyes as she turned to Milo and Daniel. "You may stay here if you wish, or you may go back the same way you came."

Milo watched sourly as Flor and the officer went to the boat. "This is too much, the way she's kickin' us around like a couple of hound dogs. I swear, I don't know why I stand for it."

"For the same reason I do—all that silver."

"I reckon. Well, friend Daniel, me and you got us an interest across the river. We better get goin'."

"I'd rather stay here." The thought of that muddy water gave him a queasy feeling.

"Stay if you want to. I'm seein' after my interests." Milo plunged off into the river. Daniel hesitated, then did likewise. He found it less of an ordeal the second time, now that he knew what to expect and how to meet it. He and Milo waded out somewhat ahead of the officer's boat and were waiting when Flor and Zamaniega came trudging up the sandy bank. Lalo and the Borregos had seen the customs officer coming and had unloaded the packs from the mules, spreading them out for inspection.

Flor worriedly told the lieutenant, "I fear we have no money with us; that was lost in the battle. Whatever the duty, we must pay it from proceeds or in kind."

The officer opened one of the packs at random and ran his hand down into the burley. He rolled the bright leaves between his fingers, bringing them up to his nose. "Ah," he sighed, "this is rare quality." He smelled the tobacco for a moment, then brought up a small leather bag. "May I?" Flor nodded, and the officer stuffed the bag with the leaves. Done, he put away his smile and momentarily took on the stiff attitude of an official doing his duty.

"*Señorita,* when I send my written accounts at the end of this month, I shall report to my superiors that I found you had three packs of very inferior goathides. Therefore I levy a duty of twenty pesos, payable upon sale of this poor merchandise. Agreed?"

"You are most generous, *mi capitán.*"

"The least one can do for a lady in mourning, and so charming a partner. And now to the boat with these packs. I think I know some merchants who will beat a pathway to your door to bid you a handsome price for these *goathides.*" He paused. "And your door will be my door. I offer you the hospitality of my own poor house."

Flor arched her eyebrows. "*Capitán . . .*"

The lieutenant hurried to alter his approach. "But only under the most proper conditions, of course. You shall have total privacy."

"I shall consider it, *mi capitán.* But first, to business, *sí*?"

They loaded the boat. Flor walked away from the lieutenant briefly to give orders to her own men. "Paley, I want you to stay here and watch our belongings. Bernardo, I want you to stay and watch Paley. If he even looks toward that river, shoot him. The rest of you follow us across and bring the mules."

Milo protested, "Flor, I don't know why in the Lord's sweet name you want to lie so shameful. The only honorable thing for us to've done would've been to smuggle that stuff across in the first place. And anyway, where's Cephus Carmody at?"

Flor looked at Lalo Talavera. "Lalo, if Milo does not keep quiet, take him to the river and drown him."

Milo grumbled as he watched the lieutenant help Flor into the boat, holding her hand longer than necessary, then stepping into the boat and seating himself close beside her. He groused, "He's workin' almighty fast."

Lalo observed, "And so is she. Trust her, Milo. She has eyes like a hawk, and talons too."

"I know all about them talons. She's dug them into me."

The river no longer held any dread for Daniel, and he led the way into it, following in the gentle wake of the rowboat. Urged on by the other men, the mules plunged in after Daniel and swam across. Before long the tobacco was on the mule's backs again, dry and in good condition. The lieutenant said he would lead the way to his house, where interested buyers could come and make their bids. "I myself shall go among them this afternoon and tell them what we—*you* have for sale."

"I hope," Flor said worriedly, "I can get enough for this tobacco that I may buy extra mules and supplies and go back for the rest."

"I believe you will be pleasantly surprised, fair lady. I think I may even find a dealer in mules who will be willing to offer you everything you need at a price better than you would expect."

Flor blinked back the tears. "*Mi capitán*, you are a comfort to me in this time of trial."

As they moved up toward the customs house, Daniel noticed a group of men trudging along afoot, accompanied by rifle-carrying horsemen. They were obviously prisoners. He heard Flor ask the lieutenant about them. The officer said, "They are from the prison. They go out to work upon the irrigation ditches belonging to the warden's brother. He considers it a mercy to the men to be allowed to get out into the fresh air and do invigorating exercise. And if thereby they can improve the fields of his brother, then everyone has been the richer for it."

Especially the warden's brother, thought Daniel.

The men were a dirty, bearded lot, many wearing clothes reduced to little better than rags. As they passed, a few shouted vivid suggestions at Flor. One of the men had a gray-laced beard eight or ten inches in length, and his long, tangled hair resembled a bush. He stopped and stared at Flor until a guard took his foot out of the stirrup and gave the man's shoulder a hard push. "Go along, old goat; she is much too young for you."

"Obviously criminals," Flor said to the lieutenant.

"To a man. The world would be better if they could all simply be shot, as *el presidente* wisely did to the *Americanos*." He glanced back at Daniel and Milo, making it plain he had intended them to hear.

In a way Daniel was glad he had heard. Earlier he had worried that Flor was about to pull some kind of swindle and knew his conscience was likely to trouble him. Now he knew his conscience would be no problem.

The customs officer led the way to his house, which to Daniel's surprise was among the larger ones in the town. Daniel wondered how he was able to afford it on the meager salary a customs officer would draw in a town of such modest size. He assumed there was additional income, though he did not speculate upon the nature of it. "The packs may be unloaded here upon the veranda where the merchants may come and examine the merchandise," he told the men. "And you, dear lady, are welcome to come into the house. But first let me go and make sure that the proper preparations are made. Will you excuse me?"

The lieutenant handed his reins to Milo, who resentfully passed them to Daniel. Daniel dropped them. If the horse wanted to wander around town, let him. Daniel looked over the front of the building and then rode to the side to see the rest of it. He saw a handsome *señorita,* obviously agitated, beating a hasty retreat out the back door. He's preparing the way for Flor all right, Daniel mused.

The lieutenant came out in a few moments, followed by an elderly dark-skinned woman, evidently a housekeeper. "My house is your house, *señorita.* The *dueña* will help you find some suitable clothes. I have a trunkful which belonged to my mother, bless her memory."

Daniel figured it was the lieutenant's "mother" he had seen going out the back door.

"You are kind," Flor smiled. "And what of my men?"

"There is a stable in the back. They may make themselves comfortable in the hay if they do not find more desirable accommodations about the town. I believe if they care to look, they can find that Colmena Vieja offers better attractions. And now I go to alert the merchants and a mule dealer. They should begin to arrive within an hour or so. I shall be on hand to see that you are not cheated."

Flor and the men watched the lieutenant ride up the dusty street past playing children and scratching chickens and barking dogs. The feigned helplessness left her face, and her mouth went hard. "He has plans for me. He'll talk the merchants into givin' me a big price to be sure I come back with the rest of the pack-train. Then they'll rob me blind."

Milo said tightly, "That ain't the only plan he's got for you."

She went into the house where the *dueña* waited. Daniel was sure she was gone an hour, possibly more. He had observed with Lizbeth that when a man waited upon a woman, time went by on its knees. She came out finally, in a shiny green dress of some fine material the likes of which Daniel had never seen. She smelled of perfume, her face scrubbed and evidently creamed with something only the women knew of, her black hair freshly combed and pulled back tightly into a bun. A flat-crowned hat sat atop her head. Daniel stared, holding his breath. She was prettier than he had imagined she could be. She bore little resemblance to the Flor Carmody he had seen scrubbing clothes on the bank of the San Antonio River, or had watched coming up muddy and wet from the waters of the Rio Grande.

Flor said, "The lieutenant's mother had good taste."

Daniel said, "I seen his mother. She's younger than *he* is. What's that pretty material?"

"Silk. Ain't you ever seen silk before?"

"I reckon not."

She shook her head. "I've seen it, but I ain't never wore any."

"It looks real fine on you."

Flor Carmody gazed at him a moment in surprise. "Farmer, I'm beginnin' to be glad I brought you along."

Daniel was flustered. "I just said what's true."

"But nobody else has said it. Not Milo Seldom, not even that gift to womankind, Lalo Talavera. Somebody brought you up right."

"I've got a good mother."

The other men stared at her, and Daniel decided he didn't like what he read in their eyes. Even Milo Seldom seemed unprepared. "I never seen you thisaway, Flor."

"If we find what we're goin' after, this is what I'll be wearin' from now on, only I won't be anyplace *you* can see me. I'll go to New Orleans or Mexico City or someplace. I'll let them high-nosed *ricos* in San Antonio take just one look at me so I can tell them to go to hell; they'll sit up and take notice."

Milo turned sour again. "They sure will. They'll figure you for one of them high-priced ones."

She flared. "What do you mean by that?"

"I mean there's somethin' undecent about them clothes. Make you look like somebody or somethin' you ain't. You know the kind of women that wears them kind of things. I like you better the way you was, just ordinary."

"You think I'm ordinary, do you, Milo?" Her voice was strained; Daniel sensed danger in it even if Milo didn't.

"You sure ain't no silk lady."

She made an angry run at him, and he turned quickly away, trying to get out of reach. She lifted the green skirts and kicked at him. Daniel saw that beneath the silks she still wore her Mexican riding boots.

Milo motioned frantically. "I see people comin', Flor. Probably the merchants we been waitin' for. You better try to *act* like a silk lady."

Flor gained control of herself, though her eyes

threatened all manner of violence. She brushed at the dress to straighten its folds and ran her fingers against her dark hair, trying to be sure it was in place. The middle-aged, heavyset *dueña* watched from the door, confused and suspicious. Daniel wondered what she might later tell the lieutenant.

Testily Daniel said, "Milo, you ought to be ashamed, hurtin' her feelin's that way. She's a lady."

"Her, a lady?"

"She's a lady to me, and you'll treat her like one."

Milo frowned as if something had just come to his notice. "Friend Daniel, I'll have to take to watchin' you a little closer."

Flor was a picture of propriety as the merchants arrived, led by Lieutenant Zamaniega, smiling and protective of the helpless girl. He halted just short of the veranda, surprised by the unexpected beauty of Flor in these fine clothes. He had trouble finding his voice. "Gentlemen, this beautiful lady is *Señorita* de Zavala y Campos. *Señorita,* I would like you to meet these honorable men of Colmena Vieja, *Señores* Vidal, Rodriguez and Sandoval. This other gentleman is *Señor* Ramirez, who may not be quite so honorable because he is a dealer in horses and mules. Nevertheless, I shall be here to see that he treats you fairly." He winked at Ramirez. The men all smiled, Ramirez perhaps the most. They bowed, each in turn.

Daniel could tell they were trying to suppress their eagerness as they inspected the merchandise. They spoke among themselves, hardly above a whisper at first but gradually louder as anger arose with the competition. Zamaniega had stood to one side, quietly admiring Flor. Now he stepped among the three, lecturing them sternly. At last he turned.

"*Señorita,* all three of these gentlemen would naturally like to buy the entire lot, though *Señor* Sandoval has come up with the highest bid. I have proposed that if his price is suitable to you, each shall pay it for one lot of the tobacco; then each will have time to consider what he may bid for the rest of the goods when you bring them."

Flor plainly did not care whether one man got it or all three. "How much?"

Zamaniega beckoned her over to one side. "Let us confer."

Daniel watched suspiciously but could not hear what he was saying. Zamaniega took one of Flor's hands and patted it protectively. Daniel could hear her saying something about the mules. Zamaniega beckoned the mule dealer over and they talked awhile. Ramirez was soon shaking his head angrily, and the lieutenant was lecturing him as he had lectured the three merchants. Ramirez finally shrugged and gave in. Again, smiling in victory, the lieutenant patted Flor's hand. "I told you the merchants of Colmena Vieja are honorable men."

"But how reluctant in their honor," she said.

When the merchants trooped off up the street, the lieutenant began trying to get Flor to go into the house with him, pointing out that the *dueña* was there to see that all was proper. Flor smilingly put him off, telling him there was much that needed to be done in the matter of selecting the mules and the equipment the dealer had promised to furnish, and in buying the supplies needed for the return.

"But," the lieutenant argued, "there should be no necessity to hurry. The good Lord gave few of us money, but He gave all of us the same amount of time.

This gift should be used to pleasure the soul as well as to enrich the purse."

"The soul does poorly when the purse is empty. There will be time later when the task is done. If we delay, someone may find our cache and take it."

"Then," he said, bowing, "I leave you and your men to finish the details of the bargain while I return to the routine detail of the bureaucrat. Until tonight."

"Until tonight, *mi capitán*."

8

Flor was pleased by the prices she had extracted, both in selling the tobacco and in buying supplies. "But they're poor liars. You can see in their eyes that they're givin' us the bait the way you'd do to catch a fish. They figure we'll be back and then they'll really jab the hook into us."

They all went together to the various merchants, delivering each his pack of tobacco, then selecting the goods they needed, taking out in cash what they didn't need in trade. Flor spread the business between all three. "If we was to buy everything from one man," she explained to Daniel, "he'd see we're takin' more goods than we'd need for a little trip like we told them about. Time they get to comparin' with each other, we'll be gone."

The way it was, the merchants were glad to trade goods rather than pay all in cash. Daniel noted a considerable discrepancy in the prices each asked for various types of goods. Daniel suspected they had a considerable profit margin hidden away. He noticed that though the general populace of the town was desperately poor, the merchants did not share their plight. Whatever little money found its way into the hands of the people evidently passed on to the profiteering merchants.

At haggling, Lalo Talavera came into most useful service; he was easy with the words, hard at a bargain. Milo observed, "A merchant is no match for a man as good as Lalo at coaxin' shy women."

The supplies bought and set aside, they went to the mule dealer's before dusk. His corrals were at the edge of town, near sprawling rock walls twelve feet high, guard towers on both sides. There was no gate on the side facing the dealer's, but there was a row of five or six barred windows. "The prison," Milo said unnecessarily; Daniel had already figured that out.

He shuddered. "Bleak-lookin' place from out here."

"Ain't none the better inside," Milo responded. "This is far and away the best view."

Daniel looked up at the guard towers, which stood perhaps six extra feet above the top of the wall. The nearest guard stared curiously at the little group of people approaching the dealer's gate. Daniel knew he looked mostly at Flor. She still wore the silks, though she rode a horse. The long skirts slipped up to show off her riding boots, which was more than most men got to see of a woman other than their wives.

The mule dealer waited, his corrals sporting a selection of animals ranging from fair to indifferent in quality. Right away Flor showed she was not so helpless as her act might have led the dealer to believe. "I have seen the *zopilotes*, the buzzards, turn away in disgust from better than these. If this is the best you have to offer, I must tell Lieutenant Zamaniega we have decided to go to another town."

The dealer quickly protested that she should not act in haste until she had seen his entire offering, that in reality these were but the culls taken out to make selection easier for her; the good mules were in a lower pen and were the ones he had intended to show her from the beginning.

"Milo," she said, "the good Lord left you with many shortcomings, but he did give you an eye for mules. And you, Daniel—as a farmer you're probably good at pickin' animals to work. I'd be obliged if you-all would select them."

It didn't take long. Daniel marveled at the easy skill the dealer's peons showed with the rawhide *reata*, roping the mules as Milo and Daniel pointed them out. The mules came without hesitation when they felt the loop; Daniel suspected they had been taught to expect the other end of the rope if they did not respond.

The deal called for packsaddles and ropes and canvas. Haggling over prices of these was again Lalo's chore; the price of the mules had been set at the lieutenant's house. By a little before dark the deal was made and the mules were led out. Lalo had exacted three extra horses, explaining that they might be needed should the party again encounter Indians.

Clear of the dealer's, Flor told Milo, "I want the supplies boated across the river tonight. We'll take no chance on losin' any of this."

Milo nodded. "You done right good on the tradin', Flor; I'll give you due credit for that. But seems to me like you've forgot one important detail. Without your ol' daddy, this whole thing is nothin' but a pleasure trip, and I ain't seen hide nor hair of him."

"Wrong. You saw him right after we came across the river."

Milo blinked.

"What're you talkin' about?"

"You looked straight at him and didn't know him. His hair and his beard were too long."

Milo's mouth dropped open. "Them prisoners!"

Flor turned in her saddle and pointed her chin toward those gray prison walls. "He's in yonder."

Milo swallowed and looked at the walls and swallowed again. "When did you find that out?"

"Six months ago. It's been nice for a change always to know where he's at."

Milo's face darkened. "How come you waited so long to tell us? We had a right to know."

"When the time came. The time has just now come."

Milo looked for a moment as if he were tempted to hit her. "If Cephus is in yonder, the whole trip is wasted."

"No, it isn't. All we got to do is get him out."

Milo was so angry that he dismounted so he could pace and kick sand. "Bust him out of that prison? You're as crazy as *he* is, and that's some."

"I got a plan. It came to me quick as I saw them marchin' him and them others down the road to the irrigation ditch. Come mornin' we'll just ride down to that ditch and take him away from the guards."

Milo sputtered. "You think it'll be like takin' milk from a baby's lips? In broad daylight, with a long run before we make the river, and with them shootin' at us every step we make, every stroke we swim? And maybe comin' after us, too? There ain't no Texan army on the other side to keep them from comin' across."

"You knew there was risk in this trip before you started."

"Risk is one thing. Suicide is somethin' altogether else."

"You think of a better way?"

"I'll study on it some."

"While you're studyin', the rest of us will be out there by daylight to bust that old man out of jail."

"More likely you'll join him inside of it. Believe me, it's no fit place for man or mule."

Lalo Talavera broke a frowning silence. "For once, pretty lady, I think Milo is right and you are wrong. You should not always keep coming up with surprises."

She held her patience. "That's a habit from handlin' men like you most of my life. The only way is to keep them off balance."

"You have *us* off balance; of that you can be certain."

She turned to Daniel, asking him with her eyes. He said reluctantly, "Milo could be right. Takin' them guards could get somebody killed."

"If it wasn't for the silver, I'd let him stay in there till he rots. But I ain't goin' back to San Antonio empty-handed; I've made up my mind to that. When I go back, people are goin' to lift their heads and take notice. Like it or not, we got to get him out."

They went by each merchant's in turn and packed the mules. That done, they headed toward the river to hire a boat which would carry the packs across and cut down the risk of soaking the supplies unnecessarily. Daniel figured they would likely soak them in other crossings of other rivers, but there would be time enough later to worry about that. He had about all the worrying he needed right now thinking about breaking Carmody out of prison.

Flor did not accompany them all the way to the river. She chose to stay at the lieutenant's house. "I want to sleep on a real bed instead of a rawhide cot or a wool blanket."

Milo said resentfully, "The lieutenant will be glad to share with you."

"Nothin's goin' to happen. The *dueña* is there."

"Probably too deaf to hear thunder and sleeps like a drunkard."

"I don't see that it's any of your concern."

It was none of Daniel's concern either, but he sided with Milo. "That Zamaniega ain't a man to be trusted."

"No man is to be trusted," Flor said, "so I never have."

She went into the house and out of sight. Daniel watched until he was satisfied she wouldn't show herself again. "Quick as we get that stuff across, I'm comin' back. I ain't just about to leave her here alone."

Milo was only half listening. A notion had come to him; he was vastly pleased with himself. "Don't worry, friend Daniel. It'll be a shorter night than she figures."

They put several packs of supplies in the boat and watched it pull away for its first trip across. Milo still smiled crookedly, keeping his idea to himself.

Daniel began to feel irritated. "You look about to bust."

Milo turned, smiling, "Boys, I got it all worked out if you'll go with me."

Daniel was dubious, for most of Milo's schemes

had gone to hell in a handbasket. But he didn't like Flor's, either. "I'll listen to it; that's all I'll promise." Armando Borrego had gone across with the boat, as had a couple of the other men. Lalo had stayed with Milo and Daniel and the mules. Lalo shrugged. "Like the farmer, I will listen."

Milo said, "I can show you easier than I can tell you. When we get the last of the goods across, we'll keep the mules here; we'll need them. We'll need all the men we got, too, except maybe Paley Northcutt. He can stay over yonder and guard the stuff."

It was dark when the last of the supplies had been boated safely to the Texas side of the river and Armando Borrego brought his brother and their two friends with him. Bernardo argued, "The *señorita* wanted me to watch after the Paley Northcutt."

"Paley Northcutt is old enough to watch out for himself," Milo said. "Right now we got need of you on this side."

He led them up the dark streets toward the prison. Daniel looked about nervously, watching the Mexican people moving like shadows, showing briefly against candlelight and then disappearing in darkness. "Whatever we're goin' to do, Milo, reckon hadn't we ought to wait till everybody has gone to bed?"

"I want us to be done *before* anybody goes to bed," Milo responded. "Especially Flor." He hauled up as the high walls loomed ahead, dark and forbidding. "Besides, we'll attract less attention now than later. There's still lots of people on the streets; us few extra won't be paid no notice of. And when it's over, we'll just get lost amongst the people millin' around."

Daniel looked at the mules and the packsaddles and the ropes. The only thing he could figure was that

Milo intended them to throw these ropes over the walls and somehow climb up on them. If that was his intention, Daniel was determined that Milo could go by himself.

Lalo voiced his own doubt. "The wall is there and we are here, and I do not think I like either."

Short of patience, Milo said, "Every prophet in the Good Book was beset by doubters."

"You been a damn poor prophet," Daniel pointed out.

Milo shrugged off the criticism and pointed. "See that barred window? That's where the cells are at. There's four big cells, all on this one wall. Other side's given over to guard barracks and cookin' area and armory and such. The prisoners are kept in these four cells right here."

Daniel demanded, "How do you know?"

"Friend, I been a guest in there."

"How do we know which one Cephus Carmody is in?"

"We don't. We'll just have to bust all four."

Daniel stared, not believing what he had heard. "Just us seven?"

"That's one man for each window and three left over. You couldn't ask for no better odds."

"The hell I couldn't." Daniel's anger began to rise when he thought how Milo had brought them to the foot of these prison walls on a fool's errand. "Milo Seldom, you've had some crazy ideas, that's fair certain. But I swear this is the worst one of all. Bad as Flor's idea was, it beats this. I'm goin' back to watch out for Flor. You comin', Lalo?"

Milo reached out and grabbed his arm. "You-all ain't heard me out. I tell you, it's easy as pourin' water out of a boot. The mules'll do all the work, and there ain't nobody takin' a chance, hardly."

Daniel glanced at Lalo and the others. They seemed inclined to listen, so he decided he would too.

Milo said, "Four windows, three mules apiece. One man will handle each set of mules. I'll take the ropes and go stroll along right by the wall. It's so dark the guards ain't apt to pay me no special attention. They're mostly watchin' the yard anyway; they sure ain't lookin' for anybody tryin' to bust in from outside. I'll pass one end of the rope up to somebody through each window and get them to tie it to the bars."

Daniel considered the plan, skeptical at first. But the more he thought on it, the better chance it seemed to have, even if it did come from Milo. *Everybody* had to win once in a while.

They were stout ropes, and there were plenty of them, so Milo took three coiled ropes per window, one per mule. He put the coils over his arms and walked slowly, falling in behind a strolling Mexican family until he had made his way across the street to the wall. He stopped there, testing to see if the guards in the towers showed any response. Daniel watched closely, holding his breath. He saw no sign that Milo had been noticed.

Milo gave the guards plenty of time, then began walking slowly again, right against the wall, until he came up beneath the first barred window. The bottom of it was a couple of feet above his head. Listening intently, Daniel could not hear him call to the men inside, but he assumed Milo must have done so. He saw a hand reach down to meet Milo's hand, and saw the ends of three ropes go up. Milo paused, again waiting for guard reaction. Seeing none, he dropped the three ropes and moved on.

It took him only a few minutes to make the four windows, though Daniel would have sworn at the time that it took an hour. He could not see any movement at the third and fourth windows because of the distance and the darkness, but he could tell from Milo's actions that all was going well. When Milo dropped the last set of ropes, that was a signal for Armando Borrego to start in with his three mules. In a moment Bernardo followed, and then Lalo and finally Daniel. Daniel felt his heart thumping, and he resisted a strong inclination to hurry. That, he knew, would stir the suspicion of the guards, for nobody tried to hurry a set of mules.

Daniel reached the ropes beneath his window and halted the mules. As casually as he could, he picked up the ropes one at a time, making sure they were not entangled, and tied each securely to a mule. He thought surely he would be seen, or one of the others would be seen, but it was as Milo had said: nobody ever tried to break into prison, only *out*.

At the window he could see prisoners clamoring to look, excitedly encouraging him to strike those mules smartly and break open this accursed stone wall. He tried to hush them, but they couldn't hear him for the noise they were making. He wondered how the guards could miss it.

"*Andolo, hombre!*" somebody shouted from inside the cell.

A guard on the center tower came awake. "*Quién vive?*" he called suspiciously. He could as easily have been looking at one of the other three, but somehow Daniel knew he was the one under surveillance.

He heard Milo's shout at the far end of the wall and broke into a trot, leading the three mules. Then he stepped aside and shouted "Hyahh!" slapping the nearest one on the rump with his hat. Before they hit the ends of the ropes, they were running.

The ropes jerked taut with a whispering sound, and Daniel heard the crunch of the iron bars being wrenched loose from the stone that held them. The mules stopped abruptly, one going down threshing. Quickly Daniel got in front of them, helped the downed mule to its feet and began tugging at them, urging them, to pull hard against the bars.

He was too busy with his own problem to do more than glance at the others in the party. He saw that Lalo's mules had broken their bars completely out of the wall at the first try, and shouting, cheering prisoners were crowding out through the hole like so many happy ants. Daniel kept urging his mules, and the prisoners in the cell pushed against the bars. Suddenly they jerked free and the mules knocked Daniel to the ground as momentum sent them surging forward. He got a hoofmark on his left ribs in the excitement, losing half his breath. But this was no time to be lying in the street. The guards were shooting indiscriminately into the darkness, among the fleeing prisoners. Fortunately they were slowed by the effort of reloading their rifles after every shot.

Milo was running up and down the wall shouting, "Cephus! Cephus Carmody!"

Prisoners came swarming out of the ruined wall through four gaping holes, clambering, scrambling down amidst the fallen stones. No one responded to Milo's call. "Cephus! Cephus Carmody, we come for you!"

One of the guards seemed to have found Milo Seldom and to have concluded that he was the source of the trouble. He fired, and Milo stumbled. For a breath-stopping moment Daniel thought he was hit, but Milo got up and began running again. He lost all sign of religion.

"Cephus! Goddamn your soul, Cephus Carmody, we're bein' shot at out here! Where the hell you at?"

Daniel was almost run over again, this time by fleeing prisoners. One grabbed and hugged him in the Mexican *abrazo* of friendship, which Daniel thought was not the brightest idea in this time of danger. He caught his mules but almost lost them again in the excitement.

In a minute the cells were empty. All the prisoners had disappeared into the night, leaving only a lingering of dust. Milo Seldom ran once more along the wall, shouting for Cephus Carmody and getting no answer.

Well, almost none. From the top of the wall now came a steadily increasing fire as extra guards came on the run, shooting at anything they saw move. They saw Milo Seldom move very rapidly, running for the other side of the street as hard as he could go. Bullets kicked up dust around him, but in the darkness the guards could not see their own sights. Milo plowed past Daniel, unable to speak but only waving his hand for Daniel to come a-running.

Guards and officers began streaming out, shouting in anger, shooting at anything which moved or seemed likely ever to move.

Somehow the seven men from San Antonio got together where they had left their horses, and all had their mules but Bernardo. Two of his had been taken from him by fleeing prisoners, and the other had been brought down by a guard's bullet. Daniel could see they had no time to talk it out or to worry over Cephus Carmody now; pursuit was on their heels.

"Armando, you and Bernardo take these mules and get across the river, and take your two friends with you," Milo said. "Me and Daniel and Lalo, we'll show ourselves and try to lure the police off of you."

Nobody took time to discuss or argue. The four Mexicans led the mules away. The other three men swung onto their horses, Milo taking the lead.

As first pursuit came around a cluster of stone houses, Milo shouted, "Thisaway, boys," and loped out, away from the direction the four had taken with the mules. Daniel and Lalo followed him as fast as their horses would run. Bullets smacked into walls beside and beyond them. Daniel didn't catch a breath until they had clattered across the flagstone floor of a big patio and through an open iron gate that put them momentarily out of direct line of fire. Shouting and shooting, mounted guards came galloping after them. Milo led them a twisting, turning chase, up one alley, back down a side street, through another patio, out into the open chaparral, then back into town.

At last he reined up, Daniel and Lalo close beside him. They could hear men shouting out in the brush.

"Lost them, at least for a little bit," Milo said tightly. "While we can, we better get Flor and swim the hell across that river."

They loped up to the front of the candlelit house. Milo jumped to the ground and hit the door in a run. Through the open windows Daniel saw Flor still in green silk, seated at a table and sipping wine with Zamaniega. Milo grabbed her around the waist so abruptly that she dropped the wineglass; it shattered on the tile. Zamaniega jumped to his feet in protest, turning his chair over with a clatter. Milo gave him a push that sent him stumbling back to fall ingloriously on his rump, cursing in a manner unbecoming an officer and a gentleman.

Flor's language was little better. As Milo carried her outside, she beat at him with her small fists, demanding that he put her down. Daniel brought her horse around. Milo gave her a boost up. "Grab ahold," he said curtly. "We got a hard ride to make and damn little time to do it in."

By now the alarm had gone up and down the streets, and shouting voices met the angry lieutenant at his front door. Milo heeled his horse into a hard run, straight for the river. Flor kept shouting for some explanation until the first shot was fired from a hundred years behind them; then she just leaned low over the horse's neck and rode.

Milo said, "We decided if we had to run anyway, we'd rather do it in the dark. So we busted the prison wall down."

"Then, where's the old man?"

"He didn't come out."

Flor Carmody cursed like a muleskinner. "Damn you, Milo Seldom, I hope we all live through this. Then I can kill you myself!"

They hit the water in a run. Daniel could hear horses running behind them, but didn't take time to look back. He slid out of the saddle to allow his horse more freedom; he held onto the tail. He heard shots, and bullets plunking into the dark, swirling waters around them.

One of the horses screamed and began to thresh; it

was Flor's. She was suddenly cast loose in the water, flailing her arms, going under and coming up gasping. She couldn't swim.

Milo Seldom cried, "Flor!" and quickly left his own horse to try to swim toward her. Then he too was splashing helplessly, for he couldn't swim either. Swimming was a talent few frontiersmen developed.

Daniel knew that if he turned loose of his horse he would be helpless too; they would all drown. But he got hold of the reins and managed to pull his horse around so that he was able to grab Flor. Her hands desperately clutched at Daniel. For a moment he thought she would drag him down. Then she wrapped her arms around his body and gave him freedom to hold onto the horse's tail.

Choking, she managed to cry out, "Milo! Somebody help Milo!"

Milo Seldom was going down for the second or third time, his horse swimming free far beyond his reach. Daniel saw no chance to reach him. It appeared to him that Milo would drown; he had sacrificed himself in an effort to help Flor.

But Lalo Talavera came up from behind and grabbed onto Milo and pulled him toward his own horse. Milo's hands closed over the horse's mane, and it was plain that only death would pry them loose.

The shooting continued, a bullet kicking up water here and there, but in the darkness it would be only pure luck if the men on the south bank managed to hit anybody or anything. Daniel was too busy hanging onto Flor and the horse to try to look back, or to worry much about the rifle fire.

They came up finally on the Texas side. Knees shaking and weak, Daniel somehow found strength to

carry Flor up the soft, sandy bank. She was still choking, coughing up water. He looked back at Lalo half
dragging Milo Seldom. Milo's horse had come out
ahead and had been caught by someone in the shadows beyond the bank.

Flor held onto Daniel long after they were out of
the water, her body trembling with cold. It was the
first time he had had his arms around her, and he
didn't really want to put her down. Even with the dis-
traction of the other excitement, he found himself
stirred by her.

But this was no time to be thinking of such things.
For all he knew, the pursuers might be swimming that
river after them. He found one of the packs of merchandise which had been unloaded earlier from the
boat, and he set her gently upon it. Her hands lin-
gered on his arms a moment while she whispered,
"Thanks." He quickly found a blanket and wrapped
it around her shoulders and the ruined silk dress. She
still coughed a little as she watched Lalo Talavera
struggle toward them, supporting Milo Seldom.

Voice thin, she said, "You saved my life, Daniel."

"Milo tried to."

"Milo!" He thought he could hear her teeth grind.
"I wish he'd drowned!"

Lalo let Milo drop at Flor's feet. He lay coughing,
spitting up water. Scathingly Flor demanded, "You
want to tell me about it now, Milo?"

He was in no condition to talk. Flor lifted her foot
as if to kick him, thought better of it and put her foot
down. "Well, Milo, you've done it again. I don't see
how one man, all by himself, can manage to do so
many things wrong."

Daniel said, "He wasn't by himself, Flor. We was all in on it. The idea didn't sound bad at the time."

"Well, it's sure knocked the bottom out from under us now. They'll be watchin' this river like eagles. We'll have to go back someplace and camp and wait till the excitement has died away before we can make another try at gettin' the old man out of there."

Milo finally had his breath back. "I'm sorry, Flor."

She gritted, "You—" and lifted her foot again. "Aw, what's the use? Your mama ought to've drowned you like a kitten the day you was born. You're like some ill-bred colt with two left forefeet that stumbles as long as it lives. Lord help you, and help all them that touch you. Let's get this stuff on the mules and leave this river before they decide to swim over after us."

The final indignity had not yet come. They found Paley Northcutt lying flat on his back, humming foolishly to himself, a jug of *tequila* sitting within easy reach.

Flor turned angrily on Bernardo. "I thought I told you to watch him."

Milo coughed. "I figured we needed Bernardo; I sent for him."

Flor walked off into the darkness to be alone, but her angry voice left a troubled wake.

9

Now and then someone came up out of the river, and Milo would tense, ready to run. But always it was prisoners they had liberated from behind the high walls, swimming over to freedom by ones and twos and threes. None showed any disposition to cause trouble, but Daniel saw to his powder. He knew some must be hardened criminals; they weren't all in prison simply because some official didn't like the cut of their sandals. How these men planned to subsist in this alien land north of the river Daniel did not know; he doubted if many of them knew. Their first concern was to secure their freedom. Bread and beans at the moment were secondary; but subsistence would soon become a primary worry, for there was little here a man could do to feed himself if he had no gun, no knife, nothing but his hands and the rags he had worn in prison.

Flor had the same notion. "It'd be easy for a bunch to jump us in the dark."

Lalo said, "They should be grateful to us; we set them free."

"Gratitude is for when a man's not hungry. We better pack them mules and move off aways from the river till we decide what to do next."

Paley Northcutt was so helplessly drunk they had to tie him to a horse. Where he had gotten the jug, no one had figured out. "A man like Paley, he has his ways," Milo said experimentally, testing to see if Flor's bitterness toward him had abated. It had not.

She snapped, "Milo, if I hear your voice once more tonight, I'm liable to lose control and shoot you."

Milo stepped back and put a horse between himself and Flor.

Having lost her own horse to a bullet, Flor used the saddle and the horse they had intended for her father. They rode north in darkness to a place where Milo knew of a waterhole, reaching it after daylight. They made camp and ate a little. At that point they gained an inkling of the source of Paley's *tequila*. Some of the coffee was gone, evidently traded to a passer-by. By now Flor was too wrung out for anger. She said the coffee wouldn't be much good to them anyway; about all they could do was give up the quest and go back to San Antonio.

Daniel spread Flor's blankets in the shade of a mesquite and stood back to watch her stretch out in the ruined silk dress. It was dried and wrinkled now, streaked by water and mud. "Anything I can bring you, Flor?"

"Just keep them the hell away from me till I get some sleep and do some thinkin'."

Milo Seldom came up cautiously, glancing back

over his shoulder as if to be sure he had room to run. "Flor, I got to tell you somethin'."

"I don't even want to hear it."

"I'm sorry things didn't work the way I figured. I can't imagine why ol' Cephus didn't come out. I'm wonderin' if somethin' has happened to your ol' daddy."

She shrugged. "I don't give a damn about Cephus. If it hadn't been for the silver, he could've stayed in there the rest of his life and it wouldn't have bothered me none."

"Honor thy father. He *is* your father, you know."

"My mother's mistake. Now go, Milo."

Milo stepped back half a pace. "I heard you hollerin' for somebody to save me out of that water. Showed you didn't mean everything you been sayin', Flor."

"I just didn't want you to drown and rob me of the pleasure of killin' you myself."

Milo looked shamefaced. "I'm right here. Fire away."

"I'm too tired to enjoy it now. I'll do it later."

Daniel watched Milo walk away and decided it was a good time to get an apology off his own chest. He knelt beside Flor. She lay looking at him with no particular expression. She had probably told Milo the truth; she was too tired even to be angry.

He said apologetically, "Seemed like a better idea than it was."

Flor just looked at him. "No need to apologize. It was all my fault."

"How do you figure that?"

"I went on a fool's errand and took fools with me." She raised her arm to examine the ruined green sleeve.

"Just look at that dress. I was goin' to have me a dozen just like it. Now even this one ain't fit to wear."

"I'll buy you a better one someday."

"With what? I bet you ain't got a coin on you."

"I *will* have, one of these days."

"Not if you keep runnin' with the likes of Milo Seldom. Anyhow, from what Milo told me, you got a girl of your own to buy dresses for."

Daniel shrugged. "I hadn't thought much about Lizbeth lately. She seems an awful long ways off."

"And I'm near, so you think about *me*. But when I'm far off someday, you'll think of that Lizbeth girl again, or some other."

"Flor."

"Don't apologize. You're a man, and you can't help bein' what Nature made you. Was it different, men wouldn't do nothin' but hunt and fish all the time, and the human race would die out. Mother Nature knew what she was doin', only it seems to me like she gave women the bad end of it all."

Daniel said, "I better go and let you rest."

"I wish you would, but first—" She caught his arm and pulled him down and kissed him. "That," she said, "is for draggin' me out of the water."

Surprised, Daniel touched a hand to his mouth where she had kissed him. "If you ever take a notion to fall in again, let me know. I'll be there."

He left her alone. He needed to lie down and rest too, but the aftermath of the night's excitement still ran too strong for him to think of sleep. He walked around camp checking the mules staked on grass, looking over the packs. He glanced at Paley Northcutt, blissfully sleeping the day away. So far as Paley knew, this was still yesterday; he probably hadn't heard a shot fired last night. Well, Daniel thought, I heard enough for both of us. Sounded like Texas and Mexico was at war again.

Lalo Talavera lay on his blanket, watching Daniel. At length Lalo said, "Lie down, *hombre*, take your rest while you can. One never knows when he may need it."

"If I could walk this nervousness out of me, maybe I could sleep."

He went up to the little spring which furnished the water for a tiny creek that almost died stillborn; the sandy soil thirstily drank it up so that the creek ran hardly more than a hundred yards. That, he gathered from what he had seen and heard, pretty well typified much of the Texas-Mexico border country. He could remember many dry spells back in Hopeful Valley, but none had lasted so long as to bring ruination. Here it appeared to be a constant condition.

The tail of his eye caught movement across the rolling prairie. Two horsemen were approaching the waterhole. Daniel hunched over to lower his profile. The longer he squinted, the more certain he was; both men wore some kind of uniform. He backed away from the spring and into the cover of brush, then sprinted down to where the others were trying to *siesta*.

"Soldiers comin'," he said loudly.

Milo Seldom raised up, blinking sleepily. "Soldiers?"

"Couple of them. The uniforms look Mexican to me."

Milo got to his feet, momentarily confused, slow in waking up. "Just two soldiers? I figured they'd bring a bunch if any came at all."

They roused Lalo and the others; Paley Northcutt

was still beyond reach. Milo was saying they had better pack the mules and be gone while the going was good. Flor Carmody went to see for herself and came back. "Runnin' from two soldiers don't hardly seem necessary."

Milo suggested, "They may be scouts for a larger troop."

She said, "So they see us run and send back for the others. Best thing is to stay low and take them by surprise."

Daniel said, "We didn't shoot nobody last night. I ain't keen on shootin' some poor soldier that's just doin' his duty."

"Any Mexican soldier over here is trespassin' on foreign soil," she said, blissfully ignoring the fact that in a sense they had all done the same thing yesterday. "Anyway, we'll just take them prisoner till we get farther from the border. They've probably never seen Texas anyhow. The education will do them good."

The Borrego brothers moved the mules farther back into the brush. Daniel and Milo and Lalo Talavera took their rifles and spread out on either side of the trail. Milo told Flor to "Git back out of the way!" She didn't; she brought her heavy old rifle and dropped to her knees beside Daniel.

The two horsemen kept coming. Daniel said, "I can't figure what they're doin' over here. They got no jurisdiction."

Flor said, "They got jurisdiction anywhere there's nobody to stop them. A lot of Mexicans cuss Santa Anna for givin' up Texas all the way down to the Rio Grande. Figure they got it took away from them, and maybe they did."

The two men were so near now that Daniel could

hear the squeak of their saddles. He leveled his longrifle, ready to fire if he had to. The two men were almost abreast of him now, no more than thirty feet
away. They reined up, suspicious. Daniel's hands
tightened on the rifle, and he held his breath.

He heard a voice say, "Now, don't nobody shoot.
We ain't Meskin soldiers."

Flor flung out a profanity and pushed to her feet.
She said roughly, "All right, boys, you can put your
rifles down."

"That's right, boys," the older rider grinned through
his graying beard. "We're harmless."

Flor declared, "I didn't say *that*. I just said for them
not to shoot you."

This, Daniel realized, was the same bearded, long-
haired old man he had seen among the prisoners yesterday on the road, the one who had stopped to stare
at Flor. This, then, was the man the whole misbegot-
ten affair last night had been intended for: Cephus
Carmody.

"Daughter," Carmody smiled at Flor, "you are a
sight for sore old eyes."

Her voice was not happy. "And you are just a sight.
Where the hell was you last night?"

Carmody took his time looking over the rest of the
group. "Well, daughter, I'll tell you all about it in due
time. Right now me and Notchy sure do need us a
drink of water. Or coffee if you got it. Or best of all,
whisky if there's any around. You don't know how
long it's been since we had us a good drink of whisky."

"It'll be a while longer," Flor told him. "You'll settle for coffee."

Carmody got down from the horse. "Coffee, then.
Even coffee ain't often come by in the *juzgado*. I

swear, daughter, you are somethin' to see. What's that thing you're wearin'?"

She still had on the green silk. "It *was* a dress, till you didn't show up last night." Her voice sounded cold, but Daniel sensed a relief she tried to cover up. Carmody gave her a tight hug. Flor protested, "After you get your coffee, you'd best go down that creek and take a bath. You smell like an old boar."

"Ain't much facilities for bathin' where we been, or any company to bathe for." He turned. "I wisht you'd say howdy to my friend and partner Notchy O'Dowd."

This time Flor's voice was genuinely cold. "I know him."

O'Dowd was a tall slim man, not unlike the outlaw Bodine. As did Cephus Carmody, he carried a beard from his long imprisonment; his hair came down to his shoulders. But despite the hair, Daniel could see how he got his name. A large piece was missing from one ear, a circular piece probably just the shape of somebody's teeth. A little eye-gouging and ear-chewing were considered fair tactics in a backwoods' barroom set-to. O'Dowd's eyes carried no friendliness as he looked over the men surrounding him. He cut his gaze finally back to Milo. "Seems like I know you. Name's Seldom, ain't it?"

Milo nodded. "I was there the night you lost a part of your ear. Wasn't me that done it, though."

"Friend of yours, as I recall. He ever heal up from the carvin' I gave him?"

Milo shrugged. "More or less, only nothin' knitted back in quite the same place as it was. In a crowd, he gets noticed."

Cephus Carmody led his horse into the camp and

rummaged around for a cup. Finding it, he poured coffee from a pot sitting on coals, held it a moment under his nose, inhaling and closing his eyes. "The prettiest woman that ever lived never wore perfume as sweet as the smell of good coffee."

Flor gave her father time to drain the cup, then she began to press him. "Where the hell was you last night, and how come you're wearin' soldier clothes? There ain't an army in the world would have you!"

Carmody cleared his throat. "Daughter, when I seen you yesterday on the road, you could've cut off my head with a sword and I'd of never bled a drop. I says to myself, I says, 'Cephus, that little ol' girl of yours has got some scheme in her head or she wouldn't be here.' Naturally I thought you'd have somebody throw a rope over the walls or somethin', so I made it a point for me and Notchy here not to be cooped up in no cell last night. I volunteered us to butcher out some goats for the guards' kitchen, and we took our sweet time gettin' her done. How was I to know you-all was goin' to bust the cells open from outside?"

He poured more coffee. "Damn, I wisht you-all had a little somethin' to lace this with. Coffee is fine, but laced coffee is *real* fine." He savored it. "Well, when all the commotion commenced, me and Notchy was as surprised as anybody. There was a couple guards standin' there worryin' awful over what was goin' on outside, so we took us a chunk of wood apiece and laid them boys away for an early night's rest. Then we put their uniforms on and walked out that front gate amongst the others. They was grabbin' escaped prisoners right and left, but they didn't pay no attention to us because we was in uniform. In the dark, what could they tell? When we got the chance, we took the borry of two good horses, and here we are."

Milo was emboldened by the fact that his plan had worked after all, even if only by accident. "All's well that ends well, it says in the Book."

Cephus Carmody looked around. "Seems to me like you got an awful lot of people here just to get me out of jail. Didn't know I was all that important." He turned to his daughter. "Ought to've figured, though. What troubled me most of all that time I was in prison was the thought of my sweet little ol' girl by herself back in San Antonio, helpless, weepin' her pretty eyes out for her ol' daddy."

Flor's voice hardened. "Oh hell yes, I cried a lot."

Cephus Carmody patted Flor's hand. "Well, girl, you don't have to grieve no longer. I'm back amongst the livin'."

"You don't smell like it. I wisht you'd take a bath."

Carmody shook his head at Notchy O'Dowd. "You hear folks say Mexicans don't care nothin' about clean, but her ol' mother was just like her—always raisin' hell at me about needin' to bathe or put on somethin' clean. That's all lies about them Mexican women; they're as bad as the rest of them to plague a man. I swear, daughter, I just got out of prison; I don't know what it takes to please you."

Flor jerked her chin at O'Dowd. "It'd have pleased me a right smart if you'd of left *him* in there."

"Why, girl, me and ol' Notchy are partners. What kind of a man would I be to bust out of jail and not take him along?"

"I expect he was the cause of you bein' there in the first place, him and his smugglin' scheme."

"Nothin' wrong with the scheme. We just had us a run of ill fortune, is all. You'll like ol' Notchy if you ever give him a chance. He's as good a friend as ever I had."

"That's damn little recommendation," she said sourly, studying O'Dowd with narrowed eyes. "We'll feed you, O'Dowd, and give you some provisions so you can be on your way."

O'Dowd shrugged. "I got nowheres in particular to go. Figured I'd stick with ol' Cephus awhile."

"No need in that. He's among his friends now."

Milo Seldom put in, "Seems to me like we could sure use an extra man or two where we're goin'."

Cephus Carmody straightened. "Where *are* we goin'?"

Flor's eyes stabbed at Milo. "I'll tell you later."

Cephus insisted, "I won't have you tryin' to run off ol' Notchy thisaway; I tell you, I won't have it. Anybody wants to be a friend of mine has got to be a friend of Notchy's too. Him and me, we been through hell together."

"We got us a plan, Papa. We don't need him."

"If there's any trouble, Notchy can give a good account of himself."

"I can tell that by his ear. Don't be askin' me no questions, Papa. Just tell him to take anything he needs and be on his way."

Cephus Carmody sat puzzling, the cup tilting in his hand until it seemed certain the coffee would spill. His eyes widened in sudden conviction. "You're after Bowie's silver! You want Bowie's silver and you can't have it without me. I knowed there had to be some reason you come to get me; you never loved me all that much."

Flor glanced quickly at O'Dowd. "Hush, Papa. You're just guessin'."

"Guess, hell! I got no secrets from Notchy. Him and me, we've talked about that silver a hundred times. That's how come we made that smugglin' trip in the first place, was to try to get us enough money together to go and hunt for that silver." He looked around the camp, seeming suddenly to realize how much equipment and supplies Flor and her party had. "By grabs, girl, I don't know how you done it, but you done it."

She said, "I didn't do it all by myself."

Milo added dryly, "That's the truth if ever the truth was told."

Cephus Carmody's grin swelled into full flower while Flor's frown grew deeper and darker. He said, "Time we get out into Indian country, we'll be countin' our guns and glad for all we got. If you want me, little girl, you got to take Notchy too."

Flor saw she was beaten. She said, "Damn you, Papa."

Cephus Carmody stretched his legs and sighed. "My, but it's good to be back once again in the bosom of my family, amongst them that loves me."

10

After putting away enough beans to have over-flowed a bucket, Cephus Carmody counted the mules and surveyed the good stock of supplies. "By George, this ain't bad at all. We've done right fine."

Stiffly Flor said, "Not *we*, Papa, *me*. This is all mine."

Carmody's eyebrows lifted. "Yours? I can't think of no virtuous way one girl could've put all this together. I hope you ain't been doin' things that'd shame an ol' daddy's heart."

"You'd of been proud. It took schemin' and under-handedness, and that's about the only thing you ever gave me."

Cephus had to know the particulars, so she told him. The old man nodded approval. "Blood always tells. Too bad you wasn't born a boy instead of a girl. We could've done big things together."

"We still can. We can go for Bowie's silver."

"Apt to be a hard trip. I've told you how it was

with me and Bowie and them others. Ain't no place for a frail little ol' girl."

"I wasn't too frail to get this far."

"But this was the easy part. You'd be better off to wait for us in San Antonio. We'd bring you your share just like if you'd gone."

"Sure you would, Papa, the first time it ever come a three-foot snow on the Fourth of July. Forget it. I got the biggest investment here, and I'm goin' to protect it."

"You figure all the leverage is on your side?"

"Without these mules and supplies, there ain't *nobody* goin' after that silver."

"Without the knowledge I got in my head, them mules and supplies ain't worth one smoke puff in hell to you. Looks to me like I got a little leverage myownself."

They stared hard at each other, neither giving an inch. Daniel watched, figuring that sooner or later one would weaken.

"You ain't goin', girl," Cephus gritted.

"Like hell I ain't. Last time you told me what to do was when I was about fourteen. I'm goin', Papa, and you'd just as well get that into your thick old skull."

Carmody finally turned away, but he hadn't surrendered; he had just let it come to a Mexican standoff. He muttered something to the effect that the new generation had no respect for anything.

Flor got in the last word. "I respect money, Papa, same as you do."

They packed the mules and saddled the horses and headed north. If they had known just where the San Saba mission lay from here, they could have cut northwest and made directly for it, but Cephus Carmody needed landmarks. These could be had only by going most of the way back to San Antonio, original starting place of Jim Bowie's expedition.

Milo Seldom fell in beside Cephus as they rode, telling him how good it was to see him again, sympathizing over the stubborn and vindictive ways of his daughter. Milo said, "She didn't inherit your kind nature, Cephus. I swear, sometimes she seems like she bites to see how much blood she can draw."

"Just like her mother was, God rest her," Cephus nodded. "A sweet and gentle woman, but *mean*. You go tell Flor we can't take her."

"*Me* tell her?" Milo frowned. "If I was to say the sun rises in the east, she'd say it comes up out of the west just to *dis*pute me. Sometimes it's hard to remember that she's in love with me."

"Well, she ain't goin'. Somehow or other we got to impress her with that fact."

Notchy O'Dowd's face furrowed. "I could impress it on her, you just give me a little slack and stay out of my way."

Daniel was outraged. "You'll have to whip me first!"

O'Dowd glared at Daniel, and Cephus turned in annoyance to Milo. "May I be shot and skinned if this ain't a fresh-mouthed farmer you brought along, Milo. I swear, I ain't too keen on bringin' strangers amongst us on an errand of this nature."

Daniel said defensively, "I got an investment of sorts in this trip."

Milo shrugged at Cephus Carmody. "Daniel's a good boy, Cephus. I wager you'll be glad we brung him, only you got to have patience. He was pulled a little green."

Cephus said impatiently, "Well, Daniel, when I was a lad your age, they always taught us to be respectful and listen to our elders, and not talk in where there wasn't no call."

"You start workin' against Flor, I'd say there was a call."

"We're workin' for her own good, boy. She's got no business out in Indian country. You know what them heathens do to a woman when they catch her? Ain't no pretty sight to see, nor to ponder over. I got nothin' but her best interests in my mind."

Milo said, "Cephus is a man with a big heart."

Daniel doubted that, but he kept his doubts to himself. As they made the long trip north, he watched old Cephus Carmody single out the other members of the party one by one and try to agitate them against his daughter. That Flor was aware of it there could be no doubt; the old man's voice carried like the squeaking wheel of an ungreased Mexican cart.

Paley Northcutt having sobered up enough, they quit tying him to the saddle, and he promptly fell off. The second time it happened, Flor commanded, "If he falls one more time, leave him. He can walk and sober up, or he can stay there; I don't care which."

Daniel felt some sympathy for him, though not as much as the other time when he had been taken out from San Antonio and forced to walk back. This time it was his own fault. Paley fell again, but Daniel helped him remount while Flor was not looking.

Paley wheezed, "I gonnies, Daniel, you right sure you didn't bring no whisky back from Mexico? Don't hardly seem natural for a man not to bring along a little drop of kindness."

"We was too busy to think about it."

Paley nodded regretfully. "Sure would ease the miseries if I just had me a little somethin' to smooth the wrinkles out of my innards. You got no idea how they can cramp up."

"I'm sorry. Maybe if you'd just leave it alone . . ."

Paley winced from the pain. "I was sober the first twenty-five or thirty years of my life. There's worse things in this world than bein' drunk." He wiped his watering eyes and caught sight of Cephus, who now was talking to Milo and Lalo. "Ol' Cephus, I reckon he's mighty worried somethin' bad'll happen to Flor."

"She's a grown woman. She's earned a right to do what she wants to."

Paley frowned. "She ain't spoke a word to me. She's got a right to be mad."

"I reckon she has."

"I made her a promise, and I broke it. But, I gonnies, I won't again."

Daniel shook his head. "I'm sure you won't," he said, though in truth he was not sure at all. He figured Paley Northcutt would stay sober only so long as he could find nothing stronger than coffee to drink.

Daniel was not with Paley the next time he fell, but Flor was nearby. She caught the horse and held onto the reins. Without a sign of pity, she demanded, "Get on your feet, Paley!"

Paley struggled onto hands and knees, got up into a hunched position, then sank back to his knees, exhausted. Daniel started to dismount and help him. Flor cast him a quick, angry glance. "You stay right where you're at, Daniel. Let Paley get up for himself."

Paley managed it, somehow. He started unsteadily for his horse, but Flor swung the animal around behind her own horse. "No, Paley, I said you'd walk if you fell again, and I meant it."

"Flor, I can't . . ."

"You can if you have to. And right now you have to." Most of the other men had gathered around. She said to them, "Don't none of you move to help him. If he's a man, let him help himself." She motioned for them all to move away. She held back until they did, then came along at the rear, leading Paley's horse. Paley staggered after her, calling a couple of times, then giving up appealing to her. He kept on walking, though his steps were short and painful. Daniel said to Flor, "Even if he keeps walkin', he can't walk as fast as these horses. He'll drop way behind."

"But he'll get cold sober doin' it. And he'll think hard before he pulls that stunt again on this trip—if he even gets the chance."

"The sun's pretty hot. It could kill him."

"You leave him alone, Daniel; let him suffer it out."

"And if he dies?"

"We'll bury him. Now you go on up yonder and leave Paley alone."

Daniel knew he ought to argue a little stronger for Paley, but he also knew she wouldn't pay attention. He wasn't ready yet to defy her altogether. He rode on ahead, as he was told. Old Cephus Carmody sat on his horse, watching, the shirt of his uniform unbuttoned all the way down and lifting with the hot wind. "Kind of got a hard streak about her, ain't she, boy?"

Daniel frowned, not caring to share Cephus' company. "She does what she thinks is right."

"A woman always does, and she's often wrong. But there ain't no reasonin' with an unreasonable woman. That's how it was with her mother. I always went ahead and done what I wanted to. She'd cloud up and thunder, and you'd even see a little lightnin', but by and by she'd pick up and come after me. Man don't ever want to let a woman take over the authority, boy. That's a lesson you better learn now; it'll save you a lifetime of grief."

"Flor's still runnin' this outfit."

"But it ain't her place. A woman's place is *behind* her man."

"Flor ain't got a man."

Cephus eyed him with speculation. "So that's it. I been wonderin' to myself why a nice young farmer like you would be along with my daughter on a dangerous scheme like this one. Now all of a sudden I think I see. You got designs on her, ain't you?"

Daniel was scandalized. "Mister Carmody . . ."

"No offense taken on my part, boy. Even if she is my daughter, I know how a man thinks. I done a right smart of that in my life, and I ain't too old to do it again given the proper opportunity. But let me tell you right now that a woman don't put out them favors free of charge; she'll make you pay if she can. Don't ever let her get the advantage."

"I got no such intentions toward your daughter, and she wouldn't think of it either."

"Boy, you got a lot to learn. But a trip like this ain't no place to learn it; we got enough other things to worry about without frettin' over the plottin' and intrigues of a devious woman. When we get close to San Antonio, we got to leave her."

"You'll get no help from me."

"Then we'll take no interference from you, either. You better study on that, farmer."

Notchy O'Dowd had dropped back to hear the last

of it, and a hard look from him backed up what Carmody had said.

Paley had fallen so far behind that Daniel finally could no longer see him. He turned his horse and back-trailed to where Flor was bringing up the rear, leading Paley's animal. He said, "I'm goin' to see about him."

"You heard what I told you."

"I don't give a damn what you told me. Give me Paley's horse."

She looked at him oddly, more startled than angry. "I'll go back with you," she said, and hung onto the horse.

Daniel took that as a bit of a victory for each of them and was willing to let her have her part of it. For his own part, he led out and stayed in the lead all the way back to where Paley was doggedly dragging himself one painful step at a time. Paley halted and swayed, tongue running over dry lips as he rubbed sweat from his face onto his sleeve. "I'd of made it, but I'm glad you come."

Daniel said, "We figured Flor had made her point with you."

"Oh, she did; she most certainly did. I'll never again lift a jug to my lips without I think of all the walkin' I done lately."

She said, "That won't stop you from liftin' it though, will it?"

"No, Flor, I'd lie if I told you otherwise."

She shook her head. "Even smallpox can be cured sometimes, but not a hard-drinkin' man. Paley, can you get on the horse by yourself?"

"I reckon I can." And he did. The heat and the walk had burned much of the alcohol out of him.

She said, "You'll kill yourself drinkin' thataway."

"But I'll die with a smile on my face. Ain't many people can say that with a certainty." His gratitude was plain. "I thank you for comin' back, Flor. You got a heart of purest gold."

"And a brain of cornmeal."

Even on horseback, Paley had trouble keepin up. As they closed in on the others, Daniel could see them bunched up, old Cephus talking and gesturing. Flor scowled. "Would you like to bet a dollar on what he's talkin' about?"

Daniel said, "They won't pay any attention to him. Not Milo and them."

"Would you like to bet two dollars?"

Cephus kept up his intrigue all the way north, hunting out the men one at a time, except Daniel, for Daniel had made it plain enough where he stood. It seemed to him that Cephus spent an inordinate amount of time riding beside Milo Seldom, always talking as if his tongue were going to fall out tomorrow and he had to get all his say in now. Flor got to carrying her rifle across her lap.

They came eventually to an old cart road that ran east and west, weaving its way through the live-oak timbered hills, seeking out the easiest passages, though these had rough places that would jar loose a cart rider's teeth. Cephus Carmody pointed east. "That-away," he said, "lies San Antonio." He turned and pointed northwest. "The road just goes a little ways, but where it plays out, and many days on past, is the San Saba mission."

Flor nodded, for she knew well enough what road this was. The country around San Antonio held few secrets for her. "All right, Papa, you lead us out."

"I'll lead, but us don't include you. We're goin' west; you're goin' east, daughter."

Flor's mouth went hard, and color surged into her cheeks. "Been expectin' this from you, Papa, but it won't work. This is my outfit, and these men are takin' orders from me."

Cephus braced his hands on the saddle and leaned back, his smiling face a picture of total confidence. "You think so, girl? Suppose you just ask them."

Flor cut a quick glance at Seldom. "Milo?"

Milo looked at the girl, but couldn't long face those sharp eyes. "Now, Flor, you got to give ol' Cephus credit for watchin' out after your safety. There ain't a one of us wants to see any harm come to you."

Flor saw her answer. She looked to Lalo Talavera. "Lalo?"

Lalo said in Spanish, "I have only respect for you, my little flower, and a warm spot for you in my heart. But a woman's place is in a man's kitchen or in his bed, not in his way."

Bitterly Flor said, "I never had much confidence in Milo, but I trusted you, Lalo."

"You can always trust me, little flower. I will see that your interests are protected. And sending you back to San Antonio will protect your person as well."

The Borrego brothers sat on their horses beside Lalo, and their apologetic shrugs showed they agreed with him. Armando said, "We shall see that you get your share of riches, Flor."

Flor saw that the other men were in agreement. All

except Daniel and Paley Northcutt. Daniel said, "I'm with *you*, Flor." Paley said, "Me too, girl. Just tell me what you want me to do."

Cephus Carmody still grinned. "A man don't have to be smart with his ciphers to know whichaway the wind blows, daughter. You got one farmer and one drunk. Everybody else agrees with me. Now, this bein' a democracy and all, it looks to me like you're pretty badly outvoted."

Flor declared, "I ain't said nothin' about democracy. I'm still givin' the orders here, and there ain't no vote bein' taken." She swung the rifle up from her lap and pointed it at her father. "We're *all* goin' west, like we figured from the start."

Cephus looked at the huge bore, but he seemed not particularly disturbed. "Another thing about you, girl, you're unstable. Now, who do you think you're goin' to shoot with that thing? Me? You wouldn't shoot your old daddy; you love me too much. Anyway, if you was to shoot me, you wouldn't have nobody to point the way to that silver. And if you don't shoot me, there ain't no use in you shootin' anybody else, is there?"

Flor's knuckles were white on the rifle.

Daniel said sharply, "Maybe *she* wouldn't really shoot anybody, but I would."

Cephus cut him a look of sharp impatience. "Who? Pick you one." When Daniel did nothing, Cephus growled, "I swear, farmer, I wonder why you ever left the plow."

Milo Seldom said, "Friend Daniel, we're doin' what's best for Flor. I'd sure be better suited if you didn't interfere."

Notchy O'Dowd pushed his horse up a little. "He

ain't goin' to interfere," he said threateningly, his narrowed eyes on Daniel.

Angrily Daniel pushed his own horse forward to meet O'Dowd. Flor reached out to grab Daniel's arm. "He's just baitin' you, Daniel. There ain't nothin' you can do but get yourself whipped."

"It'd take some doin'," Daniel gritted.

"But he would do it. You want to come out of this with just one ear, like he's got?"

"What're we goin' to do, just give up?"

Flor let the rifle sag. "Looks like there's nothin' else we *can* do."

11

Flor stood beside her horse, watching the men trail off leading the packmules, the dust slow to settle behind them in the hot stillness of the afternoon. She was saying nothing, but the set of her jaw indicated that if she did, it would not be fit for Christian ears to hear.

Bitterness churned in Daniel, reflecting on all he had gone through for a share of the silver, seeing it riding away and leaving him behind. "We could still catch up to them easy enough."

She turned on him. "And do what? They held all the cards, and they damn well knew it." The words were English, but in her fury she lapsed into a bit of Mexican accent.

Daniel flinched at the sting of her anger. "At least they promised they'd bring you back a share of the silver."

"They got to find it first. You want to bet on them doin' that? The old man'll be so busy thinkin' how to cheat everybody else out of their share that he probably never will find that mine in the first place. Milo Seldom ain't got the judgment to find a silver mine if he fell down the shaft. And Lalo Talavera will have his mind on how many pretty women he can buy; he won't be much help findin' the place. The rest of them, all they can do is lead the mules."

Daniel shrugged. "Well, me and Paley'll see you safely to San Antonio."

"Who said I was goin' back?"

"Ain't you? What else can you do?"

"I can follow them. Sooner or later they're goin' to need somebody with a brain bigger than a buzzard egg."

Daniel frowned. "You mean you'd go out there by yourself? That's too dangerous."

"I'd hoped you'd go with me, Daniel."

He hadn't expected that. "I'd be pleasured, if you want me."

"If I didn't want you, I wouldn't of asked."

His glow at the invitation was so warm that he gave only a moment's thought to the danger and even the folly of what she suggested. "Sure, I'll go with you."

Paley Northcutt volunteered, "You can count on me, too."

Flor frowned, regret in her eyes. "No, Paley, I *can't* count on you."

Hurt came into Paley's flushed face. He looked at the ground, gathering his arguments. "Even if I wasn't half a man, I'd be *that* much help to you; and you know I'm a lot more than half a man. I been *much* of a man in my time."

Flor touched Paley's hand. "You're still a good man,

Paley, at heart. But you know you're undependable. We'd be worryin' about you instead of watchin' out for the needful things."

"There ain't no whisky out there, Flor. You know it's the whisky makes me thataway."

"But the cravin' after whisky could be as bad on you as the drinkin' of it. What if we got out there a hundred miles by ourselves and you started to come apart?"

"I wouldn't, Flor. I promise you, I wouldn't."

Flor stared up at him, her anger gone and sorrow taking its place. "You know I wouldn't hurt you for all the world, Paley, if there wasn't no need. But there's no use talkin'. You can't go; we can't afford you."

Paley looked to Daniel for help. Daniel said, "Flor, maybe if—" He stopped then, for her look told him there was no use going on with it, and he sensed that she was right. Better a little hurt for Paley now than the risk of disaster somewhere out in the unknown.

Flor said, "You go on back to town."

Paley hung his head. "You know I don't want to. You know what I'll do when I get there; I'll find me a jug and a sleepin' place in some alley."

Flor looked away from him. "I'm sorry, Paley. If you push, you can make it by dark."

Paley sadly accepted the judgment. "How you-all figure to eat? They didn't leave you nothin'."

Daniel blinked, for he hadn't even thought of that. In her anger, Flor evidently hadn't either. "We'll manage."

Paley Northcutt rode east down the cart road, looking back over his shoulder as if hoping they would relent. Daniel suspected Flor wanted to, but she sternly held her ground. After a while Paley was out of sight in the live-oak timber. Daniel said, "Reckon we'd better be goin' too."

"We'll wait awhile. They may be lookin' for us to follow them. We can always track them later; I expect they'll leave a trail like the Mexican army, that damned ol' Cephus."

Daniel swung down from the saddle and seated himself against the heavy trunk of a big live-oak, the dry leaves from past seasons like a mat beneath him. "I never heard anybody talk about their daddy the way you do. Don't think much of him, do you?"

Flor sat down beside him, holding the reins. Daniel found the nearness of her aroused him a little. She said, "I suppose I talk rougher than I really feel. I love him in a way, and yet again I get so disgusted with him I could shoot him."

"Maybe it's like he says—maybe he's just thinkin' of your best interests."

"He may be my daddy, but he'd cheat me out of my own burial money if he could figure a scheme. If he found a whole mountain of silver out there—more money than he could spend in ten lifetimes—he'd still try to do me out of my share. That's why I got to be there. If he does find that silver and I'm not with him, I'll never see him again this side of hell."

"Milo Seldom wouldn't let him cheat you."

"Milo Seldom would probably lose his share too if he ever turned his back on that old reprobate. Milo's not a bad sort, but he's got a trustin' nature, like you. When they passed out the brains, he was off huntin' somethin' to eat."

Daniel considered a while, then decided to probe. "Milo has a notion you're in love with him."

She laughed aloud. "Me, with that backwoods

tramp, the seat hangin' out of his britches?" She shook her head. "I'll admit there was a time that I sort of had a feelin' towards him. That was till I knew better, till I saw how much he was like my ol' daddy—restless, no-account, keepin' what he ought to throw away, throwin' away what he ought to keep. Only difference between him and Cephus is that he ain't dishonest. Devious, sometimes, but not dishonest."

Daniel frowned. "The way you hollered for somebody to pull him out of the Rio Grande, I thought maybe . . ."

"I'd of done as much for a spotted dog."

Daniel poked at the leaves with a stick he had picked up. "I'm glad to know how you really feel."

"It makes that much difference to you?"

"It might."

He found her studying him intently, smiling a little. His first thought was that she might be laughing at him, but he decided that was not true. She simply said, "Daniel, I like you."

The smile didn't promise anything, and he wasn't asking, not yet. It was enough that she smiled.

They had sat there awhile when Flor nudged him. She pointed and whispered, "We were wonderin' how we'd eat. The Lord always provides." Daniel saw a fat doe grazing at the edge of an open grassy spot, where two good bounds would carry her back into the cover of a live-oak motte. The doe had probably seen the horses but was used to the wild ones which roamed this western country. Daniel carefully pushed to his feet, bringing up his rifle and moving cautiously to get clear of the horses before he fired. It would be no accomplishment if he bagged their supper but ran off their horses.

The doe dropped at the first shot, and he used his hunting knife to finish the work of the rifle. In a little while he had the hindquarters, the hide still on them, and the backstrap. Flor kindled a fire and drove a couple of forked sticks into the ground. She cut some of the backstrap into strips and wrapped them around a long stick, then laid the stick across the forks as the fire died down.

"Least they could've done was to've left us some coffee," she complained. "But they figured we'd make San Antonio by night."

"What do you think they'll say when they find out we've followed them?"

"We won't show ourselves till we're too far out there for them to turn us back." An expression of pleased malice came into her face. "With Cephus and Milo tryin' to lead them, they'll be in trouble and glad to see us."

The venison was done eventually, and they ate aplenty. Flor said her father and other frontiersmen of the wandering kind always ate heartily when they had it, on the assumption it might be a long wait until the next time. She broiled some more to pack for cold camp tomorrow. This done, they rode awhile. Presently Daniel glanced back over his shoulder and saw a moving figure far behind them. Flor squinted and cursed a little in Spanish. "That damned Paley Northcutt. Him followin' us, us followin' them. This is a silly situation."

They rode by a live-oak motte, cut back into it from the far side and stepped down from the horses to wait until Paley came even with them. When he did, Flor cut loose and gave him a shameless cussing that no one could have failed to understand.

Paley hung his head. "Thought I might be able to help."

"Go on back to San Antonio," she told him sharply. "That'll be the biggest help."

Paley turned around. This time, Daniel thought, he would keep going.

When Paley was well out of sight, Daniel and Flor rode again, following the plain tracks. Daniel kept his gaze sweeping the land in front of them, frequently turning, however, to look behind them. He did not really expect to find hostile Indians here, for they had not been seen this near San Antonio in a long time; but Indians were always doing what you didn't expect them to. If they had always followed a pattern like civilized people, Daniel thought, they wouldn't have been so damned much trouble.

Despite their long wait and the time they took fixing and eating a meal, Daniel found by the fresh horse and mule sign that he and Flor were catching up to Cephus and Milo's party. The two backwoodsmen seemed in no big rush to get at that silver.

"Savin' the horses," Daniel surmised.

"Savin' theirselves," Flor corrected him. "They ain't either one of them partial to sweat."

The sun went down, though the south wind continued to carry the remnant of its heat as the bright cherry-red of the clouds dulled to purple in the west. "They'll be makin' camp about now," Flor said. "I'd like to be where I could see their fire. We can make ourselves a cold camp."

Daniel was so intent on looking for sign of fire ahead that he didn't see Cephus and Notchy O'Dowd ride out of a cedar thicket until it was too late to do anything but meet them head on. Cephus looked hurt.

"Daughter, it grieves me that you don't take an order from your old daddy any more. I told you as plain as I knew how. It shames me in front of my friends for my daughter to disobey me thisaway."

"Obedience ain't in my nature, Papa. I'm that much like you."

Cephus turned his attention to Daniel. "Boy, didn't your folks teach you to obey your elders?"

"Some elders," Daniel said stiffly.

Notchy O'Dowd got down from his horse and moved toward Flor. "What this girl of yours needs, Cephus, is a good beatin' to remind her of her upbringin'." He made as if to reach for her and found himself staring into the bore of her rifle.

"You touch me," she said evenly, "and there'll be another hole in your head bigger than your mouth."

Cephus pulled his horse up closer. "Now, Notchy, ain't no need of hurtin' this little girl; a gentle talkin'-to is all she needs." He got close enough to grab the rifle barrel and give it a quick twist. Flor cried out in surprise and pain. Cephus had the rifle by then, and Flor was rubbing her hurt hand.

Notchy reached up and grabbed Daniel, jerking him out of the saddle. "A little lesson might be good for this farmer, though." Before Daniel could get to his feet, O'Dowd hit him in the face with his big fist. Daniel stumbled and went down on his back. He saw O'Dowd dive at him, and managed to roll over so that the man's whole weight didn't crush him. He lost half his breath, though, even as it was. He hit O'Dowd in the mouth and drew blood, but he sensed that he wasn't giving half as much as he was taking.

The anger surged up in him, and the hard muscles that came from farm work and guiding a plow. He got a few deep breaths to bring his strength back, then shoved O'Dowd aside so that he was able to gain his feet. When O'Dowd rushed him, the man ran into a fist as hard as a cedar knot. Daniel saw surprise as well as pain in the bloody face. He saw O'Dowd's mutilated ear and remembered what Milo had told him of this man's reputation as a brawler. It came to Daniel that O'Dowd when aroused could kill a man if given a chance. Daniel did not intend to give him one. He took a hard blow to his stomach, but in trade gave O'Dowd another taste of knuckles in the mouth. While O'Dowd faltered, Daniel swung again, catching him squarely in the right eye. It would be awhile before O'Dowd saw much through that one, Daniel thought.

O'Dowd reached down to his boot and came up with a knife. Daniel's heart jumped, and so did he as O'Dowd savagely slashed at him. The man missed by a good margin and, overextended, went down on one knee. This gave Daniel time to look around for something to use against him. He came up with a dried cedar branch. When O'Dowd tried once more to come at him, Daniel cracked it over his head. It sounded like a shot. O'Dowd went down as if it had been one.

Cephus looked ruefully at the fallen man. "Notchy," he said, "I believe you've done enough to this farmer boy. Let's let him go this time and not hurt him no more if he'll promise to behave himself."

O'Dowd raged helplessly, pushing up onto hands and knees and trying vainly to see Daniel. One eye was swollen shut, and sweat and dirt rolled into the other, blinding him. Cephus helped O'Dowd stagger to his feet and guided him to his horse. O'Dowd summoned strength to get into the saddle, cursing with every breath. Cephus turned back to his daughter and Daniel. "I hope this'll be a lesson to both of you. Don't you be followin' us no more. I'd hate to see this happen again."

Flor was immensely pleased. "I'll bet you would."

"You go on back to San Antonio now, do you hear me?"

"I hear you, Papa."

"You promise?"

"I promise."

Satisfied, Cephus rode on, leading O'Dowd's horse. It was all O'Dowd could do to stay up there.

Daniel rubbed his face and found blood on his hand. He looked at Flor in surprise. "I didn't think you'd promise a thing like that."

"Another thing I learned from my ol' daddy. I lie." She smiled. "We crossed a little stream back yonder. Let's go wash you up a little."

He lay on his stomach and cupped his hands, bringing the cool water up to his cut and bruised face. It felt good. When he was satisfied that the blood was gone, he turned over and pushed to his feet, wiping his face on his sleeve. Flor motioned for him to sit down beside a nearby live oak, and explored his face, then his hands with her gentle fingers.

"You came out a sight better than O'Dowd," she said. "I don't see anything here that ought to even leave a scar." She had cut a little tallow from the deer, and she rubbed this into the wounds. "That ought at least make it feel better."

"It feels good anyway," he said. "You know, I won that fight."

"Sure you did. You got more strength than even

you knew about, Daniel. You're *muy macho* when you need to be."

It occurred to Daniel that he had never had to prove himself back in Hopeful Valley. He had never really known how he would react when the binding got tight. Thanks to Milo Seldom and this trip, he had had several chances to find out. For that, at least, he owed Milo.

She said, "I believe you're pleased with yourself."

"Matter of fact, I am. I never much favored a man that bragged, but I can't help feelin' thisaway."

"You earned it." Touching his cheek with the palm of her hand, she stared at him a moment, then leaned forward and gently kissed him. He was surprised, but not so much so that he let the gesture go unanswered. He brought his arms around her and pulled her tight. Her hands went to his back, pressing hard. Suddenly the kiss was no longer gentle, it was hungry and urgent. The fire came up in him, and he sensed that her cheeks flushed warm.

She said, "I don't believe you've ever held a woman this way."

He had held Lizbeth, but not quite like this.

She said, "Well, you're doin' all right. Don't quit now."

Her arms tightened around him, and he knew he wasn't going to stop here where he had always stopped with Lizbeth. He couldn't have now, even if he had wanted to.

12

They had built no fire. They lay on their blankets by the little stream, listening to the crickets and the insistent calling of the night birds, staring up through the blackness of the overhanging live oak to the sparkling stars that shone through in the thin spots. Daniel said, "The more I think about it, the more I admit it's a long-shot idea, us trailin' after them thisaway. Two of us by ourselves won't be no match for any Indians we come across."

"All the tracks them others are makin', if the Indians find anybody it'll be *them*. They won't expect two more followin' way behind. If we're watchful, we won't be seen."

Daniel shrugged. "A big chance, even for all that silver."

"No chance is too big for what that silver could buy us."

"What'll it buy *you*, Flor? All I've heard you talk

about is silk and velvet dresses. I don't see how a dress could mean that much."

"It's not the dresses, really; they're just what you put up front to show. It's what the dresses stand for—money, respectability."

"Money don't mean the same as respectability. I've seen folks that had money but wasn't respectable."

"But didn't people pretend like they was, and bow and scrape?"

Daniel admitted they did.

"When I wear them silk dresses around the plazas of San Antonio, people will know I'm not just some halfbreed girl that washes other folks' dirty clothes and that they suspicion of doin' God knows what else to make herself a livin'. They'll know I'm somebody, that I got more money than they have. They'll look up to me instead of down."

"People must've mistreated you pretty bad, Flor."

"The *Americanos,* they look down on me for my Mexican blood. The Mexicans, they look down on me for my American blood. Besides, they know damn well who my ol' daddy is. If you think Americans know how to insult somebody, you ought to see an aristocratic Mexican do it; they've made it a science. You ain't been properly put down into your rightful place till you've had it done to you by some pure-blood *gachupín.* They've handled peons for two hundred years."

The bitterness was strong in her voice, and Daniel began to get some idea of how lonely a life she had led, half of one culture, half of another, not really belonging to either one. He took her hand. "To hell with people that hurt you. I'd just go somewhere else."

"If I get me a share of that silver, I'll go someplace,

but first I want to rub those people's faces in it a little."

"You ever think about livin' on a farm, Flor?"

"I've thought about it. A farmer can be as poor as
anybody else."

"But never hungry. They can't starve a good farmer
to death because he can always grow somethin' to eat.
I may not know a lot of other things, but I'm a good
farmer."

"You tryin' to ask me to marry you, Daniel?"

The thought startled him. "Maybe I am. Maybe I
was by way of workin' up to it gradual."

"Well, don't; not now. I ain't sure yet just what I
want."

Daniel frowned. "Maybe I misunderstood. While
ago I thought . . ."

"While ago I did what I felt like doin' right then.
I'm not ready to decide what I'll want to do the rest
of my life."

"You keep on thinkin' about it, anyway, and remember that I've asked you."

Though Texans usually spoke of anything beyond
the settlements as being "west," the San Saba mission
and *presidio* had actually been built as much north
as west of San Antonio de Bexar. The Spaniards had
set up the mission to convert the Apache Indians
about the middle 1700's, and had built a stone fortress just across the river to protect the mission. It did
not do its job. Comanches, enemies of the Apaches in
those days, viewed the project as an insult and sacked
the mission, leaving it a blazing ruin, priests and Indian converts lying dead in their smoky wake. The

garrison remained for several years, with its soldiers
uneasy and ineffective, but men of the cross never returned.

The way to the *presidio* had been well mapped during the years of its service, but few white men now
living had ever visited there. It was said that Jim
Bowie had paused to carve his name upon the crumbling stones at the entrance.

It seemed to Daniel that Milo and Cephus were
taking a lot of time and not making many miles;
once they paused half a day just to hunt buffalo from
among the several herds through which they passed.
Though one would have furnished them all the meat
they needed, they had left twenty dead buffalo behind
them, strung out for two miles. They had cut into
most of the carcasses only to the extent necessary to
retrieve their lead for remolding into bullets; lead was
hard to come by, and not to be wasted.

"Chased them on horseback," Daniel observed.

Flor said disgustedly, "Like kids, only this ain't no
place for kids. Where there's this many buffalo, there's
apt to be Indians."

The meat from the fat doe had not been enough to
last long. They had decided against firing a rifle and
drawing the attention of either friends or foes. Daniel had tried unsuccessfully the last couple of nights
to locate a wild-turkey roost or to catch a rabbit in a
snare. Under the shade of a big mesquite tree they
came across a young buffalo cow, wounded in the
foreshoulder and left to die.

"The wolves'll get her if we don't," Daniel said.

"I don't know how we can get her without shootin'
her."

Daniel rode up close. Maddened by pain, the cow

charged. But fevering and loss of blood had left her weak. She fell to one knee, staying there awhile, slinging her head before she mustered enough strength to regain her feet. Daniel rode in close again, circling slowly so that she kept having to turn to face him in her anger. He began moving faster, so that she had to turn faster too. Inevitably she lost her footing and went down. Daniel jumped to the ground, unsheathed his knife and plunged it into her throat, stepping back to avoid the sharp horns as she slung her head. She almost got up, then sank. In a little while she was dead.

Daniel examined the swollen wound and decided against taking meat from that area or the hump for fear of infection. He cut off the hindquarters, leaving the hide in place.

He didn't like the way he had had to kill the cow, but Flor pointed out that the wolves would have begun eating her while she still lived. "She's out of her misery now, and we may just be startin' ours," Flor worried. "If there's an Indian in twenty miles, all that shootin' and chasin' after buffalo is likely to've drawn him. By now they probably know about Milo and Cephus and them others, if they didn't before. We'd best do our travelin' by night and shade up in the daytime."

She made it as a positive statement, not asking for advice. Daniel said, "I doubt we can follow them tracks at night, even in the bright moonlight. There's too much grass on the ground."

Impatiently Flor demanded, "You sayin' I'm wrong?"

"I say you're wrong."

She stiffened, not used to being argued with. "Well,

we'll try it my way. I don't fancy havin' my hair hang in some tepee for an ornament."

They rode on, following the tracks a few more miles, then turned off into a heavy live-oak motte to build a tiny fire and cook their meat while there was yet daylight to hide the blaze. Any Indian who caught and followed the smoke smell would find only ashes, for Flor and Daniel would put the spot far behind them. The stop for cooking had given the horses a rest, so they pushed on into the dusk, and then into darkness.

The horsemen ahead of them followed a fairly straight course. But even so, in the first hour of darkness Daniel lost the trail. He and Flor both got off their horses and searched afoot for sign. They lost an hour or more.

At length Flor said sharply, "Go ahead and say it."

"Say what?"

"Say you told me so."

"I don't have to, now."

Angrily she said, "You'd better not."

Eventually it was Daniel who found the trace. He came upon droppings left by a horse or mule. On hands and knees he was able to tell where the hoofs had bruised and bent the grass. But following this thin trace in the moonlight was a slow process. In daylight they could get the trail's course and pick some distant landmark toward which the trail seemed to run. They could then make good time, pausing only now and again to be sure they hadn't lost the tracks. In the night, distant landmarks could not be seen. They followed awhile, but soon lost the tracks again.

Flor grumbled.

Daniel asked, "What did you say?"

"You wouldn't want to hear it. I was cussin' myself. It hurts to be wrong, and have the other person know it."

"I'm makin' no issue of it."

"You should. What do you think we ought to do?"

"Make a cold camp, set out again at first light."

"All right. We tried it my way; now we'll try it yours."

If they had been wary in traveling before, they were even more so now. They would try to determine the direction of the trail, then follow it in only a general way, holding to cedar and oak timber for cover as much as they could. Once in a while when they could follow a live-oak ridge down close to where they thought the trail would be, they would ride out and be sure they were still paralleling it. Always they found the tracks there, about where they were expecting them.

They stopped about midafternoon to cook up some more of the buffalo meat, careful to use only dry wood that would not put up much smoke, keeping the fire as small as was possible for it to do the job. Waiting, they watched a small armadillo digging for grubs at the edge of the motte, its high-curved shell looking like a suit of armor. Daniel pointed. "You ever watch an armadillo, really *watch* one?"

Flor shook her head. "Never was all that curious."

"Folks claim that when they have a litter, all the babies are the same—either all males or all female. They don't come mixed up."

Flor frowned, then a light of humor came into her eyes, the first he had seen in a while. "Sounds risky to me. What if the averages didn't work out? What if all

the armadillos started havin' just one or the other.
Wouldn't take long for things to get in an awful mess."

Daniel shrugged. "I reckon you just have to trus
Nature to take care of things like that."

Flor put her arms around Daniel. "I'll trust Nature
She's always been pretty good to *me*."

Daniel had spent the larger part of his life in th
gentle valleys and rolling hills along the lower Colo
rado River. The rocky limestone hills and now an
again the big upthrusts of red granite in this highe
and drier land looked like mountains to him; the
were the tallest he had ever seen. Times, in the earl
morning or late afternoon, those in the distance too
on a deep blue or purple appearance, and a fine haz
clung about them, giving them a ghostly look tha
sent shivers up his spine. Times he felt like an invade
going where the Lord had never intended him to go
reaching for things the Lord had not intended him t
have, disturbing an ageless peace, an alien land re
served for another people.

He and Flor saw deer aplenty, and doves and quai
and wild turkey. Once they saw a black bear, its roll
ing gait carrying it up a hillside into a heavy ceda
thicket. Clear streams murmured over limestone rock
at frequent intervals; cool clean water from tin
springs which broke out of the layered ledges at
thousand places.

No wonder, he thought, this beautiful, bounteou
land had long been jealously guarded by various In
dian tribes against one another, against the Spaniards
against the Mexicans and now against the venture
some *Americanos*. It gave him an awesome feeling t
know that few men of his own kind had yet beer
where he now rode. The time would come, he knew

when white men would move here as they had moved into every other Indian land so far. They would take this land and put their plows into the deep soil of these broad flats, graze their cattle on the hills, build their houses over the cold ashes of Indian camp-grounds. He wondered if any would ever know that he—Daniel Provost—had passed this way; if in any way he would leave a lasting mark on this land.

One day he and Flor came upon horsetracks, cutting diagonally across the course they were following in an effort to parallel Cephus and Milo. This new set of tracks led directly down to intercept those of the Texan silver hunters. It could have been wild horses, Daniel thought, though somehow he knew it was not.

"How many?" Flor asked him with concern.

Daniel shook his head. "Can't say for sure. Five or six."

"Well, that's not enough to jump Milo."

"It's enough to follow along and spy on them until they get a big enough bunch together." Daniel sat at the edge of the live oaks that hid him and Flor, his narrowed eyes worriedly studying the course the Indian tracks took and calculating about where they would cross that other trail. "You stay here. I'm takin' a chance and ridin' down there. It's possible the Indians came along before Cephus and Milo."

Flor stayed, nervously watching for sign of Indians, while Daniel gave the whole area a good scrutiny, cinched up his courage and rode down into the flat, where he was in broad open country except for a thin scattering of single mesquite trees. When he saw no sign of Indians, he eased a little. He followed the new tracks until they intersected the others. He swore under his breath as he saw that the Indians had come after the other party. The red men had milled around, evidently studying their discovery. One had ridden off at a northerly angle. The rest of the Indian tracks merged into those of the first group. Daniel looked around for a few minutes, then rode back to Flor.

"They're followin' Milo," he said. "They sent one man off; I expect he's gone to report to others someplace."

Alarmed, Flor said, "I hope Milo and them have got sense enough to keep awake, and not get caught by surprise."

Daniel nodded. "I think they know *that* much. Me and you, Flor, we better not both be asleep at the same time, either." He started on, moving northwesterly but taking even more pains now to stay in or near the cover of live oak and cedar. When they had to move across the open, they paused and took careful appraisal of the land around them.

As they had done before, they moved in the daytime, pausing once to cook up some meat, and kept moving until dark. The next night, dusk caught them in rough hills where rocky ground made the trail much harder to follow. For long stretches, fresh droppings were almost the only discernible sign. Daniel was almost ready to call a halt when suddenly in the moonlight he saw the ground drop away in front of him. Far below he saw a dark mass of timber and the silver sheen of a broad, winding river. He started to push forward, but the horse balked. Then Daniel realized that he had ridden out almost to the edge of a rimrock. He pulled the roan back quickly.

"Flor, that's no little creek down yonder. We've already crossed the Guadalupe and the Llano. That'd have to be the San Saba, wouldn't it?" He tried to sound matter-of-fact, but the realization brought a prickling to him, and a sudden impatience. Out yonder somewhere lay a fortune in unclaimed silver, or so people said. He started looking for a way down around the rimrock, but then he reined up, raising his hand. Across the river and some distance upstream—he couldn't tell how far—he saw a reddish dot of firelight.

Flor saw it too. "Is it Cephus' camp, or is it Indians?"

"I'm not in no hurry to go and find out." So far as he could tell, the little trailing party of Indians had crossed over the river in the wake of the treasure hunters. "I say the smart thing for us to do is stay on this side till it comes daylight and we can see the lay of the land. Otherwise we're liable to ride in on a bunch of Indians like a fly hittin' a spiderweb."

Flor followed without question as he backed away from the edge and sought cover behind the hill. It occurred to Daniel that in these long days and nights of traveling together she had begun looking to him for leadership rather than giving orders as she had done before. Up to now, at least, his leadership had not brought them into any trouble.

They backtracked a hundred yards or so from this side of the bank, where the footing was easier, and began working their way along. Daniel chose grassy ground where the horses' hoofs would not strike against rocks and make noise that might carry to the other side. At length they were about even with the fire. Daniel dismounted and led his horse into a cluster of timber to tie it. He moved afoot toward the bank. He did not have to look back to know that Flor was close behind him.

He could see the fire now, though the flames had died down to a soft red glow that put out too little light to reveal what was around it. A figure moved on the near side, but the distance was too great for Daniel to see any detail, and the glimpse was all too brief. He had no idea whether the man was white or Indian.

In the moonlight he got the impression of some large dark shadow, like a line of heavy brush perhaps, the glow in the middle of it.

Flor said, "If that's Cephus and Milo, it might be a good time to get down to them, to let them know the Indians are trailin' them."

"How we goin' to get down there without maybe runnin' into them Indians ourselves? I think we'd best hold onto what we got."

Flor accepted his judgment without argument. They sat there without thought of sleeping, watching that fire die away and the glow fade into darkness. Sometime toward morning Daniel felt Flor's weight go slack against his arm. Gently he moved her so that she lay with her head in his lap. She slept quietly, but he never did. He kept watching the point where the fire had been, trying to figure out the heavy dark shadow which seemed gradually to change in the night as the moon moved.

The moon went down, and it was dark a long time before the first light of morning began in the east, and the long shadows began to draw back toward the big pecan trees and the gnarled live oaks along the river. As dawn gradually came, Daniel watched the place where he had seen the fire. Slowly it became clear what the heavy shadows had been in the moonlight. He could see stone walls, high in places, badly crumbled in others. A chill ran up his back. His voice was shaky with excitement. "Flor, that's the San Saba *presidio*."

Flor blinked, then raised up, suddenly awake. She grabbed Daniel's hand. "We *did* make it."

"You ever doubt it?"

"Followin' my ol' daddy? You damn bet you I doubted it."

In broadening daylight Daniel could see men begin to stir, and he saw the familiar packmules staked within the protection of the walls. "That's them. I can see Milo; I can tell him even from here."

"How? Did he fall over his own feet, or somethin'?"

"We could ride down there now and they couldn't hardly run us off any more. But I'd sure like to know where them Indians are at." He realized that if he could see the men at the fortress, he could be seen too. He stretched out on his belly. He let his gaze slowly work up and down the river, through the heavy green foliage, along the riverbank. Then he saw the Indians. "Yonder, scattered amongst them big pecan trees."

Flor saw. "Wish we could go warn Milo."

"With them Indians between us, we'd better not even try."

Flor shook her head and mumbled a few cuss words. "Look at them *ladrones* down there fixin' themselves a hot breakfast. God, what I'd give for somethin' besides a chunk of dried buffalo."

It was an hour or more before the men inside the *presidio* walls began throwing packs on the mules and saddling their horses. Daniel saw Milo Seldom pour something out of a bucket near the campfire and knew it was coffee. "Damn his wasteful soul," he muttered. "Wisht I could make him eat that, grounds and all."

The men rode out the gates, bringing up the pack-mules. Daniel could see Cephus taking the lead, sitting proud in his saddle, still wearing that stolen Mexican uniform, gesturing importantly so that everyone should realize his position of leadership; he was the man who would shortly make them rich. Twenty or thirty yards outside the gate, Cephus halted his horse and carefully looked around, getting his bearings. He pointed north and a little east, then led the way up a gentle slope that seemed to promise a gentler, more even stretch of rolling hills.

Flor said disgustedly, "Puffed up like a toad, and them others makin' over him like he was the king of Sheba."

"At least he knows where the silver is at. I wisht we was down there with them."

"We got one advantage. We know where the Indians are."

"Lot of good that'll do us if they get to the mine and we're stuck up here on this high hill."

"I don't think I ever heard Cephus say how long a ride it is from the ruins to the mine—whether it's a mile or a hundred miles. All I know is that he said he had to start at the *presidio* to find it."

"If there's as much silver as they say, they can't load it all up and get away in a hurry. We'll catch up to them."

"Yeah, and maybe them Indians will, too."

The treasure party disappeared over the hill. When they were well out of sight, Daniel saw activity among the pecan trees in the river bed. Five men, all but naked, rode out taking their time.

"Reckon what they are?" Daniel mused. "Comanche, Apache or what?"

Flor shrugged. "*Quién sabe?* Indians come in two kinds: friendly and hostile. I'd hate to depend on that bunch for friendship."

Daniel watched the Indians leisurely take up the trail. They were a wild and barbaric sight to him, fascinating and yet somehow chilling. "It *is* their country," he said. "Come right down to it, we got no business here."

"I got more use for that silver than they have," Flor replied. "That silver is all I want from this country. They can keep the rest of it."

"Once white men get the silver, they'll come for the land itself."

Daniel itched to move down the hill when the Indians were out of sight and cross the river to examine the ruins. But he held himself back. There could be more Indians down there that he had not seen. He lay on the hilltop and stared a long time at the rock walls, trying to reconstruct them in his mind, peopling them with Spanish soldiers and mentally placing cannons on the four round corner towers. He knew from stories that the mission was supposed to have been on the opposite side of the river and that the Comanches had bypassed the *presidio* to attack the more vulnerable churchyard.

If any sign of the mission was left, he could not see it from here. But he could make out what appeared to be an irrigation ditch, angling away from a small man-made dam that lay partially ruined by floodwaters. The ditch led to what he judged could have been tilled fields.

"Longer I look at it," he said, "more it looks to me

like this must've been a mighty poor place. Livin' was
hard, them days. They didn't have none of our modern convenience."

"I don't expect they did."

"If they had all that silver, how come they lived so
poor?"

Flor offered no answer.

After a long time they still had seen no sign of more
Indians. Daniel said, "We just as well be movin'." He
led the way around the rimrock and down to an easy
ford which he judged had probably been used between the *presidio* and the mission. The fortress lay
just up the bank, barely past the floodline. The half-
tumbled walls brought an unexpected shiver to Daniel as he mentally pushed back the years to a time
even before his father had been born. He wondered
how many Spaniards had died here and lay buried
somewhere out yonder in a lonely, lost graveyard,
hundreds of miles from their own kind.

"Place kind of makes my back crawl," he complained.

Flor hoped to find some supplies that the hunters
might carelessly have left behind them, but there was
not a thing except one worn-out mocassin, a ragged
hole in its sole. "Milo Seldom's from the size of it,"
she gritted. "He's got a foot like a draft horse."

She's sure ridin' ol' Milo hard, Daniel thought. But
he guessed she had reason. He reminded her that Milo
had been wearing boots.

He looked at carvings on the rock at the front gate.
He made out the names of Padilla and Cos and remembered there had been a Mexican general named
Cos with Santa Anna in the big war. Then he found
the name he sought: Bowie.

Up to now all the Bowie stories had been just that—
stories. But these crudely carved letters were a reality, something he could see, something he could trace
with his forefinger.

His skin prickled, and of a sudden he could almost
see that silver—could almost taste it on his tongue.

"Let's go, Flor," he said impatiently. "That mine is
out yonder, just waitin' for us."

13

They used much the same tactics trailing Milo and Cephus as they had used the last few days, but now the brush cover was scantier as the country changed into gentler rolling hills. There were long stretches when Daniel and Flor had no choice but to risk riding out in the wide open. After a few times they eased considerably, but they rode with rifles across their laps, primed and ready.

After two or three hours Daniel found they had lost the track, trying to parallel it rather than follow it directly. He spent an hour searching, Flor moving out well to one side and helping him hunt. When finally he picked up the trail he found that the horsemen had altered direction.

Daniel suggested, "Likely ol' Cephus picked him out a fresh landmark." Offhand he could not see exactly what. He spotted a couple of hills in the line of march, but they looked about like all the others.

They moved off to one side of the trail again where

there was at least partial cover. Now and then a deer bounded off for timber. A chaparral hawk or *paisano* would sprint out of their path, building up speed and taking off to soar low across the open prairie. When Daniel decided it would be a good idea to check the trail again, it was not where it was supposed to be. Backtracking, he found the tracks leading off in a ninety-degree angle from their former course.

"Followin' another landmark," Daniel said.

Flor grunted. "Or followin' shadows. You don't know that old badger the way I do."

This time Daniel decided that if they were not to lose Milo and Cephus altogether, they would have to abandon any attempt at following the cover and just stay with the tracks. The cover didn't amount to much anyway, except sporadically.

"This runs up the odds that we'll be seen," Flor countered.

"The odds of not losin' that bunch go even higher if we don't change our ways. It comes down to a question of how bad we want that silver."

"You know the answer to that; otherwise there wouldn't neither one of us be here."

They moved cautiously across the sun-cured grass of the deep live-oak and mesquite flats, up the gentle but rocky hills, careful never to top out against a skyline if there were any other way to go. Now and again they encountered buffalo in groups of five or ten or twenty, shaggy dark beasts which edged away from the horses, for they knew what it was to be chased by bow-and-arrow hunters. Daniel had a hard time, sometimes, pulling his eyes away from the buffalo and searching the area ahead of them for sign of Indians. He had never seen many buffalo before; not many ranged down into the settled country such as Hopeful Valley any more.

"You ever see such a country for grass?" he asked, half in awe. "Drier than at home, but I bet it's sure got the strength in it. Look at them buffalo and then imagine what a man could do grazin' this country with cattle."

"First thing he'd do," Flor said, "would be to lose his hair."

"I'm not talkin' about now. The Indians can't hold it forever, not a rich-lookin' grazin' country like this. Somebody'll bring cows here one of these days, and all the Indians in a hundred miles won't run him off of this good grass."

"I'm not concerned with what's on top of the ground; I'm wantin' to get what's under it. Give me a muleload of silver and you can have all the grass from here to Kingdom Come."

Daniel said, "I bet this'd be good country for farmin', too, if it ever gets enough rain. Man, I'd like to drop a plow into one of these pretty flats."

"If there's as much silver as they claim, you'll have money enough that you won't have to drop a plow no-place unless you want to."

"I'll want to. Sure, it gets tiresome sometimes, but it takes hold of a man. If he ever gets it deep in his system, I doubt that he'll ever get it plumb out."

He reined up as the trail suddenly veered once more, almost due east this time. Daniel could tell by the tracks that the animals had milled around a good while here. He studied the skyline with sharp curiosity. "Cephus must've picked him a new landmark. But I wonder what it was?"

He saw nothing outstanding. Some hills lay yonderway, but they all looked pretty much alike, and they were little different from those he saw to the north and west, or along their back trail. "I reckon maybe Cephus knows what he's doin'."

"I'd hate to bet my life on it," Flor said, then considered. "But I am; we *all* are."

They rode perhaps an hour, following this new direction. The droppings were fresher now, so Daniel knew he and Flor were catching up. He began worrying how they could join Milo and Cephus without running headlong into those trailing Indians.

He heard a drumming sound and reined up abruptly, looking back. Flor heard it too. "Horse," she said, "runnin'."

"Horses," he corrected her, "a bunch of them." He hadn't seen them yet, which meant he and Flor probably hadn't been seen either. "We better do some runnin' ourselves. There's a right smart of timber over yonderway." He heeled his horse into a lope, looking back to be sure Flor was with him. She was. He took to rocky ground at first in hopes they wouldn't leave tracks that might be noticed. After a hundred yards or so he quit the rocks and went straight for the live-oak cover.

They had hardly reached it when he saw horsemen break out into an open flat. At this distance he couldn't count, but there must have been twenty or more, maybe even thirty. He stepped down and covered his horse's nose to make sure the animal didn't nicker to the other horses.

Flor was paling a little. It was one thing to talk bravely in San Antonio; it was something else to be out here in the midst of this unknown country, looking death in the eye. She started to say something, swallowed and stayed silent. Her wide eyes said it all.

Daniel brought his longrifle up across his left arm, cradling it for quick use. His hands trembled a little, and he found himself fervently wishing he were back in Hopeful Valley, following that plow and staring into the prosaic rear of that old brown mule Hezekiah. Why in the hell had he talked himself into coming on a wild mission like this? All the silver in Texas wouldn't do a man any good if he were lying in the sun with his glazed eyes open and his scalp gone.

The Indians held their course, loping their horses easily across the open grass. In following the plain trail left by Cephus and Milo and the others, they never saw Daniel and Flor take out for the timber. At one point they came close enough for Daniel to see the feathers in their hair and the colored designs painted on the hard bullhide shields they carried. He saw the bois d'arc bows and the feathered shafts in the quivers against their backs.

The Indians were long gone before Daniel's dry mouth worked up saliva enough for him to swallow and clear his throat for speaking. He said foolishly, "Did you see that?"

She said something under her breath and added, "I hope Milo has got his eyes open." She held out her hand and found it shaking. "What do we do now?"

Daniel did not consider long. "The Indians went thataway." He pointed. "I think we ought to go thisaway. We can still move in the same general direction but keep a hill or two between us and them."

"What if Cephus changes direction again?"

"Damn him, he'd just better not."

They had to ride two miles or more in a tangent

efore they found a saddle in the hill and could ride
p over it to regain more or less their original direc-
on. Moving down the far side, Daniel halted awhile
nd dismounted to study the land below them. He
pent ten or fifteen minutes before he was satisfied
hat nothing moved except a few buffalo. Their pres-
nce convinced him there weren't any Indians around.

"You all right, Flor?" he asked, concerned.

"You just keep movin'. You won't leave me be-
ind."

They rode most of the afternoon. They had just
vatered their horses and crossed a little creek when
Daniel once more spotted the tracks, moving at right
ngles to the direction he and Flor had been riding.
Cephus has switched again. Only this time there's a
ot more horses. That whole bunch of Indians is
ailin' after him."

Flor said, "I can't for the life of me figure why Ce-
hus keeps changin' direction so much."

"Maybe he's tryin' to shake off the Indians."

"Only way he can do that is to flap his wings and
y."

As before, Daniel gave up trying to parallel the
racks. If Cephus was going to keep changing course,
he only way to keep from losing him was to take a
hance and follow the tracks, Indians or no Indians.
Daniel kept turning his head, anxiously searching the
ills around them. Doing this, he nearly missed the
racks when they shifted yet again.

"Daydreamin'?" Flor chided him gently.

"Daydreamin' hell; I'm tryin' to keep our hair on."

They had ridden in the new direction no more than
hirty minutes when the horsetracks skirted around
cedarbrake. Any kind of cover that might hide an

ambush brought the hair to a stand at the back o
Daniel's neck. He took a long, hard look at the ceda
lifting the rifle up a little from his lap. He saw noth
ing suspicious, though a hard knot seemed to start a
the pit of his stomach. Only when they had ridde
past the brush did he finally take a deep breath an
ease the rifle back down. He turned to look ahead o
him again.

He heard a whispering sound and saw somethin
fly past him. For a second he thought it was a bird
till he saw it strike the ground in front of him.

An arrow!

"Run like hell, Flor," he shouted. "They're afte
us!"

He didn't have time to tell her twice. He heard
whoop behind them. He drummed his heels into Sar
Houston's ribs and made straight for a rock outcro
he could see ahead. It came to him that this could b
a ruse, that the Indians behind them might be settin
a trap and a dozen others might be waiting behin
those rocks. But he saw no other chance.

He heard more whooping and saw another arrov
flit past him, wide of the mark. He glanced back onc
and saw a pair of riders heeling their ponies as har
as they could go.

Daniel and Flor made the rocks and jumped dow
from their horses, grabbing hard at the reins whil
they swung around and brought up their rifles. Th
two Indians saw they had let their quarry get away
They pulled their horses up, shouting in anger.

Daniel's jaw fell. "Them ain't men, they ain
nothin' but kids. We been runnin' from a couple o
Indian kids!"

At this distance, he judged the boys to be twelve o

ourteen years old, nearly naked, each carrying an un-
dersized bow. Their feet did not reach down to the
level of their ponies' bellies. But they shouted insults
and shook their bows threateningly like men.

Flor said, "Boys or not, they could do you some
hurt."

"Damn kids," Daniel fumed, "I can't shoot one of
them."

"They'll shoot us if they get the chance."

Daniel stood up, the rifle in his hand, and tried to
wave the boys away. "You two, get the hell out of
here! We don't want to hurt you!" He knew they
wouldn't understand the words, but he thought they
should understand his gestures. When they didn't retreat, he shifted the rifle to his left hand, reached down
for a biscuit-sized rock and hurled it at the boys. It
missed.

In reply they sent two arrows at him. One missed
by four or five feet.

Flor remarked, "That boy'll be ready for war paint
by next year. You better watch him."

"I ain't taken my eye off of either one." He saw the
boys putting their heads together, hastily parleying.
Their decision was unmistakable.

"Godalmighty, they're fixin' to charge us."

The two boys put their horses into a run, each
reaching back to his quiver and bringing an arrow to
the bowstring.

Daniel swallowed. "God knows I hate to do this."
He brought the rifle up and sank to one knee for
steady aim.

Flor said, "Daniel, you wouldn't . . ."

Daniel squeezed the trigger. The powder flashed in
the pan and the rifle roared, smoke belching from the

barrel. A horse squealed and went down, its ride
pitching headlong out into the grass. The young brav
broke his bow.

"Shoot the other horse," Daniel shouted. Flor fired
The second horse fell, perhaps thirty feet past the firs
one. The boy seemed to have expected it and lande
on his feet running, trying to fit another arrow. Dan
iel stood his ground, knowing he had no time to re
load the rifle. When the boy paused to loose the arrow
Daniel dropped. The arrow struck the rock. Danie
tossed his reins to Flor and sprinted out. Using his ri
fle like a club, Daniel brought it smashing dow
across the lad's wrists. The bow fell useless.

The second boy was on his feet, rushing with
knife. Daniel parried the thrust with his rifle barre
and fetched the boy a jarring clout under the chir
The youth staggered a moment, and Daniel jerked th
knife from him. He cut the first youth's bowstring an
shoved the knife into his belt.

Breathing hard, he turned to confront the two lads
"Damn, but you try a man's patience. What's the mat
ter with you two, anyway?"

Whatever they said was gibberish to him, but he
knew he was being roundly cursed. One of the boy
rushed at him barehanded. Daniel threw him dow
and stepped aside. "You boys are fixin' to get m
mad." One boy helped the other to his feet. Danie
said sharply, "Look what you've went and done
You've made me shoot your horses, and you're ap
to have a long walk home. If you got any enemies ou
here, them shots is like as not to draw them. I know
we got enemies. Now the both of you git before I stop
makin' allowances for your age. *Git!*" He pointed
They didn't understand the words, but he though

hey got the gist of it, the last part anyway. They re-
reated resentfully, pausing first for another look at
im. If looks had been lethal, Daniel would not have
urvived.

"*Git* now!" he repeated. They retreated a little far-
her and stopped. Daniel took a hasty look around.
He saw no sign of other Indians, but he figured if any
had heard the shots, they would certainly be here by
nd by.

"Let's get out of here," he told Flor. They rode off
n a lope. Daniel looked back once and saw the two
boys watching them. "I ought to've wore out their
britches."

"They didn't have any britches," Flor reminded
im.

There was no question now that they had to abandon the effort to follow the trail of Cephus and Milo.
f the shots had been heard, it would likely be the
ndians following the silver hunters who heard them.
Daniel came to a small creek and reined up in it to
cover his tracks, Flor following his example. He
looked again to be sure they were out of sight of the
wo boys, who would no doubt put grown men on
heir trail if they had the chance.

"Of all the rotten luck," Flor blurted. "We may
never find Milo and Cephus now. Two damnfool Indian boys—two rotten kids."

"Anyway, they had guts."

"Their guts may've cost us a silver mine."

They followed the creek for two or three miles,
looking for a rocky place where they could get out
without leaving tracks. They found a good one, but
Daniel decided it was too obvious and passed it up.
He rejected three more likely places, finally climbing

up and out onto a rocky bench where he thought the
hot sun would quickly dry the water they had trailed
up with them.

"Hold to the rock as long as we can," he said
"We'll keep them confused."

"Not half as confused as we are."

They paralleled the creek always, watching for a
line of rock they could follow to get away from the
creek without leaving sign. Daniel's roan horse started
to lift its tail, and Daniel slapped him on the rump to
try to make him forget the notion. That would be all
a sharp-eyed Indian needed to see. The ploy didn't
work. Daniel had to get down, lift a flat rock and rake
all the fresh droppings under it, then fit the rock carefully back into place.

He grumbled, "People who brag about how smart
their horses are just ain't been caught in a tight like
this."

They hadn't gone much farther when he heard
hoofs striking against stone, far behind them. His
stomach went cold. "They're comin'," he said tightly
"In spite of all we done, they're comin'."

He saw fear grip Flor. For a moment he was afraid
she would cry, but she was too strong for that. The
only cover he could see was a long live-oak ridge well
above the stream. He pointed and started out, picking his way to stay among the rocks as long as he
could. He looked back frequently for pursuit.

Flor said weakly, "I wisht I was back in San Antonio, washin' other people's dirty clothes on the riverbank."

"And I wisht I was plowin' my folks' south field
But I reckon we both came into this mess with our
eyes open."

They rode into the live oaks and dismounted so they could have the use of their rifles if they needed them. Presently a dozen or so horsemen came working slowly up the creek, watching for sign at its edge.

Daniel muttered under his breath. "There's them two damn boys, runnin' along afoot like a pair of trackin' hounds."

The boys were out a little farther than most of the horsemen, bent over intently studying the ground at their feet as they trotted to keep up.

The horsemen came to the place where Daniel and Flor had climbed out, and Daniel felt his heart begin moving up into his throat. A cold sweat broke out on his face.

The Indians paused a little, and he found himself holding his breath until his lungs were in pain. One of the boys skirted close to the flat rock where Daniel had hidden the horse manure. But the Indians passed on. Daniel let his breath out slowly and wiped his sleeve across his face. He glanced at Flor and judged she was a little sick.

There was nothing to do but hold their ground, for back downstream he could see a couple of straggling Indian riders coming along behind their fellow warriors, perhaps hoping to see something the others had missed. The sun was going down when the Indians came back downstream, making another search over the same ground but a hastier one this time. Again they passed over the place where Daniel and Flor had left the stream. In the dusk, Daniel watched them move away.

He held his voice almost to a whisper. It didn't even sound like his. "They figure we went downstream. Maybe we've lost them."

"Since they're goin' downstream, I'm in favor o
goin' *up*stream, just as far as we can get."

"We'll lose Cephus and Milo."

"Right now I don't care if I never see either one o
them again, and if I never see a dollar's worth of sil
ver. I just want to breathe."

They rode long into darkness, putting the Indian
far behind them. But in so doing, Daniel more or les
lost his bearings; he had only a vague idea of direc
tion and a vaguer one yet of distance. They pulled u
into timber finally and camped, eating a little drie
buffalo meat. Daniel slept but little, and he doubte
that Flor slept at all.

At sunrise, Daniel looked upstream and saw some
thing which struck him as strange. Perhaps fifty yard
from the creek was a remnant of something built o
stone. His first thought was that it might have bee
an Indian dwelling, but he couldn't remember eve
hearing about Indians who built stone houses in thi
part of the country.

Once he was satisfied there were no Indians around
he rode cautiously toward the structure. He saw tha
at one time a rock wall had been built up in a circu
lar shape several feet from ground level. Some of th
lower side had been washed away, probably by man
successive rises on the creek. On the ground above th
circular structure lay a huge rock that six men coul
not have lifted. Grooves had been carved into it. A
rotted log lay beside it, badly broken, hardly enoug
of it left to indicate that once it had been all in on
piece.

Nearby lay more stone and the ruins of what ha
been some type of platform. These rocks were black

ned as if they had been burned repeatedly over a
ong period of time.

He found Flor as puzzled by it as he was. He asked,
"You ever seen anything like this?" She hadn't.

Then her eyes brightened in sudden realization.
"But I've heard about it. Daniel, I think this is an ore
melter."

He blinked. "What's a smelter?"

"Where they crushed the ore and then melted the
ood stuff out of it. That circle over there, I'll bet
hat's the ore crusher. They'd dump the ore in there.
That big rock was tied to a log with rawhide, and the
og was laid across the top of the wall. Them Span-
ards, they'd make Indian slaves push down on one
nd of the log to raise the rock up, then step back and
et it fall on top of the ore. When they had it all busted
p, they'd wash it out and then melt down the heavy
tuff over yonder where the rocks are burned." Her
oice was excited. "You know what this means?
We've come onto the place where they melted the sil-
er down."

Daniel's skin prickled. "Then the mine must be
around here close. They wouldn't of carried that ore
any farther than they had to."

She began to laugh. "That stupid Cephus—while
he's off runnin' around over the country like a lost
hounddog, we're findin' the mine." Her laugh became
ouder, and a little wild.

Daniel looked around worriedly. "There might be
Indians back there somewhere behind us."

"And there's a fortune in silver somewhere ahead
of us. Come on, Daniel, let's go and find it!"

14

It occurred to Daniel that if this had indeed been a smelter and the ore had been brought here from a mine for any great length of time, the foot traffic should have beaten out a trail that probably would not have healed even yet. He discerned what might have been several, but he knew they were as likely to be game trails as any path beaten out by silver miners.

He looked carefully for Indians. Seeing none, he motioned to Flor that he intended to follow one of the trails and see if it led to anything. She nodded eagerly.

This trail led up a slope, through a thin scattering of live oaks, and over the top. He hesitated to go up over the hill and stand the risk of being skylined to the view of searchers far away. Instead, he skirted around and picked up the trail on the other side. It began meandering and breaking down into smaller trails, and before long he realized it was nothing made

y man. This was a path the deer and the buffalo had
ong used working their way down to the water.

Flor was disappointed, but he reminded her there
vere more trails to try. He picked up another which
lso played out before long. Daniel and Flor then
vent all the way back to the smelter and picked up a
hird that he thought looked possibly heavier-traveled.
3efore long he realized it was less crooked than the
thers. Anticipation began building in him again, for
e had a feeling about this one. He looked at Flor and
aw she had caught the excitement; she had lost her
lisappointment over the other two. "Don't build your
lopes too much," he warned her. But he knew he was
vasting his breath.

He heard something ahead and stopped to listen.
3rush crackled somewhere up the slope. Quickly he
ignaled Flor and they pushed their horses down into
l clump of close-grown cedar, stepping down to the
;round and getting ready to clamp their horses' noses.
)ry-mouthed, Daniel watched through the heavy ce-
lar.

At length the tension drained out of him. "Buffalo,"
le said in relief, "goin' down to water." The animals
valked slowly without sign of alarm, which he took
is a good omen. He let them plod by before he started
o move out of the cedar.

His eye caught something lying on the ground in
he cedarbrake. He took it at first for a small, dead
mimal, then decided it was something else.

Flor said, "Come on, let's find that mine."

"In a minute. I want to see what this is." He led his
lorse through the close-bunched timber where the
till heat seemed tightly held by the dense foliage; his

pushing through it shook accumulated dust from the greenery, and he sneezed.

What he found was a scattering of black metal roughly molded into wedge shapes, each bar just a few inches long. He picked one up and found it much heavier than it looked.

Flor pushed up behind him. "What you got?"

"Lead, looks to me like. Lead bars to be melted down and poured into bullets."

Flor hefted one experimentally. "What're they doin here in the middle of a thicket?"

Daniel picked up a few more of the bars and found beneath them a remnant of badly rotted rawhide. "I'd say they was in a rawhide bag. Rats or somethin' have chewed up the bag except what was underneath." He found a few pieces of ancient wood, which he thought were oak, pieces of a packsaddle. Amid the bars was a flint arrow point, the wooden shaft long since rotted away.

"I'd guess they had this lead on a packmule or a burro. When the Indians hit them, this mule probably got shot with arrows and ran off into the thicket to die. That was a long time ago. Everything has been eaten up or scattered except the lead bars and a little of the packsaddle."

"I bet them Spaniards was wishin' they had this lead cast up into bullets."

"We're liable to all be wishin' the same thing before this trip is over with. I got a notion to load some of this in our saddlebags and carry it with us."

"What we're lookin' for is silver, not lead."

"We may need the lead to let us get the silver and leave here alive."

He found their saddlebags inadequate and rolled

ome of the bars in their blankets, tying them behind
he saddles. "A lot of extra weight," he admitted, "but
we get in a tight, I reckon we can always drop the
lankets off and run."

Even so, they left a good number of bars where
hey had found them, on the ground in the thicket.

The trail led a couple of miles up from the smelter.
He almost missed the point where it suddenly turned
p a hill. Rains through the years had washed down
he rocky hillside, all but wiping out the traces. He
ointed. "Up yonder, Flor. I think we'd best tie the
orses in the brush and climb up there afoot."

At the crest of the hill he found a large mound of
dd-colored earth and rock which did not quite match
he ground around it. Part of this had washed down
he hillside, leaving a smear of light color which con-
asted strangely with the rest of the earth. He nicked
p a piece of rock three times the size of his fist and
ound odd scratches on it. Chisel marks.

Flor made the guess first. "This has all been dug out
f the earth. The hole it came from has got to be right
ere someplace." Her voice was high-pitched with ex-
itement. Daniel cast the rock aside.

He missed the hole twice before he found it. A bush
ad grown up at the edge of it over the years, all but
iding it. When Flor saw Daniel had found it, she
ushed over and began hacking at the bush's trunk
vith a heavy Bowie knife. Daniel thought she was not
ar short of being hysterical. He took the knife from
er and warned her not to get too close; she might
all in. The hole appeared to go almost straight down.

When the bush was cut away and cast aside, he
ound the hole to be roughly oval in shape, three to
our feet across. It was not quite straight down, but

the sides were too steep to climb without a rope or some other help. He picked up a small rock and pitched it into the hole to get some idea of its depth, for he could not see bottom. From the sound, he judged it to be twelve or fifteen feet.

"And us without a rope."

"A blanket," Flor suggested, trembling. "We can cut a blanket into strips and tie them together."

Daniel judged Flor's blanket to be the strongest and ripped about half of it apart, testing the strips for strength, then tying them together. He tested the stump of the bush they had cut away and thought it would do for an anchor. Tying one end of the strip to the stump, he dropped the rest down into the hole. "You stay up here," he warned Flor. "If something goes wrong, we don't want to both be caught down there." Cautiously he began a descent. Halfway down he found that footholds had been chipped into the rock wall. That made it easier.

The bottom was farther down than he had thought, possibly twenty feet. He was in what he first took to be total darkness. After he had been there a couple of minutes and his eyes adjusted themselves from the bright sunshine, he could make out the general form of the walls, if it was too dark to see details. He moved cautiously across the room toward a spot where he thought he could see light. There he found another shaft going straight up from the ceiling, barely wider than a man's body. An air-hole, he decided.

He went back to the main shaft and shouted up to Flor. "I got to have light, Flor. Find me something that'll burn."

She dropped down three or four bundles of dried broomweeds, which she had crushed and tied tightly

o make them burn longer. Daniel took out his flint
nd struck it several times until one of the bundles
tarted to blaze. He held it up and got his first real
ook at the room in the wildly dancing firelight. It was
wenty-five or thirty feet across, just tall enough for
man to stand. He half expected to find a cache of
hining silver bars against a wall, but in this he was
isappointed. He found nothing but the rubble of
ard work. He thought perhaps he would see silver
eins sparkling in the walls, but in this also he was
isappointed. He saw nothing but rock, the chisel
narks still as plain as if they had been made yesterday.

Off in the far side of the room he saw a tunnel, and
is heartbeat quickened again. Maybe that was where
he silver was stored.

He felt pain and realized that the weeds had burned
own to his hand. He dropped them on the floor and
vent back for a second bundle, setting them ablaze
rom the remnants of the first one. With the new light
e paused in the mouth of the tunnel. He would have
o crawl on hands and knees to negotiate it. He looked
ubiously at the ancient timber shoring. He feared it
vas largely rotted away. It wouldn't take much to
ause the timbers to fall in, and part of the walls or
eiling might come down with them.

He heard Flor's voice behind him. "Where's the sil-
er?"

He turned and demanded, "I thought I told you to
tay up yonder!"

"I couldn't. I just had to come down."

He decided there was no point in scolding her; ex-
itement had such a grip on her that she wouldn't
near a word. "Go bring them other bunches of weeds.
We'll need them for light."

With Flor following close on his heels, he wen
down on hands and knees and began to crawl throug
the tunnel, careful not to brush against the shoring
Breathing was not easy, for each move raised long
settled dust that threatened to choke him. He sav
the end of the tunnel just ahead and reasoned tha
beyond it was another room, maybe the place wher
the silver came from. He crawled out of the tunne
and tried to stand but bumped his head against th
low, rough ceiling. He took a third bundle of weed
and set them ablaze to throw light across the room.

"Where is it?" Flor demanded. "Where's the sil
ver?"

This room was smaller than the other, no mor
than ten to fifteen feet across. Here again was an ai
shaft going up to the top, laboriously chiseled by hand
through many feet of rock.

There was no other tunnel; this was the last room
It was as bare as the first. Daniel reached down and
picked up a steel chisel about six inches long, its poin
pounded to a ruined mass. Halfway across the room
lay an old steel hammer, its oak handle broken. Other
than that, nothing.

The place was as barren as a robbed tomb.

Flor began to sob, and between sobs she cursed
She took the ruined chisel from Daniel's hand and began to hack at the rock walls until her hands were
bruised and bleeding. "Where's the silver?" she cried
"Goddammit, what did they do with it?"

Daniel swallowed a bitter disappointment. "Look
to me like if there was any here in the first place, they
got it all."

He studied the walls, thinking perhaps there was a
vein of silver here and he didn't know how to recog-

 size it. But he decided he had been right the first time; whatever might have been here, the Spaniards had mined it out before they left. They might have found nothing at all. He fired the last bundle of weeds. "Come on, Flor, we better get out of here while we still got some light."

The weeds burned away before he reached the end of the tunnel, but enough light came from the main shaft so that he could see his way to finish crawling out. Flor came close behind him, crying. On the floor he found a bundle of weeds she had failed to pick up and carry through the tunnel. With his flint he fired these and took a final look around, trying to tell himself he might have missed something. But he knew he hadn't.

Flor bitterly hurled the old chisel against a rock wall. "Fraud," she cried, "that's what it is, a fraud! These damned stupid old men and their damned stupid old stories about buried silver. They're dreamers and frauds, every last one of them!"

The weeds were rapidly burning down, but Daniel was held in morbid fascination by the look of this place. He found one thing half covered with dust: a set of leg irons, badly rusted. He recalled the old stories about Spaniards using the *padres* to Christianize the Indians, and chains to be sure that they did not lose religion. No telling how many had worked and died here. There might not even have been any silver; all that misery might have been for nothing. The place had a smell of decay and death about it. It made him cold.

"Let's get out of here, Flor. This is a bad place."

They climbed back on the dangling blanket strips, Flor going first so that Daniel could catch her if she slipped. Daniel sat outside and rested, letting his lungs fill with the good clean air. Flor sobbed softly again. Daniel decided to hold her and keep silent; maybe the best thing was to let her cry it out and be done with it.

At last he said, "I doubt we can ever find Milo and Cephus again."

He heard something then, in the distance. Gunfire. Flor looked up suddenly; she had heard it too.

Daniel said, "Looks like *somebody* found them."

"Milo!" she cried. "They'll kill him! They'll kill Milo!"

15

Milo and Cephus and the others were in bad trouble. Crouching on the crest of a hill, Daniel saw that the San Antonians had taken refuge in a live-oak motte. It appeared to Daniel that they had dug in, shoveling up some kind of hasty breastworks.

They needed them, for in the tall dry grass and scrub oak shinnery around the motte, Daniel counted at least thirty Indians. He thought more likely there were forty, all afoot and well positioned to direct arrows at the men they had surrounded. The Indian horses were being held in safety two hundred yards away.

If the beleaguered Texans had any advantage at all, it was simply that the timber helped deflect the arrows. So far as Daniel could tell, only a couple of Indians seemed to have any kind of firearms. The rifle fire was desultory now. Now and again an Indian would fire a bullet into the trees. Once Daniel heard the scream of a wounded mule. It appeared that Milo and Cephus had lost most of their packmules and even some of their horses before they reached the motte.

Flor cried, "What can we do? They're trapped."

Daniel shook his head. "Be damned if I know."

"We got to do somethin'. We can't just sit here and not lift a finger to help."

"I don't know that a whole hand would do them much good. Looks to me like them Indians'll keep them bottled up till they get them all. Far as we know, there may be more Indians on the way."

"From where we're at we could shoot a bunch of them."

"And wind up dead before the others. We ain't even got a stand of timber."

"Well, think of somethin'. We got to save Milo."

"Seems to me like you're suddenly almighty worried about Milo Seldom. Your ol' daddy is down there too."

"My ol' daddy brought this on himself by bein' greedy and mean. Milo Seldom is just dumb; he can't help himself."

Daniel watched, but no idea came to him. For a while it wasn't much of a fight; it was more of a standoff. The Indians were unable to get closer without undue exposure to rifle fire, and the San Antonians were unable to get out of the timber. Now and again someone fired out of the live oak, or an Indian loosed an arrow at what he considered to be a target. It seemed to Daniel that neither side was getting much done.

But in the long run he knew the Indians held all the advantage. Time was their ally, and they had plenty of it.

To one side Daniel saw a wisp of smoke. He took t for gunsmoke from an Indian rifle, but it began to grow. He grabbed a short breath. "Flor, one of them has fired the grass."

The wind was in the Indians' favor. The tiny flame grew, moving slowly through the grass toward the motte. Indians began shouting their enthusiasm, a number setting fires of their own, blowing on them to get them started, watching them build in the heavy, summer-cured grass. Shortly a dozen fires and a dozen smokes were crackling inexorably toward the timber. The men entrapped there began a faster pattern of rifle fire, trying to keep the Indians down and to halt their grass-kindling efforts.

Tears ran down Flor's cheeks. "They'll burn them out of there. When they try to run for it, the Indians'll cut them to pieces."

Daniel pushed to his feet. "That fire idea ain't bad at all. Maybe we can give the Indians somethin' to worry about. Let's gather up some dry grass and brush."

He had saved the makeshift rope they had made from blanket strips. When he and Flor had quickly gathered a mass of combustible materials, he tied them into two large bundles with rawhide and had enough strip left to drag them by. "Bring up the horses, Flor."

He took out his flint and struck sparks. It required a minute to get the first bundle afire. When he had it burning, he used it to touch off the second. He swung into his saddle and pointed. "You go yonderway. Don't get too close to them." He veered off, putting his own horse into a steady trot down the hillside and onto the long slope that led down toward the motte,

the burning grass and brush bouncing along behind
him, here and there touching off a blaze. It seemed
that the Indians hadn't noticed him yet. He hoped for
time. He had to ride slowly enough to let the burning
bundle behind him fire the grass; dragged too rapidly, it wouldn't work. He rode straight toward the
Indians.

One of them saw him and shouted. Half a dozen
arrows were hurriedly sent at him. They would miss,
but if he got much closer, they wouldn't. These were
no boys. He cut back at a right angle into the thick-
est of the dry grass, looking over his shoulder. Behind
him he was leaving a trail of smoke, the sun-cured
mat of ground cover flaming up quickly, the wind
rapidly whipping it into a full blaze. He took one
glance at Flor and saw she was moving ahead of him
on the same general course, moving a little faster and
bouncing the burning bundle higher, leaving a more
ragged pattern of fire.

Suddenly the Indians on this side of the motte
found themselves afoot between two lines of fire—
one they had set themselves and the other touched
off by Daniel and Flor. Shouting in anger, they sent
futile arrows searching after the man and woman. A
rifle-carrying Indian shot at them but did not come
close.

The Indians were running after them afoot now,
some almost as fleet as a horse. Daniel moved into a
hard lope, catching up to Flor. "Spur him," he shouted
at her. "They ain't overly happy."

Ahead of them was the Indian horse herd. Two Indians guarding it came riding out to meet them, fit-
ting arrows to their bows. Daniel could tell these were

young, green warriors, not a great deal older than the
two he and Flor had set afoot. Maybe their aim wasn't
polished yet.

Flor's bundle of brush and grass burned free of the
blanket strips and fell off, but Daniel still had his. He
could tell it had the full attention of the Indians'
horses, for they stood watching, ears forward, eyes
highly nervous as this ominous fireball bounced
toward them. The Indian guards' first arrows missed,
and Daniel and Flor rushed past. Daniel shouted at
the horses, and Flor took up the yelling. Daniel
plunged headlong into the horse herd, the flaming
bundle close behind him.

That was all it took. The horses broke into a sudden frightened run, tails high, manes streaming. Daniel looked back for the two young Indians and saw
only one still on horseback. The other sat on the
ground, his horse pitching away in panic.

Daniel felt something hot bite into his shoulder
and knew an arrow had struck him. He let the blanket strip go, for the fire was largely burned out. He
brought his horse around and painfully reined to a
quick stop, bringing his rifle up. He took no time to
aim, for he saw the Indian draw the bowstring back.

Daniel fired, and the Indian's horse fell. The arrow
went astray.

The horses were in a good run now. It would take
awhile for the Indians to round them up. Flor cried,
"Daniel, you're hit."

It was beginning to hurt now, the long shaft bob-
bing up and down with every move he or his roan
horse made. He got down from the saddle. He could
feel blood flowing warm inside his shirt. Flor jumped

to the ground, knife out, and ripped part of the shirt away. "It's not in too deep," she said. "Hold onto somethin'."

She didn't give him much time. He grabbed his saddle, and she yanked at the arrow shaft. It held the first time, and he almost sank to his knees from the pain of it. Before he could do more than cry out, she jerked again and brought it free, breaking the shaft.

He was dizzy for a moment, and realized he was still bleeding. Somewhere in his subconscious he knew some bleeding was good for him because it would wash the wound clean.

He heard a sudden increase in firing but could not focus his eyes to see what was happening. Flor said, "Milo and them, they're breakin' out of the timber. Here they come, runnin' like the devil was after them."

"He is," Daniel gritted, fighting down the sickness that welled up. "I halfway wisht he'd catch them."

"I'll help you on to your horse," Flor offered.

"I'm able to do for myself." But he almost fell over on the other side. He grabbed the saddle and caught himself. Through blurry eyes he saw the men riding toward them, stringing out in a broken line. As his eyes cleared a little, he could tell they had left most of the pack animals behind. They were riding for their lives, and they weren't worrying about baggage.

Angry Indians ran after them afoot, loosing arrows and shouting all manner of insult.

Daniel couldn't see the men clearly enough to recognize them individually, but he knew old Cephus Carmody's voice. "I swear, daughter, when first I seen you ridin' down off that hill, I thought I was killed and gone to heaven. Nary angel ever looked prettier to mortal eyes."

"That's the nearest you'll ever come to seein' an angel, Papa. Everybody make it all right?"

"Bruises and scratches, but nobody killed. Come on, we need to be puttin' distance behind us before we pause to parley."

Cephus jabbed spurs to his mount. Daniel's horse jumped forward to keep up, and Daniel almost lost his seat. He felt strong arms come around him and hold him. A familiar voice said, "Hang on tight, friend Daniel."

Daniel gritted, "Goddamn you, Milo, let me fall and I'll stomp the liver and lights plumb out of you."

He gave all his attention to staying in the saddle. Eyes blurred, he sensed rather than saw the broken land flying by beneath his horse's long-reaching legs. At length he was aware that Cephus and the others ahead of him were slowing down. He heard splashing, and he felt Milo Seldom stopping his horse. "All right, friend Daniel, ease down here into this creek. The wetness of it'll do you good."

The cool water did help. They ripped the shirt some more, and he felt gentle hands washing the wound. He heard Flor say, "It's about quit bleedin'. He won't die on us." Then her voice changed from confidence to sudden concern. "Milo, your face! You're wounded too."

Daniel's vision cleared some. He could see Milo shaking his head, and he could see it streaked with blood and swollen and blue. "Indians didn't do this. I was havin' me a fight with your ol' lyin' daddy when them Indians come up and hit us unawares."

"A fight? What about?" she demanded.

Milo said bitterly, "Tell her, Cephus."

The old man began to back away. "Now, daughter,

you don't want to be listenin' to the likes of Milo Seldom. The truth was never in him."

Milo said sharply, "What would you know about truth, you ol' whisky-soak? You never told it in your life."

Flor had taken charge again. "All right now, you two, I want to know what happened. Somebody tell me before I take and shoot you both!"

Milo said angrily, "We wasn't two hours from the San Saba ruins till I knowed the old reprobate was lost. All of yesterday and this mornin' he took us ever' whichaway, cuttin' back and forth like a rattlesnake track. He kept sayin' he knowed what he was doin', but he didn't. Finally me and Lalo Talavera shook the truth out of him. That's when me and Cephus had our fight. I tell you, I smote him hip and thigh."

"The truth?" Flor pressed. "What're you talkin' about?"

Lalo Talavera said in Spanish, "The truth, my pretty little flower, is that your father never was with James Bowie on that expedition. He wanted to go, but they would not let him; they knew him too well. He trailed them, but somewhere near the ruins he lost them, and he never did find them again. When Bowie and his men were having their big fight with the Indians, your fine, sweet father was wandering around out here by himself, lost."

Flor took two angry steps toward her father. "Papa . . ."

Defensively Cephus backed off some more. "Now, daughter, I always knowed I'd been within a hundred yards of that mine. I could feel it in my bones. I always figured if ever I could come back, I'd find it; you know I've always had a sixth sense about such things.

could find it yet if I just had a little time, and people wouldn't be bayin' on my heels like a bunch of mean hounds. You got to have a little faith, daughter."

"You know as much about faith as you know about truth, Papa." Daniel thought for a moment that Flor was going to strike her father, but instead she gave him a cursing the likes of which Daniel had never heard in his life, using every possible invective from two languages. When at last she was wrung out, her arms went limp at her sides. She paused for breath.

"Papa," she said, calmer now, "do you know what you've done? You've kept us fired up for years on false hopes about a mine that don't even exist. You've led us out here and put all of us in danger of bein' killed for a wild dream. Your rich mine is a lie. Me and Daniel, we found it. It's as empty as a promise from Cephus Carmody."

Old Cephus' mouth dropped open. "You found it?"

"We found it. There's nothin' there, Papa, nothin' but just a hole in the ground."

Milo Seldom slumped. "There's *got* to be somethin' there, Flor."

"Lies, that's all we found there. Wild stories dreamed up by people too lazy to work and dreamin' of findin' somethin' they could have free for the takin'. It's just a dead empty hole in the ground."

Daniel could see the impact hit them all, the bitter disappointment of a dream shattered at their feet like glass. Lalo Talavera turned and walked away slump-shouldered, muttering about all the *señoritas* that could have been his. Notchy O'Dowd stood in building anger, fists knotting as his face reddened. Of a sudden he bawled aloud and lunged at Cephus Carmody, and the two men went down together in a rolling, punching, gouging heap. Milo Seldom pushed forward to stop it, but Flor caught his arm. "Leave them alone. One's about as dirty a fighter as the other one is, and they both deserve whatever they get." Her voice softened. "You all right, Milo? You sure you didn't get hurt none?"

"Sure, Flor, you know nothin' ever happens to ol' Milo Seldom. I'm too smart to let it." She touched his leather sleeve and found a fresh hole there, and a thin edge of red.

"Oh, that," he said sheepishly, "just a little scratch is all. One of them Indians had a rifle, and he sort of nicked me a little when I was gettin' Armando Borrego out from under his shot horse. Nothin' serious."

Voice soft and concerned, Flor said, "Take that shirt off and let me look at it. You never know how bad somethin' like this can turn out."

Daniel watched them, listened to the care and softness in Flor's voice, and knew that the arrow wound was not the only one he had suffered here.

One of the Borrego brothers had ridden out on a short scout. He soon came back to the stream in a trot. "Some of the Indians have recovered horses. They are trailing after us."

Daniel thought he had regained enough strength to hold himself in the saddle. Now that he could see clearly, he discovered that several men were riding double, their horses lost. Only one packmule had been salvaged.

The Indians had come out of this thing with a considerable net gain, he thought with an odd detachment; they had a dozen or so packmules and evidently several horses as well. The hell with it all!

The fugitives rode into the night. So long as day-

ght lasted, they could always look behind them
nd see fifteen or twenty Indians trailing just out of
fle range. Old Cephus complained, "Ain't they had
nough yet?"

Milo told him dryly, "They're lookin' for a gray-
aired scalp of one lyin' old windbag to hang up on
shield so the wind'll blow the bullets away."

The horses were tired, and so were the men. Shortly
fter dark, they made dry camp in a protective rock
utcrop which gave them a view of sorts across an
pen flat and might keep the Indians from slipping up
n them in the night. Daniel's shoulder was fevered,
ut in spite of it, he managed some fitful sleep. The
ist thing he clearly remembered was hearing Milo
ell Flor they had lost most of their ammunition on
ne packmules. Through the night a vague worry
bout ammunition kept coming back to Daniel. At
ther times, in a fevered haze, he would see Lizbeth
Vills, and that farm they had planned to own.

The pain of the shoulder brought him awake be-
ore full daylight. He looked out across the flat and
aw no Indians, but a feeling in his bones told him
hey were there. He got up stiffly and scooped out a
mall hole, gathered up some dry grass and small
ieces of wood and built a fire in it. He got his bullet
nold form his saddlebag, and a wedge-shaped bar of
he black metal he had found near the old Spanish
nine. He ringed the little fire with stones so he could
•alance the ladle across it. He put the bar into the
adle to melt the lead down.

Flor came up and sat quietly beside him. "You all
ight?"

"Fair to middlin'. How's Milo?"

"You know him; you couldn't kill him with a club."

"Yesterday," he said, "I was sore tempted to try, th
way you carried on over him. I thought you said you
didn't have no feelin' left for him."

"I thought I didn't. But then when I saw there wa
danger of him bein' killed—" She looked away. "I'n
sorry if I led you astray, and gave you notions abou
me and you. I really thought I was shed of him, but
reckon the feelin' has been there too long to get ri
of it. God help me, it looks like I'm stuck for life."

Daniel said, "You know how he is; he's got a restles
foot. He don't have nothin', won't ever have nothin
won't leave nothin' permanent when he's gone."

"He leaves tracks. He goes where other people ain'
ever been, and they see it can be done. They follov
him, and *they* make somethin' permanent. I reckor
he serves the Lord in his own way."

Daniel shrugged, and the shoulder hurt hin
"Maybe so. I think this trip kind of got the roamin
out of *my* system."

"If we get out of this—if them Indians don't get u
all—what'll you do, Daniel?"

"Go back to the farm, I reckon. Work for my daddy
or work for somebody else, and hope someday I'
manage to save enough money to take up a place o
my own."

"That sweetheart back there—is she a good farn
girl?"

"Lizbeth?" He hadn't thought much about Lizbetl
lately. Last night was the first time in weeks she hac
intruded even in his dreams. "Farmin's the only lift
she's ever known. She's always said she'd be patien
and wait. It's always been *me* that was impatient tc
have a place of my own. But I don't know if I coulc
ever go back to Lizbeth now, not after me and you . . ."

"You'll forget me once you're with her again. We're not made right to live together, Daniel. You're a man who'll have to have your own way, and I'm a woman who's got to have hers. You need a woman who'll follow you but not push you. Milo needs a woman who'll follow him but yank him up short when he goes the wrong way; he needs a woman who'll mother him when he needs it and give him hell when he needs *that*. And I need a man who'll let me do that and get away with it. You wouldn't, Daniel, not very long."

Daniel guessed she was right, but he couldn't be that objective about it yet, not till he'd had some time. He didn't want to talk about it. He looked impatiently at the bar in the ladle. "I don't know what's the matter with that lead. Ought to be meltin' by now. Maybe the fire's not hot enough."

He put a little more wood under it. He saw Milo stirring, crawling sleepily out of his blankets. "Marry him and he'll drag you all over hell and half of Georgia."

"Only when I want to go. I'll give him enough rein to roam where he has to, but keep it short enough that he'll always come back to me. I'll never turn him that aloose like my mother did with ol' Cephus."

Still the bar showed no sign that it was going to melt. Daniel took out his hunting knife and poked at the part resting down in the hot ladle. "Not even soft," he said disgustedly. "Them Spaniards sure did use a sorry grade of lead."

Flor's eyes widened. "Let's see that bar."

Daniel lifted the ladle off the fire and set it down on the bare ground. Flor dumped the bar out into the dirt, took Daniel's knife and began to scratch at it. He

saw that her hands trembled. She looked up, her eye
excited. "Daniel Provost, me and you are blind!"

"What do you mean?"

"We were lookin' for big silver bars, nice and shin
But if you put a piece of silver up for a long time, yo
know what happens to it?"

"It turns black."

"It just came to me; I've heard San Antonio me
chants talk about the silver bars the Indians used t
bring to trade with. They didn't look like silver ti
they was polished up. They was rough cast, and the
had sat so long they had turned black on the outside
She kept scratching at the bar until some of the in
side was exposed. "Daniel, this ain't no lead bar. Th
is silver!"

"*Silver?*"

"Sh-h-h, not so loud! No use lettin' everybody hea
about it."

"But if this is silver, I reckon they got a right to
share."

"Why? They cut us off, remember? They didn't fin
this stuff, *you* did. By rights it's yours, ever bit of it."

Daniel swallowed. He had no idea how much thes
silver bars might be worth. He hadn't even counte
to see how many he had brought along. Of a sudde
he remembered the many he had left behind where h
had found them, and he felt sick.

"Flor, I couldn't find that place again, not in a hun
dred years."

"You won't need to. Maybe you got enough to ge
you that farm. Let the land give you its own treasure
one crop at a time."

His head swam with the intoxication of the idea.

"Half of it is yours, Flor. Don't argue with me;

ouldn't have it no other way." She seemed inclined
· protest but didn't. He said, "You can have them
k dresses after all."

She thought about it awhile, then shook her head.
No, I've done without them this long; I reckon I'll
e without them the rest of my span. But Milo ain't
er to know, Daniel. You know how he is; there'll
me times we'll really be in need and I can go dig
a bar. He won't ever know but what he provided
r me himself. He's not too smart, Daniel, but he's a
an with pride."

Milo Seldom knew how to make a healing poul-
e to put on Daniel's wound. He shaved bark from
ung live oak trees, boiled it down to a syrupy mix,
unded up some charcoal from last night's fire and
ut it into the syrup, along with a little cornmeal for
ickening, then slapped it on the wound, binding it
p with buffalo hide. "Now, friend Daniel," he prom-
ed, "when we take that off in four-five days, you'll
e as good as ever was."

They knew San Antonio lay southeastward, so they
ruck a straight course in that direction. For the first
ur days they were never out of sight of Indians, who
ailed behind them like wolves after a handful of
rippled buffalo. Every so often some young warrior,
erhaps trying to prove his bravery and bring up his
atus in the eyes of the tribe, would charge forward
lone and send an arrow flying after the fugitive sil-
er hunters.

The first time, Notchy O'Dowd brought his rifle
p. So sternly that he surprised himself, Daniel com-
anded, "Don't shoot him. No use killin' one with-
ut need; they'd swarm over us like bees."

O'Dowd obeyed him without question, which also

surprised Daniel. He had not intended to take charg
but he found that he had; he found the others wai
ing expectantly for him to give the orders. It occurre
to him that no one else in the party had any bett
right, or was better qualified. He found himself si
ting straighter in the saddle.

Late on the fourth day the Indians fell away. Da
iel learned the reason shortly before dark when l
saw a group of horsemen approaching on the tra
ahead. He ordered his party to dismount in a sma
stand of timber and prepare to fight if necessary. Bu
presently Milo Seldom said, "Friend Daniel, the
ain't Indians; they're white men."

The bedraggled party remounted and rode forwar
They found Paley Northcutt there with twenty me
from San Antonio; a mixed group of American
Mexicans, a Frenchman and a black freedman.

Paley Northcutt was the first to speak. "Milo," h
asked eagerly, "whichaway's the silver mine?"

Sheepishly Milo said, "Boys, we never found no si
ver mine. Oh, there was a mine, all right, but ther
wasn't no silver in it."

The San Antonians were disappointed. It develope
that Paley Northcutt had gone back into town afte
Flor had sent him away. He had proceeded to ge
drunk and tell about the planned expedition to th
Bowie mine. In no time he had collected a set of ea
ger volunteers, ready to share in the glory and th
wealth.

Daniel said, "It's a good thing you came, Paley, eve
if there ain't no mine. I don't know if them Indian
intended to let us get back to San Antonio alive."

It didn't take long for Milo Seldom to tell the whol
story, upon which some of the newcomers were of

otion to hang Cephus Carmody to a nearby live oak.
ut Cephus talked them out of it.

"Boys," he said, "I know there wasn't no silver in
e mine that my daughter and Mister Provost found,
ut that don't mean there ain't another one. Stands
 reason them Spaniards didn't dig one hole and quit.
 ands to reason they had more than one mine—
 aybe a *dozen* of them. Somewhere out yonder is a
 ine with a pile of silver bars taller than a man's head,
 gger'n a Mexican *baile* room, maybe bigger'n *two*
 them, just waitin' for the taker. I swear, boys, soon's
 :an get me an outfit together and some good men
 ride with me, I'm goin' back out there and find that
 ine. I'll go right to it the next time; I got a feelin'
)w that I know just where it's at."

He got them out of the notion of hanging him. Be-
 re he was through talking, half of them were of a
 ind to turn around and go back with him.

Milo had his arm around Flor's shoulder. "You
 low somethin', Flor? Ol Cephus makes sense. I bet
)u, the next time we can . . ."

Flor looked hopelessly at Daniel and shrugged.
 Milo . . ."

"What, *querida?*"

"For God's sake, Milo, take me home!"

Forge

Award-winning authors
Compelling stories

. . . .

Please join us at the website
below for more information
about this author and other great
Forge selections, and to sign up for
our monthly newsletter!

. . . . . www.tor-forge.com . . . .